W9-AZJ-276

WITHDRAWN

IRREPLACEABLE

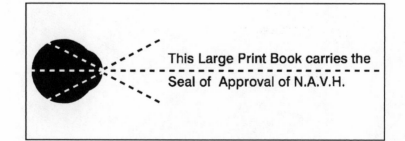

This Large Print Book carries the
Seal of Approval of N.A.V.H.

IRREPLACEABLE

STEPHEN LOVELY

THORNDIKE PRESS
A part of Gale, Cengage Learning

GALE
CENGAGE Learning

Detroit • New York • San Francisco • New Haven, Conn • Waterville, Maine • London

GALE
CENGAGE Learning‑

LIBRARY OF CONGRESS CATALOGING-IN-PUBLICATION DATA

Lovely, Stephen.
　　Irreplaceable / by Stephen Lovely.
　　　　p. cm. — (Thorndike Press large print core)
　　ISBN-13: 978-1-4104-1488-5 (alk. paper)
　　ISBN-10: 1-4104-1488-4 (alk. paper)
　　1. Heart—Transplantation—Fiction. 2. Donation of organs,
tissues, etc.—Fiction. 3. Bereavement—Psychological
aspects—Fiction. 4. Family—Fiction. 5. Psychological fiction. 6.
Large type books. I. Title.
PS3612.O85I77 2009b
813'.6—dc22　　　　　　　　　　　　　　　　　　　　2009001356

Published in 2009 by arrangement with Voice, an imprint of Hyperion,
a division of Buena Vista Books, Inc.

For the family
whose decision to donate
their boy's organs
inspired this book

nose practically touching her forearms. She shifted her weight back and mashed her legs through their strokes, holding her cadence, fighting her way up. For the first twenty yards she felt like an engine — a sleek, powerful, perfectly calibrated device clipped onto the bike to crank its pedals. Then she ran out of gas. This was a long, steep hill, and she wasn't yet in shape. It was only her third ride of the season. Her lungs felt singed, her thighs heavy as iron. The bike wobbled beneath her.

She looked up and saw the crest of the hill approaching, not ten yards distant. A field of soybeans dipping toward a farm. Goats huddled in a barn doorway.

She struggled to the top, where the wind lunged and bullied, its sound sharpening to a whistle at the peaks of the gusts.

The roar of an engine lunged out of the ground behind her, and she felt a jolt of panic: in the fraction of a second before impact she realized she was too far out into the road.

■ ■ ■ ■

PART I

■ ■ ■ ■

April 2006
One

Alex Voormann slouches in a folding chair in a basement room of U.S. Exam's corporate campus wishing he could call his wife. He'd like to vent, perform a little comedy routine called "My Shitty Day." *You wouldn't believe the inanity we've got going over here, Iz.* He used to enjoy calling Isabel at the lab and luring laughter to her serious surface. She'd giggle and protest. *Alex, I am so busy.* Still, she'd be tickled, and glad he called.

Alex would like to call Isabel, but Isabel's dead. She's been dead now nearly a year.

Diane Topor, director of U.S. Exam's SCAT Project (Secondary Composition Advancement Testing), appears at Alex's side dressed in one of her citrus-colored power suits. She inserts a piece of paper into his field of vision. "Remember this essay? You gave it a zero. The Quality Control Panel gave it a unanimous score of three. Can you account for the discrepancy?"

Alex is used to Diane bringing his work back to him, querying his scores, defending inept young essayists. He leans back in his chair for a better view of the essay, wanting Diane to notice his wrinkled, untucked polo shirt, his faded jeans with the fringy tear in the knee. He rakes his fingers through unkempt hair and tries to remember the essay and author. Of course. Tina Criswell. Age thirteen, of Fort Collins, Colorado. In response to the essay question — *What do you think is America's biggest problem? What can be done to fix it? Use details and examples to make your writing vivid to the reader* — Tina wrote, *Teen pregnancy. Abstain until marriage.* Her script is neat, tight, curlicued. Beneath her words she drew a winking smiley face. The smiley face is provocative and impossible to interpret. What does it mean? Sex will be hot when you finally have it? Abstinence is a joke?

Alex encountered this essay just before lunch, and felt it a perfect candidate for the zero score. *The student does not attempt to address the question and/or the student's answer is illegible and/or written in a language other than English.*

He looks up at Diane, hoping she'll take his bewilderment personally. "A three?"

Diane raises her eyebrows, a direct challenge to his intelligence.

Alex rummages through his papers for the Holistic Scoring Guidelines and reads aloud from the description of a three. " *'Vague focus.'* I didn't see any focus. *'Content limited to a listing of ideas.'* Where do you see ideas? *'Inconsistent organization.'* Organization of what? *'Repeated weaknesses in mechanics and usage.'* What mechanics? What usage? Diane, this girl didn't *write* anything. She didn't take the question seriously."

Diane places her hand tenderly over Tina's words. The sleeve of her blazer slides up her wrist, revealing a stiff white cuff and a gold watch with a butterfly-shaped face. "We consider this an attempt. A minimal attempt, but an attempt nevertheless. There is focus. The focus is teen pregnancy. Two ideas are listed and organized. One, teen pregnancy is a problem, and two, a possible solution is to abstain from sexual activity until marriage. There are no weaknesses in mechanics and usage. Indeed, we have a sophisticated use of the imperative verb form."

Alex surveys the basement room's sulfur yellow walls, the urine-colored window overlooking the back of a shrub. Is it possible that this is all a bad dream from which he'll eventually awake?

15

He scoots his chair back to face Diane more directly. "I can't believe the panel gave this a three. Do the guidelines mean anything? Are you sure the QC people aren't working off the guidelines for first and second graders?" He's exaggerating his dismay; he really doesn't care about anything except bucking against Diane and U.S. Exam and this whole dubious enterprise of branding adolescents with numerical scores. "You're rewarding this girl for doing nothing. We know she's smart. She used the word 'abstain,' and spelled it correctly. She blew this test off. She told you to take your test and shove it."

Diane draws a long breath meant to display how much oxygen her response will cost her. "One of our concerns, Alex, is that you seem to have difficulty recognizing effort when you see it. You consistently score lower than the panel by two or three points. This is unacceptable, in the long run, but in the contemporary we're willing to work with you."

Alex tries to calm down. He does need the job, after all. He allows penitence into his voice. "Look, I made a judgment call. I don't call this an attempt. Not for a seventh grader. See this space here?" He touches his hand to the exam booklet, the blank answer space. "This should be filled with words, thoughts, ideas."

Diane nods, a perfunctory display of understanding. "Revisit this essay and see if you can't surface its merit. That was the imperative verb form, in case you didn't recognize it."

"I believe you've committed a usage error, Diane. You don't revisit something you've read. You might revisit, say, Italy, but when it's a book or other piece of written material the correct term is re-*read*, I'm pretty sure."

"Re-*grade* the essay," Diane says, and slides it onto the table.

Before meeting Isabel, armed with a bachelor's degree in anthropology and a master's in archaeology, Alex worked doing rescue excavation for the Iowa State Archaeologist. He and his team, over which he was proud to have been awarded a supervisory role, traveled to the sites of future roads and highways and dug up fields and abandoned lots, making certain, before bulldozers rolled, that there was nothing present of historical or cultural value — remnants of a prehistoric settlement, say — that might be destroyed.

Alex liked the work, the days spent in the

17

country kneeling on dry, hard ground, brush in hand, his fanny pack stuffed with tools (soup ladle, teaspoon, dental probe), his primary concern a meter-wide square of the Earth's surface. He liked the solitude — his square meter, his province — and the safety net of camaraderie, the other excavators close by, kneeling over their own square meters, respectful of his need to concentrate but available to chat if the occasion arose.

He would come to appreciate a similar blend of solitude and easy communicativeness with Isabel. Sitting in a room with her, reading or studying, he had the silence and space to conduct his inner life, but it wasn't the barren, unbounded space of loneliness: Isabel was right there carrying on her inner life, which she had linked to his in what seemed to him an astonishing act of love and generosity and confidence, and when one of them sensed a need or receptivity in the other they would set out talking, populating each other's minds with thoughts, ideas, theories, connections. They shared a spirited affection for science — Isabel was working toward a PhD in plant biology — and during their days apart, while he was kneeling over some remote patch of ground, Alex liked to think of her back in town peering through a microscope at a spore or out in a field taking pollen samples — liked to think that they were engaged in a joint venture, a collaborative investigation of the physical world.

He'd enjoyed playing in the dirt for as long as he could remember. As a child he liked its grittiness and fragrance, the feel of soil in his hands, under his fingernails, the excitement of not knowing what he'd find if he dug down even an inch: a blue glass perfume bottle the size of a thumb, a copper bullet, an arrowhead. Twenty years later he was still just playing in the dirt, the way he saw it, only with more sophistication, more technology at his disposal, and a better sense of what he was looking at, looking for. Each layer of soil was a flypaper-thin page that might present to him — in the language of its color and texture, its stones and tiles, bones, seeds, glass, mineral deposits — glimpses of animal and plant and microbial life, of the planet's tumultuous geophysical history. Over millions of years frost and ice had shattered exposed surfaces, rain and wind dumped mud and dust into hollows, water seeped, roots groped, bacteria and fungi fed on debris, insects dug burrows, worms inched through the soil passing millions of tons of it through their bodies. It gave Alex quite a feeling, kneeling on top of all that — all that *work*. He felt integrated with the onward march of centuries. He wasn't floating in a cold, dark universe: there in the dirt was the drop of sweat just fallen from his nose.

Two years ago there were budget cuts in Des Moines, layoffs at the Office of the State Archaeologist. Alex's attempts to find another job — with a cultural resource management firm, an environmental canvassing organization — led nowhere. He was forced to wait tables to pay rent and bills. Relocation didn't appeal to him. He and Isabel had married by then, and Isabel was midway through her doctoral program. They had constructed a life together that seemed to depend so much on the stately limestone university and its ongoing cultural bazaar, the familiar coffee shops and bookstores, restaurants and bars, the tree-lined pedestrian mall, the quiet streets longing to be aimlessly walked — all the things that had conspired to bring them together.

When Isabel died, Alex lost the hopefulness and assurance necessary to search for serious work. A dense weight settled in his forehead. Concentration, once a talent, was impossible: filling out a form, reading a job description, his brain went white, failed to engage, as though all the neurons involved had been clipped and cauterized.

He took to buying *People* magazine. The stars were marrying other stars, the stars were conquering cancer, the stars had never been happier. Alex spent whole days lying on his back on his living room floor, limbs sprawled, feeling nauseous and doomed.

In the evenings he walked a mile to a shopping mall and played pinball in a video arcade stuffed with teenagers. In his favorite game, Tentaclon, the player was charged with defending the planet against an invasion force of gigantic, mutant octopi. There were bells and buzzers, flashing lights — white, blue, red — chutes and tubes through which the shiny silver ball arched with incredible speed, slots that opened, panels that flipped, a pulsating display panel that proclaimed in huge orange letters OCTO-POD DESTROYED! and BONUS PRO-JECTILE!

The machine had so many parts and components that Alex felt, after thirty minutes at the flippers, like a much less complex organism than he was: a spineless polyp feeding on sound and light. He played for hours. There was no doubt, no ambiguity in this game about what you were supposed to do. When the ball approached the flippers, you flipped. *Thwack.* Again: *thwack.*

When you lost three balls, the machine shut down, but you could resuscitate it with a pair of quarters, and — miraculously, it seemed to Alex — with a ringing of bells and a flourish of lights it would shake itself to life.

Two

At five o'clock, along with a crowd of coworkers, Alex squeezes out the main door of U.S. Exam.

He's lean, slim-hipped, fit. He walks slowly, shuffling in his sandals, twirling his car keys on a carabiner. He's ready to get some distance from U.S. Exam but otherwise has no particular urgency, no purpose or desire. This used to be one of his favorite times of year. Spring. April. There's a breeze. The air is flimsy and sweet. Clouds cling like moss to a bold, Caribbean-blue sky. Nice to see the sky in its entirety, unobstructed by the grading room's urine-colored window — though there's something about that bright blue that wants to make light of the mess below, like a funny hat on a dying person.

In the parking lot, a legion of cars sparkles with sun. Alex finds his weathered brown Jeep, whose cargo space and four-wheel drive were better put to use out in the field. He pulls out of the parking space, inches down the driveway with the logjam of cars. Turns left onto Dorchester Road, heads toward Athens. The sun, low on the windshield, warms his face and neck. Air flaps in the open window. The air smells like manure from the surrounding countryside. Cars approach, gasp, whip past. The road glimmers with a silvery metallic sheen. Is that a trash bag on the shoulder? No. An animal. A dead . . . possum?

Dorchester curves left past the convenience and grocery stores, dips, levels, shoots under towering oaks and maples. A piece of paper tacked to a telephone pole: HAVE YOU SEEN MY CAT?

While Alex is stopped at a red light in a mausoleum of trees, the afternoon's stillness settles in the Jeep's open window. Nothing moves except low-hanging branches and leaves, stirred by a breeze that seems in league with the continual fading and resurgence of the light, with whatever the clouds are doing overhead, as though in some brave, persistent respiration.

Alex turns left on Radcliffe, a moonscape of potholes and crumbling curbs. A perimeter of bright orange tape encloses five tanned backs dug deep into the street. For weeks now this work crew has been moving up and down Radcliffe, engaged in an underground project whose objective is unclear and seems unrelated to the decay on the surface. To the right, overlooking a creek, surrounded by trees, is Alex's apartment building — tall, ark-shaped, brick. Alex parks in the gravel lot and heads across the bridge. The creek is slow, trickling through mud and rocks and fallen branches. A red laundry detergent jug, caught in the crook of a branch, pitches and bobbles. Isabel used to study up in that room there, Alex's living room, close by the window at the broad Spanish desk, her head bent low over journals and books, which were mostly about spores — her area of interest. *Selaginella selaginoides. Osmunda regalis.* Cells that looked, under a microscope, like miniature pies and tarts.

The building's front door jams against the stiff, rumpled doormat within. Alex presses his shoulder hard against the door, forces his body through the narrow opening. His mailbox used to have squarely affixed to it a card on which Isabel had written, calligraphically, in blue permanent marker, *Isabel Howard & Alex Voormann.* Now there's a yellow Post-it that reads, faintly, in pencil, *A. Voormann.* Inside the mailbox Alex finds an electric bill, a phone bill, and a small white envelope addressed to him in a crisp, energetic hand — a hand he thinks he recognizes. The postmark confirms it: Chicago APR 15. And the return address: Corcoran, 2014 West Wabansia #4.

An ache develops in Alex's stomach. He feels bristly, bitter toward these Corcorans, who seek so quietly and persistently his — forgiveness? blessing? friendship? — his acknowledgment, certainly, though they seem willing to give him their sympathy in exchange. And they are grateful, so grateful Alex sometimes feels he donated the heart himself. Still, he can't believe these people expect him to be enthusiastic about a correspondence or a friendship rooted in an event that may have been a gift for them, a stroke of luck, a windfall, but was the worst thing that had ever happened to him.

He leans against the wall of the foyer, claws at the back of his neck. He tells himself, *Throw it on the floor,* but can't bring himself to do it. After all, this woman, Janet Corcoran, a thirty-four-year-old high school art teacher, wife, and mother of two, is walking around the city of Chicago with Isabel's heart beating in her chest. The alleged reality of this floats high above Alex's day-to-day existence in a bubble of abstraction he can't lift his head to look at, much less penetrate. He doesn't have the brain space to process this bizarre outgrowth of his tragedy, to determine how and where it might be accommodated in his life. He'd need to sit down and think. He'd need to read books, talk to people. How do they do it, transplant a heart?

There were opportunities to learn. That evening in Zambrotta's Pizzeria, for instance, the summer after he and Isabel were married. She arrived directly from a routine physical. Her long black hair, which was usually tied into a ponytail, hung loose on her shoulders. She tossed her blue alpine backpack onto the seat across from him, sat down, and produced from the front pocket of her shorts a pamphlet on organ donation. Her narrow, finely carved face drew inward — her eyes, eyebrows, mouth — and focused an invisible beam of interest upon the pamphlet, which she held open before her. She read to Alex. Statistics: how many thousands of people died every year waiting for hearts, kidneys, livers, lungs. She said, "I've got one of each, at least. I could save a life. Maybe a few."

"Do we really have to discuss this? Can't you just check a box on your driver's license or something?"

"We're supposed to discuss it. It says so right here: *'Discuss your decision with your loved ones. Make sure they understand your wishes.'* You are my loved one, aren't you?"

"Look at this," Alex said. "There's like, tar or something on my menu."

Isabel reached over and removed a blue ballpoint pen clipped to the neck of his T-shirt. She tore loose a small perforated card from the organ donation pamphlet and laid it flat on the table before her.

Alex panicked. "Hey, can I at least *see* that first?"

ORGAN/TISSUE DONOR CARD. A line for a signature. *In the hope that I may help others, I pledge this gift to take effect upon my death.* A space below to specify which organs or tissues you were willing to donate, or to indicate that you would donate any and all needed.

Alex asked, "Are you sure you want them carving you up and taking out your insides? It's going to be messy."

"It's not like I'll be awake. I won't feel it."

"Sure, but . . . isn't signing away your body, your anatomical parts, isn't that a kind of premature slackening of resolve? A contravention of your . . ." He groped for the term.

Isabel said, "Blah, blah, blah."

"Your substantially endowed biological project?"

"Depends on what you think the biological project is. I don't think it's a personal project, that the individual is necessarily the point. The evolutionary parade is broader than that. Sure, the individual is the *point*, but the individual is finite. The individual should look beyond her own existence, beyond her death. You know, go for some solidarity with the group. Take an interest in how things turn out. Give to the fund."

"Yeah, but Iz, we're talking about medical personnel cutting into your body with sharp implements."

"The implements have to be sharp or they won't cut."

"Stop it," Alex said, distressed.

"I really want to do this. I've been thinking about it."

She was serious. And, Alex saw, unstoppable. "What if your kidney or heart or whatever ends up going to some wacko? Some crazy right-wing nut who shoots illegal immigrants for sport?"

Isabel gave him a bemused look. "Maybe there's a place on here," she said, flipping the donor card over, "you know, where you can specify Democrat or Republican . . ."

She signed. Alex signed too, on a companion card whose purpose was to state that he understood what Isabel wanted to do and would inform the appropriate authorities if the circumstances arose. He signed mostly so they could set the subject aside and get on with their dinner. He buried the card in his wallet, thinking, *It'll never see the light of day.*

The light was the color of butterscotch. The light radiated heat and descended in a powdery, conical beam from an examination lamp set in the ceiling above the thick, sloping bed on which Isabel lay mostly naked, her cycling shorts and jersey gone, her head shaved to the scalp, her eyes shut to syrupy slits. Her lips were swollen, her face was bruised, there was a pinkie-sized gash above her right eye that someone had sewn up. A clear plastic breathing tube was jammed between her teeth, hard to one side so her upper lip curled back and she appeared to be sneering, snarling, pissed-off, even though she wasn't anything — she was brain-dead. That is, her body was still alive: a ventilator at the bedside gave her breath, and a drug running through an IV in her wrist helped her heart pump. But her pupils, when Alex lifted her eyelids to look, nearly filled her irises, and were fixed motionless, staring, terrified, as though she were trapped at the climax of a nightmare.

Isabel's mother, Bernice, leaned low over the bed stroking Isabel's forehead. *Hey, honey . . . Isabel, it's your mom.* The intentness, the fervor with which Bernice addressed her daughter's ear suggested that through the labyrinth of the inner canal she hoped to locate some undamaged region of the brain that would respond to her, the mother, where it had not responded to the EMT, the neurosurgeon, or any of the other hospital staff and, like a circuit breaker, with the flip of her voice, bring the whole operation up again. *Hey, honey, Isabel, can you hear me? Baby? Let us know.*

Helen Pagano, the attending physician, thin and decorous, dressed in a white lab coat monogrammed with her name in red script, explained to Alex and Bernice that because Isabel's brain showed no signs of activity she was, for all practical purposes, dead. A short while later, after being left alone to absorb this news, Alex and Bernice were approached by a gentle, fawnlike woman who blinked and winced and prefaced nearly everything she said with a thoughtful breath and an exhalation of air that counseled resignation to a higher power. She introduced herself as Susan

Downing, from the Iowa Organ Procurement Organization. Susan Downing expressed her sympathy and then suggested that it was time to consider the delicate issue of organ donation. Had Isabel ever expressed interest in such a thing? As if to answer her own question, Susan Downing handed Alex the organ donation card Isabel had signed. The EMTs had found it in her wallet. If donation were to proceed, Susan Downing explained, steps would have to be taken, people notified. Most important, Alex would have to give his consent.

Alex stared at Isabel's signature. The blue ink had faded slightly, and dampness had blotted the bottom of her "I." He couldn't help feeling, at that moment, that she had courted her own death, even signed off on it. He looked at her body laid out in the bed. Her shaved head was as still as a stone and strangely beautiful. He was angry at her — angry at her goodwill.

Bernice wanted to see the card. Alex gave it to her. "I never had any idea," Bernice said, and asked Alex, "Did she talk about this with you?" Alex wasn't ready to say. He asked Dr. Pagano to join the conversation. He told Dr. Pagano he found the concept of brain death confusing. If Isabel's brain was dead now, and her body would die later

— in the operating room, after the harvesting of her organs, when the ventilator was shut off, as Susan Downing had explained — then when would the whole of Isabel die? Would she die more than once? Another thing: if the flow of blood and fluid and air through the body didn't constitute life, what did it constitute?

Dr. Pagano explained that ever since physicians had become capable of diagnosing brain death independently of cessation of heart function, brain death had become the primary criterion. If the brain was dead, the person was dead.

Alex thought of lying, of telling them Isabel had never mentioned anything about organ donation. And of letting the companion card, soft and frayed after nearly three years in his wallet, remain where it was. But he wasn't capable of the betrayal. He confessed that Isabel wanted to donate her organs — any and all needed, just like the card said — and that she had told him so. He took out his wallet and handed the companion card to Dr. Pagano. "Her signature's on this one too," he said. "So is mine."

After Susan Downing and Dr. Pagano left the bedside, the nurses in the bay began to circulate more quickly. Phones appeared at people's ears. An organ-procurement specialist had been called in. A countdown had ensued. The first step was to certify that Isabel's brain was legally dead. Apparently there was not only a distinction to be made between brain-dead and totally dead, but between brain-dead and *legally* brain-dead — a distinction that would be made by a "Brain Death Committee" composed of two doctors called in from home. These doctors took some time in arriving. They read Isabel's EEG, shined a light into her eyes, wagged her jaw from side to side, prodded her lip with their fingers, squirted ice water into her ears. The consensus: Isabel was certainly brain-dead, but the brain-death doctors couldn't legally pronounce her so until the amount of a certain drug in her brain — pentobarbital, administered hours earlier to minimize brain swelling — had decreased slightly. The thrust being that Isabel's EEG, though flat, could not be interpreted as such until the pentobarbital was largely gone. There was some rancor about this from one of the brain-death doctors: why had he and his colleague been called in before the pentobarbital level was acceptably low? Dr. Pagano explained that she had expected the level to be low enough by now, but that the latest level had come back from the lab surprisingly high. Another level

34

would be sent, and everyone, including Alex and Bernice, would have to wait patiently for the results.

It was not a matter of patience, but of fearlessness and resolve. The experience of Isabel's death, which Alex and Bernice might swiftly and mercifully have lived through, was now further prolonged, and they had to stand close against it without letting their legs go slack. Alex managed to endure only by reminding himself that donating her organs had been Isabel's wish, and that she must have had some idea of what she might be in for. But had she known what her husband and mother might be in for? Had she known they would be forced to sit contemplating the glossy film of saliva on her lips; her ribs showing through her skin at the crest of each sudden, pneumatic inflation of her chest — a skeleton emerging from her torso with each breath? Her body was covered with bandages and patches, wires and tubes, lines through which bars of blood inched toward syringes dangling like Christmas lights. Droplets of urine trickled down through the catheter between her legs to the transparent plastic sack hanging from the side of the bed.

From other parts of the bay, from other

bedsides, from the nurses station, came talk, laughter — voices that showed no trace in their tone of pain or sorrow. The flatulent banter of TVs.

The organ-procurement specialist arrived. Ray Albuta was a large cask of a man with flushed cheeks and curly, apricot-colored hair. Ray bobbed around Isabel's bed, examined lines and tubes, the IV pumps, the ventilator. Ray wanted labs, tests, consults. Acronyms and cryptic multisyllabic enunciations flowed from his mouth. He questioned Isabel's nurse — quiet, industrious Emily. What was Isabel's gentamicin running at? Her cefamandol? Her dobutamine? Alex thought Isabel would have liked these names. Ray wanted to keep her bacteria-free, her fluid levels up, her heart beating healthy and strong. *Toned,* was the word he used. Isabel was his girl now. You could see the eagerness in his face, not so carefully concealed as Alex would have liked. Ray was *treating* Isabel, as though she were a patient who might get better, live, go home, and Alex felt a sharp coldness each time the illusion slid to the floor, each time he realized that all this effort was not being directed toward Isabel's life, but toward the lives of other people, people he didn't even know. Ray asked Alex and Bernice to step

36

outside to the waiting room so a cardiologist could do an ultrasound of Isabel's heart, after which he, Ray, planned to help Dr. Pagano put in a CVP line — Central Venous Pressure — to monitor Isabel's volaemic status. Alex didn't even know Isabel had a volaemic status. He returned to find a thin tube curling from an incision in her chest.

Ray Albuta was growing impatient with the brain-death doctors, who were out at the nurses station awaiting news about the pentobarbital from the lab, where there was some confusion: the pathology resident, who had performed the first pentobarbital level, had gone home and was just now being called back in to perform the second level. The lab was saying another hour, minimum. The brain-death doctors went downstairs to the vending machines.

At one thirty in the morning word came that the pentobarbital level was acceptably low. The brain-death doctors read the EEG — again, flat — pronounced Isabel legally brain-dead, signed some forms, and went home. Ray wanted to take Isabel to the operating room in ten minutes. There were surgeons en route from other hospitals to harvest her organs. They planned to take Isabel's heart, her kidneys, her liver and lungs, even skin and corneas. Would Alex and Bernice think about saying their final good-byes?

The pronouncement struck Alex senseless. After standing beside her body for five hours, gradually, imperceptibly developing a desire to let her go, get it over with, get out of there — for wouldn't the pain of leaving be less than the pain of staying? — to reach this point and then be told he *must* leave, in ten minutes — he was undone. Couldn't the pentobarbital come back? He stroked Isabel's forehead, concentrated solely on that. He untangled an IV line caught in the bed's side-rail, arranged other lines and tubes in a sensible order, which he imagined might make Isabel more comfortable, though he understood she couldn't feel a thing. He wiped saliva from her lip, a spot of blood from inside her right ear. Cleaned her up. Got her ready for the big night — or morning. He had no idea how long the operation would last. Where on her chest would they cut? Would they cut her stomach, too? He tried not to think where else. He hoped they would be gentle and slow. He hoped they wouldn't speak. He knew it was a ridiculous hope, that surgeons chattered and fussed and played music. But he would always envision them bent in silence over Isabel's body, carefully cutting through skin and muscle, delicate with their hands and tools, concentrating, reverent, amazed, as he would be, were he to stumble on such valuables.

Inside Alex's apartment, Otto is waiting, his silky muzzle wedged between door and frame, mouth dropped open, the big meaty tongue draped over a lower front tooth. "OK, sweetheart," Alex says, petting the dog's head, pushing the door slowly open. Otto is a great golden heap of dog. Alex and Isabel got him from the animal shelter five years ago, just after they moved in together. At that time Otto was a puppy, a little blond otter. Now he's the size of a sea lion. He has a sea lion's frumpy bulk, that sloppy way of sitting with his front legs and paws splayed outward and his white, thrushy chest sagging between. He peers past Alex into the hallway, sniffs the air and, when he fails to detect any sign of Isabel, follows Alex into the living room looking demoralized. In this way Otto and Alex are alike: after all this time, they still expect Isabel to suddenly appear. They can't get it through their heads that she's gone.

Alex sets the mail down on the coffee table and says to Otto, who is sniffing the envelopes, "That's a card from Janet Corcoran. What do you think about that? Are we excited? Are we happy-clappy? Do we honestly give a fuck?"

Otto's tongue slides in and out with each breath. He wants to go out, but Alex isn't ready to make the effort. The sight of the answering machine's blinking red sliver quickens his heart rate, makes his breathing go shallow. He inhales deeply, calming himself, and closes his eyes, then pushes Play, genuinely hopeful — though he knows such hope is ridiculous, embarrassing — that one of the messages will be from Isabel, will deliver her voice calling from the ends of the earth, a phone booth in some East Asian metropolis, a Siberian mining outpost where she's been trapped all these months, held hostage by a rare, inexplicable flap in space-time. *It's me. Really. I'm OK. Can you wire me some money for a plane ticket?*

One message is from his dentist, reminding him of an upcoming appointment. The other is from his friend Rob, who wants to know if he's interested in going rock climbing Saturday.

Otto is standing near the door, his tail sweeping wide arcs. "In a minute, Otto," Alex says. He sinks onto the couch, leans back, rests his head against the cushion. He hears footsteps ascending the stairs outside his door, and again his heart quickens. He holds his breath waiting for the sound of a key in the lock. The footsteps continue up the stairs. Alex's imagination insists she come in the door, and the reunion scene, with all its amazement and gushing love, occurs. A year ago, around this time of day, she would have been arriving home after meeting him downtown on his way to work. He would have been starting his evening shift waiting tables at the restaurant. Isabel, tired from a long day in the classroom and lab, would have gone first into the kitchen to feed Otto his Science Diet and make sure he had water, then into the bedroom to change into her cycling gear: the shiny black shorts, the fluorescent aqua-green jersey, the Styrofoam helmet and fingerless gloves. Her elfin cycling shoes had hard plastic soles that made a hollow knocking sound on the floor. This sound always alarmed Otto, sent him stumbling away from Isabel as she walked out into the living room on her heels and stood for a moment trying to make sure she hadn't forgotten anything, hands on her hips, head bowed, one downward-pointed foot lightly resting on the back of her opposite ankle.

Otto, who wandered into the bedroom, now reappears with one of Isabel's black pumps held loosely in his mouth like a dead bird. With a thud he collapses on the floor, positions the shoe between his paws, and gently gnaws the toe. From the delicacy of his chewing, the tender strokes of his tongue, the dog appears to know well who the shoe belonged to. Otto has been mysteriously attached to Isabel's shoes ever since her death; the black pumps and the Birkenstocks are his favorites, though sometimes he'll bring out an oxford or a hiking boot. Alex saved them all.

Other things Alex saved: Isabel's Turkish kilim, a handwoven rug hanging above the Spanish desk, its central design a pistachio green diamond inlaid with flowers and hourglass shapes. Books: *Topics in Cell Motility; Morphology, Taxonomy, and Ecology of Pollen Grains and Spores* — in which, a kind of miracle, he found one of Isabel's eyelashes. Novels by Agatha Christie, Ursula K. Le Guin. Isabel's brown leather recipe book, which used to be an address book until it became so jammed with recipes — scrawled on index cards, cut out from magazines, written on the pages of the book itself — that the transition naturally occurred. Her Captain Kirk poster, signed in black Sharpie by William Shatner himself. On Alex's dresser, in a cushioned jewelry box, earrings and bracelets and necklaces, her engagement ring and wedding band.

At times Alex feels he should get rid of these things, as each reminds him, upon catching his eye, of Isabel. But these are the sacred objects of her affections, and he is their custodian, their curator — a task he takes seriously, and that keeps her close to him.

Otto has abandoned the black pump and taken up position near the door, breathing hard, eyes wide. Alex hoists himself from the couch, goes into the kitchen, drags the sack of Science Diet out from under the sink — this will keep Otto happy for a while — and dumps a scoopful into Otto's bowl. Otto plunges. Alex pours himself a glass of grapefruit juice and returns to the living room couch.

The card from Janet Corcoran, still un-opened on the coffee table. Alex's name and address look as though they were written not for the meager purpose of addressing an envelope but for a place card to mark his seat at a banquet. *Alex Voormann.* The "A" is bold, towering. *Voormann:* solid, purpose-ful, a Roman aqueduct. There is respect, even admiration, in the structure of the two words. It's strange: he can't imagine signing his name like that — feeling like doing so. It's like a signature on the Declaration of Independence. Alex tries to get his mind around the idea that these words were written by a hand whose veins were pulsing with blood pumped by Isabel's heart. He tries to picture this Janet Corcoran, addressing the card, sitting at a desk or a kitchen table in a bathrobe some morning a few days ago with her bare ankles hooked beneath the chair, but it's Isabel he sees, sitting at the Spanish desk, her face contemplative, peering down at photographs of spores.

He tears open the envelope. It's a nice card — firm, glossy white paper, arty, a painting on the front, a cabinet or something full of flowerpots and paintbrushes in jars, green and orange and yellow. *Matisse: Open Window, Collioure, 1905.* He opens the card. *Feeling sorry for you at this tragic time, but boy we're glad your wife was an organ donor. Thanks!* No. The message reads: *Dear Alex Voormann, Thinking of you, as always. Love and courage, The Corcorans.*

Love? They don't even know him. How can they love him? And Alex isn't sure he wants this woman thinking about him *as always.* Otherwise he has to admit there's a directness, a sincerity in the message's brevity. Janet's name is signed below, boldly, like the word *Radcliffe* on the envelope. David, the husband, signed beside her. The children, Carly and Sam, also signed: each letter carved separately, painstakingly, though the end effect is to make the words appear loose, disjointed.

Alex sets the card down on the coffee table. Carly. David. *Thinking of you, as always.* Who are these people? He'd like to talk to Isabel, wherever she is, just to let her know her generosity had an unforeseen consequence: she linked him with these Corcorans, who otherwise would not have existed, who wouldn't be threatening him now with their curiosity, their vitality, with a gratefulness close to adoration. He can't blame them for seeing Isabel as an angel or a saint, or for wanting to know more about her. He'll agree she deserves better than the oblivion of an anonymous benefactor. But apparently he's to introduce Isabel to these Corcorans. To be the courteous host.

The pleasure would be all theirs.

THREE

The banana's long, curving body isn't round — not like a carrot is round. The banana is ridged, multisided. One side, two sides, three . . . the girl loses track. She's a slight, pixieish five-year-old standing in a grocery cart, facing aft, her legs spread for balance. The banana dangles by its stem from two pinching fingers. She tells her mother, who is pushing the cart, "It's not round. The sides are flat, here, here."

"Hey, you're right," says Mom, truly interested. Only recently has she learned to use her brain for what is surely its most rewarding and neglected capability: processing the observable into astonishment. Fruit: an amazing thing. Food that grows on trees, in different colors and shapes, in natural protective packaging, for people to eat!

Janet Corcoran is tall, broad in the shoulders, dressed tonight in a light blue silk shirt that drapes over black capris. The capris

46

used to fit comfortably, but now they cling snugly to blocky hips. Janet would shop for larger sizes if she didn't intend to lose the weight. She's especially eager to lose the extra flesh in her cheeks and under her chin, though that extra flesh is concealed now by the light blue surgical mask she's wearing to guard against infection. She doesn't enjoy wearing the mask. People avoid her when they see it, even though they're the ones who are a threat to her, with their coughing and sneezing. She tells herself the mask makes her look mysterious, and that her green eyes, fair skin, and rambunctious red hair, bound today into a sprout on top of her head, distract and compensate. If she wants to dazzle — at a party, say — she dispenses with the mask, lets her hair flow loose, slips on a black dress, and strides like a giantess. When introduced, she likes to open by declaring that she ought to be dead. "It's incredible that I'm standing here talking to you at all," she'll say, and then, depending on the level of interest — she doesn't require much — explain how just over a year ago she was an inmate in a large metropolitan hospital, and before that, bed-bound at home, sleeping fifteen hours a day, for the other nine mostly lying around in her pajamas watching movies checked out from the library: *Holiday, Indiscreet, His Girl Friday* — Cary Grant's boyish babble turned up high, a wall of yakkety-yak-yak erected against the question threatening from the shadows: how long would she live?

The enormity of the transformation between that woman and this one, and Janet's success at surviving it, have more to say about who she is than anything else. When asked, she tends to overestimate people's curiosity and describe in detail how she had her sternum cut down the middle with an electric saw, her chest cracked open, her diseased heart cut out and replaced with another. She makes no effort to hide the scar: tonight, in the grocery store, the top inch of ten rises from the crevice of her open shirt collar, a thin pink strip, slightly raised, firm to the touch.

Carly, the girl in the cart, points to a box of cereal on a nearby shelf. "Count Chocula has chocolate in it."

"Yes it does," Janet says. "That's why we don't eat it for breakfast. Isn't muesli on our list? Cross off muesli. There."

The shopping list is a piece of notebook paper safety-pinned to the front of Carly's T-shirt. Carly grips a forest green crayon attached to a string around her neck and crosses out the word, drawing the crayon's

48

wedged tip horizontally across the paper.

Janet says, "Honey, you're getting your T-shirt green."

"Is a green T-shirt bad?"

"Two hands, please."

"I don't need two." Carly displays a free hand, five fingers splayed wide. "Except if we're turning. Then I do this. Mom. *Mom.*" She grips the cart's edges with both hands and crouches. "I'm versatile." Her word of the week, picked up from a minivan commercial.

Carly, born prematurely, is smaller and more delicate than her brother, Sam, was at this age. For this reason, Janet has always been especially — her in-laws would say excessively — protective of her. For a long time, beginning when Janet was admitted to the hospital prior to her transplant and continuing through the precarious months afterward, Carly was quiet, uncommunicative, distant. It's a joy to see her spunky again, absorbed in the world around her, bubbling with questions and observations.

Janet thinks, squinting into the distance, *It's beautiful,* these shelves loaded with food packaging, the gaudy plastic, the garish colors — though the unrestrained barrage of color creates a cloudy, silvery shimmer, like that of burning fuel, up and down the aisles. Unless the prednisone's screwing with her vision again. She squats low to the floor and plucks two twenty-four-ounce canisters of raisins off a bottom shelf, loads them into the cart, lifts Carly out so she can look at the reflection of her face in a hanging skillet, lifts Carly back into the cart. No breathlessness, no exhaustion, no frantic knocks of protest from her heart. Unnerving, to think one's health is dependent on that single muscle. Assaulted by a virus — in all likelihood it was a virus — Janet's old heart couldn't contract forcefully enough to pump the required blood to her body, couldn't empty its chambers after each filling. Fluid backed up into her lungs, usurping precious space: when she tried to breathe, the air seemed to go no deeper than the bottom of her throat, and her chest felt as though it were wrapped tightly with packing tape.

She reaches down into the cart, rescues a plastic cup of boysenberry yogurt that Carly's foot has nearly crushed, and places it safely atop a heap of bananas and oranges and celery, albacore tuna, kidney beans, brown rice, couscous — food she must ingest with Eucharistic seriousness of purpose. Sometimes she feels *she's* the one who's been transplanted; as though she, and not the heart, is the one doing all the work. Sure, the heart will support her, but it requires her support in return, and its demands are particular, unequivocal. The heart nags her, the heart says, *Please, no more than 2,000 milligrams of sodium per day, 40 milligrams of fat, 200 of cholesterol. It's nine a.m. Have you taken your cyclosporine? Your prednisone? Your Oscal-D? Don't whine to me about side effects — about your nausea and your flatulence, your cramping and your constipation, your dry skin, mood swings, the hair in funny places. Would you rather be dead? Check your blood pressure. Write it down on the clipboard beside the medicine cabinet. Check your temperature. Write it on the clipboard. Clean the thermometer. Wash your hands. Brush your teeth. Is your sputum green or blood-tinged? Is your skin red, dusky, or swollen? How long have you been coughing like that? Go wash your hands again. As long as you're in there, brush your teeth. How many times do I need to remind you? You're an infection waiting to happen. Go take a walk — you need exercise — but don't walk too vigorously, and wear a mask, and stay away from people with coughs or colds, stay away from construction sites, large crowds, public phones, bathrooms, cold drafty areas, smoke- or dust-filled rooms. Welcome home: that wedge of smoked cheddar in the fridge has mold on it. Tell David to throw it out.*

Sam, Janet's eight-year-old son, dispatched earlier for bread, appears ahead of Janet and Carly at the end of the aisle, his arms stuffed with loaves. He runs up to the cart and dumps the bread onto the accumulating pile. "They didn't have Crunchy Oat. I got Honey Wheatberry. Actually, Honey Wheatberry's better for you, because of the honey."

He's standing with his feet together, fingers fidgeting at his belly. On the crown of his head several strands of fine blond hair, charged with static, reach upward.

"Where have you guys been?" Janet's husband asks, appearing from behind a huge stainless-steel oven in which charred pieces of chicken revolve on a rotisserie. He's carrying four cartons of orange juice, two in each arm, and though he could set them down in the cart he continues to shift and boost them, as if to impress Janet with how burdensome they are. Finally he dumps the cartons into the cart with a self-pitying recklessness that leaves two toppled on their sides. "I've been lugging these things all over the store," he says.

"Hello," Janet says. Carly, bless her, is dealing with the toppled cartons.

David inspects the contents of the cart, reaches down and lifts a bag of celery to see what's underneath. Kidney beans. Tuna. Brown rice. "Fun," he says.

Janet tells him, "Get some junky stuff, I don't care."

"You will when we're all chowing down."

"I may express frustration at not being able to join the free-for-all, sure."

Sam is gripping the cart's handle with both hands and leaning way back, his butt shoved floorward, trying to raise the cart into a dangerous wheelie.

"Hey, cool it," Janet tells him.

Carly says to Sam, "You got the *wrong* kind of bread." With regal composure, standing firm and unshaken in the cart.

Sam, in a voice equally incriminating, says, "You don't even know where the bread *is*."

"It's near the health food," Carly says, correctly.

Sam says, "What you call health food some people call junk."

Janet's been alarmed to hear, lately, in conversations between Sam and Carly, echoes of her more acrimonious conversations with David. She settles a firm hand on the back of Sam's neck and says close to his ear, "We discuss, but we don't get nasty, do we?"

"No," Sam says meekly, and tells Carly he's sorry.

David says, "All right, let's get moving here. What's left on the list?"

He's prepared to push the cart off down the aisle, but two sluggish women and three lumbering men are blocking the way, all chattering at once, shuffling from side to side with little discernible forward movement. David says, under his breath, "All right, come on, it's not a cocktail party."

It's the kind of thing anyone might say — indeed, Janet often said such things herself, she could be as impatient as the next person — but it strikes her ears as coarse, senseless, and a mechanism inside her, recently installed, flinches. After getting her heart she walked out of the hospital onto a new planet. The surface was green, the sky blue, the air drenched with light and sweet to the palate. People, their faces symmetrical and intricately designed, shaped phrases with their mouths and touched one another with elegant, five-fingered hands. Janet's conception of what was beautiful and valuable, once nearly identical to David's, had evolved, and she refused to hurry past that beauty or to let others hurry her past it.

Only weeks ago, confronted with a situation like this, she would have taken David's arm and tried to slow him down, soothe him, encourage him to relax. But she's tired of making the effort. She sings, imitating Mick Jagger, *"Life's just-a-cocktail-party on-the-street."*

From the look on David's face you'd think the world outside the grocery store was a smoking gray ruin — that he was checking his family into a fallout shelter, and that the grocery cart contained all their worldly possessions.

When Sam clutches Janet's hand and says, "Mom, look over here, Mom," she feels rescued, and gladly follows. She lets Sam lead her to an installation of transparent plastic bins, five high and five across. Peanut-butter logs, Gummi Bears, jelly beans, chocolate-covered raisins, malted milk balls. Each bin decorated with a jazzy cartoon depicting pieces of candy exploding outward from a central point. With Janet's permission, Sam detaches the clear plastic scoop magnetically attached to the Gummi Bear bin and begins filling a small bag. He takes only five or six Gummi Bears per scoopful, handles them like uranium pellets, prolonging the experience in a way that makes Janet think, *Yes, right, that's the way to take in the world.* She's pricked with a craving for Good & Plenty but sees that the oblong caplets, half pink and half white, look too much like her 2-milligram prazosin tablets, which taste like dish soap. This visual similarity spreads rapidly outward until the entire rack of candy bins is transmogrified into a gigantic pill container, each bin stocked with a lifetime's supply of one of her medications — with tongue-colored cyclosporine capsules, yellow binocular-shaped Imurans, white aspirinish prednisones and furosemides, pecan-sized K-DURs, Bactrims and Oscal-D's. Each bin with its own magnetized scoop. A preview of all the swallowing she'll have to do to stay alive.

David and Carly are around the corner in the frozen-foods aisle, hand in hand in front of an open freezer door, vapor creeping over their faces. David's height still appeals to her, as does his thick shock of black hair, graying at the temples, and his ruddy handsomeness. The way he's standing stooped in front of the freezer door makes her think to remind him of his posture, which is continually worsening. Not that she's a model of physical perfection. She drags a finger across her right eyebrow, which is thick and bristly — one of several

56

side effects of the prednisone. Walking toward David, she feels her pants clenching her thighs and ass, fat straining against fabric. She's a clumsy, lumbering disturbance, a hormone storm, a battle-battered dray horse. She's got a grisly scar between her breasts, meaty low-slung hips (the prednisone gives her a ravenous appetite), a persistent film of oil on her forehead (prednisone again). She farts and throws up regularly. She gets teary and irritable without provocation. But she doesn't feel the pervasive self-pity she once did. She feels proud and tough. *Take me as I am,* she beams telepathically toward David's head. She feels edgy, adrenalized, as though she's going into battle.

David's mood has grown more cheerful since their last exchange, thanks no doubt to Carly's immense capacity to amuse. "We're wondering what the status is on fish sticks," he asks. "Too much fat?"

"Too much sodium," Janet says. "Let's get some fresh fish and bake it."

"We want the kind of fish you can dip in ketchup," Carly says.

"Mom can't eat ketchup," says David.

"Get some fish sticks," Janet says. "Get some ketchup. I'm not the food police."

A boy careens around a blind corner and

collides hard against David's leg. "Whoa, big fella," David says, palming the boy's head like a basketball.

The boy's mother appears, winces at David by way of apology, and drags the boy away. "Garth, there is a *world* around you, young man. There is a world around you and you must orient yourself *to* it."

David waits until the pair are out of earshot. "Yet another American child named after a country music star."

"It's the cities in Texas that bother me," Janet says. "Austin. Dallas. Houston. What's the next hip baby-name state going to be?"

"Seattle. Spokane," David says, trying out Washington.

Sam opens his mouth and displays for David a green Gummi Bear impaled on one of his incisors. "Why didn't you name me after a country music star?"

"What's country music?" Carly asks Janet.

"It's music people listen to in the country," Sam says.

Carly thinks for a moment. "What country?"

"This country," David says. "It's a certain kind of music that certain people like."

"Do you like it?" Carly asks her father.

"Not particularly," David says.

Sam asks, "Do you like it, Mom?"

"Sometimes. When I'm in a ramblin', heck-raising, Southern-girl kind of mood."

Janet misses them already, these children of hers. She hopes that in ten or fifteen years, after she's gone (even if she stays healthy, transplanted hearts don't last forever: sooner or later an incurable vasculopathy will clog the coronary arteries), there will be a second mother for Carly and Sam, a stepmother who will grow to love them, who will shepherd them safely through rocky adolescence and into adulthood. Janet also worries. What if this woman can't follow her act? What if she does a lousy job? What if her children grow to love this woman as much as they love her? It's agony, the thought of parting with Carly and Sam. She takes in her boy with a slow sweep of her eyes: his feet bare in the canvas compresses of his shoes, the stubborn smudges of dirt in the shallow wells on either side of his ankles, his calves smooth as dolphin skin, elbows knobby, the soft fuzz on the back of his neck, the haphazard swirl of his hair. What will he look like when he's thirty?

They finish their shopping, and though they have enough groceries to cook ten dinners, they decide to eat across the street at Dominic's. Dominic himself flops three gyros and a garden salad onto flimsy paper plates and slides them forth. Four fervent thank-yous bloom from Janet's mouth. David, irritated, wanders away from the counter. Dominic says, "Hey, thank *you*. No problem. No — thank *you*." Janet doesn't bother explaining that her outbursts are actually dispensations of a much larger reservoir of gratitude that has little to do with Dominic or his food — a gratitude dammed off from its rightful recipient, a woman named Isabel Howard. So people like Dominic have to absorb a little extra.

Through the window, on the street, two streams of cars glide in opposite directions. Janet, mask off, enjoys the cool air on her face. She devours her salad, allows her attention to slide free from all subject matter into clear, white thoughtlessness. Isn't this one of the privileges of life, to take life for granted? To disengage, to let time pass unexamined? What's it all been for, otherwise? A woman's brutal death, the grief and suffering of her family, hours of work by doctors and nurses, not to mention Janet's own labor and suffering — all that she might spend these last precious years burdened with the impossible task of living every moment to the fullest?

She hopes Isabel Howard would understand. Isabel Howard: what would Janet do without that name? Of course she understands why the organ procurement organization doesn't want donors' families and recipients discovering one another's identities. There have been cases of donor families making unreasonable demands, monetary and otherwise, as well as instances of harassment, threats, unannounced visits, general unpleasantness. But Janet believed from the outset that the potential benefits of contact outweighed the risks, and with a combination of luck (a surgeon's dropped remark about Iowa and a "bike versus car"), the Chicago Public Library's newspaper archives, the Internet, and too many phone calls to count, Janet broke through the barrier of anonymity. If she hadn't broken through, she would have had to invent a name for this woman who alternately cheers and reproves her from the grave in a voice that sounds uncannily like Ingrid Bergman's in *Notorious,* and who tells her now, feeling generous, *Take it easy. We've earned it. Don't even think of me.*

But Janet does. She wishes Isabel could be here breathing the air, looking out at the world. Eating one of Dominic's gyros.

"One year Saturday," she says, addressing

whoever wants to listen. "One year since Mommy got her new heart. What do you think about that?"

Sam's dangling a strip of lamb in front of his nose with sour-cream-pasted fingers. "Are we going to have a birthday party?"

"We'd have an anniversary party, if we had anything." Janet trains her eyes on David, passing him the burden of explanation.

David plucks a scrap of onion from his lip and flicks it into his mouth. "Sure. Let's have a party to celebrate the anniversary of a horrible, violent death."

"That's not what we'd be celebrating," Janet says, annoyed.

"Of course not. We'd be celebrating *you.*"

Janet doesn't want to engage on this front. Not just now. "I hope her husband's OK."

"I'm sure he is."

"How are you sure?"

David sets his gyro down on his plate, wipes his mouth with his napkin, and wads the napkin into a ball. "It's been a year. He ought to be moving on. Or trying."

"Would you be moving on right now if I'd died?"

"I wouldn't be . . . maybe not *now,*" David fumbles. "I can tell you one thing, I wouldn't be interested in getting cards and letters from the people who got your organs.

How creepy is that?"

"The heart was a gift," Janet says defiantly. "Not from him."

"He supported his wife's decision. He gave the go-ahead. Otherwise the whole thing might not have happened. Otherwise I might not be here."

"So you thanked him. Aren't two cards enough? Two cards and a four-page letter?"

"Three pages." True, that first letter had been long, and writing it had been one of the most difficult things Janet had ever done. How did you go about explaining to a man without sounding too grateful or too ungrateful, without entirely highlighting or ignoring the harsh injustice of the transaction, that his wife's untimely, tragic death, while causing him excruciating pain, had permitted her, a complete stranger, to live? She spent a week scribbling and scratching out, and in the end felt like she had made a noble effort even though the letter weighed in at a meager three pages that seemed to contain nothing more than a faint condensation of all the gratitude and confusion and guilt in her head.

"I'm sure he appreciated the letter," Janet says. "I don't think it was intrusive. And the anniversary card was a gesture. It would have been unconscionable not to send something. If he doesn't want to read it, he can rip it up. It's not a subpoena."

David chews his gyro, temporarily silenced. Then he says, "What are you going to do if you ever get the chance to talk to this guy?"

"I don't know, to tell you the truth."

"What if you meet him? How are you going to look him in the face?"

In the hospital, close to death, waiting for a heart, Janet often envisioned — indeed, hoped for — car accidents in which a donor might be killed. "If you're trying to make me feel guilty, I already do. Maybe that's what I'll tell him. How guilty I feel."

"If it's a gift, like you say, there's no need to feel guilty."

"It's all so easy for you, isn't it?"

"I just don't see the guy as such a big hero," David says defensively, and with a kind of anguish. "His *wife* is the hero. Or was."

"She's done suffering," Janet says. "He's still alive. He's still paying the price."

David rolls his eyes, chafing against her incisiveness. "Aren't we all."

FOUR

Sometimes in the evening after work, for company and consolation, or for the lack of anything better to do, Alex walks over and visits Isabel's mother.

Bernice lives on the east side of town, east of the university, just outside the perimeter of perennial student rentals. Her neighborhood is one of modest houses, four-squares and bungalows and Craftsmans. The sidewalks and streets are shaded by old trees. There are vegetable and flower gardens, tool sheds and log piles, cedar fences and lattices. Isabel grew up here. Superimposed over all Alex sees is the afterglow of Isabel's childhood. A fall from a lower branch of that white oak, there, broke the third and fourth fingers of her right hand. She and Sally Serbousek displayed their fledgling sixth-grade breasts to each other in the dark, cramped interior of the Serbouseks' doghouse, there. On the other side of that hedge, in the Cavanaughs' yard, a trampoline was set up through the warm seasons, upon which neighborhood children jumped and tumbled, shrieked and sang, injured themselves.

Bernice's house is a brown-brick Tudor, cloistered in trees. The high, steeply pitched roof looks designed to impale anything — clouds, aircraft — that might descend upon it from above. The walls are hairy with vines, thick as cable, which sprout teaspoon-sized leaves. The windows are dark, tinted green by the reflections of trees: the house appears to be filled with pond water.

The doorbell produces a mellow, chiming tone within. Eventually the door opens and Bernice floats out of the murk, dressed in black jeans and a white Joffrey Ballet T-shirt whose short sleeves she's artfully rolled up into thin cuffs. She places one hand, visor-like, over her eyes as though Alex were blasting her with a harsh light. Her bare feet look fragile and so pale as to appear nearly translucent, their veins dangerously exposed. "Hey. How's it going?" she asks. "Hello, Otto." She reaches down and musses the hair on the dog's head. "What a good boy."

"Did I wake you up?" Alex asks.

"I've been on the computer." Bernice

studies the sky, which is still light — a fine, luminescent blue. "It's gorgeous out here. Please tell me what I'm doing sitting inside staring at e-mail."

"I don't know. But why sit inside staring at e-mail when you can sit inside staring at" — with a dramatic flourish he removes a video from behind his back — *"Jason and the Argonauts?"*

A few weeks ago, after seeing the original *Godzilla* on TV, Alex and Bernice started renting other Japanese monster movies: *Godzilla vs. Mothra, Rodan, King Kong vs. Godzilla.* But the genre was getting boring, and Alex thought it might be nice to branch out. Unfortunately Bernice doesn't seem interested. "Oh. Huh," she says, like the victim of unwanted solicitation.

Alex moves in for the hug. Bernice snaps onto him: her hands clutch his back, her chin digs into his collarbone. Such complex events, these hugs. Each is a release of grief, a confession of loneliness, a soaking-up of reassurance.

Alex follows Bernice into the house and unleashes Otto, who heads for the kitchen, knowing he'll find crumbs on the floor. Bernice pauses in the foyer to smooth a throw rug with her bare foot, then continues into the living room and studies the walls with a kind of abstracted uncertainty, as though they're unfamiliar to her — as though she's seeing this room for the first time. She turns to face Alex, smiles, slips her hands together, all ten fingers interlocking. Bernice is sixty. Her age is confirmed in her face — a pretty face, the skin like crinkled paper around the eyes and mouth — but confounded by her body, which is trim, sturdy, muscular in the arms and shoulders from working out with handweights. Years ago, when Alex first met Bernice, he thought rather proprietarily that he'd be lucky if Isabel turned out to look as good as her mother did in her midfifties: as lean, as fit, as clear-complexioned.

Bernice inserts her hands into the front pockets of her jeans and scratches the calf of one leg with the toe of her opposite foot. "I was thinking of heading over to the school before it gets dark to see how they're doing on the new playground. They're tearing down the monkey bars and putting up a whole new deal."

Alex can't get enthusiastic. It's been another long day grading the obtuse scrawlings of seventh graders. He wants to plant himself on Bernice's couch and vegetate. Suck down a few beers. Travel the Mediterranean with Jason. "What's wrong with the monkey bars? I liked the monkey bars. I had a lot of great times on the monkey bars."

"They're worried about injuries and litigation. The new equipment is supposed to be safer. Although some people say the new equipment's less challenging, and just as hazardous, potentially, in different ways. Who knows. I just want to take a walk. I've been staring at a screen all day."

Alex, knowing he should try to please Bernice, smiles in acquiescence. She gives his upper arm a grateful pat and as an afterthought bends and tugs one of the threads dangling from the hole in his jeans. "Did you go to work today? You look like you were attacked by a cougar."

"Technically we're only allowed to wear jeans on Friday. Dress-down Friday. I try to dress down every day. It's my little way of rebelling. Dress-down Friday is supposed to be this big boost for morale, but it just shows how pathetic management is. They lay off a hundred full-time people and replace them with temps, and pay us less money and don't give us health insurance or benefits or any job security, but they figure, Hey, if we let them wear jeans on Fridays, they'll be happy."

"If they didn't hire temps, you wouldn't have a job," Bernice observes.

"Some days I wish I didn't."

"Have you looked into any PhD programs?"

Alex isn't particularly interested in pursuing a PhD in archaeology. He'd rather move into private enterprise or government work, do cultural resource management for an environmental firm, or for the Forest Service or the National Parks — a job that would allow him to spend time outside. But one night a few months ago he mentioned the PhD option to fend off one of Bernice's periodic inquiries about his future, and since then he hasn't been able to shake it. He'd like to tell Bernice that just because Isabel was getting a PhD doesn't mean a PhD is the only direction available to him. He gets the sense that Bernice is pressuring him — consciously or not — to measure up to Isabel's potential, to follow Isabel's dream, to adopt Isabel's ambitions and goals. To accomplish what Isabel would have accomplished, had she lived. "If I decide to get a PhD, and that's a big 'if,' I need to look into some programs, yeah," Alex says. "And get in touch with some professors. And do a zillion other things. *If.*"

"You know, that's a silly expression, 'dress-down,' when you think about it," Bernice says. "As though you somehow dress *down,*

70

like going down or falling down or maybe sort of leaning down as you put on your clothes. Well. Dress up. Of course it comes from dress up. Speaking of which, I need to go upstairs and put some shoes on."

The stairs creak under her feet. Alex goes through the living room and dining room to the kitchen, where Otto is lapping vigorously at the floor — probably the most thorough cleaning it ever gets. Alex grabs a beer from the fridge and wanders back into the living room. He knows he must learn, as Isabel did, to be patient with Bernice's concern, her prodding, her high hopes. Bernice believes she wasted her own life, that twenty-odd years ago she missed the launch of the feminist boat. According to Isabel, Bernice wasn't sure it was seaworthy. She wasn't sure where the boat was going, or whether she belonged on board. Her husband encouraged her doubts. Her children demanded attention and food. Suddenly Bernice was fifty and her husband was gone and she decided she belonged on the boat, but it was too far out to sea. Personnel directors eyed her down and up in her middle-aged-lady clothes and told her she didn't have enough education and experience to be an assistant editor, a reference desk clerk, even a secretary — which was true. She had a BA in home economics from the University of Kansas and thirty years of homemaking experience. Still, she managed to get a job working in the Accounts Receivable department at US West, and then, many years later, the job she'd long coveted, designing costumes for the university's opera and dance productions.

The curtains over the living room windows are a pale cinnamon color, and drawn so that only a faint, tinted light reaches the carpet. Alex sits on the chunky tan couch, runs a hand over cushions glossy with wear, props his feet up on the coffee table — a big slab of driftwood covered with glass, a relic from a primeval family vacation, a summer's station-wagoning along the Oregon coast. A philodendron spills from the mantel. Beside the philodendron is a bronze bust of Mozart with a green and white Pioneer Hi-Bred Seed cap tipped jauntily on his head. Isabel set the cap there years ago, when she was a girl, as a joke; Bernice felt it expressed something. On either side of the fireplace are bookshelves: the left sparsely populated with older books, *Adam's Rib, The Sensuous Woman, The Female Eunuch*. A Time-Life set about the ocean, missing volumes two and five. The right shelf is a squalid tenement of paperback science fiction, novels, and story collections stacked and crammed in every which way, many with split, chafed spines and shiny with tape Bernice has used to repair them. Bernice's ancient stereo receiver is also here, and a newer CD player, and lower down, in drawers that remain partially pulled out, Bernice's CD collection, which is eclectic in taste — jazz, classical, folk, world music, Broadway — but dominated by opera, dozens of little boxed sets with librettos in Italian and French and German.

How does Bernice stand it, living in this house where her family grew, passed its brief golden age, and swiftly declined? Todd, Bernice's husband, left first, when Isabel was thirteen, and a few years later Isabel's older brother, Clancy, went off to Stanford, from which he rarely returned. Now Clancy is an investment banker in Hong Kong. He hardly ever calls or writes, and when he visits the country he stays in San Francisco with his father and stepmother, with whom the divorce left him allied. Alex gets the impression that Clancy's defection and continued absence hurt Bernice far more than Todd's. For a while Bernice had Isabel, who stayed close to home and loyal throughout, but now, except for Bernice's estranged older sister in Kansas, Alex is it.

Sometimes Alex feels he and Bernice are alike in this — in their isolation, their lack of close family. Alex is an adopted, only child, and he's never been close to his parents. His father is the president of a bank in Council Bluffs, and together with his mother they run a hostel for wayward youth out of their sprawling Victorian house. Alex visits once a year, usually at Christmas, for a perfunctory day or two, and occasionally if Herman and Gena are traveling east on I-80 they'll drop in to see him. He doesn't miss them the rest of the year, and as far as he can tell they don't miss him. On the contrary: they seem absorbed in their life — their books, their philanthropy, their boarders — and content to have raised him and sent him on his way. He spent his childhood searching, and failing to find, assurance that he was more than just Herman and Gena's first and longest-staying boarder, and in the clear light of retrospect he feels that although he may have been more, he was not much more. He feels more gratitude toward Herman and Gena than love.

In the den, on a desk in front of a window overlooking the backyard, Bernice's computer hums. Alex flicks the little eggy mouse with a finger. Words flood the monitor:

I am truly interested to learn that you harbor an interest in bird watching! Or, as the more devoted enthusiasts term it, birding. I derive great peace from observing birds in the wild and recording their behavior with my Panasonic Palmcorder — an invaluable accoutrement. Trust me: care in selecting the proper equipment will ensure you propitious rewards in the wild. Actually, if you are truly interested, I recommend beginning with the Audubon Society's Field Guide to North American Birds (Eastern Region). This is a very thorough, well-organized guide with lots of gorgeous color plates and descriptions of birds and their habitats.

Janet is fine. She mentioned having a little blurry vision at the grocery store the other night, which is no doubt due to her prednisone. On Friday she's taking one of her advanced art classes on an outdoor excursion to do some drawing, which she's excited about. It's been two years since she's been able to do this. They walk a few blocks to a busy street near the high school and draw some of the old Czech-style buildings.

Take care/Talk to you soon,
Lotta.

Lotta. Alex feels a cool lightness trickling through his chest, as though from a burst capsule of icy fluid. He was disturbed to find out, several weeks ago, that Bernice had struck up an e-mail correspondence with Janet Corcoran's mother, who had somehow managed to track down Bernice's e-mail address. He feels — is it silly? — that Bernice is betraying him. Going over to the other side. Consorting with the enemy. He doubts that Lotta has Bernice's interests foremost in mind, and suspects Lotta is hoping to lure Bernice, and maybe him, into a meeting with Janet, who will want to talk about — guess what — Isabel. *Give me the rest of her, will you?* The history, the personality, the lore. Apparently the heart wasn't enough.

There are footsteps on the stairs, and presently Bernice shuffles into the den. Her cheeks and lips are pinkish: she's put on makeup. "I should turn that off," she says, nodding at the computer. "I don't even — oh. Reading my e-mail, are you?"

"This woman's got a problem with the English language," Alex says. " 'Propitious rewards in the wild'? What's that?"

Bernice sits down in front of the computer, gazes into the screen, lays her hand on the mouse. She looks as though she's holding the computer's hand. "I don't think there's anything wrong with 'propitious.' "

"So you've got this major interest in birds all of a sudden?"

Bernice shrugs. "It's easy to get interested in things when the objective is to sustain a conversation."

"I hate to tell you, but this woman is a nut. 'Propitious rewards in the wild.' 'Invaluable accoutrement.' I'm a paid expert at interpreting human prose, and I can tell you, this language is symptomatic of a disjointed relationship with reality."

Bernice gives Alex a sly, doubtful look. "I think she's nervous, to tell you the truth. And so what if she has a florid writing style. I don't understand why she bothers you so much."

"She doesn't bother me," Alex says, thinking, *Not as much as you do, constantly talking about the Corcorans, thinking about the Corcorans, wondering about the Corcorans, giving me stupid trivial news about the Corcorans.* "She's the greatest. Send her a cyber-smooch for me."

Bernice folds her arms low across her stomach and claws at her elbows; she looks as though she's trying to unscrew them from her arms. Isabel used to do this, exactly this, when she was irritated or upset.

Even Bernice's posture resembles Isabel's: the shoulders stiff, the head dipped and held perfectly still as though at the request of a hairstylist. Would he and Isabel have been like this, Alex wonders, in thirty-odd years? Bickering? Sniping? He doesn't like to think so.

"I got another card from Janet Corcoran a few days ago," he offers.

Bernice sits perfectly still, uncertain of his intentions. "Did you bring it?"

Why would he *bring* it? "It's at home. A whole bunch of people signed. I can't remember the names. Carly?"

"That's Janet's daughter. There's a boy, too. Sam. He's eight."

"I thought Sam might be the dog. You know how some people sign for their dogs and make the letters all crooked and sloppy so it'll look like it was actually the dog holding the pen?"

Bernice, not amused, moves the mouse in slow circles around its pad.

Alex asks, "How old is Carly? Younger than Sam?"

"Carly's five. You want to see a picture?"

It takes Alex a moment to understand that she means a photograph of the Corcorans. He's never seen a photograph of the Corcorans, and wasn't aware Bernice even had one. He feels tricked. Bernice goes into the other room and returns with a small manila envelope, from which she removes a 3 × 5 photograph. In the foreground are a woman, a man, and two children, all standing straight and unnaturally erect, lungs filled with air — hold those smiles! Sweepstakes winners. The man is tall, black hair. The boy's thumbs are hooked in the front pockets of his jeans. The woman is holding the girl's hand and leaning slightly over her as though to shadow her from the sun. The girl is small, cute, dressed in a blue T-shirt. There's a stretch of grass in the background, and farther off, rising from a bank of trees, buildings — silver and bronze pillars.

So this is Janet Corcoran. Tall, broad-shouldered, big-boned. A black stocking cap. Ribbons of kinky red hair shoot to her shoulders. Alex stares at her chest, telling himself Isabel's heart is right there underneath her T-shirt, underneath skin and bone, but he can't make himself believe it. "She looks like Frankenstein's monster. What does she weigh, like, two hundred? She's got to be six-two. It's got to be a strain on the heart, being that big. Seriously."

"It's *because* of the heart that she's heavy," Bernice says, exasperated. "She has to take special medicines."

"What do you mean it's because of the heart? It can't be the heart. Are you kidding — all that exercise Isabel got? It's a great heart."

"No, you're misunderstanding. The heart — she has to take steroids to take care of the heart, and the steroids make her gain weight, is the way Lotta explained it. There's nothing wrong with the heart itself."

"She'd better be taking good care of it," Alex says, though it occurs to him there's not much he can do to enforce this. He stares at the faces in the photograph. The faces stare back. "I don't feel a connection."

Bernice tips her head back as though trying to catch a scent in the air.

Alex says, without concealing the incrimination, "You do."

Bernice nods. Her expression is one of nostalgia, as if for some other, better life.

FIVE

Bernice has trouble sleeping. Every night around ten or eleven, lying exhausted on the living room couch, she sinks into a delicious doze: her body warm, cheeks numb, vision gauzy, as though she's been given a dose of morphine. But when she rouses herself and goes upstairs and tries to continue sleeping in bed, flat on her back in the dark, she can't drift off. Haunted by memories, anxious and distressed, she twists and thrashes long past midnight. In the morning she wakes on her stomach like a pinned wrestler, chest and cheek pressed to the mattress, a penny of drool on the sheet.

She wipes her mouth with the sleeve of her T-shirt and swings her legs over the edge of the bed. She stands at an east-facing window basking in sunlight, having read in a women's magazine that sunlight improves your mood — something about photons hitting your retinas.

It's Friday, April 21. Isabel died a year ago tonight. Bernice is dreading every minute of this day, but she's determined to face it full-on, with courage. She'll have a busy day at the costume shop to distract her. Then, tonight, she and Alex are having dinner together here.

She pulls on a pair of jeans, takes off her T-shirt, and fastens on a bra. She's overdue for a breast self-exam but can't get interested, perhaps because the prospect of death no longer frightens her. In her family, where grandmothers and grandfathers, her father and mother, and now Isabel are dead, dying is like being confirmed, or lettering in a high school sport, or going to college: everyone has done it. Bernice feels left out, left behind, unproven. *You sure you won't give it a try?* Bernice answers *No.* She's never been able to contemplate suicide — swallowing pills, swiping a blade across her wrists — though she does wonder if she might find Isabel on the other side. Recently she's been reading books with soft, fuzzy covers, ethereal bursts of light in the background, the titles in raised gold lettering: *Closer to the Light, Transformed by the Light, Saved by the Light, Embraced by the Light.* She keeps these books upstairs on her night table, where she hopes Alex won't see them. He's agnostic and would think they're silly. She imagines him making some smart-aleck remark: "Is this something from your science-fiction collection?" Bernice wouldn't call it science fiction. She believes there's a good possibility that what she's reading is true, that these people who have near-death experiences in emergency rooms and operating rooms and intensive-care units really do rise above the crowd of frantic doctors and float through a tunnel into a haze of well-being, a light-steeped reception chamber where deceased relatives await. Bernice wonders if Isabel is there, wherever *there* is. Some of the more evangelical authors want her to believe it's the Christian heaven — a big, jubilant love fest for a wise, Michelangeline God. But Bernice has her limits. She rejects these books as propaganda. They're light on evidence, and shoddily thought out: the authors, like Moses descended from the mountain, relate intimate, privileged conversations with a professorial deity. Bernice laughs her way through these books, retitles them in her head. *Christianity: It's All True!* or *Everything Fits Together!*

The stairs are covered with a sand-colored runner of carpet and creak loudly beneath Bernice's feet. The living room is dark, the curtains drawn. Mozart's gaze is particularly zealous and uncompromising this morning, peering out from underneath his green-and-white cap. Bernice would gladly have gotten rid of the bust ages ago if Isabel hadn't come home one night several months after Todd left and stuck the cap on Mozart's head. Todd had insisted on buying the bust one summer at an antique show, then argued it should be displayed prominently in the living room — a position of which Bernice didn't think it worthy. The bust is dingy, and the sculptor didn't get Mozart's face right: the expression is too heavy, too ponderous, the jowls like saddlebags. This Mozart looks like Churchill.

She picks up a pair of socks she left on the floor the night before. She was sitting on the couch watching *Alien* when her feet felt clammy, so she stripped off the socks and jammed her feet down between the couch cushions. Now she wads the socks into a ball and uses it to wipe up a ring of condensation left on the coffee table by her iced-tea glass. Without any particular cue or inducement she sees her son, Clancy, sitting with a crowd of lively, honey-skinned Asians around a table littered with thimble-shaped porcelain cups, bowls of steaming rice, platters of fish. Somewhere in the hive of Hong

Kong. She understands clearly what he has against her, what he blames her for. The divorce. Throwing his early adulthood into disarray. But his unwillingness to forgive her, to see a more complex picture, to accept her mistakes as the unintended blunderings of a well-meaning adult trying to live a life for which there is no trial run, bewilders and angers her.

She opens the living room curtains, the windows. The air is cool, moist, fragrant with blossoms. A man in a blue anorak walks past on the sidewalk with a stringy-legged black Lab. A woman jogs by wearing shimmery orange leggings, ponytail swishing. Bernice tries to suppress a vision of Theresa Skarda — the woman Todd had an affair with. Short, compact, a body like India rubber. The perfect all-weather accessory for the Distinguished Man of Fifty. In bicycle shorts and jogging bra, a snack-pack of sex. In her gray cashmere cardigan and black cat glasses, the fashionable, acute graduate student. It's funny, the thought of Theresa doesn't bother Bernice the way it used to. Neither does the divorce. What's a divorce compared with a death? Losing Todd, which at the time felt like a mortal wound, feels in retrospect like a glancing blow. People who have survived coronary artery bypasses and brain surgery and organ transplants, people like Janet Corcoran, must feel similarly blasé about the torn ligaments and broken bones they suffered earlier in life. Not that losing Todd wasn't debilitating. Bernice felt betrayed and deceived. But the damage was confined to a few tender, exposed regions of her soul. When Isabel died, the devastation charred every hill and valley. Bernice emerged into nuclear winter.

It's inspiring to think back on that period from her current vantage. She's come a long way. Here she is, moving briskly through the dining room, awake, alert, dusting with the wad of damp socks, the edge of the sideboard, a lampshade, spots where the ubiquitous membrane of dust has thickened to fur. She feels composed, tranquil. She's looking forward to seeing Alex tonight but doesn't crave his company like she used to back in the days when she called him constantly and showed up on his doorstep at odd hours, teary and fierce. *Will you* please *go for a walk with me?*

The kitchen is a mess. The sink full of dishes, the counter strewn with used glasses and mugs, plates and bowls, cupcake wrappers, empty yogurt cups. Bernice dumps yesterday morning's coffee grounds out of the filter, rinses it, measures in three scoops of Fair Trade Guatemalan. She stands at the counter waiting for the coffee to brew and preparing mentally for an arduous day at the costume shop: a last-minute fitting, cuffs to be sewn on two of the men's coats, a gold braid to be repaired on a turban, more work on the Act II costume change. She'll be lucky to get out of the shop by seven. She was smart to do her grocery shopping last night. She wonders whether she ought to buy a third bottle of Shiraz. Neither she nor Alex are big drinkers, but she likes the idea that they'll spend a long evening talking over liberally refilled glasses. She'll put on music, something jazzy and cheery, Ellington or Armstrong. She tries to hear it now from the living room but instead hears creaking on the stairs. Young Clancy, twelve or thirteen, appears in the entryway to the kitchen, fresh from his shower, damp splotches on his shirt and khakis. He was going through a phase in which he refused to dry off with a towel, insisting his clothes were a sufficient absorbent, that toweling off was a waste of energy. Already he was preoccupied with efficiency, with maximizing returns. Isabel, precocious and hyper-confident, sixth grade, floated around in her blue knit polyester pants and matching shirt, orange fringed vest, and some long necklace with a medallion — a rabbit's foot or a chunk of red clay studded with plastic rubies. How Bernice loved those hectic weekday mornings! The kitchen floor cluttered with book bags, news yabbling on the radio, everyone chattering and chomping English muffins and slurping orange juice and rushing to get out the door, or not rushing enough: Isabel tended to dally over her food, experiment on it, dip her finger into her orange juice and fish for pulp, prod the craters in her English muffin with her fork. Bernice rarely rushed or chastised her, feeling that Isabel's curiosity should be protected. Bernice was also cultivating trust, intimacy, having sensed early on that Isabel, more than Todd or Clancy, was her most likely candidate for an ally. She and Isabel were close, devoted, affectionate, *simpatico*. Chummy. In the early years Isabel was permanently attached to Bernice's hip. At the grocery store they huddled beside the cart, heads bent, voices low, Isabel struggling to read the ingredients of a juice or a cake mix or a soup, Bernice jumping in on words like "fructose" and "hydrogenated." They went bowling together, tromped around in the funny shoes, spent too much time choosing their balls, invented variations on the game in which you bowled standing on one leg or imitating a certain animal. On blazing summer afternoons they rode their bikes to the city pool and splashed in the cool water until Bernice, worn out, sprawled poolside while Isabel did flips off the low board or scurried off to intrigue with her giggly pre–junior high pals — girls with whom she would shortly be going to the pool alone. Bernice was astonished that these girls didn't entirely supplant her as Isabel's companion. True, as Isabel got older Bernice no longer spent as much time with her, but they still talked, and Isabel still confided in Bernice.

The divorce tore them apart. Both Clancy and Isabel seemed to conclude, from their father's rejection of their mother, that she had serious shortcomings, grave flaws — that they ought to be wary of her apparent goodness. Isabel moped around the house with the cowed, disbelieving look of a slapped dog. She hardly spoke. She spent hours alone in her room reading comic books whose violence astonished Bernice, and when she was downstairs gravitated toward the television and sat staring at the screen like a street child receiving the enticements of a cult leader. The cult, as it turned out, operated out of the high school where Isabel was a newly minted freshman. The Ghoul Girls, as Bernice called them, were a sulky, abrasive bunch who dressed exclusively in black, dyed portions of their hair orange or blue, and listened to wild, frantic music that sounded like hordes of screaming men massacring one another with automatic weapons. The Ghoul Girls hung around on the pedestrian mall downtown, their arms yoked around each other's necks, sucking clove cigarettes and slurping black coffee from old lunchbox thermoses decorated with pictures of superheroes: Cat Woman, the Incredible Hulk. They were quirky, the Ghoul Girls, and might have been endearing without the searing looks, the foul mouths, the disdain for parents and teachers and police officers who made them pick up their cigarette butts off the ground. Bernice had no doubt that the Ghoul Girls were guilty of more serious violations of the law, but she couldn't come by hard evidence. Isabel, mornings after meetings of the coven, was evasive and sarcastic, dressed typically in black sweatpants and a black T-shirt with a gruesome image on the front — a worm-infested skull, a blood-drenched crucifix — her face pale as a vampire's, eyelids tinged purple, torturing a piece of toast with long, talonlike silver fingernails and rolling her eyes as she parried Bernice's questions. *A drunk guy drove me home. Who? Ted Bundy. Son of Sam. Rob Kutcher, if you have to know. No, he's not my boyfriend. He's my pimp.*

Bernice, who felt like a totalitarian dictator, was nevertheless afraid to ease up on the interrogations and curfews; she worried Isabel would disappear some weekend at a slam-dancing concert and turn up months later in Milwaukee or Detroit living in a basement apartment with a man whose lower lip was pierced with a safety pin. Fortunately Isabel never defected. Somewhere in the fall of tenth grade she grew disillusioned with the Ghoul Girl ideology, whatever it was, and came in from the wild. Ghoul Girl pessimism and gloom were wearing her down, narrowing her options. The Ghoul Girls were too dismissive of interests Isabel secretly, blasphemously desired to pursue: sports, schoolwork, a certain handsome, mild-mannered boy who sat behind her in geometry. Soon this boy was taking Isabel to university basketball games and coming over on Friday nights to watch rented movies (Bernice gladly made herself scarce). Isabel stopped dyeing her hair, stopped wearing black, and rediscovered the primary colors. In school, her C's climbed to B's, A's in biology and chemistry. She went out for the swim team, undeterred by the fact that she'd never swum competitively before. It turned out she had a knack for the backstroke and enjoyed the long hours in the water frantically wheeling her arms while a man stalked her up and down the length of the pool shouting into her face through a bullhorn.

Bernice went to the home meets and to any of the away meets within driving distance. It was a triumphant return, of sorts, to their pre-divorce, pre–junior high excursions to the city pool. Bernice sat in the bleachers with the other parents and fans and shrieked her lungs out at the rapidly gliding tumult of spray in her daughter's lane. After the meets Isabel was glorious and elated and starving, and Bernice took her out for cheeseburgers and milkshakes. They talked openly, at length, over ketchup-streaked plates and perspiring water glasses. Isabel didn't gawk at the ceiling or nibble on her fingernails when Bernice voiced ideas or opinions. Isabel watched her mother's face. Isabel was serious and receptive. A miracle: the curiosity Bernice had spent so long cultivating in the girl was being turned on her.

Bernice was ecstatic when Isabel decided

to attend the university in Athens. Bernice had been careful not to force the decision on her, even though she'd wanted to drop to her knees several times and beg Isabel to stay close to home. Clancy had been at Stanford for three years and had rarely visited, preferring to spend his breaks with Todd and Theresa in San Francisco. If Isabel chose Michigan or Wisconsin Bernice would be completely alone. But Isabel seemed to understand. Not only did she stay close to home, but she was careful not to vanish into the whirlpool of student life; she called or dropped by the house whenever she could. Some of Bernice's fondest memories of Isabel date from this period: sitting in Café Apollinaire over foamy café au laits, talking about Isabel's courses, her professors, her interests and ambitions and quandaries. Bernice was inspired to enroll in classes at the local community college: Introduction to Computers, Basic Lawn Care and Fertilization, Beginning Aikido. Isabel would say to her, *Way to go, Mom,* with sincerity and pride. Bernice quit her bill-processing job at US West and found a costume-making job at the university. She cleaned out her basement, unloaded all the old junk with a series of festive garage sales. She wrote to friends she hadn't seen since high school or college, related her recent travails, told them, *Now the fog is finally lifting and I'm having my own personal renaissance.* She was proud to write to those same friends a few years later, *Isabel is engaged to be married to a man she's been seeing for some time now. His name is Alex Voormann, and he's wonderful, he works as an archaeologist for the state. They're thinking about a date in the spring. I'm so happy she's not making any of the mistakes I made!*

And then one evening, while slicing a lemon, the phone call from Alex at the restaurant, his voice rushed, his meaning barely comprehensible. There were red lights all the way down Burlington Street, every intersection, six agonizing stops. Pouring rain. She arrived at the same hospital her daughter had been born in. And now here was that daughter laid out like some kind of beautiful slaughtered animal.

Bernice is standing exactly where she was when that phone call came, her coffee mug on the counter in front of her, thinking that at least nothing will ever hurt her that much again. She always used to suspect that the price for happiness, the price for enjoying the company of a person you loved, was the steadily increasing risk of losing them, and at times, when she considered the possibility that she might lose Isabel or Clancy or, in the early days, Todd, Bernice didn't think she could stand it, didn't think she could go on living in a universe whose laws forced her to submit to such a terrible fear. Now she sees what a small price it is to pay, what staggering joy she received in return. You should be willing to pay that price for as little as a few days or hours with a person you love, she thinks, rubbing her fingertips across a patch of linoleum the years have worn down to a cloudy smear.

Six

It's exciting for Janet, every spring —
especially this spring, she has her old energy
back — to hustle her advanced drawing
students out the rear door of Benito Juarez
High School and up Ashland Avenue to
Eighteenth Street. It's quiet at this hour,
nearly one, the traffic light, sidewalks clear,
a few young mothers pushing strollers,
pretty, well-dressed women with caramel
skin and raven-black hair. A trio of scruffy
hipsters heads for the Jumping Bean Café.
A new arrival from Mexico rides the invisible, lethargic current that hugs the storefronts, dressed in an old flannel shirt and
paint-splattered jeans, the brim of his
baseball hat pulled down low, fists shoved
deep into the pockets of his jacket.

It's a gorgeous day, the sun high and
bright, a breeze that pulses every ten or
twenty seconds to brush accumulated heat
off the skin. Janet wishes Isabel Howard

could be here to see this day, feel this breeze — Isabel, who died a year ago tonight. Of course if Isabel were here Janet probably wouldn't be, which is the reason Janet's been thinking about Isabel ever since she opened her eyes this morning and why, every few minutes, she closes her eyes and bows her head and whispers under her breath, *Thank you.*

"OK, spread out!" Janet shouts to her flock, who are dreamy, tipsy with freedom, and would rather have a day party than draw buildings. Janet is an aggressive shepherd, and within minutes her students are nicely spaced along the shady south sidewalk of Eighteenth in front of the *taquerías* and *fruterías* and *panaderías,* sitting on benches or stoops or cross-legged on the ground, drawing pads open on their laps, pencils poised, eyes on the streetscape: the tall, elegant buildings with their funky-shaped gables and castellated cornices — buildings that might have been transported intact from nineteenth-century Prague and that were, in fact, built by Czech immigrants near the end of the last century, years before the first Mexicans arrived.

Julia Perez, pretty and model-thin, dressed in black vinyl pants and a maroon sweater, sits slouched against a wall with her drawing pad closed on her lap. A bored, worldly grimace radiates downward from her sunglasses.

"How's it going?" Janet asks. "Rough day? Tired?"

Julia's purple frosted lips pull back to reveal slick white teeth, a gray raisin of gum impaled on a lower incisor. "Nah . . . I don't know."

"You're doing *la psíquica,* right?"

Julia opens her pad, thumbs through pages of doodles and scribbled notes, and locates a few faint lines that appear to constitute the preliminary skeleton of an awning. "I didn't get any of that stuff we did about perspective."

"Forget perspective." Janet crouches beside Julia. "Let's look."

The awning is a pale, weathered blue. The word PSÍQUICA is written across it in bright yellow letters, flanked on one side by a yellow moon and on the other by a yellow sun. Above the word PSÍQUICA are three fanned tarot cards, also yellow. On either side of the cards, in yellow letters, are the words LAS CARTAS and LA MANO.

"So what do you see?" Janet asks. "What interests you visually?"

Julia fiddles with one of the silver studs

that circle the waist of her pants. "A building."

"Look, Julia, when you were buying these pants" — Janet nips the black vinyl between two fingers — "it wasn't just because they were a pair of pants, was it? You saw the material. You liked the vinyl. You probably touched it. You liked the black. You noticed these silver studs around the waist and thought they were cool. You tried the pants on. You liked the way they hugged your hips and legs, defined your shape. Right?"

"They make me look thin," Julia says.

"You *are* thin. Now look across the street. What are the silver studs on the psychic's shop? What's the black vinyl over there? Don't look at me like I'm a crazy person. Aim your eyes. Engage your brain. Take your sunglasses off, for a start."

With a gameness that takes Janet by surprise, Julia removes her sunglasses, sits forward, crossing her legs beneath her, and focuses her attention. "I like the letters. That's why I decided to do it. They're up letters, you know? Happy."

"Yes! They promise you a good reading, a good fortune. You're off. Start with the letters. What makes them happy? The color? The shape? You've got to get excited about what you see, and convey that excitement,

99

get whatever excites you onto the paper. I'll be back."

Score, Janet congratulates herself, moving on. She wouldn't have had the patience or the tenacity to connect with Julia in the old days. When Janet first started teaching at Juarez, six years ago, she was young and puffed up with idealistic notions about educating the underserved. She'd already taught for two years in the glamorous high school of a moneyed fiefdom north of the city. There, her students were adolescent aristocrats — trendy, well-scrubbed sons and daughters of the nobility. Janet, who had inherited from her mother an extraordinary abundance of energy and stamina, began to feel that she was wasting it on the anointed, on kids who were destined for lives of security and comfort no matter who taught them art. She wanted to teach where she could make a difference.

Invigorated with missionary spirit, she took a staggering pay cut and started teaching downtown, at Benito Juarez High School, in Pilsen. She liked everything about her new job that the old warhorses in the faculty lounge complained about: the numb, distracted students — yes, but needy and endangered; the Byzantine bureaucracy of the Chicago Public School system, which

Janet found fascinating in its absurdity, a challenge to outwit; the long, arduous, unpredictable workdays, the rough terrain and spiky obstacles across which Janet rumbled like a Humvee, exhilarated, all systems peaking, shedding sparks.

She stumbled at first, of course. How many young teachers didn't? Desperate to make her students like her — to win their hearts — she threw herself at each boy or girl like a zealous, love-struck suitor, only to be dismayed when she was rebuffed. Her students had other things on their minds besides learning how to draw and paint and sculpt. On top of the usual adolescent preoccupations — identities, relationships, sex, alcohol and drugs, and gangs — these students came from families struggling to eat and clothe themselves, pay bills, keep up with ever-rising rents brought on by gentrification. Many students worked in the family business and came to school exhausted. Many dropped out to work full-time, with their parents' permission. These students always seemed to disappear just as Janet was beginning to get a response from them, just as they were beginning to show promise.

At the beginning of her fourth year at Juarez, just as she was beginning to get the hang of things — she had recalibrated her expectations, accepted some of her limitations — she got sick. A breathing problem, an inability to fill her lungs with air, stopped her in her tracks. Janet slumped against tables and panted like an emphysemic. The rumor spread quickly: *malo corazón.* Her students developed a fascination with her illness that was partly touching and partly morbid. How serious was it? What had caused it? Was it curable? She wrote the word "cardiomyopathy" on the blackboard. She drew a diagram of her heart, illustrating the inefficiency of her enlarged left ventricle. For a few months her students became fantastically attentive, perhaps because they expected her to drop dead right in front of them. But she didn't drop dead. She dropped out. She vanished. *Mrs. Corcoran has taken a leave of absence.*

Rudi Villarreal perches high on the back of a bench, pad open on his knees, pencil on the move. His streaky, dyed-blond hair is gelled back, and a trio of gold studs glints along the upper ridge of his right ear. His ambitious drawing attempts to cover a long stretch of Eighteenth Street: the buildings begin large at the left and diminish in size to the right. His use of perspective is skillful, and the foreground blooms with detail:

trees, lampposts, parking meters, cars.

"Wow," Janet says. "From now on I'm just going to call you Pissarro. Do you know who Pissarro was? Pissarro was one of the Impressionists, a group of painters in late-nineteenth-century France, and he did these great, sweeping, incredibly detailed Paris street scenes. I'll show you one in class tomorrow."

Rudi screws up his lips and cocks his head at the sky; he looks as though she's just asked him a riddle. "Was he astonished by what he saw? Did he convey his astonishment to the viewer?"

Janet laughs. He's making fun of her. That's what she tells all her students, repeatedly, incessantly. *Learn to be astonished, and to convey your astonishment to the viewer.*

"Hey, you think I can frame this?" Rudi asks. "I want to frame it and hang it in my room."

"We're matting and framing the last week of school. Why don't you concentrate on finishing it first."

"Si no me molestarias . . . ," he says. *If you'd leave me alone.*

Janet gives Rudi a gentle shove on the shoulder before moving on. She adores Rudi. His seriousness, his good sense, his smart-aleck wit, his talent. She likes the idea of Rudi's framed streetscape going home with him, likes to think that one day his drawing will move with him to an apartment of his own, hang on another living room wall while his children grow and his grandchildren visit until one day long after Janet is gone *abuelito* Villarreal will point to the drawing and tell one of those grandchildren *I did that in high school,* and the child, looking up, will experience a configuration of emotions due partly to her, to Janet's existence, to her effort and encouragement.

Janet wonders if Isabel Howard had a similar longing to have an existence beyond herself, to secure an intimate connection with a person and a time she would otherwise have been unable to reach. *I'm a work of art myself,* Janet thinks — a creation, a product of her donor's foresight and will.

Learn to be astonished, and to convey your astonishment to the viewer.

Janet's not sure she *can* convey her astonishment. Not to anyone who hasn't had the same experience, who hasn't had a heart transplant. She fails continually to impress her amazement on David. When she refers to her life as a miracle, he reminds her that they've paid dearly for it with fear and suffering and hard labor. He reminds her that the heart is a tremendous burden. As if she doesn't know. As if she doesn't often think of it as a needy, cloying, untrustworthy infant who requires constant vigilance, consumes all available resources, dictates schedules, and restricts her, and her family's, freedom of movement. But the rigors of caring for the heart haven't blinded her to the transaction's complexities and mysteries. The inner disjointedness, the mixed feelings of blessedness and encumbrance, the quiet, haunting sensation of carrying in her body not just a piece of another human being but the only piece — well, one of the only pieces — of that human being still alive.

It's not a physical sensation, not really. The predominant physical sensations are side effects of her medications. Her new heart doesn't *feel* very different from her old one — her old one when it worked. It's in the same place. It makes the same muffled *lub*-dup, *lub*-dup when she listens to it with a stethoscope. True, the new heart is denervated — the surgeons couldn't attach it to her nervous system as intricately as her old heart had been, couldn't accomplish in four hours what had taken nine months in the womb — and because of this,

Janet's heart's slow to get going when she launches into a brisk walk or a run. She has to start gradually, let the heart keep pace with her, give the hormones and chemical messengers in her blood time to do the nerves' work. If she doesn't, she'll get light-headed. More seriously, if something startles her, her heart takes a minute or two to react; then, just as she's calmed down, her heart gets the news as a rush of adrenaline and starts beating frantically, scaring her much worse than whatever originally startled her. She has to breathe deeply, she has to tell her heart, *Relax, it's OK.* The poor, confused thing.

Apart from these peculiarities the heart's a mean, lean piece of equipment. The strangeness, the fascination, is up in Janet's mind, fueled by curiosity and imagination. This heart in her chest, it's a heart someone *else* was born with. Janet gets queasy thinking about that — that a part of her body once popped out of a stranger's uterus. Sometimes she thinks about this woman, Bernice Howard, Isabel Howard's mother, the heart's mother: a thin, pretty woman with short, artfully cropped gray hair, locally handcrafted silver bracelets on delicate, bony wrists. It's just a guess. Who knows where that vision comes from. And who knows what Bernice Howard looked like years ago, pushing Isabel down a shady sidewalk in a stroller. Janet would have been six or seven, living in Minneapolis, enthralled by the Beatles and just recently permitted to operate the family phonograph, prancing around the basement rumpus room singing "Yellow Submarine" into a cherry Popsicle while three hundred miles to the south her future heart rolled down the sidewalk with an infant girl packed around it, neighbors bending to marvel at her flushed cheeks, her pudgy pink fingers. The heart was tiny then, plum-sized. Still, at that early age, a master of perfusion. So much activity to support, all that little-girl growth and development and hysteria: running and jumping and spinning, clambering and climbing, lifting and throwing and smashing. The heart never complained or asked questions. Such an obedient muscle. It fueled cries of exhilaration and distress, pounded in the agitated states of excitement and fear, and all the while, every few seconds for days and months and years, its ventricles clenched, battling gravity to get blood to Isabel's brain so she could learn to speak and think and formulate unanswerable questions. Why isn't snow blue, like the sky? Why don't trees grow in through the windows of houses? So she could learn to read and memorize multiplication tables and develop crushes on boys. Go on field trips. Make collages out of leaves. Well — Janet's substituting her own childhood now, knowing nothing about her donor's. But she can feel it, she's crowded inside with the accumulation, the prematurely arrested potential of a life.

She walks back up Eighteenth Street, checking on her students, most of whom are squinting dutifully into the middle distance and drawing. Julia's head is down, her pencil moving; she appears to have bitten off something to chew on. Janet gazes over at *la psíquica.* Even the three fanned tarot cards on the awning look cheery and hopeful. Janet wonders if she ought to stop in there some afternoon, seeing as she has so many unanswered questions. Will her relationship with David heal? Will he come around to accepting her need for a relationship with Isabel Howard's family? Will she, Janet, stay healthy enough to take care of her children? She worries about this a lot. If she dies, will David be able to raise the children on his own? What if he meets another woman? Will she be good with Carly and Sam? What if she's too good?

Last night she and David had another

heated discussion about leaving the city. David wants to migrate to one of the western suburbs — he's currently enamored of Elmhurst and Wheaton — but she won't hear of it; she's already decided which radiator she'll chain herself to. She adores Wicker Park: the energy, the eclectic mix of people, the ethnic restaurants and coffee shops and used bookstores. David, on the other hand, is tired of congested living, wackos and freaks, homeless people who hit him up for change and then piss on the same sidewalk he has to walk on — the continual assaults on his personal space. He sees threats everywhere. Janet traces his heightened concern back to the children's births, after which he began to complain that there was no filter in the city to keep out undesirables — in short, the poor — who were more likely to be desperate and unhinged, more likely to hustle and steal and get high and drunk and drive recklessly, putting everyone, especially children, at risk. Also — incidentally, as far as Janet is concerned — David doesn't think an urban environment is good for her fragile health, her weakened immune system, her reduced energy level. He thinks she'd be better off in a quieter, more peaceful place without all the hassles and crowds and germs.

Janet nearly ventured an observation about which one of them had a reduced energy level but decided to hold her tongue. David was the one already stretched out in bed at nine o'clock in his gray Northwestern T-shirt and L.L. Bean pajama bottoms, groggily flipping pages of Paul Kennedy's *Preparing for the Twenty-first Century.* Janet, who had just cleaned up the kitchen after getting Sam and Carly to bed, now sat on the edge of the armchair, stripping off her clothes and changing into a tank top and sweatpants. She had decaf tea going on the stove and planned to plow through some paperwork before going to bed herself. "I don't want peace," she said. "I nearly got eternal peace, and it scared me shitless. I want densely populated urban madness. I'd rather catch a virus on the street and die suddenly a year from now than waste away safely in milquetoast suburban convalescence."

David smiled, and his face assumed the smug, bemused look it always assumed when confronted by her pluck. "So you don't have any qualms about raising your children in densely populated urban madness?"

"What, you want them to grow up as little soccer-ball-kicking country squires? People *do* raise their children in the city, you know. Just because it's not where you or I were raised . . ."

"Hey, I like where I was raised," David said. "And we're not talking about Highland Park or Lake Forest. We're talking Elmhurst or Wheaton. We can talk Oak Park, too. Or Evanston. What's wrong with Evanston?"

"What's wrong with the city? Why do we have to defect?"

" 'Defect'? What kind of crazy talk is that? The kids would be happier in the suburbs. Give them a yard to run around in. Space. There'd be more kid-oriented activities. Better schools. More opportunities and advantages. For them and for us. Again, two words: property values."

Janet tried to remember if they had ever agreed to this, as David seemed to imply, that their life would take this course, this trajectory: a few years in the city, until the kids were old enough to start school, and then a move to the suburbs. What else had they agreed on that she didn't know about? Summer homes? Retirement communities? The colleges Sam and Carly would attend? "What about the value of life?" she asked. "Are property values going to dictate the course of our existence?"

"Look, let's not get too philosophical,"

David said, letting out a heavy breath, reaching his arms behind his back and adjusting his pillow chaise. "It's not just schools and property values. It's been a rough couple of years. You getting sick, all that time in the hospital, major surgery, huge upheavals and scares. Let's not even get into your first few years at Juarez. I'm ready for greener pastures. Tranquility. I'm ready for a break."

She wanted to ask him what he was getting right now, propped up on all those pillows. She wanted to say, *I have a chronic illness. There will be no break.* She said, "Great, so you need a little R and R. Take it."

"I see open spaces. I see grass. Trees." He extended his arms as if before a panoramic vista.

"You see Lincoln Park," Janet said, annoyed at his whimsy. "It's ten minutes on the El. Go there."

"I need to go further."

"What exactly are you trying to tell me?"

"I'd like to get further away from downtown."

"I'd call that a preference, not a need. Whereas in my case it really is a need, to stay downtown, in addition to a preference."

"So we live right here forever, tethered to

112

that hospital of yours? Parkland-Wilburn isn't the only major medical center on the continent, you know. There's Evanston, there's Loyola. They all have good heart-transplant programs. I've checked."

It disturbed Janet that David continually failed to respect what was most important to her, and that he appeared to do so willfully, as though he felt entitled to prevail. "Not *my* heart-transplant program," she said coolly. "Not my doctor, my nurses. Do you realize how lucky I am to have Lenka?" She was referring to her cardiologist, who had diagnosed her with heart disease two and a half years ago and seen her through all the rough patches since. "Do you realize how fortunate I am to have a doctor I like and trust, and who hasn't left for a better job somewhere else? I'd be crazy to dump her. And she's not the only one out there. I know just about everyone at Parkland-Wilburn, and they know me. Do you realize how important that is?"

"Yes, I realize," David answered obediently.

"Then why can't you be more flexible and accommodating?"

"Why can't *you* be more flexible and accommodating?"

"I'm the one who's sick, that's why."

113

"You're sick when it suits you. The rest of the time you're Miss Tough-as-Nails. So why can't you be tough as nails at a new hospital?"

"I've toughed enough. You owe."

"Owe?" David sat up and twisted to face her, his face crimped with anger.

Janet felt a rush of exhilaration: was this the conversation into which all the bruising diatribes she had rehearsed in her head were finally going to emerge? Was it time to go live with all that dark, pent-up disappointment?

No. She would resist the urge, which was as overwhelming as the urge to empty a full bladder. She went into the kitchen and poured her tea, slopped hot water onto the counter. She sat down on a high stool at the counter and doodled in her assignment notebook, drew — or more accurately, carved — triangles and hexagons, pressing so hard with the pen that the paper grew moist and concave with ink.

She waited for an apology or retraction or last-ditch overture of conciliation to come from the bedroom, but none did. Janet wondered how successfully David's eyes were traveling down the pages of *Preparing for the Twenty-first Century.*

She wouldn't live to see very much of the

114

twenty-first century, in all likelihood. Was the book preparing him for that?

SEVEN

Shortly after Isabel's death, tired of waiting tables but too demoralized to force himself through the obstacle course of inquiries and interviews necessary to secure a job worthy of his education and ability, Alex caved and joined the growing legions of the temporary workforce. He worked for a different company every few weeks, answering phones and typing letters and filing documents. When a five-day assignment at U.S. Exam turned into an open-ended assignment, Alex accepted, eager for some consistency.

Today Alex and the other galley slaves at Table E are working on a shipment of seventh- and eighth-grade essays from Colorado on the subject of America's Biggest Problem.

"I'm so fried on Iraq," says Grier Kuehl, his cheek mashed into his palm, his elbow propping his head up. "Iraq, crime, education, Iraq, terrorism, immigration, Iraq, health care, the deficit, Iraq. You know what scares the shit out of me? They all know how to spell it. I haven't seen one kid yet who's missed. No Iraqs with a *k*, a *c*, a *ck*."

Grier is a graduate of the university's playwriting program, and while his career isn't exactly taking off — his most recent play, *My Life in a Glass of Milk,* was deemed "unperformable" by the judges of a contest in Minneapolis — he does have his own breed of artistic look: long, wild, Germanic chieftain's hair, round glasses, flabby arms.

"I'm working on mutant frogs," says Mavis. Mavis is thin, angular in the shoulders, long in the neck like a gazelle. She does graduate work in African languages at the university. "Frogs with extra feet and heads. I'm giving it a five."

"OK, please tell me what I should give this kid." Alex drums his hands on Charlie LaFosse's essay. His initial instinct was to slap Charlie with a one, but there was something unquantifiable in the kid's tone, an earnestness, that made him pass it to Grier, who read it and then made the mistake of passing it to Mavis.

Grier asks, "Read that one sentence again?"

Alex reads: " *'If we wood take more money of the goverment uses for defence for police*

117

this wood be good because of goverment waist' — he spells it W-A-I-S-T."

"Poetic," says Grier. "The image of a bloated government waistline. Still, no great friend of the English language. I'd say we're in the presence of a classic one."

"I concur," Alex says.

Mavis looks up from her work. "Considering that the argument is fairly sophisticated, he deserves a three, at least. You can't say he has an *absence of focus, absence of relevant content, no apparent control over sentence structure and word choice.* There are mechanical and usage errors, sure, but not so many that his ideas are impossible to understand. And syntax isn't everything. Diane made that clear."

Though Alex doesn't let on, he's continually amazed by the agility and power of Mavis's mind: by the speed and thoroughness with which she reads and comprehends the essays, by her photographic memory of the scoring guidelines.

"Speaking of our fearless leader," Grier whispers, and presents his head like a plastic flower, stiff and glazed, for their approaching supervisor. Diane is wearing a peach blazer with padded shoulders, tugging at the cuffs as she promenades past them across the carpet.

Alex can't say what makes him want to stab deeply into Charlie LaFosse's young life. It occurs to him that Charlie may be the victim of fate, or more specifically, of his grader's foul mood. It's the year anniversary of Isabel's death, and Alex would have called in sick if the prospect of staying home alone in his empty apartment had seemed the more endurable of the two miseries.

Charlie LaFosse: unscarred, his whole life ahead of him.

Alex gives him a one and tosses him onto the heap.

Grier leans forward, peeks at the grade. "Well done."

Mavis can't resist looking. She turns on Alex with distaste; it's clear she's making an effort to restrain herself. "I can't believe you. That was totally undeserved."

"Wasn't it?" Alex says.

There's music on the stereo, jazz, a swingy big-band thing that Alex feels is too cheerful for the occasion. Though maybe that's the point. The dining room table has been cleared off, dusted, polished: the dark wood shines. Bernice has arranged two place settings facing each other across the table's width, pretty plates ornamented with orange, yellow, and blue floral patterns. Two wineglasses. A bottle of Shiraz. Two tall, thin, white candles, planted in crystal, unlit, flank the place settings.

Bernice is busy in the kitchen, scrambling to launch the meal, spinning and lunging from refrigerator to counter, sink to gas range, stopping short every so often to straighten her back and press a finger to her lower lip and concentrate hard, eyes darting among her projects.

"Matches," Alex says, squeezing past. "I thought I might light those candles."

"Above the sink. Open the wine, too. There should be a corkscrew in that top drawer."

Alex goes back into the dining room, lights the candles, turns off the overhead light. He's created a dark, borderless space in which the place settings float, glazed in flame-light.

Bernice brings in a salad of romaine lettuce, tomatoes, apples, and mushrooms. She sets it on the table. "This is nice," she says, meaning the atmosphere.

"Too dark?"

"It's fine."

Alex, working with the corkscrew, checks out the label on the back of the wine bottle. He was hoping to find a poetic description of the wine's character, but there's only the standard government warning: *According to the Surgeon General, women should not drink alcoholic beverages during pregnancy because of the risk of birth defects.* Sharp, distinct focus, specific content — a solid six. Alex doesn't like the word "pregnancy," which sounds lacy and precious, like a gift he'll never receive. He looked forward to having children with Isabel. They discussed the issue frequently in the months leading up to her death, and though they didn't exactly see eye to eye, they planned to wait to get started until after she finished her dissertation.

"Hey, this stuff impairs your ability to operate machinery," he says to Bernice, who has gone back into the kitchen. "What if we want to run the dishwasher after dinner, or make toast?"

"One of us will have to stay sober and be the designated dishwasher operator."

A few minutes of hustle and portage and they're seated at the dining room table taking their first bites of tagliatelle. Alex notices, and tries to conceal that he's noticing, how Bernice, apron off, has dressed tonight. A black short-sleeve blouse with a faint shimmer in the fabric. A necklace with a jade cabochon set in the pendant — a necklace Isabel gave Bernice several years ago for her birthday. Jade earrings. A trio of silver bracelets on her right wrist.

"That necklace looks nice on you," Alex says.

Bernice laughs uncertainly. "Well, thank you." She casts her eyes down, gives herself a once-over. Rubs the pendant of her necklace between forefinger and thumb. "I'm hardly ever dressed up enough to wear it."

"Isabel was crazy about jade."

"I know. So's her mother."

Bernice sits motionless except for a tremor in the tip of her fork. Alex is visited by a vision of Isabel walking toward him along a snow-swept street, dressed in her puffy blue down jacket, a black scarf wrapped snug around the lower half of her face — mouth, nose — compressing all her allure into her eyes, a blue tri-peaked hat with a long swinging tassel, black leggings and hiking boots below. She does a burst of the Slavic dance step, four little outward kicks, alternating feet, which means she's excited to see him.

Bernice's face, with no animation, no movement, looks sunken, deflated, slung on the bones. "You know, I was thinking today, and maybe this is ridiculous. We're so used to having a certain chunk of years with people we care about, because of natural life spans or whatever, but if you think about it we're amazingly lucky even to encounter one another, considering how vast time and space are. Don't you think? That's my little philosophical thought."

It's a pleasant sentiment, and mildly inspiring, but it hardly alleviates the physical pain of Isabel's absence, or the anger and bitterness Alex feels at the thought of other men his age whose wives are still alive and will be for years. "I know what you mean. Still, I wish I'd had longer with her."

"Of course. Of *course*." A tightening in the musculature of Bernice's face looks like it's going to produce tears.

Alex refills her near-empty wineglass.

"When Isabel was eight or nine," Bernice says, "she saw a special on TV, some news report about Honduras, or maybe El Salvador — one of those Central American countries — and it *really* got to her, I mean really sank in. She started wandering around the backyard pretending to be a poor peasant girl. She'd walk with these tiny, clumsy steps, you know, like she was weak with hunger or disease or whatever, like she was about to fall down. Sometimes she *would* fall down. Isabel always had a flair for the dramatic. She had this patter, I'd hear her out there murmuring in a breathless foreign accent, *We have no water in the village. We are very poor in the village.* The accent was Eastern European, is the thing. I never did figure that out. I'd call her in to dinner and she'd tell me we couldn't have dinner because there was no food in the village. I can tell you, I got pretty damn tired of that village."

It's bittersweet, painful, to learn more about the woman he lost — to learn he lost that much more than he knew. "So how are things at the costume shop?" he asks. "Isn't the opera coming up soon? Which one is it again?"

"*Così Fan Tutte.* Mozart. Opening night's a week away. It's a zoo." Bernice describes her ordeal of the day, doing the final fitting for a pretentious undergraduate diva who complained that the costume made her butt look big. "You should have heard her carrying on about the imperfections of her derrière. As if she'd been cursed with some hideous physical abnormality."

"Wow," Alex exclaims, feeling as though what he has to contend with at work isn't half as bad. "Couldn't you jab her in the ass with a pin or something?"

Bernice laughs. Her cheek, in the candle glow, looks smooth, burnished, like copper.

It's uncanny, Alex thinks, how Bernice shares, to a degree, Isabel's ability to make him feel at ease being purely, utterly himself.

"I got an e-mail from Lotta today," Bernice says. "Actually it just came a few hours ago. An anniversary note. Condolences. It was sweet. I'm impressed she thinks about us. That she remembers."

"It's no great mystery. If Isabel hadn't died, Lotta would be gearing up for the anniversary of her daughter's death."

Bernice stares down into her half-eaten salad, prods a lettuce leaf with her fork. "It can't be easy for her to think about us. I think she's brave. To keep the channel open."

"It'd be harder to close the channel. Keeping it open makes them feel better. Less guilty. If they keep thanking us and writing to us and hearing back that we're OK, that we haven't been devastated, which we'd never reveal to them anyway, they can go on with their lives."

Bernice falls silent with a deliberateness and reverence that make Alex realize, as she clearly has, that the exchange is getting bristly.

"So what's this mysterious dessert you've got planned?" he asks. For several days, since they began planning this meal, she's

125

been teasing him with it, tantalizing him with the prospect of a surprise.

"Oh. It's not quite time, is it?" Bernice, taken aback, surveys the table, measuring their progress. "Are you in a hurry?"

Alex gives Bernice a funny look, pointing to the preposterousness of the idea that he might have somewhere else to be, something else to do.

"I don't know," Bernice says. "Maybe you have a date."

She says this offhandedly, with traces of titillation and suspicion in her voice. Immediately she clamps a hand to her mouth. "Oh my God. What an awful thing to say. What's wrong with me?"

Alex feels chilled and dizzy-light, as though he's just lost a few pints of blood. "There's nothing wrong with you," he says, trying to understand. "I don't have a date. You're my date."

Bernice laughs — a lurching, uncontrolled cackle — and falls sharply silent, meditates on her plate, her face flushed with embarrassment. "That was an absolutely horrible, inconsiderate thing to say. Will you forgive me?"

She's looking at him plaintively, and with an intensity that betrays her attachment to him. He knows she's worried about the possibility that one day — not soon, but one day — he'll start seeing another woman, drift into another family, leave her behind. When that happens, will she forgive him?

"Of course," he says.

EIGHT

It's nearly midnight when Alex gets home, and he still has to take Otto for his evening walk, a prospect he's not looking forward to. He feels bloated and tipsy. He ate a huge serving of Bernice's surprise dessert: raspberry chocolate cheesecake — one of Alex's favorites — from the best bakery in town. He and Bernice both drank too much wine. By the end of the evening they were silly, slap-happy, making jokes as they cleared the table and loaded the dishwasher.

Alex squeezes in the front door of his building, shuffles across a crazy-quilt of discarded junk mail, clasps the handrail, and hauls himself up the steps. As he approaches his floor, he sees, in the upper reaches of his vision, a pair of large eggy blobs that condense into running shoes. There is a man attached to the shoes, sitting hunched over on the landing with his knees drawn up to his chest and his hands clasped to his shins. His head rests sideways on one knee, the kneecap shoved into his cheek, deforming its shape. A step creaks beneath Alex's foot, and the man looks up, flutters his eyes to life.

Alex stops.

The man is Jasper Klass.

Anger floods Alex's body, rushes to the extremities.

Jasper rises quickly to his feet, sways unsteadily, steps back up onto the landing and wipes his mouth with his upper arm. "Hey. I'm sorry to bother you, Alex."

His hair is a frazzled tuft clinging to the big white rock of his head. His ears are small and leafy, his cheeks flushed. His body is hefty, walruslike. He's wearing a peach-colored polo shirt untucked over a pudgy stomach. The running shoes are, upon closer inspection, expensive cross-trainers with tectonically interlocking plates and swatches and pads. In the heels are large transparent air bubbles in which one might expect to see goldfish swimming. Jasper's making good use of these shoes, bobbing up and down on his feet, shifting his weight from one to the other, as though he's standing in a line he's been waiting in for days. He says to Alex, "I know, I'm the last person you want to see right now. I'm the last person you ever want to see. But hear me out. I'd seriously appreciate it."

There's a despondent reverence in his voice that makes Alex feel tyrannical and commanding. He continues up the stairs to the landing, forcing Jasper to move aside, and positions himself outside his door. "I want you to leave," he says.

Jasper nods sympathetically, as though recognizing a reaction he anticipated. "I'd like to talk to you. Just for a sec."

"I don't want to talk to you. Not even for half a second. I've got to walk my dog."

Jasper presses his hands flat against the wall and bows his head between his arms. Suddenly he springs upright and jerks his head back and says, "I couldn't walk *with* you while you walk your dog, could I? Or would that ruin your night?"

Alex fishes his key out of his pocket, inserts it into the lock. "I don't see what we have to talk about."

"Oh." Jasper looks startled. "Well, when you've done something like I've done, when you've had the kind of accident I've had . . ." He stalls, concentrates. "I just want to apologize, make amends, make things right."

"You can't ever make things right," Alex says. "Unless you can raise the dead." He unlocks his door, slips inside, and slams the door behind him.

At first, from the hallway, through the door, silence. Then, finally, the whine of a floorboard, one step after another squeaking under the weight of Jasper's descending body.

Alex pets Otto's hard, bony head, accumulates a film of fine, powdery grit on his hand. "Hey, baby. What's up? Miss me?" Otto's been alone for hours, and really should go out immediately. But Alex waits a few minutes, until he's sure Jasper has had time to get some distance away. Then he takes Otto's leash from the closet doorknob and hooks him up.

Down the stairs, out the door. Alex revolves his head like a radar dish, alert. No sign of Jasper. The walk, the bridge — all clear. Then Alex sees a figure standing in the shadows of a tree. Jasper's staring up into the branches, holding a twig between his fingers, lightly scratching the opposite palm. He sees Alex and straightens, drops the twig. "Hi," he says cheerfully.

"All right. Listen." Alex tries to control his anger. "You're going about this in a really bad way."

Without warning, in a characteristic outburst of friendliness, Otto gallops toward

Jasper, dragging Alex with him. Alex reins Otto in, but not before the dog jams his muzzle into Jasper's groin.

"He's a beaut," says Jasper, stepping back, hesitant to pet the dog. "I think he likes me."

"He likes everybody. Otto, come on." Alex yanks the leash and jerks Otto away from Jasper — an act Alex is instantly sorry for. Otto topples precariously to one side and has to scramble to regain his footing. "Sorry, baby," Alex says, stroking the dog's neck.

"I'm going to walk with you," Jasper says, "and you can talk to me or not. It's up to you. It's a free country."

Alex considers going inside and calling the police. He's being harassed. But he'd prefer to deal with this one-on-one, at least for now.

He hauls Otto away. They cross the parking lot, leaving Jasper behind, and start down the sidewalk. The air is cool. The sky is clear, the stars crisp as sparks. The moon casts the houses and driveways in aqueous blue light. A breeze rustles bushes and bends the branches of trees, making shadows creep and slide.

Jasper catches up, appears alongside. He removes a thick, rolled-up magazine from his pants, where it was jammed, and after allowing it to uncoil in his closed fist he raps it against the open palm of his opposite hand. *Killer Pentatonics and Modal Jams for Guitar.* It's some kind of music book. Jasper overestimates Alex's interest and holds the book up for a clearer view. "Great stuff," he says. "Treasure trove. A complete guide to mode construction theory, with some scale stuff thrown in. I play guitar. Blues. You should come down to the Blues Jam at Calamity Jane's on Monday night. Good scene. I'm a pretty big attraction down there, modesty aside. You'd be impressed. I could get you free drinks."

Alex cuts across the street past the perimeter of bright orange tape that surrounds a pit in whose depths are chunks of rock and sections of concrete pipe.

"This isn't a half-bad neighborhood," Jasper says, keeping pace. "Buddy of mine used to live over here. Bass player. Talented dude. We had a band called Animal Instinct. I'm talking ancient times."

Otto makes a desperate lunge for a dead bird in the gutter. One of the bird's tiny beadlike eyes is choked with blood — a squashed huckleberry. Dragging Otto away is like dragging a sack full of rocks.

Jasper asks, "What's the weight on that guy, anyway?"

133

Alex ignores him. He's thinking how many times he and Isabel walked Otto around this block. Hundreds. Hundreds of evenings. Hundreds of conversations.

A car approaches — its headlights searing white holes that blind Alex — and passes. Slowly, like a photograph developing, the world reappears. Shapes, contrasts. Windows: pictures of light hanging on the houses.

Alex turns sharply right at a corner so that Jasper, uninformed as to which direction they're going, must jog again to catch up. "OK," he says, out of breath. "So you're wondering, like, what the hell. Well. I wanted to let you know, to set the record . . ." He laughs uncomfortably. "Incredibly sorry. Is what I'm getting at. There's no way to describe it."

"Hey, no problem," Alex says. "Don't worry about it. Seriously. I'm much happier alone."

"It happened so fast. She came out of nowhere. Suddenly there she was in the middle of the road."

It occurs to Alex that he's speaking with the accident's only eyewitness. "*Was* she in the middle of the road? Or were you too far to the right? You and your huge fucking tank."

"She was in the middle of the road."

"The middle of the road or the middle of the lane? The middle of the road is the center line. Don't tell me she was riding on the center line."

"She was in the middle of the lane. The right lane. My lane. If you want to get technical."

"I want to get technical."

"It was the wind. I'm telling you. It was gusty."

"Still, you had a second to react."

"I never understood how they figured one second."

"Math. Time elapsed between the moment you had a sightline and the moment you hit her. One second. One, one thousand."

"One one thousand."

"You're saying it too fast. One, one thousand."

"That's too slow," Jasper says, anger rising.

"It's exactly right. One, one thousand."

"Hey, if you want to ease up, feel free."

Alex wishes he had more hard evidence with which to attack Jasper. He wishes Jasper had drunk two or three beers, or that Jasper was driving ten miles over the speed limit when he hit Isabel. But according to

Jasper's court testimony, which was impossible to disprove, he was essentially sober, driving fifty-five, and paying attention to the road. Not that Alex buys it. He's convinced that Jasper might have reacted more quickly if he had been completely sober — if he hadn't had anything to drink — or if he had been driving more carefully, at a slower speed, and paying closer attention, especially coming over the crest of a hill, the other side of which was invisible to him. But the jury didn't agree. The jury felt that Jasper had been adequately cautious, and that his reaction time hadn't been impaired. They felt that Isabel had been far enough out into the road to bear part of the blame.

"People tell me I look like Oliver Stone," Jasper says, presenting his face in case Alex wants to inspect it. "You know Oliver Stone? *Platoon, JFK, The Doors*? Actually I got a new one the other day. I was in Java Jolt," he says, referring to a local coffee shop, "and this barista said, 'Has anyone ever told you you look a little like Russell Crowe?' I was like, *Hello.* I think she was coming on to me."

Alex is having an experience, a moment of total removal from the cockpit of self, a kind of massive psychic whiplash: he's sitting in the very back row of the balcony, looking out across an expanse of darkness through his eyes at the sky, trees, strange houses, a dog attached by a leash to his hand and beside him a babbling, unfamiliar voice — *I think she was coming on to me* — none of which seems to have any connection to him. Is this his life?

They've reached his building — an event Alex has contrived to bring about swiftly by choosing to walk around only one short block. They stop on the sidewalk near the entrance. Jasper appears unsettled by the abrupt termination of their walk, which he's managed to establish as his justification for being in Alex's company. He clasps his hands behind his back and rocks forward onto his toes. "I quit drinking. Did I tell you that? I don't drive anymore either. Only when I absolutely have to."

"I'm going in now," Alex says.

"Listen to me shoot my mouth off. Hey, nice hanging with you. Maybe I'll see you around?"

"Stay away from me."

Alex and Otto go quickly up the stairs and into his apartment. Alex closes the door and locks it behind him. Unhooks Otto from his leash. He doesn't turn on any lights, worried that Jasper may have found a vantage from which to spy on him through the windows. He sits on the couch, stupefied. He can't believe Jasper's nerve, waiting outside his apartment, bothering him tonight of all nights, when it should have been obvious that Alex would want to be left in peace. Doesn't the man have any respect? Doesn't he have any sense of decency?

After a while Alex goes to the window and stands in the dark, scanning the lighted walkway below, the bridge across the creek, the parking lot, each progressively dimmer. No one in sight. Which isn't to say that Jasper might not be out there somewhere.

"You wouldn't believe this, Iz," he says out loud. "You wouldn't believe what just showed up on our doorstep."

NINE

All right, Jasper thinks, walking away. Things could have gone worse. Alex might have attacked him verbally or even physically. But Alex was civil. Friendly, even. Not a bad guy. Jasper could definitely envision spending more time with him.

Jasper wishes he'd been more articulate, done better delivering the apologies and explanations. He wishes he'd found some way to bring up the heart. On the other hand, he's got to be careful. Establish trust. Which he did. Lay the groundwork. Establish a rapport. He can't rush it. He definitely scored points with the dog.

He climbs onto his motorcycle, a red Kawasaki Vulcan, and fires it up, looks both ways before pulling away from the curb. He might have been more specific when he told Alex that he didn't drive anymore. What he meant was, he doesn't drive a truck or car. He tried, after the accident, to continue driving his Dodge Ram, the truck he'd hit Isabel with, but whenever he got behind the wheel and started driving down the road he heard the raucous metallic crash of the bike hitting the front end, and his body reexperienced the event: his legs jumped, his arms locked rigid, his windpipe shrank until his breaths burned. He sold the Ram and test-drove some cars, but even a Ford Focus gave him the symptoms. Being a passenger in someone else's car was a struggle too. Only when he climbed onto a motorcycle at the suggestion of a friend and felt his body in a completely new posture on a completely different machine did he feel removed enough from his previous experience of driving to feel relaxed, in control. Of course he was more of a danger to himself than he had been — motorcyclists, his friend warned him, were not only more likely to get into accidents but to die in them — but Jasper felt this was appropriate. He had killed a woman. As penance, he would risk being killed himself.

It's Friday night, and even though it's nearly twelve thirty Jasper doesn't feel like going home. He'll stop by Mendocino's and squeeze in a drink with Ryan and Blake. It's been a long week at work. He's an audio specialist at Best Buy. He recently won

Salesman of the Month two months running. He considers himself an expert in stereo equipment: CD players and recorders, receivers, amplifiers, speakers, headphones, home theater systems, MP3 players, satellite radio, car audio, you name it. He loved amassing components as a teenager, hooking them up and tinkering with them, and in college his system was the envy of his dorm. He had few other successes in college; he dropped out after his second year. Reading and writing bored him. He liked talking in class, but neither his professors nor his fellow students listened to him. They were all pretentious idiots. He went to work at Radio Shack, where he was encouraged to talk all he wanted, and did, charming and persuading and selling. He quit after he was passed over for a promotion. He worked at Circuit City until he got tired of his manager's constant sales coaching. Jasper knew how to sell; he didn't need lessons. His next gig — his longest and best, nearly two years — was at Custom Sound Design, a high-end audio boutique. Jasper did home evaluations and installations for customers with thousands of dollars to blow. Unfortunately many of them ignored his advice or failed to respect his expertise. The final straw came when a customer complained that Jasper had been "aloof and unhelpful." Jasper's boss told him to improve his attitude. Being criticized was one thing, being insulted another. Jasper kicked over an eight-hundred-dollar speaker and stormed out of the showroom.

At an intersection, at a red light that just turned green, the driver of a black Toyota Tundra directly in front of Jasper is too busy on his cell phone to notice that the light has changed. Jasper guns the engine, swings into the left lane, and surges past the Toyota, glaring in through the open window at the driver and thinking, *Get off that phone before you kill somebody.*

He heads downtown and pulls into the lot next to Mendocino's. He revs the engine before shutting it off. The growl turns heads in the crowd outside the bar, and Jasper relishes dismounting in the gaze of a cute college girl. He gives her a look on his way into the bar. She turns away. She thinks she's out of his league. She is. On the other hand, Jasper's last girlfriend, Yvette, a smoking-hot yoga teacher with whom he went out for a record three months, told him he was a generous lover. She also told him he was deluded and manipulative, but he'd heard that from girlfriends before.

He walks into the bar with his cell phone

to his ear, listening to his messages — or more accurately, since there are no messages, pretending to. The place is loud with music and laughter. Cigar smoke floats under the lights. Mendocino's is the newest bar in town, to which Jasper and his friends, none of whom smoked cigars, were attracted by the talent — the glammed-up women who flock here to meet business students and law students. This is the fourth or fifth time Jasper has come. The decor is upscale, dark wood and leather, and the drinks overpriced. Jasper scans the room for Ryan and Blake. They're not here. He can't believe it; they assured him they would be here all night. He checks his phone to see if he missed a call. He didn't. He dials Ryan, gets his voice mail, leaves a message. *Where are you guys?* He gets Blake's voice mail and leaves a similar message. *I'm at Mendocino's. You guys coming?*

He goes to the bar and stands waiting for the bartender, a muscled pretty-boy named Mike, to recognize and serve him. Jasper stretches his mouth open dentist's-chair wide; his jaw continually feels tight, sore, like some hinged thing in need of oil. His left eyelid flinches uncontrollably, spasms that feel like a tiny leaping frog sewn into the skin. Mike points to him from a distance and Jasper calls out, "Jim Beam, thanks Mike." Mike brings it to him and says, "There you go, buddy."

"Dude, don't you remember my name?" Jasper asks.

Mike stares blankly.

"Jasper. *Jasper.*"

"Four dollars, Jasper."

Jasper hands Mike four singles and doesn't tip. He's surprised to be asked to pay; he'd have expected some free drinks by now. How many times does he have to come in here, how much money does he have to blow before the bar staff knows who he is? He moves away from the bar and sips his Jim Beam. He keeps a hand on his phone, set on vibrate, in case Ryan or Blake should call. Fifteen minutes pass and neither does. Jasper orders a second drink — a consolation. *When you've been through what I've been through,* he thinks, *accidentally taking a life, taking a life through no fault of your own, you've got to be nice to yourself.* He remembers telling Alex that he'd quit drinking and feels a twinge of shame. He *did* quit drinking, before the accident, when he realized he was having trouble getting out of bed for work. Actually he quit drinking only during the week, but that was something, seeing as he'd been going out nearly every weeknight and having three or four beers. He slipped once or twice — no one was perfect — and a third time that Thursday evening last April just before getting into his truck and killing Isabel Howard. He would have hit her anyway. The alcohol isn't what made the difference. Still, he suspects he drinks too much, and plans to cut back. Not now, though. Not during his time of need. Alcohol dampens his anxiety, boosts his confidence, makes him feel less numb to the world around him. Alcohol helps him sleep. True, alcohol sometimes makes him feel even more guilty than he normally does, but in these instances he tells himself he's drinking not for relief but as penance — to make his guilt feel more intense and genuine.

The crowd around him is boisterous and sloppy with alcohol, the laughter loud, bodies unsteady, couples touching and nuzzling. There must be a hundred people in the bar, but Jasper doesn't see anyone he knows, and no one is paying attention to him. He feels invisible, detached, as though he's watching this entire scene from behind a two-way mirror. He'd never admit it, but during his trial, back in November, even though it was the most frightening period of his life — he would have faced jail time if found guilty —

he enjoyed the limelight, seeing his picture in the newspapers, seeing himself on the local news. People knew who he was. People recognized him. True, many of these people blamed and despised him, but there was compensation, even occasional exhilaration, in feeling that he had achieved notoriety. He was a personage. He walked around in the new suit he had bought for the courtroom. Reporters crowded around and asked questions. He felt important standing next to his attorney, who gave most of the answers and referred to Jasper as *my client.* Jasper got letters and phone calls from women who told him that he was attractive, that they knew he was innocent from the goodness in his face. Jasper went on dates with several of these women and soaked up their sympathy. He became skilled at telling a version of his accident story that omitted the crucial self-incriminating detail and portrayed himself as a sad unfortunate, a victim of circumstance. His sex life spiked.

His attorney told the same version of the accident story to the jury. He put several people on the stand: a waitress at the restaurant where Jasper had been just prior to the accident, who testified that he had only ordered one beer, and a chemistry professor who testified that Jasper's weight and height, in conjunction with the buffalo wings he had eaten, would have prevented the beer from being rapidly absorbed into his bloodstream. The jury bought it. Jasper thrust his fist jubilantly into the air. Outside the courthouse his supporters — few, admittedly — swarmed around him. Reporters wanted to know how he felt. There were TV crews.

Now all that has evaporated. Jasper's thankful he was acquitted, that he's not in jail. On the other hand, returning to normal life hasn't been easy. He's come out of the whole thing empty-handed. Surely such an awful event, such an upheaval in his life, should have transported or transformed him, should have been a gateway to advancement or reward. Instead he got dumped right back into his mediocre job, his stale social life, his loneliness — none of which interests anyone or attracts any media coverage. Even his friends seem to have lost interest in him. Lindsay and Vinnie, Daniel and Robert and Rebecca, now Ryan and Blake. Didn't they hear the verdict? Didn't they watch the news? *Innocent. Acquitted.*

Why does this always happen with his friends? Why does he go through them so quickly? The crowd in Mendocino's is thinning. It's nearly one thirty. Jasper, feeling self-conscious, doesn't want to be the last one in the bar, so he finishes his drink and walks purposefully out the door.

On his bike he resists the urge to gun his engine and parade past the revelers on the sidewalks. He's had three drinks. He's a prime target for the cops, who are out in force patrolling for DUIs. He drives home slowly, carefully, using side streets and alleys. His apartment occupies half the basement of an old converted house. The entrance is around back. The neighbor's dogs, alerted by the sound of the motorcycle's engine, bark from upstairs. Dying embers glow in a fire pit in the backyard, surrounded by a dozen plastic Adirondack chairs and a spread-out blanket. At a picnic table littered with beer cans and wine bottles, a man and woman, obviously the survivors of a party held by other tenants of the house, sit side by side, close, talking. Jasper, who's seen the woman before, parks his bike and approaches the table and chats. It's soon clear that the couple, though friendly, would rather he leave them alone. For exactly this reason Jasper doesn't, and rhapsodizes about the warmth of the night, the stars, obliquely flirting with the woman, who's too good for this guy. When the couple stands and leaves, Jasper feels a sinking in his stomach, a kind of despair. He eats a potato chip that's lying on the table, pockets a disposable cigarette lighter — God knows what for. He doesn't smoke.

Inside his apartment he pours himself a glass of water from the tap and sits down on the black leather couch. Sets his phone down on the coffee table. Framed posters on the walls: B. B. King, Buddy Guy, Jimmy Reed. His electric guitar in its case in the corner, next to his amp and his effects box. His acoustic guitar, a pretty blond thing, out for show. He's proud of his CD collection, mostly blues and rock, and his DVDs, among them entire seasons of *X-Files* and *Saturday Night Live.* His home theater system is state-of-the-art, purchased at Best Buy with his employee discount. A Yamaha receiver, a set of 7 RBH speakers, an HSU Research subwoofer, a high-definition DVD player, and the king of the castle, a Pioneer 42" High-Definition Plasma TV. *You are what you watch.*

Jasper turns on the TV and spends a minute flipping through his deluxe package of channels. He doesn't find anything appealing. He switches on the DVD player and starts the DVD, a recent episode of *NOVA* called "The Miraculous Human Heart," which he checked out from the public library. It's hardly typical fare for Jasper. He prefers action movies and sci-fi. But since hearing a piece of conversation between Isabel's mother and husband on the night of Isabel's death, he's been curious about organ donation. The conversation took place at the hospital, where he had gone to apologize (without success), and he distinctly heard Alex say that Isabel's organs would be donated. As time passed, this remembered conversation took on significance to Jasper, began to emit suggestions and possibilities. Isabel Howard's organs — her heart, liver, kidneys, lungs, who knew what else — had gone somewhere. They had *traveled,* found new bodies to inhabit. Jasper was most interested in the heart. No disrespect to the other organs. The heart evoked thoughts of love and compassion and generosity. Thinking about the heart gave Jasper a sense of promise and possibility, and he had the notion that if he could find the person who had received it — he envisioned a woman — she might respect and appreciate him, maybe even forgive him for killing Isabel Howard.

"The Miraculous Human Heart" is a three-part, six-hour program, but Jasper's only interested in the second hour of part two, "A Change of Heart." This is the fourth

150

or fifth time he's watched it. He's learned that the earliest heart transplants were done on dogs. The first human heart transplant was performed in South Africa in 1967 by a surgeon named Christiaan Barnard, but the procedure didn't become common until the 1980s, after the drug cyclosporine, discovered by a Swiss scientist collecting soil samples on vacation in Norway, was developed and approved for use.

This is all prelude. "A Change of Heart," for which Jasper now settles in, tells the story of a forty-five-year-old woman named Ellen whose heart is damaged beyond repair. She's in a Boston hospital waiting for a new heart. She waits and waits. Apparently hundreds of people die every year waiting for hearts. Finally she hears that a donor has died in a drive-by shooting in Baltimore, and that a heart has become available. While her nurses prepare her to go to the operating room, a team of surgeons from the hospital races in an ambulance, sirens blaring, to a nearby airport, where they board a small jet and fly to Baltimore. In Baltimore they get into another ambulance and race to a hospital. There, in a crowded operating room, they harvest the heart from a young black man. Back in Boston, Ellen is anesthetized on the operating table. When the surgeons in Boston hear from the surgeons in Baltimore that the donor heart is healthy, the Boston surgeons open Ellen's chest and remove her heart and put her on bypass. By this time the harvest team is flying back from Baltimore with the donor heart packed on ice in an Igloo cooler. When they arrive in Boston, they race to the hospital and there's a dramatic scene when the heart arrives in the OR: the doors of the operating room swing open, a surgeon rushes in with the cooler, the surgeons around Ellen's body lift their heads, the crowd parts to let the heart through.

Jasper can't get enough of this scene. He reverses the DVD and watches it again: the doors swinging open, the heart making its entrance. A year ago this morning there must have been a similar scene somewhere in the Midwest when Isabel Howard's heart made its entrance, and a dying woman — or so Jasper imagines — lay waiting for it. Jasper watches the personnel in the operating room step aside to let the cooler through, notices how the chief surgeon carefully lifts the donor heart out of the cooler, inspects it, and fits it snugly into Ellen's chest.

A few days later Ellen is home from the

hospital walking around in her garden with her husband and children.

True, Jasper killed a woman. But he also saved one.

Everything he's done in life — college, jobs, relationships — has turned out a mess. But now, out of his worst mess, has come something extraordinary.

PART II

SEPTEMBER 2003
TEN

A breathing problem, an inability to fill her lungs with air, had joined the entourage of minor ailments — aches and pains, cramps, mysterious bruises, paper cuts, hangnails, dry knuckles — that followed Janet through her days.

She would have described the problem, which occurred at first only sporadically, as a tightness, a clenching in her chest that made her feel as though she were holding her breath, even if she was breathing deeply. She got light-headed, too, though whether from lack of oxygen or anxiety she couldn't tell.

This was the beginning of the end of her first life, of her first heart.

She had just started her fourth year teaching at Juarez. After three stormy years of being perplexed and mortified by the social problems afflicting her students, and by the inability of so many of these students to transcend their afflictions in the name of Art, she had decided to chill, settle, take the difficulty in stride. Not that she was backing off. She was working harder than ever. Her workload had nearly doubled since spring. She was teaching a new class, History of Mexican Art. She had inaugurated an after-school mural-painting club for at-risk students — kids who would otherwise go out and get into trouble, shoplift or deal drugs. There was a new attendance policy that required her not only to keep inordinately meticulous records but also to phone the homes of absent students every afternoon — *Su hijo no está en esquela hoy. ¿Por qué no?* — even though she knew what answers she would get in nine cases out of ten. *He's working. He's got a court date. She's on bed rest. We don't know where she is.*

So naturally Janet wondered if her breathing problem had been brought on by stress. Her other theory was that a work crew, which had done some fumigation near one of the stairwells over the summer, had left behind an irritating and possibly toxic chemical residue. There was an odd, medicinal odor in this stairwell, and it was while climbing these stairs, which her routine forced her to do several times a day, that Janet's breathing problem usually struck:

158

the shortness of breath, the clenching in her chest, the light-headedness. One day Tom Eugenides, the life-sciences teacher, caught her leaning against a banister. She asked him if he thought the air smelled weird.

Tom sniffed the air hopefully. "Pot? Why don't they ever offer me any?"

Janet might have stuck with her fumigation theory if the breathing problem hadn't followed her home and pestered her through the nights, over weekends. The problem remained quietly and portentously in the crowd of assorted aches and pains, pushing to the front whenever she exerted herself — when she went jogging along the lakeshore or played basketball Wednesday nights or took a Saturday hike with David and the kids in Lincoln Park. Soon the breathing problem attacked whenever she dashed up the stairs to the El platform to catch an approaching train or climbed the long, straight, steep set of stairs to their fourth-floor loft. Or, when shopping, she tried to cover too much distance carrying too many bags. Dashing for a bus. When she lifted Carly up onto her shoulders, arm-wrestled with Sam. When she and David had sex.

A doctor diagnosed Janet with asthma and sent her home with an inhaler. She spent the months of November and December squirting albuterol down her throat. The breathing problem went about its business with the bold insouciance of a heckler. Having sabotaged Janet's strenuous activities — she was exhausted and feeble in the classroom, she couldn't jog farther than twenty yards, one night she blacked out for a few seconds on the basketball court — the breathing problem now advanced upon the sedentary. This advance coincided with the holiday season. With rigorous shopping, perky relatives, big meals. Traversing the vast, tiled expanses of Water Tower Place, Bloomingdale's, Marshall Field's (was it her imagination or did her shoes feel tight?), wrapping packages, removing a ham from the oven, loading the dishwasher, explaining to David's mother why she hadn't gotten around to replacing the mirror in the bathroom, which was slightly cracked along one edge, big deal — in the midst of these activities Janet found herself panting like a jogger. She began to suspect that anxiety about the problem was now enough, on its own, to bring on the problem's symptoms, for she would sit for long stretches on the couch, her body rested but her mind crackling with fear, drawing huge gulps of air that wouldn't go down into her lungs unless she manhandled them with the muscles in her throat — unless she swallowed each one like a snake swallows a mouse.

"Maybe you should see another doctor," David suggested.

It was 4:21 a.m. Outside the bedroom window, snow sprayed across ginger-colored light. A dry, gritty cough had clawed Janet out of sleep. She sat on the edge of the bed, sucking on her latest inhaler. David was up too, sitting close behind her, rubbing her shoulders.

She said, "I think my feet are bigger than they used to be."

David slipped around in front of her, took one of her feet in his hands, and studied it from several angles, massaging. "You have pretty feet. You come from the family of pretty feet, and I come from the family of ugly feet."

"Who in your family has ugly feet?"

"My mother. She doesn't have arches. You have nice arches," David said, tracing the underside of her foot with his fingertips.

"I've never noticed your mother's feet."

"She wears shoes."

"Akk!" Janet jerked her foot away from David's probing hand. "That tickles."

"Wait a minute." David took hold of her foot again, wrapped both hands around her sole, compressed. "They are a little meaty, aren't they?"

"If they get any meatier they'll look like Cornish hens."

"Since when does asthma make your feet bigger?"

Janet wished he hadn't posed the question with such unnerving clarity. She threw her inhaler at the wall.

Dr. Lenka Maslowcya, the cardiologist to whom Janet had been referred at Parkland-Wilburn Medical Center, and who had given Janet a variety of tests, motioned for Janet and David to sit on the two chairs in the examination room. Dr. Maslowcya sat in a third chair, adjusted her lab coat, and squinched up her nose, causing her gold-rimmed glasses to rise on her pretty, olive-skinned face.

"What we have with you, Janet, is an impaired ability of your heart to contract with necessary force to ensure proper circulation. Your cells don't get the required oxygen, hence your fatigue. Because blood fails to move with necessary force through your body, we see fluid accumulation at the extremities. Edema. You were right to notice a swelling in your feet. As for the cause of your difficulty breathing, blood from the lungs that should be pumped by the left

162

ventricle directly to the body backs up in the heart and causes fluid seepage into the lungs. Asthma is a common misdiagnosis. Asthma would be nicer for all of us."

Dr. Maslowcya stood and moved to a dry-erase board and drew a picture that looked like a highway interchange sprouting out of a baby's bottom. "On each side of the heart is an atrium and a ventricle. The left ventricle does the pumping of blood to the rest of you. We observed a marked insufficiency of left-ventricular contraction. A virus, probably, has caused a hardening of the muscle of the ventricular myocardium, which impairs its ability to contract. The beleaguered left ventricle, to compensate, has enlarged to hold more blood, but the enlarging ventricle loses its elasticity and contracts even more poorly. Think of a rubber ball growing harder and larger until you can no longer squeeze it so easily in your hand. The condition is serious. The disease is called dilated cardiomyopathy. We see high mortality within five years of onset, the speed of deterioration various from patient to patient."

The danger seemed to reside not in Janet's body but in Dr. Maslowcya, in the brain that knew of such a disease and possessed the language to describe it. Janet felt that if she could just dash out the door into a stairwell, race down three flights, and burst outside into the day, none of this would be true. She didn't have dilated cardiomyopathy, or whatever it was called. Dr. Maslowcya was *giving* it to her.

Dr. Maslowcya drew another diagram on the marker board. Janet watched her marker-hand operate with marvelous facility. "That's a wonderful drawing, Dr. Maslowcya. I hope you don't mind me saying so. You've got a great line."

Dr. Maslowcya studied the tip of her marker as though it, not Janet, had spoken to her. "Thank you."

"Do you draw? Other than pictures like that? If you do, I'd love to see some of your work."

"I think we'd better pay attention here, babe," said David.

Dr. Maslowcya set her marker down on the ledge at the base of the board and slipped her hands into the outside pockets of her lab coat. "You are a strong woman, I think, Janet? I hope? With your heart you have a serious difficulty. I will need to see some of *your* work."

Following Janet's diagnosis, in which her fatigue and inability to breathe were matched up with a name, a disease, a clinically documented condition — with science, history, the experience of other human beings — Janet felt she had acquired some degree of understanding and control. She took the medications prescribed for her. She still got tired and out of breath, but not very often, and usually late in the day, so that after a few weeks she was inspired to declare to David, "I'm fixed! Seriously. I think I've got this thing licked."

A tentative tranquility had returned to the household. Carly and Sam, who had been showing their own symptoms of Janet's mysterious illness, began to recover. Carly had been fussy and clingy, sensing not only a disruption but a threat to her preeminence, and sullen, bewildered Sam, who understood that his mother's heart was being attacked by a small bug, had taken to approaching her with fantastical, convoluted schemes to save the troubled organ, schemes that involved everything from ingesting magic crystals to soaking a washcloth in insect repellant and sleeping with it on her chest. It was a relief for Janet to see him back at Legos and Nintendo, unconcerned about her. Carly was perky and elfish again, mothering her stuffed duck, Ocean, and raiding the Tupperware cabinet for containers to drum on.

Janet, had she been offered the opportunity to grade David on how well he was handling her illness, would have given him an A. He was encouraging and supportive, and even when she was at her worst — tired, depressed, scared — he managed to stay buoyant and hopeful. He pitched in generously around the house, picked up more than his share of tasks: shopping, laundry, cleaning, fixing meals. He gave the kids their baths at night, got them dressed in the morning. Most impressively, he made a concerted effort to educate himself about her condition. He bought *The Physicians' Desk Reference* and gathered all her pill bottles from the medicine cabinet and made a study of each drug: its purpose, properties, side effects. In bed at night he read articles about heart disease downloaded from the Internet, reading key passages aloud to her or, if she wasn't interested — some things she didn't want to know — kept them to himself. He marked passages with a pink highlighter. He jotted down notes on a legal pad. Janet took to addressing him as the Nation's Foremost Scholar of Cardiomyopathy. "Does the Nation's Foremost Scholar of Cardiomyopathy have time to mop the kitchen floor this week-

166

end?" "Does the Nation's Foremost Scholar of Cardiomyopathy have any desire to make dinner tonight?" "Would the Nation's Foremost Scholar of Cardiomyopathy like to put down that boring article and get it on with the Nation's Sexiest Art Teacher?"

"Hell, yeah," David always said to that one.

"A transplant?" David nearly lost control of the car. "You mean they want to take it *out?*"

"They don't *want* to take it out," Janet said, trying to sound calm. "It's just that they might have to take it out, and I suppose they'd like to replace it with something, so Dr. Maslowcya wants to get me all worked up and on the list."

David was driving her home from the hospital through rush-hour traffic. She was exhausted and lay nearly horizontal, the passenger seat tipped back to a dentist's-chair angle, staring up at passing buildings, the sky like milk mixed with iron. She'd just had a cardiac catheterization, during which Dr. Maslowcya had discovered that Janet's ejection fraction, the pumping ability of her left ventricle, was fourteen percent. A normal ejection fraction was sixty percent. Not that Janet had expected good news.

Despite the medications she'd been taking in increasing doses all through the winter, her health had deteriorated with a stealthiness akin to the deterioration of eyesight. Her energy, her ability to perform the routine business of everyday life, was diminishing by imperceptible increments, each of which she learned of only after a delay, and by indirect channels. One morning David asked her why she was spending so much time in the bathroom. Was she? The answer, though she didn't say so, was that she no longer felt like getting up off the toilet and flushing. Long lines at the ATM and the grocery store, which had once made her crazy, were now tolerable, even pleasant, especially if she had something to lean against. When had she, Janet Corcoran, a committed stair-taker, started walking into every elevator that presented itself?

"So what's this list?" David asked.

"There's a waiting list for hearts."

David glared out the windshield; he seemed already to be thinking about how they might circumvent such an obstacle. "But it's basically a contingency plan, right?"

"Sort of." Janet figured this impression was accurate enough for the time being. Why add to his anxiety? His anxiety only compounded her own. "Dr. Maslowcya's in a hurry to get me on the list, though."

David lunged left around an indecisive driver. "How is it . . . I got the idea the drugs were supposed to keep you going for a long time, with — what do they call it? An alteration in lifestyle."

Janet tried to remember if David had been present when she and Dr. Maslowcya discussed the likelihood of a transplant in her future. Because of obligations at work, David had missed most of the clinic visits and discussions, and had fallen behind even though he usually debriefed her. Also, she'd been reading up on her disease lately — she felt like an initially reluctant student who was starting to get interested in the course — whereas the Nation's Foremost Scholar of Cardiomyopathy, alarmed by much of what he'd found in all the articles, had backed off. "My heart's getting worse more quickly than she expected. 'Options for treatment are narrowing.' That's what Dr. M said."

"Great."

"It's not great."

David sighed: a seepage of air long enough to inflate a balloon. "We'll be fine."

He sounded discouraged.

"One more time, please, with enthusiasm,"

Janet said.

David let out an uncomprehending, hope-less laugh that gave her a sinking feeling in her stomach. "We'll be . . . fine," he said with idiotic musicality, as though it were a refrain from a children's song.

The purpose of Janet's evaluation was to make sure she had no preexisting conditions that would make her a bad investment, or any diseases that might take advantage of her immunosuppression to stage an uprising in her body and destroy whatever health a new heart brought her. But the two days felt to her as though they had been orchestrated by the hospital staff to frighten her into staying healthy so that she might never have the misfortune of ending up here. A phlebotomy technician spent fifteen minutes jabbing a long needle into her arm searching for an artery whose existence Janet began to doubt until blood spurted all over the tech's chalky white gloves. A cheerful, muscular nurse forced her to walk on an ever-inclining treadmill until her lungs burned. A dentist filled two cavities. A gastroenterologist shimmied a scope up her colon and then snaked a second scope down her esophagus into her stomach. A young physician did a vascular ultrasound of her leg and neck veins. When Janet reminded this young physician that she would be having a heart transplant, and that they weren't planning to do any operations on her legs, he explained that her leg veins needed to be good enough to replace the veins in her heart in case there were complications during surgery. The answer terrified Janet. She saw, with the shock of a person unwittingly unearthing a conspiracy or deciphering a code, the reality, the substantiality of what they were preparing her for. They were going to cut into her chest, much as she had cut into pieces of steak. They were going to cut out her heart. They were going to lift it out of her body with their hands.

A few days later Janet returned to Parkland-Wilburn to meet with a cardiothoracic surgeon, Dr. Karl Ballows. Dr. Ballows reviewed Janet's test results and cleared her for takeoff. She was advised to be patient. The wait might be a week, it might be a year. The wait would be much worse than the operation, if she were ever fortunate enough to have the operation. They might not find a heart for her at all. There was something piercing and ruthless about Dr. Ballows's demeanor. His delivery, unlike that of the staff Janet had been in contact with so far, was brisk and merciless and made no attempt to conceal from her the brutality and injustice of life on this earth. Dr. Ballows had triumphed over this brutality with his short, stocky body, his thick arms, and his aggressive cologne. His gray hair was clipped short. Janet wouldn't have been surprised to learn he'd served in the Marine Corps. He told Janet, "A large percentage of people die waiting. You'll be relatively high on the list, but you're not critical yet, not like some. Good-bye. With any luck I'll see you again."

ELEVEN

A change occurred in Janet's relationship with her telephone. Once it had been her dull, obliging servant; now it had the magnetism and power of a lover. She moved the phone from the living room to the bedroom and awarded it a prominent position on the night table. She cleared away all the books and magazines and pill bottles that might obstruct her reach when the transplant coordinator called with news of a heart. She had been advised to forget about the heart, if she could, and immerse herself in distracting activities, but she found this difficult. True, school was out, for her and for Sam, and the two of them were free, with Carly, to engage in as many distracting activities as they pleased. But Janet had no energy. Her heart, that pathetic wad of muscle in her mediastinum, was still reluctant to pump, despite steadily increasing doses of drugs. In the early part of the day, recharged from sleep, she felt strong, and after David left for work she usually took Carly and Sam down the street to Wicker Park, if the weather was nice, to play on the playground. They might run a few errands, head home for lunch. By midafternoon, when Carly was ready for her nap, Janet was ready for one too: she felt drained and clumsy. A baby-sitter would arrive to watch the kids or take them on an excursion while Janet slept. Or tried. More often she lay awake worrying that she was shortchanging her children, having so little energy for them.

She decided she had to get a heart this summer. Her fear of dying was equaled, if not surpassed, by the fear that she wouldn't be able to teach in the fall. She lay in bed admiring the phone's smooth, curved, unblemished surface, its mellow beach-sand color. She called out to it in her mind, *Ring for me!* The receiver was cool to the touch. She lifted it and checked for a dial tone. Set the receiver gently down. With a forefinger she wound the curly cord into a kinked clump. Now and then in the middle of her reverie the phone would ring and she would have a brief, halting conversation with a telemarketer. "Take me off your list!" she'd shout, fuming at the irony.

Her friends came to visit when they could.

Ana and Tom and Sondra, her teacher friends from Juarez. Nina Fontenot, a college roommate, now an assistant curator at the Museum of Contemporary Art. Lequetia Hayslett, from Wednesday-night basketball. Tall, elfin Whitney, owner of Whitney's Antiques on Damen. One by one they climbed the four stories to her sick chamber and listened patiently to her bitching and cheered her with their jokes and stories. Unfortunately they were rarely able to stay very long. They were too busy. They rushed back out into the world, out into the bright, busy days. Janet envied them. Did they know how lucky they were? Actually, after an hour or so with her, she got the feeling most of them did.

Some afternoons Janet went stir-crazy and had to get out of the apartment. She clipped her pager to her front pocket and descended the long flights of stairs to the street, stepped out into sun dust filtering down through the trees. Into a glorious summer. Blue sky. Lordly processions of clouds. A world undaunted by the possibility of her departure. And here she was lovesick, smitten by her runty little street with its warehouse-district dinginess, the ashy brick buildings with bars on the lower windows, couples walking wolfish dogs, foreign cars tipped at the curbs. She smelled wet paint but couldn't place the source. She petted the cat lurking in the doorway of the video store. In front of the store were three parking meters whose heads had been covered with red vinyl hoods cinched at the necks. The hooded meters made Janet think of detainees about to be tortured or executed. Attached placards warned not to park in the designated spaces 6/22 through 6/26, as street repairs were planned. *Next week,* Janet thought. *Easy. I'll live through that.*

She drew encouragement from reminding herself that there were people all over the city, state, and country who were prepared to donate their hearts to her, who had signed their donor cards. Janet tried to pick them out on the street, at the grocery store, at the park. Walking down Wabansia, she thought, *Is she a donor? Is he?* as she passed a woman in a red miniskirt and black tank top, a young man peering under the propped-open hood of his Toyota. She stared covetously at the bare chests of construction workers. She wished organ donors would wear bright green T-shirts that read READY TO GO TO WORK FOR YOU! Then again, it might be dispiriting to see how few people wore the shirts. Janet knew there weren't many organ donors out there.

Not many people were that brave and generous and forward-thinking — big-picture thinkers who'd come to terms with the inevitability of death and the subsequent decomposition of the body, with the sad fact that they were not indispensable, that the human endeavor would lumber on without them.

The chilly air of fall made an advance appearance early in September, slipping into an open window during the night and gripping Janet's exposed body sprawled on top of the covers. When it became clear that the drop in temperature was not a climatic aberration, that the coolness planned to accompany the day, and soon all days, Janet experienced a jarring into clarity, an acute consciousness of time draining. Her health was draining too. She'd taken a leave of absence from teaching, a painful but unavoidable relinquishment. It no longer took any significant physical exertion to exhaust her: walking across a room, lifting a gallon of milk out of the refrigerator. Once she'd fixed huge, ambitious lunches for Carly and Sam — turkey sandwiches, quartered apples, grapes, carrots. Now she slid by with frozen entrees. Sometimes she nodded off while Carly and Sam were eating and woke to their burbly voices or a prolonged slurp from a cup and saw faces wobble into focus, her children as puzzled by her listlessness as she was by their fortitude: how did they hold their bodies upright, lift their hands to their mouths? She held her fingers up to her face and imagined millions of cells crying out for oxygen. It really was all about oxygen. She'd never had proper respect for the stuff. It wasn't just an invisible, pleasantly tasteless treat for the inhabitants of Earth to snack on. It kept her body from rotting. It kept things from turning black and falling off.

At Janet's weekly clinic visits, Dr. Maslowcya gave her increasing IV doses of milrinone, a drug that temporarily made her heart beat more strongly. Unfortunately the doses couldn't go much higher. Dr. Maslowcya worried that Janet could suffer a potentially fatal arrhythmia at any time. Janet checked into the hospital for two days to have an ICD, or internal cardioverter-defibrillator, surgically implanted beneath her collarbone. The ICD, a metal device the size of a cell phone, had leads that attached to Janet's heart muscle, and would shock her heart back to normal in the event of an arrhythmia.

The onslaught of every new day, the sinking disappointment of another phone call—less night. She told David she was going to buy a rifle and climb onto a roof across the street from one of the local health clubs and gun down the first healthy specimen who walked out the door. ("Don't aim for the chest," David said.) She watched the Weather Channel, watched storm fronts gather out west and rooted for them to sweep eastward across Illinois. When it rained, she went on high alert: checked the phone for a dial tone, made sure her pager was on, packed a night bag. She saw the twisted metal and contorted, bloody bodies. She'd read somewhere that a person would be killed in a car accident every fourteen minutes. The imminent possibility of death had activated a cold competitiveness in her, an uncompromising self-devotion that told her, *You* must live, *your* life comes first.

Two days before Thanksgiving Janet was lying on the couch under a blanket watching the Weather Channel — a huge cold front was sweeping across Nebraska and Iowa toward Illinois — when she got tired of looking at the grit strewn across the carpet before her. David's parents would arrive the next day, and even though they planned to stay in a hotel, Janet was determined that the loft should be clean, since everyone would spend most of their time here. She could have asked David to vacuum, but a few minutes ago he'd caught Carly doing some illicit exploration among his toiletries, and now they were in the bathroom together washing shaving cream out of her hair. Anyway, Janet was tired of feeling helpless and burdensome.

She untangled her legs from the blanket and struggled to lift her body from the couch. She walked to the hall closet, breathing heavily, and got out the vacuum, unwound the cord, plugged it into the power strip next to the fish tank. When the motor whined to life, David poked his head out of the bathroom looking concerned, but she waved him away.

She felt strong and capable watching specks of debris vanish beneath the vacuum. A pebble, which had surely ridden into the room on the bottom of Carly's or Sam's shoe, put up a tough fight, snapping and rattling until it was sucked up into the workings. The vacuum's handle felt slippery. Janet turned her hand over and discovered a glistening palm. She wiped it dry on her sweatpants, which she thought she'd exchange for shorts when she finished the job. She vacuumed under the coffee table, lapping at the floor with short strokes. After only a few strokes she stopped to rest, leaning on the vacuum's handle. She felt tipsy and boneless. Her heart was galloping. She coughed hard, coughed again, trying to reset her rhythm. She called for David but undershot the volume: the sound of the vacuum muffled her. She reached for the power switch. The room shrank to the size of a capsule. A cannon-slam to the chest — her ICD firing — yanked her conscious, ears popping, to the sight of David's frightened face. She blacked out again, and again a cannon-slam blew her ears and heaved her up and rattled her in convulsing light.

Twelve

A cold front had swept across the Midwest, dumping several inches of snow. At the reservoir north of town, the hiking trails were mottled with footprints, but all else was a pure white duvet from which gray-black trees stretched and sprawled and tangled, their branches sleeved with white.

Alex and Isabel and Bernice walked in a tight pack, bundled in coats and scarves and hats, sluggish from Thanksgiving dinner. They walked high on a trail overlooking the reservoir, a vast sheet of snow-dusted ice. No Jet Skis or powerboats or water-skiers, as in summer. An ethereal hush, broken only by the sound of boots crunching snow, the huff of breathing, the jingle of Otto's tags.

Alex took Isabel's hand but the clumsy, skinless grip of her glove failed to satisfy him. She snaked her arm around his waist and walked close to him for a few steps, briefly allowing her head to rest on his shoulder. For several months, since September, they'd been traveling on separate tracks, largely out of touch during the days while she was at school teaching and working and he was waiting tables. Also, he had taken to going out after hours with his coworkers, more often than Isabel liked. She interrogated him when he came to bed, but he was often too drunk to participate in the discussion. This compounded her anger. It didn't help that he reeked of Bushmills and cigarettes. "You think it's cool to fill your body with toxins?" she'd reproach him over the phone the next day, from the lab. "How cool is it going to be when you die of lung cancer at forty?"

Over the course of several inquisitions and arguments, he admitted that he was dissatisfied. Not with her. Not even with his life. With his employment. He missed fieldwork, rescue excavation, being outside all day, being an archaeologist. He was sick of waiting tables, of serving graduate students and professors — people thriving in their disciplines, earning money for pursuing their interests. He knew he was capable of better, yet no one in a position to employ him seemed to agree.

Isabel, relieved to learn the problem

wasn't her, sympathized, even when he broke the news that it wasn't easy, in his downtrodden state, being married to a woman who was succeeding magnificently at her teaching and studies and writing and research. She suggested that maybe he could be looking harder for a job. Alex dropped his head into his hands and told her she wouldn't know anything about the frustration of looking for a job, having never experienced it. "That's not true," she said, and then, dodging a fight, "I'm sorry I haven't been more supportive. You give me so much support." Burden me, she told him. Burden me if it'll stop you drinking and smoking and staying out until two in the morning.

So Thanksgiving break, like a gift from the gods of spousal harmony, had arrived at the perfect time. The restaurant was slow, and Alex was able to take a few nights off. He and Isabel went to a new animated movie called *The Incredibles,* which they agreed was incredibly ingenious and funny. They shot pool afterward in one of the bars they had frequented during their early days together. They slept late the next morning, went for a walk with Otto, took a nap followed by long-overdue sex. And now this, walking through the woods after Thanksgiving dinner. The snow was beautiful. The upper branches of trees bent calligraphically, like fragments of Chinese characters. Otto romped through the woods chasing squirrels, living out his predation fantasies.

"Think he's having fun?" Isabel asked Alex, nodding at Otto.

"He's got so much turkey on board, it's a wonder he can move."

"Don't look at me," Bernice said. "You were feeding him too."

"You were *serving* him," Alex said. "You may as well have set your plate on the floor."

They stopped at Vanguard Video on the way home. The place was jammed. What would the pilgrims have thought, Alex mused out loud, if they had been able to know that one day in the distant future millions of sleepy, gluttonous Americans would spend Thanksgiving afternoon watching movies? "They would have been jealous," Isabel said. The three of them wandered the mazelike aisles. They could watch a drama, they agreed, as long as it wasn't too serious. "Death, disease, war — I'd like to avoid all that," Bernice said. A comedy would be OK as long as it wasn't unwatchably goofy. Horror was out. Foreign was out: they were already sleepy enough. They needed something to keep them awake. Alex suggested action. "As long as there isn't a lot of violence and bloodshed," Bernice said.

"What kind of action movie doesn't have a lot of violence and bloodshed?" Alex asked.

"The kind I want to see," Bernice said.

"Good luck."

Isabel said, "Stop yakking and start looking."

A fine idea, in principle. They split up. Isabel and Alex rediscovered each other in New Releases and slipped into an embrace. Nearby, a little boy, three or four, unattended, was studying the cover of *Playboy 2004: The Party Continues,* which depicted a group of scantily clad blondes gathered around Hugh Hefner. The boy wore a puffy down jacket and a blue stocking cap with a tassel on top.

"Nice choice," Alex whispered to Isabel.

Isabel was amused and aghast. "Where's his mother?"

Alex and Isabel found Bernice and settled, eventually, on *The Last of the Mohicans.* " 'Epic adventure. Passionate romance. A frontier wilderness ravaged by war.' " Bernice read the plot description. "Well, I guess I can waive my no-war rule."

At the counter, during a long wait in line, they watched *Roman Holiday* playing on the

TV overhead. Isabel told Alex she didn't think Gregory Peck and Audrey Hepburn were having nearly as much fun as she and Alex had had on their trip to Venice earlier that year. A friend of Bernice's from the costume shop — Ralph, a slender man wearing black jeans with some kind of silvery gloss on the thighs — brushed past on his way to the depths of the store. "You'll enjoy that," Ralph said, eyeing the video in Isabel's hand. "Daniel Day Lewis is hot. His shirt comes off in the first five minutes. You'll love him."

"I already love him," Isabel said.

"The Hottest of the Mohicans," Alex said.

It was early enough in winter, and soon enough after the repeal of daylight saving time, that the premature darkness unsettled Alex as he left the store, fleetingly giving him the impression that there had been a nuclear attack or a comet impact. But it was only humankind fiddling with the clocks. The bill had come due for summer's long evenings. Perhaps for this reason it was pleasant to see a coppery glow in Bernice's downstairs windows as they pulled up in front of the house. They had forgotten to turn off the lights. Walking in the front door, Alex felt warmed, welcomed by the lighted rooms and the lingering scents of dinner and cooking and candles, as though they were guests arriving to join earlier versions of themselves. In the kitchen Alex poured a bowl of water for Otto, who had hydrated all afternoon on snow. Bernice made coffee. Isabel set some M&M'S and chocolate chip cookies out on the coffee table and cued *The Last of the Mohicans* on the VCR. "Showtime!" she called out as she extinguished lights.

Hawkeye — Daniel Day Lewis — sprinted through the dense, gloomy forests of Colonial America, dressed in flowing buckskin, his musket as long as a spear. He was accompanied by two men, his adoptive father and brother. They killed a deer. They supped with a family of white settlers. There was talk of war. The room where they ate was cramped and cozy and fire-lit against the perilous frontier, and Alex was conscious of his own cozy surroundings: Bernice's living room, now flickering blue-green in the glow of the television. Bernice sat beside Isabel on the couch, legs extended across the driftwood coffee table, re-sewing two loose buttons onto one of Isabel's shirts. Alex sat on the floor in front of Isabel with his back propped against the couch, his head resting on a spare cushion between Isabel's legs, which stretched out beneath his arms so that her feet, stripped to the socks, could rest on his lap. He had begun massaging them, and whenever he stopped she spurred him to continue with little toe pokes and heel prods.

Otto lay pitched on his side like a dead horse, legs fully extended, front right paw twitching.

The movie, which had started out so simply, three men running through a forest, complicated with new characters, war, factions, schemes, betrayals. Isabel slipped a hand into Alex's hair. He tipped his head to one side, propping it against the back of the couch, and closed his eyes. He woke several times to loud voices and gunfire, and each time drifted off again. Finally Isabel woke him to credits scrolling up the blackened screen. He wished the movie weren't over, even though he hadn't been watching it. He'd been enjoying his nap. He'd been enjoying the peace, the feeling of safety and belonging, curled up in the denlike dark with his wife and mother-in-law and dog.

Later, months later, when Alex thought back on *The Last of the Mohicans,* he would remember only the first scene, when the three Mohicans shot the deer. He remembered Daniel Day Lewis's face after he had felled the enormous buck: serious, grave, without a flicker of exultation. The three men approached the carcass slowly, with awe and trepidation and unease, like three boys who had in their rashness committed a profane act for which they might be severely punished. The oldest man spoke to the animal, apologized to it. *We're sorry to kill you, Brother. We do honor to your courage and speed, your strength.* The men knelt in front of the animal and admired it. Though it wasn't shown onscreen, Alex could imagine them exploring the animal's skin with their hands, pressing the powerful haunch muscles.

One of the men inhaled the animal's scent.

THIRTEEN

She woke up biting air, ripping off rough chunks of it and grinding them between her teeth. If there was an easier way of getting at the stuff, she had forgotten. A man was telling her to relax. He was dressed entirely in green. He was telling her about his crazy idea that if she relaxed the air would go into her mouth by itself. Where was David? She decided to stand up. The gravity had hands. The green man said *Noooooooooooo* with a voice that seemed to have the voices of other people inside it.

Her next waking took place gradually. She ascended through a nether space of sounds and voices and touches into a troubling but reliable clarity. She was bound to a high, broad bed by a tangled matting of tubes and wires. Drugs dribbled through IV lines in both arms. A catheter in her right arm dispensed blood like a faucet. Nurses drew syringefuls and went away rustling papers.

A stiff, transparent tube emerged from an incision below her left breast. Its purpose, a nurse explained, was to drain fluid from her lungs.

At some point David lurched into focus. Riding a crest of panic, he came directly to the bedside and stroked her head, held her hand, whispered *You'll be all right* over and over into her ear. Janet got the impression that he had never realized until this moment just how sick she actually was. It was proof of the severity of her illness that she had ended up in this place where nurses rushed in and out, where urgent voices filled the hallway, where the air vibrated with pinging alarms and warbling phones. His unease was palpable. He soon thought better of his initial rush to the bedside and began to keep his distance, as though one of Janet's lines or tubes might lash out, tentacle-like, and strangle him. He preferred to isolate himself in the middle of the floor, where he stood craggy and stiff, like some kind of sputtering volcanic butte, fumes of anxiety rising from his head.

How could Janet explain to him that he shouldn't worry, that she felt comfortable here? She felt lucky to be alive, to be an inpatient in this huge metropolitan medical center, tended by professionals, her decrepit body rescued by drugs and machines. She had felt for some time that the burden of her illness had become too heavy to carry alone, but she hadn't realized until now how ready she had been to hand herself over. Lenka Maslowcya, who had been a constant presence since Janet's admission, explained to her that she had experienced several runs of ventricular tachycardia, or racing of the heart, which had deteriorated into ventricular fibrillation and acute cardiac failure. She would have to stay at Parkland-Wilburn until she got a new heart. The good news was that Janet had gone from Status 2 to Status 1 on the transplant-candidate list, which meant she was top priority: if a heart became available, she would be among the first considered for it.

Janet spent five days in Cardiovascular Intensive Care basking in narcotized obliviousness. She wished she could sink back into it when Carly and Sam were finally allowed to visit. She was overjoyed to see them, but they were more terrified and confused than they had ever been in their lives, and the woman who would have normally taken them in her arms and hugged them close was not only restricted in her movement and zonked on drugs but responsible for their fear. David was too nervous and disoriented to be much comfort to them. On the contrary, without intending to, he took out his frustration on the children, mostly Sam, snapping at him to get away from the bed, keep his fingers off of the pumps. *How many times have I told you not to touch those buttons? Calm down.* David didn't seem to have noticed that calm Sam simply stared at his mother's perforated body and picked his lip till it bled.

Janet thanked God for her mother. Never before had Janet so appreciated this stocky, robust woman who motored about on thick ankles, her pockets stuffed with hospital and city maps, comforting Carly and Sam, shepherding them through their days, fixing them meals, getting Sam to school, watching Carly while David worked — trying to create for her grandchildren an atmosphere of normalcy, a sense that all the scary stuff happening to their mother would soon pass.

Janet left the CVICU for Medical Cardiology, right next door, where she was to settle in for the long wait. There were nine other Status 1's on Medical Cardiology, all in the end stages of heart disease, all waiting for new hearts. Janet's roommate was a fifty-eight-year-old welfare case worker named

Nora Lomanto. Nora was short and burly, and looked like a battle-hardened Roman centurion in her fuzzy red bathrobe, gripping her IV pole like a lance. Her belly was swollen, her arms bruised blue, and she negotiated the pod's flat, carpeted terrain with a doddery uncertainty. She was a determined walker, though, and took it upon herself to show Janet the "track" when Janet was well enough to exercise. They left Medical Cardiology, pushing their bulky, fully loaded IV poles (Nora called them Christmas Trees) and turned right into Parkland-Wilburn's main corridor. Nora pointed out the short black nubs protruding from the ceiling every ten feet or so and explained that these antennae relayed signals from their telemetry boxes to the bank of monitors at Medical Cardiology's central nurses station. They were on an electronic leash. They turned back into Medical Cardiology, where the walls were off-white and the carpet a blueberry houndstooth. They stopped to peer into dark doorways, where Nora introduced Janet to heads that rolled on mounds of pillows and gazed at them across seas of linoleum. In other rooms they found people up and about and ready to walk with them. Sherman was a short, sinewy man in his mid-sixties, blood Type

B. His gray hair was buzz cut to a smooth pelt, and he had a blunt, bony face like something you might stick on the end of an ax handle and use to smash rocks. Jim was somewhere in his late forties, bald up top, Vandyke-style beard, dressed in knee-length red basketball shorts and a white T-shirt that didn't quite reach all the way down across his volleyball-shaped belly. His legs were milk-white pegs, but his arms and shoulders were burly, and in fact he turned out to have spent most of his life repairing drilling equipment on oil platforms in the Bering Sea and the Gulf of Mexico. Brad was a tall, big-boned twenty-four-year-old whose college football career had been cut short by idiopathic cardiomyopathy. "Now I quarterback my own church," he told Janet. "We witness Friday nights in the conference room if you want to join us. We're up to fourteen venerators." Phil, a stocky African American man dressed in a navy blue bathrobe, white hospital pants, and expensive-looking brown leather slippers, reminded Janet that they had run into each other briefly during her transplant evaluation, a year ago. "I was the depressed-looking guy coming out of Ballows's office just as you were going in."

They formed quite a spectacle, the whole

pack of them out on the exercise circuit, shuffling through Medical Cardiology in their bathrobes and hospital gowns, sucking at the air, eyes staring, determined, hopeful. Like athletes in training for some rugged individual event, they respected and cared for one another while discreetly harboring the knowledge that if someone proved unable to go the distance, devastating as it might be, the field of competition would be advantageously narrowed.

One January evening the Status 1's were hanging out in their after-dinner spot, in a cozy nook by Elevator H in front of a tall window overlooking a canyon between two twelve-story pavilions. It was quiet except for the muted ding of the elevator bell and the occasional pneumatic tube scudding through the ceiling overhead. In the distance, to the east, rising from the grizzle of low buildings, they could see downtown skyscrapers, great dark towers flecked with light. Tonight the lights were obscured behind blowing snow. The Status 1's were excited and alert. They were discussing organ donors. Specifically, how few people out there actually signed donor cards. According to Jim there were only five or six thousand cadaveric donations a year, and that was spread across the entire United

197

States. "You may get hundreds of car wrecks, hundreds of fatalities, but what are the chances of any one victim being a donor? Slim."

"What we need," said Sherman, propping a bony white elbow on the steering ring of his Christmas Tree, "is an eighteen-wheeler careens off an overpass and squashes a bunch of cars — like, five cars full of O negatives, and everybody inside goes, quick and painless."

"Let's not have any children in any of the cars, OK?" Janet said, thinking of Carly and Sam and David, out there somewhere driving toward her.

"Oh, absolutely no children," Jim said. "Only adults. Healthy young adults who've signed their cards, and they aren't enjoying life anyway, they've decided it really sucks and they want to pack it in."

Nora's husband, Walt, a thin, reedlike man dressed in brown corduroy pants and a red argyle sweater-vest, had been following the conversation with a kind of dismayed amazement. But now he seemed to develop an interest. "I'm worried that truck of yours isn't going to be big enough, Sherm. You folks need a plane crash on I-294 out there by O'Hare. That way you get eight, nine, ten cars. Maybe more. Remember, you can't count on a donor in every car."

"Let's not get into planes," Phil said.

"How about two boats?" Nora offered. "A couple of passenger liners?"

Sherman raised an eyebrow, tantalized. "Nice body count."

"Recovery problem," Jim said. "How you going to fish everybody out?"

Nora said, "How about a meteor lands on the Super Bowl?"

There was another round of laughter, and then Phil, in what Janet sensed was an overture to Brad, changed the subject to football: would the Patriots win the Super Bowl? During the ensuing debate Janet traveled back over the conversation they'd just had and tried to decide what kind it had been. Were they savages? Were they greedy, scavenging vultures? It wasn't pure savagery, she decided. It was a practical morbidity, an attempt to get a feel for gruesome, tragic events — car wrecks, strokes, drive-by shootings — that she and her fellow Status 1's were now forced to accept as their only hope for survival. The black humor paved a descent into this grim marketplace and also served as a stabilizing fixative into which they could mix their desperation and hopelessness and fear. Otherwise these feelings would bubble up into despair, into tears.

And Janet sensed an unspoken rule against tears — against any display of emotion that might demoralize the troops.

Janet and David had discovered a way to converse without exchanging any distressing information. When David arrived at the hospital after work, in the evening, he typically asked her, *How are you doing? How do you feel? Anything big happen today?* with a fatigue in his voice that let her know he didn't feel up to a complicated answer — that he would be grateful for a brief, upbeat assurance of her well-being. So Janet told him she was fine, that she felt OK, and that nothing "big" had happened. She did her best to censor out troubling or ominous news, even though it was hard to conceal her anxiety. On the upside, she spared herself the compounded anxiety of seeing David upset.

On several occasions she attempted to break out of quarantine and honestly tell David how she felt, to let him know how scared and frustrated she was, but whenever he sensed unpleasant revelations on the horizon, he resisted or shut down. He'd insist he was tired. He'd insist he was thirsty. He'd insist he needed to use the bathroom. He'd say, *Just a sec, I'll be right back* and go down the hall to the vending machines or the restrooms. When he returned he'd open a new topic of conversation, as though wherever he'd gone and whatever he'd done had conveniently induced amnesia. Janet suspected his resistance wasn't due to fatigue or thirst or a continually full bladder. She suspected fear. He'd developed a cold, reluctant way of looking at her, as though she had betrayed him. As though she were dangerous. It was disturbing to realize that she *was* dangerous, a threat to his peace, his happiness, his well-being. "Come here," she'd say. "Hold my hand. I won't bite you." It was difficult to lure him close. He shied away as though she were a homeless woman on the street, and possibly infectious. When she did reel him in, he was awkward and paralyzed, strangely inept at both giving and receiving comfort, like a high school boy confronted for the first time with a naked girl. He didn't know what to do with his hands, what part of her to touch or how. "Easy," she'd say, rolling her head to one side. "Here. Can you scratch the back of my neck?" It helped to give him something to do. He'd settle into a project, relax. Recognize her. But any genuine, intimate conversation, if they happened to luck into one, was difficult to sustain in an environment where there always seemed to be an aide slipping through the curtain to take Janet's vitals, or a nurse to change one of her IV bags, or a rounding wolf pack of doctors and residents and medical students encircling the bed and making a seminar out of her, or the same people barging in on the other side of the curtain to work on Nora. The unit tended to quiet down later in the evening, but at that point David and Janet were usually so tired that conversation was disjointed and snippy. Better to shut up, split up, and recharge for another long tomorrow.

If only they could have slept together. Janet had never realized how important sleeping together was. Their bedroom, their bed, that warm loaf of linens in which they could lie together under soft light stripped of all armor and speak without distraction or disturbance, or not speak at all; that place where all explanations and apologies and assurances could be compressed into a look, a touch, a hand on skin. Some nights David did sleep with Janet at the hospital, on a cot between the bed and the window. Janet's mother, who was more or less in permanent residence at the apartment, watched the kids. The ambiance in Janet's room was hardly romantic. The air smelled like disinfectant and sweat. The walls shook when the Life Flight helicopter landed on the roof six floors above. Nora hacked up sputum in her sleep. Janet, who had grown numb to all this, slept adequately, but David had trouble drifting off and ended up spending most of the night awake, reading under a soft light or watching TV with a pair of headphones on. Janet woke to find him sprawled out in one of the big padded rocking chairs, eyes blinking from deep hollows, balancing a foam cup of coffee on his knee. Strangely, he was at his best at that hour. "Morning, sunshine," he'd say cheerfully. "You missed some great infomercials last night. They're making big strides in the world of ab toning. If you want to know about the latest technology, I'm your man."

He would be exhausted later, and grumpier than he would have been if he'd slept at home, but in these quiet dawns he seemed happy to see her, pleased to have her to himself in this tranquil, secluded space that was curtained off from the nurses and doctors and children and in-laws who would flood over them during the oncoming day. Even Janet's illness seemed absent at this early hour — distant, inattentive — and they played behind its back, chatting and joking, flipping through channels, poking fun at the miracle mattress, the wax-complexioned evangelist, the perky morning news show hosts fawning over their celebrity guests.

There were times late at night when Janet waded deep into her conscience and questioned what she was doing, what she had signed on for. Was it right to conspire with all these doctors and nurses and assorted professionals who were determined to steal her away from a death that had been directed to her naturally, though prematurely, by the same overarching ecology responsible for her birth and development, and for all the pleasures she had enjoyed in life? It would have been one thing if she were fighting tuberculosis or hepatitis, if she only required medicine. But she required the death of a member of her own species. She wanted to feel brave and justified in defying her own death, but sometimes she felt like an audacious, tampering coward. She had a recurring vision of herself as a greedy bitch scheming to shove a fellow passenger off a life raft just to get his or her bottle of fresh water. Wouldn't it be more noble just to slip quietly over the side?

Come now, Janet. We can't have you taking that attitude. We're physicians. The physician speaking in Janet's head had the indefatigable optimism and unassailable authority of a Cold War propaganda film narrator. *This isn't Haiti or Uganda. This is the United States of America, the Home of the Brave. American ingenuity and gumption settled this harsh, untamed land, defeated Hitler's armies, landed a man on the moon. Now that same American ingenuity and gumption are going to put a new heart in your chest. You just sit back and watch!*

But Janet was proud, and felt an equally American impulse not to take handouts. She felt guilty receiving so much attention for her disease when so many people in the world, including tens of thousands of children, died every day of common, curable diseases without getting any attention. And what happened one day when American ingenuity and gumption could accomplish anything, when surgeons could increase intelligence with microchip implants or slow the aging process with stem cell infusions? Would Janet get in line?

By April the status of the Status 1's was this: Sherman had suffered a severe angina attack, which had taken three nitroglycerin pills and lidocaine to stop, and had been so painful, even through the morphine, that he had wept. Jim had been declared temporarily ineligible for a transplant. All the blood transfusions he'd been given during his previous surgeries — a triple bypass, an LVAD placement, a sternum repair — had overloaded his blood with antibodies, and according to Dr. Maslowcya he would instantly reject any heart he received. She'd started him on plasmapheresis to clear out his blood, but in the meantime he would be ineligible for a transplant. Phil had had a run of V-tach so intense that he passed out. Brad had got his call and gone off to the OR to receive a heart that might have gone to Sherman, had it been smaller. He returned to Medical Cardiology a few days later, a celebrity, making little kicking and dancing motions with his feet, rediscovering the most trivial capabilities of his body. His smile, when he lifted his surgical mask, was like something that had been accomplished with champagne. He wore his pink skin like an expensive new suit.

Nora had died.

One afternoon after Janet had been out walking with Brad, envying his newfound health, they returned to find Janet's room thick with nurses and doctors. Janet couldn't see her roommate through the hedge of green scrub backs. The cardiologist on call stood at the bottom of the bed, eyes on the monitor above Nora's head, giving instructions in a quiet, deliberate voice. Nurses fiddled with infusion pumps and IV bags and tore open sterile packages of clinical weaponry. A fist gripped a huge syringe, the heel of the opposite hand shoving hard against the plunger. Two nurses bent so low as to practically touch their noses to what Janet recognized as Nora's bare right foot, now a poking ground, three slim, latex-gloved hands holding it steady while the fourth angled a needle toward the skin. Carla Dickerson, one of the shortest nurses on the unit, looked abnormally tall, Janet realized, because she was kneeling on the far edge of the mattress, leaning forward over Nora's body, doing compressions on her chest.

Then it was over. Voices dropped like shot birds. Nurses emerged shell-shocked, wiping sweat from their foreheads, refastening loose strands of hair into ponytails, tucking in the dislodged hems of scrub shirts, cleaning their glasses, their faces slack and consciously expressionless as if to say, *This is what happens, I will not let it crush me.* They lined up at the sink to wash their hands. They hugged one another and wept. Janet felt blunt with disbelief. She knew perfectly well what had just happened in that room but couldn't accept or feel it: her limbic system had thrown up a firewall. She watched an environmental aide wheel the crash cart out of Nora's room — out of *her* room — straight toward her. The emergency drug tray, which rode on top of the crash cart and was normally a neatly wrapped bundle of blue plastic, had been torn open and disemboweled. A defibrillator paddle hung loose from the defeated machine. The cart's drawers were ajar, its normally pristine surface littered with empty yellow epinephrine boxes, plastic syringe casings, ribbons of EKG tape, a squashed packet of defibrillator jelly.

When Janet had left for her walk with Brad, twenty minutes earlier, Nora had been sitting up in bed eating tapioca pudding and watching *The Young and the Restless.* Now she lay motionless, her body tucked in a white sheet, her face gray, her eyelids and lips tinged purple.

One morning a few days later Janet was in the exercise room doing curls with a three-pound barbell when she felt a suspicious insubstantiality in her upper body, much like the feeling she had had just before her Christmas V-tach. Wiser now, she put down the barbell and informed a nearby nurse that she felt dizzy. Within minutes she was tachycardic in bed, surrounded by doctors wearing expressions of uneasy annoyance. The stethoscopes were out, and everyone wanted a grope. Janet's nurse gave her a dose of amiodarone. An aide wheeled the crash cart into the doorway. Janet was hot and light-headed and scared. Was this it? Was she going to die suddenly, like Nora? Then all at once she broke: her heart scudded back into a normal rhythm, *lub*-dup, *lub*-dup. A deflation passed through the bodies around her, one expelled breath after another. Someone cracked a joke about weightlifting being good for your health. Janet's nurse gathered up a wad of EKG paper from the floor and handed one end of the strip to the cardiologist and they stretched it out like a banner across Janet's bed: seven feet of black, thatchy scrawl, the line leaping and plunging just short of vertical.

"That's a lot of V-tach," said Janet's nurse, amazed.

Janet was terrified. "Too much?"

The cardiologist put a hand on her shoulder. "Just don't do that again."

FOURTEEN

Three hundred miles to the west, Alex walked briskly toward downtown Athens. Otto strained at the leash. It was four thirty on a Thursday afternoon. Alex planned to meet Isabel on her way home from teaching, pass off the dog to her, and go to work at the restaurant. Isabel would walk Otto home, then go for her bike ride.

Alex felt cheerful, optimistic, prepared to endure the servility of waiting tables. This morning he'd gotten up before sunrise and driven four hours to Omaha, Nebraska, for an interview at a company called Enduring Ecosystems. Enduring Ecosystems had a contract to manage the construction of two road networks across the Rosebud and Yankton Indian reservations in South Dakota. They needed a principal investigator for the project, an archaeologist with experience in rescue excavation and cultural resource management. Alex's qualifications were a near match. The interview had gone well. Alex had liked the people who interviewed him, and he was pretty sure they had liked him. If he got the job, he would have to travel extensively but he would not have to relocate. The money and benefits would be nice. He'd been promised a decision by next week.

Alex was excited. It felt great to get his hopes up, as dangerous as that could be. He couldn't wait to share his excitement with Isabel. He felt an intense love for her, which rose on the swell of his sudden hopefulness, a belief in the possibilities of his life.

The pedestrian mall, only two blocks long and half a block wide, aspired, in its humble way, with its redbrick surface and wooden benches, its trees and flowerbeds, to the majesty of a great public space. People sat with their arms hooked over the backs of the benches, talking and laughing. Alex spotted Isabel sitting on a bench near a tall stone sculpture inset with translucent green glass. She waved and smiled. She was wearing dark jeans and a black, fitted, button-down shirt with big square cuffs — French cuffs, Bernice called them. Isabel's hair was tied back into a ponytail. Alex felt a twinge of envy for her students, the lucky undergraduate biology majors who had signed up for Survey of Land Plants and got to stare at her for fifty minutes every day.

"Hey, you," she said, tipping her face upward to receive Alex's kiss.

Otto wanted to climb onto her lap, and she held him back, stroking his head.

Alex moved her brown leather bag out of the way — it was heavy with books and papers — and sat down. "How's it going?"

"Fine. Tired. So tell me everything."

They had discussed Alex's interview earlier, briefly, on the phone. Now Alex gave Isabel the whole story, describing the offices of Enduring Ecosystems, which were located in an old renovated loft in Omaha's meatpacking district, and the people, who struck him as busy but relaxed. The interview had been informal and inspiring, a lively conversation in which Alex felt he'd done well answering most of the questions put to him. "I can't imagine how it could have gone any better. Unless they'd said to me, 'Alex, you'll be pleased to hear that the other candidates have withdrawn their applications out of deference to your experience and intelligence. Congratulations. You're our guy.' "

Isabel laughed. "They'll say it soon enough."

"I hope so."

"What did they say about travel? How often would you be going back and forth?"

Isabel had specifically asked Alex to bring up this issue in the interview, but Alex, who had gone in determined to do so, changed his plan when the conversation reached a pleasant cruising speed and the atmosphere in the room became genial and he entered an acquiescent trance in which he was confident that getting the job would be so glorious as to make any related hardships — like spending days and possibly weeks away from home — acceptable. "The subject didn't really come up. I'm sure it'll be cool. They were really reasonable people."

"Are they going to move Omaha to Eastern Iowa so you don't have to drive four hours to get to the office? Are they going to relocate the Native American tribes from South Dakota to Cedar Rapids so you don't have to drive ten hours to get to your work site?"

"I think relocating the Native Americans is out of the question. They had to go through enough relocation back in the day."

"Alex, I think this is going to be logistically impossible if you're gone all the time."

It seemed to Alex that Isabel, who had urged him to be more aggressive in his job search, and who had chastised him for his

213

inaction, shouldn't be allowed to set conditions and restrictions. "It'll work out," he said. "I'll pull my weight at home."

"You can't pull your weight at home if you're never there."

Alex nearly said *Look who's talking,* but refrained. Isabel spent long, full days on campus, and when she got home usually went right back out again for an hour or two of swimming or biking. The confounding thing was that often she still had the energy, later in the evening, to cook, clean, run errands. So he couldn't honestly accuse her of neglect. "It's not like I'll be working in Montana," Alex said. "I'll be around."

Isabel laid her head on his shoulder. "I'll miss you. Otto will miss you."

"They haven't offered me the job yet."

"When they do, get some specifics about travel, OK? For me?"

"Sure. I promise."

"Thanks."

"Did I mention what they're paying?" Alex said with a twinge of glee.

"Forty thousand?"

"We'll be rich. Compared to what we are now."

"Easy there, big spender."

"I'm going to spend it all on you."

"Now you're talking."

They sat quietly for a while. The evening was cool and breezy, an occasional scent of blossoms in the air. The sky in the west was overcast. Alex massaged Isabel's neck, scratched her head with slow, lazy contractions of his fingers. A thin, middle-aged man strolled past, eating an ice cream cone and taking careful, conscientious bites. A college-age girl sat on a bench getting intimate with her cell phone, curling up around it. Two children played nearby, the girl around three, the boy around five. They were chasing each other around a sculpture of a tornado made out of one continuous strand of silver wire spiraling out of the ground. The children's parents sat off to the side exhorting them not to run. Run they did, around and around, giggling hysterically. Alex glanced at Isabel to see if she was watching the kids. She was, but when she realized he had noticed, she looked away.

"Cute, huh?" Alex asked.

"What?" She waited for Alex to nod at the kids. "Oh, sure. In principle."

"What about in reality?" Alex said suggestively. He reached over and squeezed her thigh.

Isabel said, "Consider the tornado sculpture as a metaphor for what will slam into

215

our lives."

"You have awesome DNA. It would be a crime for it to go to waste."

"It's not going to waste. It makes up *me.*"

"Yeah, but combined with my super-awesome DNA we could make a veritable superhuman. A cute one, too. A cute little plant to grow in our greenhouse."

Isabel smiled with a mixture of affection and exasperation. "I need to finish my dissertation. I need to finish my course work. I need to finish *me.*"

Alex shrugged, chastened, a little hurt.

"I'm sorry," Isabel said, "but I feel like I need to start pressing back. You've been bringing this up more and more — which is OK, I want you to talk to me about it — but it's clear from your tone that you've assumed we've settled the question of *if* and moved on to *when.* I'm still stuck back at *if.*"

Her worries, Alex knew, were the usual. She didn't want to be constantly harried and exhausted, like most mothers of young children. She wasn't sure she was willing to make such an enormous sacrifice of time and energy. There were so many other things she enjoyed doing, activities and pursuits that had nothing to do with children and were in fact hindered by their presence. Work. Research. Teaching. Reading. Writing. Exercise. Travel. She worried her relationship with Alex would suffer. On the other hand, she also worried her relationship with Alex might suffer if they *didn't* have a child — if Alex was unhappy. This made Isabel reluctant to commit one way or the other. The problem with her silence and uncertainty, Alex was coming to understand, was that when his hopes were left to themselves, unchecked by any explicit correction from her, they inflated into expectations. Alex wanted children. Most of the time, when he saw or talked to a boy or girl he liked, he was smitten enough to have a taste of the immense, powerful love he might feel for that child, were it his own, and how much fun they would have together.

He glanced up at the bank clock across the street. It was 4:56.

"Shit," he said. His shift began at five. "Blake is such a sleazy, disingenuous fuck," he said, referring to his supervisor, the restaurant's manager. "One of these nights I'm going to dump a bowl of lobster bisque on his head."

Isabel patted his knee as though he were an overanxious child. "Wait until you get your new job. And then make sure you let me know when you're going to do it so I can come in and watch."

Alex liked the way she said *your new job.* She sounded pleased, approving, proud. He pulled her close and kissed her. "I love you," he said.

"I love you," Isabel said. "I was thinking maybe I'd stop by later and have a drink."

"Sure. Come witness my humiliation at the hands of impatient diners."

"Another kiss, please." Then she said, "Turn on that big-tip smile."

Alex made a goofy, mocking face — a parody of solicitous service staff. He bent down in front of Otto and cupped the dog's head in both hands and gave him a smooch on the muzzle. "Thanks for the walk, buddy. You be good on the way home. Don't eat any dead animals off the sidewalk." He told Isabel, "He went for a dead squirrel on the way over here."

"Did he get it?"

"No. Watch out going back, though. It's near the intersection of College and Lucas. North side of the street, light blue house, in the grass near the sidewalk." Otto would remember, and be quicker this time.

"We'll walk on the south side."

"See ya." Alex shuffled away.

"Bye," Isabel called sympathetically after him.

Alex walked across the pedestrian mall to the intersection where it met the street, traffic stopped at a light. He looked back at Isabel just to look at her, and to let her know he was thinking of her. He made a funny, exasperated face. She smiled. She leaned down and lifted Otto's paw and made it wave good-bye. She was quite a picture sitting there in her dressy black shirt among the trees and newly blooming flowers with the great golden dog obediently at her feet. Both of them watching him go.

What would he have said, what would he have done, had there been any way of knowing this would be the last time he would ever see Isabel alive? He would have run to her, he would have thrown his arms around her body and his legs and tucked her head to his chest and tried to shield her from whatever blow the cold, black universe intended to deliver.

But there was no way of knowing. There was no warning. One presumed a future.

FIFTEEN

Janet was ecstatic. She was terrified. She was distraught, for it was news of a death.

"Don't be anxious," said Lenka Maslowcya, touching Janet's hand. A minute earlier Dr. Maslowcya had slipped into the room, knocked lightly on the door frame, and asked if she could turn on a light. It was ten o'clock on a Thursday night, and Janet had been lying in the dark trying to sleep. Dr. Maslowcya turned on a soft light and stood beside the bed without saying a word, tapping her fingers on the mattress and grinning mysteriously. She was wearing suede boots, blue jeans, a burgundy wool sweater. Street clothes. Janet's first tip.

"I think we have found a heart for you," Dr. Maslowcya said. "Are you interested?"

Janet knew from experience that the prudent response to such news was guarded optimism. Often the heart turned out to be too big or too small or too fatty. Sometimes the heart had a bad valve, or the donor was diagnosed with hepatitis or HIV. But there was so little in this gray prison to take joy in, and Janet was desperate. She clutched Dr. Maslowcya's arm. "Are you serious?"

Dr. Maslowcya nodded. "Everything looks good in terms of size, so we are going to proceed, hoping that everything else will fall into place. You are going to be a busy woman for the next couple of hours. I'm sorry you won't get any sleep, but I can promise you some anesthesia."

Janet reached David on his cell phone. He and the kids had left the hospital half an hour earlier, and were three blocks from home. "Turn around," she told him. He took the news with an outburst of excitement and apprehension. She was glad; she couldn't remember the last time she'd said something that pleased him. She heard him announce to the kids over the whoosh of traffic, "Hey, your mom's getting a new heart!"

Angie, a short, cute, sparky nurse, burst into Janet's room looking thrilled and harried. "We have got a *shitload* of work to do."

Angie got Janet naked and scrubbed her skin from chin to toes with a sponge soaked in disinfectant. A second nurse, Krista, helped shave Janet's legs, groin, and chest.

Then Angie and Krista painted the shaved areas with betadyne, an antibiotic solution that made Janet's skin glisten orange-bronze. Angie drew blood to send to Micro for cultures, to Core Lab for a general screen and CBC, to the blood bank for a type and cross. A pharmacy tech arrived with a basket full of syringes and IV bags. Angie passed two pills to Janet, along with a cup of water. The pills were huge and smelled like skunk, but Janet muscled them down. The suppression of her immune system had begun.

A short, wiry physician who introduced himself as Dr. Bruce Taggart, Cardiothoracic Surgery, scrubbed at the sink, gloved, laid out supplies on a table next to Janet's bed, and spent a few minutes inserting an arterial line into her left arm. The stick was deep, and it hurt, but Janet was impressed that Dr. Taggart managed to strike bright arterial blood on the first try. Then Dr. Taggart transferred his attention to the right side of her neck and set to work with Dr. Maslowcya, inserting a Swan-Ganz catheter into Janet's right internal jugular. Just before this procedure got under way Janet heard Dr. Taggart mention something to Dr. Maslowcya about the heart being from Iowa, a bike versus car.

David and the kids had arrived, and Janet's mother. Angie let them into the room and explained that Janet was now officially immunosuppressed and extremely vulnerable to infection. She washed her own hands to demonstrate proper technique: how to scrub the ends of the fingers, scrub between the fingers, scrub high on the wrists, let the warm water run down off the hands into the drain. Carly and Sam were rapt, fascinated, staring down at their hands as they sloshed them around in the foamy lather. David was too distracted to pay attention. He'd come into the room flushed and huffing for breath, his eyes skittering along the walls. Janet coaxed him to the bedside for a kiss, then told him where to stand out of Angie's way. David moved obediently to the spot but couldn't calm down; he rocked back and forth and shifted his hands between his pockets and a clasped position behind his back. At one point he lost his balance and took a lurching, corrective step. Angie asked him, "Would you like a chair?" What he needed, Janet understood, was something to do. She instructed him to lift Carly into bed with her and hold her lines clear so Carly didn't snag.

Carly worried the new heart wouldn't love her as much as the heart her mother had now. Janet assured her that loving came from the brain. Sam wanted to come to the OR and watch the surgeons operate. Janet told him gently that he couldn't. She hooked an arm around Sam and the other around Carly and hugged them close. David snapped a picture of their entangled bodies, arms flung everywhere, Christmas-morning smiles.

Well-wishers poked their heads in the door, proceeded to the sink to wash their hands if they wanted to come closer. Nurses and doctors, Status 1's, families of Status 1's, environmental aides, unit clerks, technicians, medical students. A dietary worker. A security guard. A *This Is Your Life* of people Janet had met over the past three months at Parkland-Wilburn. The atmosphere was hurried and festive, the air cracking with quips and laughter.

Three anesthesiologists arrived and closed in around Janet's bed. They studied her circuitry, her arterial line and Swan-Ganz catheter. They traced her IV tubing back to pumps, scrawled notes and numbers on pads of paper and on the thighs of their scrub pants. The lead anesthesiologist riddled Angie with questions about Janet's medications. The more they discussed her and tinkered with her fittings, the more

224

Janet felt detached from the proceedings, like a piece of cargo.

Launch. Two fifteen a.m. The ceiling twisted and slid. New textures and lights and faces. Janet's bed, heaped with medical records and infusion pumps and syringes and vials of meds and a portable Propac monitor, all carefully arranged around her arms and legs and feet, resembled the *Kon-Tiki,* that cluttered, balsawood raft Thor Heyerdahl had sailed from Peru to Polynesia. The anesthesiologists took Janet out through the unit's main thoroughfare, past all the assembled nurses and a few of the more nocturnal Status 1's. *Good luck, Janet! Go for it, Janet! You go, girl!* Angie and Krista wished Janet well and dropped back.

In the hallway they gained speed. Janet's mother followed behind the bed with Sam and Carly in tow. David walked alongside, even with Janet's head, jogging occasionally to keep pace. Janet tried not to think too hard about his anxious, hovering presence. She tried not to think about *infection, bleeding, cardiac arrest, death* — the risks of the surgery listed on the consent form she'd signed an hour earlier. As she hurtled toward a sleep in which she would leap across a chasm from one life to the next — at one point there would be nothing in her

225

chest except the sawed-off cuffs of her old heart — she saw with incredible, penetrating clarity, through the mist of her sedation, the damage done to David by fear and stress over the past year and a half, as well as the crust of courage he had applied to cover it up. He looked frail and peaked. Janet reached up toward his face. He lowered it to hers. She ran a finger along his jaw. He guided her hand back to her side. "Relax," he told her, his own hand trembling.

"*You* relax," she told him. "I'm going to be fine."

"I'll be OK," he said tentatively, as though trying to convince himself. "It'll be nice to get this over with."

Janet smiled to reassure him. "Take care of the kids, OK?" She meant during the period of her surgery and recovery, but also if she never came back.

She thought of Nora, wished Nora had gotten a heart so she could be here now to tell Janet, "Relax. Don't worry. You'll be fine."

At the doors to the OR, Janet's mother and the kids closed in for final kisses. Sam was crying. David gave Janet a sweet smooch on the lips that made her think of old times. Courting days. "See you soon," he said.

"See ya."

And she rolled. Rounding a corner into the OR, she looked back and saw her mother and children wave. David was leaning into a wall, overcome by anxiety and emotion. Janet ached to comfort him. As the automatic doors shuddered and closed it occurred to her that despite the prevailing myth of a second life, she would be going back to the exact same life — and to what she now recognized, in this odd, preoperative clarity, as the same complications and difficulties. She would need a strong heart. She hadn't prayed since childhood, but she came close now, closing her eyes and silently intoning to whoever or whatever pulled the strings, *Please let this heart from Iowa be a workhorse.*

Isabel lay on her back in the middle of the night, slit from neck to pubis, her body covered with a blue, sterile drape except for the trough of pulp where the hands were. The hands were from Minneapolis, Madison, Peoria, and Chicago, and they were here for the liver, pancreas, kidneys, and heart. Faces were masked: you could be in the room for hours and never see a mouth. Arthur Wood had learned to gauge others by their voices, their eyes, the agility of their hands as they probed and groped and snipped at connective tissue. In this particular case Arthur Wood and the liver surgeon, Matteo Inzaghi, had worked together before, at a recovery back in the fall — neither could remember where — so the mood was amiable as they stood across from each other, one at the chest and the other at the abdomen, inspecting and palpating.

"Not a lot of fat on this girl. Good-looking liver."

"Heart's nice. Nice contractility."

"When do you want to cross-clamp?"

It was two forty-five a.m. Arthur Wood stepped over to a phone on the wall and called Chicago. He spoke directly with Karl Ballows, the surgeon who would perform Janet Corcoran's transplant. Wood gave Ballows Isabel Howard's medical history and described the condition of her heart. "Let's take it," Ballows said.

Wood and Inzaghi decided to cross-clamp at three forty-five. There was nothing to delay Wood: within half an hour Ballows would have Janet Corcoran asleep on the table in Chicago. Wood and his partner, Jim Tully, a first-year Cardiothoracic Surgery fellow who had never done a heart recovery, completed their initial dissection of Isabel Howard's heart, freeing the aorta and two large veins from surrounding tissue. Inzaghi needed forty-five minutes to complete his preparatory dissection — the liver's hookup was more complex — and the heart needed to stay in place to perfuse the abdominal organs with blood. Wood and Tully scrubbed out. In the hallway they chatted with the kidney team, who had also scrubbed out. Kidney dissection required significant manipulation of the intestine, which caused blood loss and liver damage. The kidney team would have to wait until the liver was removed, and the liver couldn't come out for another hour, at least, when it would be removed immediately following the heart. So the kidney people were in for a long night.

Wood and Tully scrubbed back in at three forty-five. Inzaghi was running behind. Tully stapled the superior vena cava just above the right atrium. Inzaghi asked Wood, "Where are we cutting the IVC?" He was referring to the inferior vena cava, a large vein that returned blood to the heart from the lower portion of the body. Inzaghi wanted the inferior vena cava cut near the heart. Not only did he want a substantial section of the IVC to take with the liver, but after cross-clamp the girl's bloody renal drainage would flow from the severed end of this vein, and Inzaghi preferred that it flood the pericardium, where Wood and Tully would be a few simple cuts away from having the heart in their hands, rather than the abdomen, where Inzaghi and the pancreas surgeon had a trickier series of cuts ahead.

Wood agreed to cut the IVC just below the right atrium. He instructed Tully to cross-clamp the aorta high on the arch, immediately below the three arteries that delivered blood to the brain. If there were any moment in the entire process in which Arthur Wood felt a twinge of uncertainty as to the nature of what he was doing, this was it. They had just cut off blood flow to the girl's brain — not that the brain was feeling or thinking anything — and now they were going to cut off the blood flow to her body. Tully prepared to inject the heart with a chilled cardioplegic solution, and Wood instructed him to do so at the moment just after the heart had contracted and expelled its blood load. Tully got the timing perfect: the heart drew in the cardioplegic solution, twitched briefly, and arrested. A few seconds earlier the heart had beaten hard and warm against Wood's palm; now it lay still and cold as an uncooked roast. The blood in this woman's body, which had flowed continuously since she was an embryo, would now stay where it was, unless it was flushed out. Its circulating days were over.

Wood told the anesthesiologists, "You can stop ventilating her."

Tully cut the inferior vena cava. The liver and pancreas teams were off on their own synchronicity now, irrigating the blood out of their organs, severing ligaments, dissecting and cutting complex tangles of veins and arteries. They'd be at work for another few hours, mostly on the back table, where, having removed the liver and pancreas from the donor's body, they would separate the two organs and undertake the lengthy process of trimming and cleaning them, preparing all the veins and arteries to hook up to corresponding ones in the recipients' abdomens. Wood was glad to be in the heart business: the heart was basically hooked up to a couple of garden hoses. Already Wood and Tully were nearly finished cutting it free. While a nurse suctioned blood that was gushing into the pericardium and a second nurse poured cold saline onto the surface of the heart to preserve the outer tissue, Tully and Wood removed the catheter from the aorta and severed the remaining arteries and veins and tissue connecting the heart to the body. Then Wood lifted the heart out of the woman's chest with two hands. With a quick swivel of his body and several careful steps across a floor strewn with cables he carried the heart to a nearby table, where he set it down in a metal bowl. He and Tully gave the heart a good once-over to make sure they had everything and then packed it in a clear plastic bag full of cardioplegic solution, sealed the bag, double-bagged that bag, and stowed the heart in a cooler.

Once they had thanked the room and written a brief note in the woman's chart, they were free to leave. No one expected the heart team to stick around. The heart could only survive four to six hours without a blood supply — the shorter the ischemic time the better — whereas the liver could survive eight to sixteen, and the kidneys two days. Still, Wood paused near the door and sent Tully ahead with the cooler. Wood never felt comfortable turning his back on the cadaver and rushing out. He watched the huddle of blue gowns around the table. The kidney surgeons were rummaging around in the abdomen, assisted by several nurses. More surgeons and procurement specialists waited in the wings to take skin and corneas, cartilage and bone, tendons and veins, lymph nodes for cross-matching. Feet sheathed in polypropylene shoe covers moved across the floor. One of the kidney surgeons was leaning over the donor with an arm sunk to the elbow in viscera, grousing, accusing Inzaghi, who was busy at the back table, of not having left enough infrahepatic vena cava, a vein necessary to transplant the kidney. "I left you a perfectly nice cuff," Inzaghi said without looking up from his work.

Wood leaned against the wall, bowed his head, and closed his eyes. To anyone else in the room he might have looked like he was stealing a nap or recovering from a dizzy spell; they wouldn't have guessed he was praying to God never to let this happen to a member of his own family. He wouldn't want a team of surgeons going at one of his daughters like this. He wouldn't be able to watch. On the other hand, would he be able to watch one of his daughters being cremated? Would he be able to watch one of his daughters' bodies decomposing, if a light and a camera were installed in the casket? What he could or couldn't stand to watch might not correspond with what was or wasn't an ethical or worthy enterprise. There was no question it would be a terrible waste to burn or bury all the magnificent organic devices in this room, to reduce the heart and liver and kidneys to ash or abandon them to decay just because their compatriot and leader, the brain, had been senselessly destroyed.

But philosophizing, in this instance, was irresponsible. The heart needed to get to a blood supply. Wood went out into the hallway and found Tully. "Let's go," he said.

She lay on her back early in the morning, slit at the sternum, her body covered with a sterile blue drape except for the incision between the arms of the rib spreader — an incision that looked like a big, bloody, open mouth.

Bruce Taggart, a first-year Cardiothoracic Surgery fellow, had clamped the aorta and was now ready to detach the left and right atria. Under Karl Ballows's supervision, Taggart hooked the thumb of his left hand into the heart's left ventricle, hooked his forefinger into the right ventricle, and lifted the heart upward. With his right hand he reached underneath and snipped away at the atrial septum, detaching Janet Corcoran's heart, leaving a rim of tissue at the bottom of the pericardium.

The heart-lung machine — which took the patient's blood as it entered the venae cavae, oxygenated it, and returned it through a cannula in the aorta just above the clamp, completely bypassing the heart and lungs — gurgled nearby.

Cut free, the diseased heart was lifted. "What a whopper," Ballows said, placing the bloated wad of muscle in a nearby bowl. He experienced something like vertigo looking down into Janet Corcoran's empty pericardium, which was bare except for the rim of the old atria on its back wall (Ballows thought this resembled the two halves of a vertically cut, seeded red bell pepper lying side by side, insides up), and the twin jutting hoses of the pulmonary artery and the aorta, which were waiting for something new to be hooked up to.

"We're ready for the graft," Ballows announced.

A nurse brought over the donor heart and handed it to Ballows, who showed Taggart how to trim its aorta, pulmonary artery, and atria to interlock precisely with their corresponding parts in the pericardium below. Then Ballows and Taggart fit the graft into the chest and set to work stitching the back walls of the donor atria to the remaining rim of the old atria. Ballows let Taggart do most of the stitching. This was only Taggart's second transplant. Ballows interrupted periodically to give instructions while Taggart sewed together the aortas — taking large, deep bites of tissue with the sutures — and then stitched together the pulmonary arteries. Ballows didn't think Taggart appreciated how crucial it was, at every juncture, to be sure that all residual air was evacuated from the heart. "The last thing you want is an embolism," Ballows said. "Good way to waste a lot of people's time and effort."

When the moment was right, Ballows instructed Taggart to remove the aortic clamp, allowing freshly oxygenated blood from the heart-lung machine to flow into the coronary arteries and irrigate the muscles of the heart, which was thirsty after nearly three hours — a respectable ischemic time, given the distance traveled — deprived of blood.

"OK, suck it down," Ballows said.

He could never help being a little apprehensive about whether the graft would start. Sometimes — not often, but sometimes — it didn't. This one was reluctant to begin its rhythm. The surface muscle twitched and rippled in fleeting, disorganized wavelets. The heart looked like a plastic bag full of squirming worms. Ballows told Taggart to give it a shock, and Taggart touched two tonglike paddles to the muscle. The worms stopped squirming, then started. Taggart shocked the heart again, and again the heart slipped back into fibrillation. Ballows had to remind himself that this heart had suffered the concussion of an enormous impact and labored under the whip of inotropic drugs, that it had been cut out of its body and packed on ice and flown three hundred miles — all in the past ten hours. "Let's go up to fifty," Ballows said. Taggart increased the joules and shocked the heart for the third time. Still, the graft failed to take on a rhythm. "Stubborn," Taggart said. "Hang on," said Ballows, who was watching more closely and had an eye for these things. Ballows pointed a blood-spackled, white-latex finger at the heart muscle. "See that?"

Taggart concentrated. Ballows smiled under his mask. It was quite a thing to see: all that twitching and rippling beginning to organize around single, detectable contractions.

PART III

MAY 2006
SIXTEEN

Schools. What if rooms have as many kids that you do'nt know what if the teacher sees you? We could get a book every class but there's not so we share. I go to Tri-County. It's OK that I don't have the nice close. We don't have as much for close because of our bujit. But Dad needs a new dog for hunting.

Alex tips his head back and turns it carefully from side to side, stretching his neck. He unfastens a strap on his wrist brace, scratches the skin beneath, refastens the brace more securely. Two weeks ago, rock climbing with his friend Rob, he struck out on a free climb for which he probably ought to have been belayed; he lost his footing and fell six feet to a hard, rocky slope. His left wrist broke the fall, or tried. Sprained, it burns when he bends it, though every day it hurts less.

Ah, but what are his sufferings compared to those of Aleisha Drechney? He has to

241

admire her brave, persevering tone, the way she describes her deprivation without self-pity or despair. He's touched by her innocent linguistic fumblings. *We don't have as much for close.*

"Got a winner?" Grier looks up from an essay that's clearly boring him.

"Not exactly," Alex says.

Grier reaches across the table and snatches Aleisha's essay. He tips his chair back, braces a knee against the table's edge, and reads, emitting dismissive mouth-cluckings and groans. "Yuck. Yikes. So . . . who cares whether the kids go to school half-naked, as long as Pa gets his coonhound."

"I'll take that back," Alex says.

"May I?" Mavis, intrigued by Grier's comment, takes the essay from him and positions it on the table in front of her. Her hands are busy unwrapping a peppermint just beneath her chin. She holds the peppermint in front of her mouth, poised for entry, until she's finished reading: then she pops it in. "So what are you going to give her?" she asks Alex. "Negative one? Negative five?"

"I was thinking a two, actually," Alex says.

"A two? Are you crazy?" Grier flips through papers on the table in front of him, searching for the scoring guidelines. When he finds them he reads. " *'Absence of focus, absence of relevant content, severe mechanical and usage errors'* — need I continue?"

"Hold on," says Alex, feeling inexplicably lucid. "Are the mechanical and usage errors *'so severe that the writer's ideas are difficult if not impossible to understand'?*"

"Yes," Grier says brusquely. "Don't get technical. It's the spirit that steers us, the spirit of Thanatos. And like I said, there's no focus."

"Keep it down," Alex says, watching Diane Topor float by in a cherry blazer, head swiveling, alert for discord.

"This girl's focus is schools," Mavis whispers to Grier, joining the defense. "It's a confused focus, but it's present. Her mechanical and usage errors *seriously interfere* with her purpose. That's a two."

Alex reads Aleisha Drechney's essay again. This time he finds her whiny and irritating. She thinks she's suffering, does she? He feels it roiling within, a charge to be released, a fierce, adrenal urge to answer the world's random violence with random violence of his own.

He marks Aleisha with a one, pressing down hard with his pencil.

Grier peers at the score. "Nice. I thought you'd lost your touch."

Mavis checks the score too. Alex is nervous, steeled for rebuke, but Mavis doesn't say a word, doesn't even glance at him. Casually, as though nothing has happened, she goes back to her work, chewing her peppermint.

His mailbox is jammed. Electric bill, water bill, a big blue envelope stuffed with Val-Pak Coupons. Two credit card offers (3.9% APR! Double Cashback Bonus!) and, sandwiched between them, a little square envelope with a Chicago postmark, the energetic handwriting, the familiar return address: Corcoran, 2014 West Wabansia #4.

Alex holds the envelope like a Frisbee, roughly parallel with the ground, forefinger on a corner. He imagines the arty card within, the robust handwriting, the grateful, well-composed sentiments. Maybe it's the company in which the envelope has arrived, but there's something about its weight and his apprehension of its contents that makes it feel like an overdue notice for a bill he's already paid. He ought to write back to Janet and tell her to stop writing to him. *Please take me off your mailing list.* Then he looks at his name and address written on the outside of the envelope and thinks of blood pumping from the heart down through an artery into this stranger's hand, her fingers gripping the pen, as well as, higher up, eyes reading the words, brain choosing them, all powered and sustained by that brave, resilient fist of muscle formerly his girl's — *still* his girl's, now relocated — beating in some other chest a few hundred miles to the east.

He mounts the stairs quietly, peers around the corner toward his landing. Since Jasper's nocturnal visit Alex has been nervous coming into his building. He's been nervous everywhere. Walking Otto, running errands at the mall or downtown, going to the grocery store, the video store, the public library — every time he gets out of his car, every time he rounds a corner, every time he goes through a door, Alex is prepared to see Jasper. So far his vigilance hasn't led to a sighting. Thankfully. But he's hardly ready to let his guard down.

Inside the apartment, Otto huffs, excited, a chicken-flavored Nylabone dangling from his mouth like a cigar, the big plume of tail sweeping a broad arc. Alex is glad Otto likes his new Nylabones. Last week Alex finally motivated himself to throw away all of Isabel's old shoes, which Otto had been licking and chewing for over a year. Alex had been tempted to continue indulging Otto's taste for fine leather, but it couldn't be good for Otto's stomach to continually ingest it, and it couldn't be good for Alex to come home every evening to find Otto waiting inside the door with one of Isabel's old sandals clutched in his mouth. "We're moving on," he told Otto as he scoured the apartment for the Danskos and the Keens, the Børns and the Nikes, lying flat on floors to squint and grope beneath furniture while Otto, thinking it a game, jammed his head down next to Alex's and scraped at the floor with his paws. Alex stuffed all Isabel's shoes into one of two kitchen trash bags, one for shoes that Otto had destroyed and another for shoes that were still wearable. As Alex carried the bags downstairs he tried not to look at all the toes and heels and soles straining outward through the thin white plastic. He threw the bag of ruined shoes in the Dumpster. At Goodwill he handed the other bag over to the attendant unceremoniously and, driving away, tried not to think of the women who might buy and wear those shoes, tried not to think that someday he might walk past one of them without realizing.

Alex tosses Janet's unopened card onto the coffee table, where it will be gradually buried under a sediment of future mail:

246

bills, catalogs, magazines, newspapers.

The answering machine flashes. One message. Alex breathes deeply through a tightness in his chest. He still feels it's possible he'll press Play and hear Isabel's voice, tiny and distant, reaching out to him from the ends of the earth. *I'm in Phnom Penh. I'm in Algiers. There's been a huge mix-up. Will you come and get me?*

The message is from Bernice. "Hey, it's me. Just called to see what you were up to. I thought maybe you'd like to try out this new Indian restaurant I've been hearing about. It's supposed to be great."

In her voice Alex hears a cheerful veneer over urgent loneliness. There's something about the way she addresses him — a directness, a familiarity — that makes him feel very close to her.

"Oh, by the way," she says, "I just got a card from Janet Corcoran. Apparently she got out of the hospital about a year ago. After getting Isabel's heart. She said she jogged two miles along Lake Michigan the other day. I thought that was pretty great. Anyway, give me a call if you're not too worn out from the young budding authors."

By the way. As if that were enough to conceal Bernice's intentions. Alex is irked at the way she mentions Janet Corcoran as though she, Janet, is a member of the family, some overachieving older cousin he's supposed to be impressed by. He can't believe Bernice doesn't find it freakish and disturbing that Isabel's organs are coming back to talk to them. That wasn't part of Isabel's plan, was it? Did Isabel sign a clause on the donor card that said, *In the event of my death I permit the recipients of my transplanted organs to hunt down my grieving husband and mother and send them arty cards and tell them where and how far I went jogging?*

He listens to Bernice's message a second time. When she says *I thought maybe you'd like to try out this new Indian restaurant* Alex feels an agenda in her voice. It's not just an invitation or a suggestion but a comment on how he might otherwise choose to spend his time. Is it his imagination, or has Bernice been hounding him to get out more during the past few weeks, ever since the first anniversary of Isabel's death? It used to be she'd invite him to spend a quiet evening at her house watching TV or a rented movie, eating pizza or takeout. But apparently quiet evenings at her house are no longer enough. She wants to go out for walks, drives, lunch, dinner, coffee, ice cream. Maybe she figures they both need to get out more. Or maybe it's May. The warm weather, blue skies, trees and flowers in bloom, everything coming alive after another long, bleak Iowa winter.

What Bernice doesn't understand is that he *is* getting out. Just not with her.

He goes into the kitchen, dumps a scoop of Science Diet into Otto's bowl. He fills a glass with ice and Coke. Returns to the living room, glimpses Janet's card on the coffee table. What is it about first anniversaries? Is Janet going to send him or Bernice a card on the first anniversary of everything that happens to her? Did Jasper specifically choose the first anniversary of Isabel's death to appear on his doorstep? Why has Bernice evidently decided that one year of drinking beer and watching rented movies in her living room is enough — as opposed to, say, one year, two months, six days, and five hours? Why would anyone attribute so much significance to a denomination of calendrical time that marks nothing more than three hundred and sixty-five revolutions of the planet, a single orbit around the sun, and that has no connection with the revolutions and orbits of the self, and certainly not with Alex's clock of grief?

Lately he's been rereading a book on grieving rituals that he read years ago for an upper-level anthropology course. Among the Native American Yokuts of Northern California, the widower doesn't eat meat for three months after his wife's death, wash any part of his body except his hands, or engage in any social activity — and then it's his dead wife's family who decides when his mourning period will end. Alex won't mention this to Bernice, and certainly won't mention the case of the Trukese man of the Central Caroline Islands who, after losing his wife to a prolonged illness, grieved alone in his house for three months, shunning all company, until his dead wife's mother came and told him he must get out and walk around or else he would get sick and die too.

He's tempted to call Bernice back, he feels compelled and obligated, but he doesn't feel up to an evening with her. Lately he finds himself shying away from her company. It's not just that she's likely to talk about Janet Corcoran and try to convince him to be more receptive to her overtures. Self-preservation wants to spare Alex the sadness that pools around him and Bernice when they're together. Sometimes he feels they're each a reminder of the other's loss, each a poor substitute for the missing. They weigh each other down, keep each other submerged, like a pair of objects that might each be buoyant if only they weren't lashed together.

So he calls Kelly.

"Why did you go for the six?" Kelly asks him. "The two-ball was just waiting to be sunk, it was, like, yelling at you from right next to the pocket: 'Pick me! Pick me!' " She waves both hands frantically.

Alex takes a consoling sip of beer. "I thought I could sink the six."

Kelly looks doubtful. She lines up her shot. The cue ball, struck hard, fails to connect with anything except bumpers and finally drops into a corner pocket. Kelly tosses her head back and puffs out her cheeks and blows air at the ceiling.

Alex asks, "Going for anything specific there?"

"I don't want to talk about it."

"You did achieve the somewhat difficult objective of managing to hit absolutely nothing."

"Don't get cocky." She points to the table — to his six balls, her two. "Got a victory plan?"

Kelly is funny, smart, animated. She has thatchy brown hair, fair skin overrun with freckles. A tiny nose stud like a droplet of mercury. Thin, waiflike, she wears flared jeans that pinch her knees and colorful T-shirts. One night a few weeks ago, shortly after his anniversary dinner with Bernice, Alex was in the basement of his building doing laundry when he discovered a red Elvis Costello T-shirt clinging to the inside of the washing machine. He removed it and hung it up to dry. An hour later he came downstairs to move his clothes to the dryer and found Kelly taking Elvis Costello down. He told her the story of the shirt's rescue. Kelly seemed grateful he hadn't just thrown her wet, wadded shirt onto a folding table. A few days later he ran into her on the stairs. Her right forearm was smeared with grease; she'd had some kind of mishap putting oil into her car. A few days later on a balmy evening he saw her sitting out by the creek drinking a beer. He ventured out to talk with her. She lived on the fourth floor, on the opposite side of the building. She and her roommate had just moved in. They were MFA students in sculpture. They were having a party Saturday night. A sort of housewarming. Did he want to come?

The party was small, the crowd young. Alex found himself at the upper end of the age range. Kelly was attentive. Late night, he and Kelly and several others drank red wine and passed a bong. At some point Kelly took him by the hand and led him into a bedroom hung with tapestries and lit by Japanese paper lanterns and readmitted him to a world from which he had long been absent: nibbles on lips, tongues, nipples, a sweet fumbling tussle that left them tangled naked in bed.

The next day, recovering, replaying several of the previous evening's delicious highlights in his mind, guilt set in. Sitting in the apartment he had shared with Isabel, he had a nagging sense that he had betrayed her, moved on too soon, too casually, too randomly. Though he wasn't sure he ought to pay attention to this nagging. Would Isabel really have disapproved of what he had done? After all, it had been a year since her death, a duration of suffering that seemed to offer permission. Maybe she would have said, *Hey, go for it. You've got to move on. I know you loved me. I know you still do.*

What worries him, what's more disturbing, is his suspicion that Isabel would have been critical of Kelly. Even now, watching Kelly sashay around the pool table to the music from the jukebox, looking for a shot, pausing to sip her whiskey, Alex sees Isabel's appraising face, hears her mildly disdainful tone. *Huh. Young. Kind of dippy.*

Are you sure she's substantial enough for you?

"Substantial"? That's funny coming from a dead person.

I'm just saying I wouldn't have pegged her as your type.

She's different from you, it's true. Which isn't easy to accept. Believe me. It's like getting used to a completely different climate.

Don't compare her to me. It's not fair to her.

Talk about arrogant. Also, you just compared her to you. You called her dippy and insubstantial.

Oooo . . . defensive.

Leave us alone.

Kelly has sunk her two remaining balls, and now nudges the eight-ball into the side pocket with a deft, oblique shot. She looks at Alex and bugs out her eyes, stretches her mouth into an O, anticipating and mocking his astonishment.

"Nice game," Alex says. "You crushed me."

"Well, you *were* handicapped," Kelly says, feigning obsequious sympathy, lightly rubbing his injured wrist. "Macho rock-climbing stud."

They leave the bar and walk toward a party Kelly has been invited to. The evening is warm, the air still. The pervasive quiet makes the surrounding darkness feel vast and depopulated. If one didn't see lights in windows, if one didn't hear the occasional car engine or barking dog, one would think this part of the world had been abandoned.

"When you were a kid, did you ever wish you had superpowers?" Kelly asks. "When I think back on it, I spent so much time wishing I had superpowers, and thinking about which ones I wanted, and ranking them in order of preference, and daydreaming about what I'd do with them."

"You probably felt powerless," Alex says. "Most kids do."

"I don't remember feeling powerless. Did you?"

"Definitely. I was adopted, and I was the only child. My adoptive parents ran a kind of hostel. Our house was the hostel. People coming and going all the time. Distant relatives, friends of friends, exchange students, immigrants, random travelers. They slept in the bedrooms, the attic, on the screen porch. There were always suitcases and duffel bags everywhere. I remember this one guy who could make a spoon move without touching it — seriously — and a girl from Cambodia who didn't know her own age. I think I wanted to stand out. To my parents. I remember this guy who rolled in one night when I was in high school, and we were hanging out on the back porch, and he asked me, 'So, where are you from?' I was like, I *live* here. This is my house."

Kelly nods thoughtfully. "Sounds like you needed attention."

"It's not like my parents ignored me. It's just that there were a lot of people competing for their attention."

"I didn't know you were adopted," Kelly says.

Alex speaks in a mysterious tone: "Ahh . . . there are all kinds of things you don't know about me."

"Like what?"

Alex hasn't told Kelly anything about Isabel. It seems to him that now is an opportune time. "I was married. My wife died a little over a year ago. She got hit by a truck while riding her bicycle. Her name was Isabel."

Kelly stops walking and stares at him, her expression sympathetic. "How long were you married?"

"Nearly three years. We were together for three years before that."

"That's terrible. I'm so sorry."

"I'm OK."

Kelly takes his arm and gently squeezes. "Don't play the tough guy. Honestly, when

I first met you, you seemed kind of lost."

Alex takes a moment to reconcile himself to her perceptiveness, and to the fact that he's more transparent than he thought. "Did you find that attractive?" he asks with a smile.

Kelly shrugs. "I'm not sure I'd go for *any* lost-looking guy."

After a silence she asks, "Am I a Band-Aid? For the wound?"

"I haven't really classified you in my head as any type of bandage."

Kelly laughs. "Good answer."

"What about me?" Alex asks. "What am I to you?"

"A boy-toy. A cheap plaything."

"Cool."

"Seriously? In light of what you just told me?" Kelly studies him with a mixture of concern and affection. "Don't take this the wrong way. But you might turn out to be more of a project than I expected."

SEVENTEEN

When word came down from the higher-ups at Best Buy that a new "Employee Retention and Advancement Incentive Policy" was being implemented and that all shift managers and department managers would receive — among other perks — an "at cost" discount on all merchandise, as opposed to cost plus five percent for regular employees, Jasper could have taken his concerns to his supervisor (the department manager in Audio) or to one of the shift managers or even to the store manager. But these petty functionaries were hardly the brightest lights in the Best Buy constellation, and they tended not to appreciate the particular blend of skills and talents that Jasper brought to the operation. So when Jasper heard that Luke Payne, Eastern Iowa area manager for Best Buy, would be making a store visit on a Wednesday afternoon in early June, Jasper made sure to be working and to have a strategy in place.

As misfortune would have it, Jasper was tied up with a hesitant, needy couple who were curious about home theater systems and ready to shell out when he saw Luke Payne, dressed in jacket and tie, coming toward him through Cameras & Camcorders. Jasper recognized him from a previous store visit. Escorting Luke was the store manager, Steve Schultz, wearing the official uniform: blue polo shirt and khakis. Jasper waited until the two men made their way into Movies and started down an aisle between high shelves of DVDs. Jasper excused himself from his customers and slipped into the aisle from the other end. Here he was lucky: there was only one customer in the aisle, a middle-aged woman, and no other blue shirts in sight.

"Mr. Payne," Jasper said boldly, extending his hand. "Jasper Klass. Audio. I was salesman of the month two months running. I wanted to make sure to have the honor of meeting you, and to offer you a personal tour of Audio, if no one else does."

Luke Payne seemed both surprised and impressed by Jasper's assertiveness. "Nice to meet you," he said, shaking Jasper's hand. "Congratulations on salesman of the month. Or maybe I should say salesman of the two months."

Jasper laughed. "Thanks."

Steve Schultz smiled broadly, settled his hand firmly on Jasper's shoulder, and told Luke Payne, "Actually, Jasper was salesman of the month for two months running over a year ago. Lately he's" — Steve glanced uncertainly at Jasper — "refining his skill set."

Luke Payne folded his hands in front of his belt buckle and nodded gravely. "Glad to hear it."

"I wanted to bring something to your attention, Mr. Payne, on behalf of all the employees," Jasper said. "I've had a look at the ERAIP, and it's an excellent, excellent plan. Did you have anything to do with putting it together?"

"Very little."

Steve spoke to Jasper sternly. "Luke and I have pressing business, and not a lot of time. Maybe you and I could discuss this later?"

"Just a sec, Steve." Jasper held up a silencing finger. "Mr. Payne, nice idea giving shift and department managers an at-cost discount, but the other worthy staff, worthy of *incentive,* are being overlooked. What you should do is, just hear me out here, extend that discount to the top salesman in each department. Or saleswoman. Nothing against the women. That way you encourage retention *and* sales. I'd be encouraged. Of course I'd already have the discount, given my top salesman status. But others would be inspired."

Luke Payne lifted an eyebrow but offered no comment.

"Luke, you should understand this," Steve said, irritation rising. "Jasper, you *were* the top salesman, at one point, but now Christie is top, and you're sixth out of seven full-time staff. So I think it's inappropriate and frankly presumptuous for you to be asking for special consideration. Let me emphasize, Luke, that Jasper is not advocating for the staff."

A cool sweat was breaking out across Jasper's forehead, and his left eyelid had begun to twitch. "Top salesman status should be permanent, once you get it. Doesn't that seem right? And when I refer to myself as top I'm not saying top just in numbers but in qualities that are harder to quantify: integrity, expertise, attitude, customer rapport."

Steve lets out a disbelieving laugh and glances at Luke as if to say, *I'm sorry you're having to put up with this outrageous shit.* "Why don't you get back to work, Jasper.

You've expressed your opinion and I'm sure Luke will take it into account."

"Don't mock me," Jasper says. "Don't think there aren't plenty of places where I'd be appreciated."

"I'm not mocking you," Steve insists. "I'm simply asking you to do your job."

"I'm sure you're appreciated here, Jasper," Luke Payne says.

Jasper gives Steve a fuck-you look and heads back to Audio. He's smart enough not to fight with the regional area manager. Anyway, it's clear that he and Luke Payne have mutually recognized each other's superior intelligence and initiative over the top of Steve Schultz's pointy head. Probably Jasper will get a call from Luke one of these days with a job offer higher up the food chain. In the meantime he'll deal with Steve and the big steel rod up Steve's ass. Every time they've butted heads over the past few months — when Jasper went AWOL in the middle of the day, when Jasper got caught watching a movie on one of the big high-def plasmas, when Jasper came in buzzed and fell asleep in back — in every case there was a perfectly good explanation for Jasper's actions that Steve failed to accept.

People were mistrustful, Jasper thought. If

262

only people would believe him, buy into his version of the truth. *He* buys into it. He finds himself persuasive and compelling.

He leaves work at five o'clock feeling underappreciated and disrespected. He takes the Vulcan out onto the highway and gets up to ninety miles per hour, weaving through traffic, helmetless, the wind pressing his eye sockets and roaring like a chain saw in his ears. In front of him in the right lane, a semi's brake lights come on and the truck seems to stop in its tracks. Jasper swings into the left lane, but there's an SUV right there in the space he's trying to occupy; the SUV brakes hard to avoid hitting him, strains forward on its chassis, and lays on the horn. Jasper tweaks the throttle and he's gone, he's out of that mess like a rocket. Bones buzzing. Head light as a balloon. *You could have taken me there,* he thinks, silently addressing whatever higher power ordains the shit that happens. *I held myself out. I gave you a chance.*

On the way home, sticking with his routine, he drives past Alex's apartment and looks for Alex's Jeep in the parking lot. It's not there.

Jasper parks the Vulcan a few blocks away and walks back to a bus stop near Alex's building. The bus stop is perfect: he has a clear view of the parking lot and the building's door, about fifty yards away, and he can stand here doing nothing without looking suspicious. There's even a small shelter he can step into for extra cover. Today he leans against a tree and watches the lot. While he waits, he clenches and unclenches his right hand, repeatedly pressing the tip of his thumb into the fleshy pads on the insides of his fingers. Usually Alex gets home between five fifteen and five thirty, though several times he's come home later. He'll go inside and emerge a few minutes later with the dog. The walk might be a quick jaunt around the block, or it might be a long, rambling sojourn across town. There's no way to tell at the outset. Jasper has to be ready for anything.

It's a mild, breezy afternoon. The elderly woman in the pink split-level is on her knees in the front yard weeding a flowerbed. In the backyard of another house two boys have coaxed their cat into a red milk crate they've tied to the end of a rope; they've thrown the other end of the rope over the low branch of an oak to make a pulley, and they hoist the cat up.

When Alex's Jeep appears, Jasper conceals himself behind the tree and watches, processing every detail. Does Alex pull into the parking lot at a normal, relaxed speed or careen aggressively? Does he slam the Jeep's door? Does he shuffle, shoulders drooped, like the living dead, or walk briskly, as though he might have something to look forward to? Today he pulls into the lot slowly and takes some time getting out of the Jeep. He looks glum, defeated, weary. Still, he's alive, awake, breathing, putting one foot in front of the other, shuffling across the bridge, dressed in jeans and a light blue button-down shirt, the red North Face backpack slung over his shoulder. He's not weaving or staggering. He's not muttering to himself. There are no gaping purple circles under his eyes, no unsightly stains on his clothes — no outward signs of debilitation or ruin.

Five minutes later Alex and his dog appear and head out on their walk. Jasper follows cautiously, keeping at least a block behind. It's an absorbing game, not to lose Alex and not to be seen. Jasper enjoys the challenge, ducking evasively into driveways and alleys in the rare event that Alex reverses course, keeping him in sight despite visual obstacles — trees, garages, houses — while shadowing him on a parallel path. Jasper does have experience at this, having once pursued a tall, willowy brunette with haunting eyes all around town — he spied on her in coffee shops, bars, in the university classroom where she taught — until one night she caught him standing in the courtyard outside her ground-floor window and called the police. She used that ugly word "stalking." He insisted to the cops that he'd meant to impress her as romantic and smitten, not threatening. If only he'd brought along his guitar and serenaded her! The whole business ended unpleasantly after he made a second attempt at talking to her — he waited by her car while she was getting a haircut — and she got a restraining order. It turned out she was from France. She taught French. He decided that if he had pursued her in France, where the authorities were no doubt more enlightened about matters of love, there wouldn't have been a problem.

Jasper follows Alex west toward town, then a few blocks south to a park. Alex lets the dog off the leash to chase a squirrel, which escapes easily up a tree, then tosses a tennis ball for the dog, who is a fetching machine. Jasper watches from across the street behind a concrete wall. He's going to make another run at Alex, but the circumstances have to be exactly right. The encounter needs to look accidental, and should happen in a public place. That way Alex can't ask Jasper to leave. Jasper figures he only needs ten or fifteen minutes to execute his plan — to drum up enough sympathy to get Alex to reveal the key information. Jasper's confident he can pull it off. On the other hand, Alex won't be an easy nut to crack. He was tough and resilient. What will Jasper do if he can't break him? Is there any way to force Alex to tell him what he wants to know? Anything Jasper can use for leverage?

He has a vision, a recurring daydream in which he's standing in front of his lucky beneficiary, the woman he's rescued from the brink of death, and his skin shines with the glamour of it, with a self-regard he's never experienced. She's an attractive woman, and in her eyes there is reverence and gratitude and sympathy, a suggestion of kinship. She's looking deep into his soul, and there she sees things no other woman has had the patience or faith to see. She understands him. She can help him, as he helped her. She reaches out and touches him, kisses his face. The kiss is spiritual, like a blessing. This is her answer to his wordless confession. A new universe opens up to him — a universe in which he is revived and refreshed. Reborn. Given a second chance.

He doesn't want to play rough with Alex.

Watching him tossing the tennis ball to the dog, calling out and clapping his hands in encouragement as the dog bounds back toward him with a big yellow mouth, Jasper feels a strange tenderness for this man, this man whose life he's damaged and, on top of the tenderness, affection, goodwill, even a strange protectiveness. When Jasper first started taking his walks with Alex, he was interested mostly in Alex's general movements — where he went, what he did. Now he finds himself paying attention to specific aspects of Alex's behavior. The clever way he inserts his hand into a plastic grocery bag and uses it like a glove to pick up his dog's scattered defecations, then reverses the glove into a bag and seals it with a knot. The gentleness with which he lifts Otto's front leg when the leash gets trapped underneath. The way he cleans dog slobber off the tennis ball by wiping it briskly against his thigh.

He really does love that dog.

EIGHTEEN

Bernice stands in a flowerbed in back of her house and holds the ladder tightly as Alex climbs up to the low, shallowly pitched roof of the screened porch. There are two skylights in the roof of the porch, and one has been leaking, dripping into a bucket below during anything more than a light rain. Bernice got a commitment from a roofer to come out at the end of June, but that's three weeks away, and there's rain in the forecast. She was reluctant to ask Alex for help, given his injured wrist, but when she mentioned the roof problem to him and her proposed, temporary solution — climbing up there and tacking a tarp down over the skylight — he assured her that his wrist was healed enough for the job, and that if he was careful and didn't lift anything too heavy, he could do it.

Now, watching Alex step from the ladder onto the roof, momentarily bending and planting both hands on the shingles to ensure his balance, Bernice wonders if he's taking too great a risk. "Please be careful," she says. "Watch your step. It might be slippery up there. Are you *sure* your wrist is going to be OK? Maybe you should wear your brace."

"I'm fine. Don't worry."

Bernice hands up the tarp, the roof tacks, the hammer. Alex unfolds the tarp, which is stiff and unwieldy and much larger than either of them expected. "Jeez. We could cover the whole house with this thing." Alex folds the tarp in half and arranges it over the skylight. "I'm still not sure your roofer's going to approve of the way we're handling this. I'm worried we'll damage the roof, driving tacks into the shingles. Can't you live with the bucket for another week?"

"I'm sick of the bucket," Bernice says, essentially dishonest. The roof-patching project is the first good excuse she's had in weeks to spend time with Alex — rather, to compel him to spend time with her. Lately she can't help feeling that he's been avoiding her, resisting her overtures, responding to her invitations with mysterious excuses and evasions, as though she did something to offend or repel him. Bernice prefers to think it's not personal — that Kelly, his new girlfriend, is the real reason for his inaccessibility.

She tells Alex, "Take a look at the skylight before you get started. Just see if you see anything. The bottom left corner is where it leaks. There, by your right foot."

Alex kneels and lifts the corner of the tarp and inspects the skylight. Moves his head close. Squints. Prods the seal with his fingertips. "I don't see anything. Doesn't mean there's not a leak, though."

"Oh, there's a leak, trust me," Bernice says.

Alex sets to work driving in tacks. Bernice is impressed by his agility, the ease with which he maneuvers around the tarp while keeping his balance against the slope of the roof, stepping and pivoting, squatting and kneeling, plucking tacks from the package and plocking them in with only a blow or two from the hammer, which he wields with his strong hand. Behind and above him the sun blazes in a vibrant blue sky, trees assert their green, neighborhood noises pepper the fringes — children's shouts, a dog barking, a distant lawn mower. It's not déjà vu but a more intricate interplay of environment and memory that gives Bernice a flash of the fresh, undamaged optimism of her youth — more precisely, her young womanhood —

in which Isabel and Clancy might have been playing in the backyard, and Todd repairing something on the house while she watched admiringly. She recalls, and fleetingly experiences, the conviction afforded by youth that pure, unalloyed happiness was achievable, up there just around the bend, over the horizon. The irony was that the falsity of the hope did nothing to detract from its power to inspire, to motivate, to make one feel bold and determined. To make one feel . . . *happy.*

Alex drives in the final tack, stands up, and steps back toward the edge of the roof to inspect his work. The tarp fits snugly and squarely over the skylight, the tacks along the edges driven in at regularly spaced intervals.

"Thank you *so* much," Bernice says. "You have no idea how nice it's going to be to sit out on the porch and not have to listen to Chinese water torture."

"You could have done it yourself," Alex says, confident in her handiness.

"It would have taken me two or three hours to do what you just did, and I probably would have fallen to my death before it was over. How's your wrist?"

"Fine." Alex hands the hammer down to her, handle first, and then the empty package of tacks. Bernice insists he be careful as he steps precariously near the edge of the roof, turns, and bends low over the incline like a sprinter at the starting block, fingers pressed to the shingles. Bernice grips the ladder with both hands as he climbs down. As soon as he's low enough she takes hold of his waist, thumbs in his lower back, to steady him and support his weight. Alex freezes.

"You're OK," she says. "I've got you."

"I'm fine. Hold the ladder."

She does. "Got it."

Alex turns and glances down into the space he's being asked to descend into — a narrow space enclosed by her arms and chest. He starts down cautiously, elbows tucked in, body flattened to the ladder, as though the slightest misstep would cause him to plummet hundreds of feet. His long legs and slim waist, his rangy torso, the tiny sweat-dewy hairs on the back of his neck all scroll past her. When Alex reaches the ground he stands still and strangely rigid, both hands gripping one of the ladder's rungs. Bernice is still holding the sides of the ladder, her arms extended around him, her chest inches from his back. They're practically spooning. Embarrassed, Bernice lets go of the ladder and backs away. Alex moves sideways. She watches him take a deep, necessary breath. She takes one too, thinking how strange it is that she feels both spared and disappointed.

In the kitchen's dim cool they raid the fridge for drinks — Bernice joins Alex in a Bass — and carry their bottles out onto the screened porch to inspect their work from below. Alex glances briefly at the skylight before moving deliberately to a wicker armchair and collapsing into it like a man who hasn't been off his feet for weeks. He strokes the chair's raised arms. "I guess the real test will come when it rains."

Bernice sits in a wrought-iron chair alongside a glass-topped patio table that was, in ancient times, the site of pleasant family dinners on summer evenings. "If the weatherman's right, we won't have to wait long for that."

"Is it supposed to rain tomorrow?"

"I think they said Monday."

Alex nods with satisfaction.

"Got plans?" At this moment Bernice feels nothing more than curiosity.

"Nothing big. Kelly and I were thinking of going to the pool."

Bernice pictures Alex poolside, lying on his side, propped up on an elbow, arms lithe and tanned, a slight pudge to his stomach, belly button glistening. She's never met Kelly, so she can't fill in her details, and manages only a faceless shape cross-striped with two wisps of sheer fabric.

"If you'd like to bring Kelly over to dinner sometime, I'd love to meet her," Bernice says.

Alex nods minimally.

"What does she like to eat?" Bernice asks.

"She's a quasi-vegetarian. I think she eats fish. I know she eats shrimp. She ordered some the other night."

Bernice nods agreeably. "We can deal with that. I'll cook something shrimpy."

That noncommittal nod, grimmer this time. Why, when Alex looks at her with tender, measuring eyes, does she sense that he foresees some eventuality that will cause her pain?

"What?" she asks. "What's that look?"

"Nothing."

"There's something."

Alex lets his head collapse back as though the tendons in his neck have snapped. "Don't you think it would be awkward? I can't believe you'd really enjoy meeting her, much less spending a whole evening with her."

"Is she that unbearable? Is she rude? Does she smell?" Bernice is trying to be game.

Undaunted. Fun. Worth introducing one's girlfriend to. The truth is, she's terrified. "Let me decide what I'll enjoy. If I didn't think I'd enjoy it I wouldn't have asked."

"I'm worried it might be awkward for Kelly." Alex gives her a sympathetic, beseeching look that wants to spare them both further awkwardness. *Dinner with the new boyfriend's ex-mother-in-law. Mother of the new boyfriend's dead wife.*

Bernice feels insulted. "You're worried it might damage your relationship with her."

"Wouldn't you? If you were me? Be honest. Put yourself in my shoes. Put yourself in Kelly's shoes."

"*I'm* flexible and groovy. If you're worried about anything, you should worry she and I will hit it off and she'll start to find you boring."

Alex sighs deeply. "I don't exactly want to emphasize that I was married. For her sake."

"A mature woman will accept your history."

"She does accept my history. She knows I was married, and she knows my wife died, and how. But she's not under any obligation to *live* my history. More to the point, neither am I."

"So I'm history. I'm not part of your present."

276

"Of course you're part of my present."

"Then don't be so weird about bringing your girlfriend over for dinner."

"Hey, ease up, OK?"

What does he want? *Not* to be asked? Does he wish she'd said, *Don't ever bring your slutty new girlfriend into my sight; how can she possibly measure up?* "We can go out for dinner. If eating here is weird. I'll wear shades and a fedora so she won't know who I am. Or I'll pretend to be the waitress. That way I'll at least get to speak to her. No, wait. I'll pretend to be your history professor. You can tell Kelly you want her to meet your old *history* professor. Who is part of your *history*."

He's lowered his face into his hand, ashamed or fed up with her or both, but when he emerges Bernice is pleased to see he's smiling. Amused. Abashed.

Later that night, after reading a few chapters of a science-fiction novel, falling asleep on the couch, waking with a terrible headache, and eating a bowl of cereal, Bernice turns on her computer and checks her e-mail. There's a message from Lotta.

Greetings, Bernice! Has spring's boisterous uprising of breezes and color ended in Iowa? Most of our trees have passed through their bloom, and now reluctantly join the common darkening green of the grass and bushes in making preparations for summer.

I saw a bird the other day, a Pied-billed Grebe, which can disappear beneath the surface of a pond without causing a ripple. Such a sleek diver! I managed to capture several of these sublime submergings on my Palmcorder, and will send you a copy of the video — the footage certainly does the Grebe justice.

Janet is doing well. She's done with school now for the year, so she'll have more free time, which she plans to spend with David and the kids. The other night she went to a karate class with Carly, and last Saturday she and David took the kids to a Cubs game. She and David are still discussing the idea of leaving the city and moving to the suburbs — an idea Janet isn't crazy about, to put it mildly.

This weekend David is off delivering Sam to eco-camp in Michigan, where he'll delve into all the vicissitudes of the natural world. I think Janet will enjoy the time alone with Carly. Next weekend she and David are dropping the kids off here at Hotel Grandma and going to Door County for a few days. Should be a nice little break for them.

How is Alex doing? I hope he's well. Please give him my regards if you feel they'll be appreciated.

By the way, Janet has mentioned lately that she's thinking about calling Alex. Do you think this would be a bad idea? I told Janet she probably ought to hold off. I don't know if she'll take my advice or not. She can be headstrong.

Well, that's all the news from the North. By the way, did you ever pick up the Audubon Field Guide to North American Birds? Just curious.

Hope you're hanging in there. Take care.
— Lotta

Bernice hits the Reply button, writes:

Hello up there! The weather here is hot going on hotter. It's funny you mention Sam going to eco-camp. Just yesterday a boy banged on the door from some kind of environmental group and wanted me to sign up to turn off all my electrical devices, including air conditioning, on July 6, which is "Global Warming Action Day." I'm not supposed to drive my car, either. I signed up. May have to dust off the old bicycle. Oh my gosh! I just realized that July 6 is Alex's thirty-first birthday! So much for my environmental convictions. I may have to break the rule about driving.

Congratulations on your spotting of the Pied-billed Grebe. Please send me a copy of the video. That way maybe I'll be able to recognize a Pied-billed Grebe if I ever see one. I saw a very pretty cardinal this morning. He was perched in a tree just outside one of the windows in the den.

Glad to hear Janet is well. I hope she and David enjoy their vacation. I'm always so cheered to hear about Janet. Nothing reminds me quite so forcefully that there could have been two women dead, but that there's only one, because of Isabel — that even though Isabel's life was lost, the sum total of life was increased, and that it was my daughter's doing. I'm proud of her.

I wish I could bring Alex around to my way of seeing this, but I'm not sure I'll be able to. I mention Janet to him from time to time, but not as aggressively as I used to. It's too contentious a subject. For this reason I'd have to advise against Janet calling him at this point. I'd hate for her to get a bad reaction. Maybe at some point in the future?

I hope we can meet sometime, Lotta. I'd love to talk to you with real voices in real space.

A warm hello to Janet & Co.
— Bernice

NINETEEN

A balmy evening, mid-June. Alex walks Otto along tree-shaded sidewalks past houses stirring with life after their long day unoccupied, people tinkering in yards and flowerbeds and garages. A breeze is sweeping away some of the day's heat. The uprightness of trees, the elegant arcs of branches: audacious displays of endurance and grace. The world flaunting itself, insisting on its ability to survive. The world wants to show Alex how easily it accepts a single human death, how easily it goes about its business. It's a taunt, a challenge. *Can you do it?*

Alex wants to shout back, *You don't feel emotions, you don't have a memory.* The natural world has no idea what it's like to slog through the detritus of a former age, to steer one's body among the living while one's mind plunges down to earlier strata where the beloved moves and speaks, where fragments of conversations and experiences lie in shards. This gazebo in College Park where one Saturday afternoon Alex and Isabel sat eating sandwiches when they were approached by a dazed, unsteady homeless man who asked for change. Isabel gave him half of her sandwich. The homeless man took a few bites of it and then, partly out of gratitude, partly flirting, he rattled off all the helping verbs — *may might must be being been am are is,* etc. — in a dazzling display of grammatical prowess. Here, this sprawling white house on College Street with dormer roofs and long, deep, wraparound porches — Isabel said it looked like it ought to have a Chekhov play going on inside. They went to a dog party once at this lemon-colored ranch with the fenced-in backyard, a party to which they'd been invited by a couple they encountered regularly while walking Otto. There were twenty or thirty people there, and about the same number of dogs running and playing. Alex and Isabel drank margaritas from plastic cups. Otto sprawled like a walrus in a plastic wading pool. A muscular yellow Lab named Baryshnikov did miraculous leaps and spins while catching a Frisbee.

Sometimes it's too much, and Alex wants to disinfect the entire town, scrub clean whole city blocks, vaporize all evidence of the deceased. In primitive cultures the dead person's property is typically given away or destroyed, the dead person's dwelling burned. Among the Abipones of Paraguay, the dead man's utensils are burned, his horses and cattle killed, his hut torn down. There's a story about a Shavante man of Central Brazil who went to fantastic lengths to obliterate all signs of his dead wife: not only did he destroy her personal belongings, but he walked the path of the last trek they had taken together and burned down all the shelters they had built along the way, just so he wouldn't happen on them again.

Alex could never destroy Isabel's personal belongings — her books, her shoes, her Turkish kilim. He tries to imagine what it would be like to set fire to his apartment, where he and Isabel began their life together. Would he enjoy watching from the parking lot as flames spewed from the windows? What about other places where he and Isabel used to hang out? Would he enjoy watching flames lick the walls of Café Apollinaire, where they studied and bumped into friends and chatted for hours? Would he enjoy the sight of black smoke unfurling from the windows of New Prairie Coop, where they bought their organic fruit and vegetables, their meat and fish, their beer and wine? Would he enjoy torching the gazebo in College Park? The dog-party house? How would he feel watching fire consume University Books, in whose labyrinthine aisles they wandered and idled? Would he enjoy creeping around the pedestrian mall in the middle of the night with a can of gasoline and a pack of matches torching every bench they ever conversed on?

Alex doesn't think any of these conflagrations would bring him solace. True, the memories often feel like an infestation and haunt him with his loss. At brighter times, though, they seem to be his last remaining connection to Isabel.

On the pedestrian mall, Alex sits on a bench near the information kiosk, where tacked-up flyers advertise the performances of bands, apartments for rent, calligraphy workshops, aromatherapy. Otto paces and circles near Alex's feet, alert to passersby, willing to be stroked. Every so often Otto's ears lift at a high note from the Peruvian musicians playing over near the fountain. The Peruvians are dark, slight, delicately boned men conjuring an ethereal birdsong with charangos and panpipes. Their audience, fed and drained by streams of wanderers, sits cross-legged on the ground, crammed together on benches and on the low walls of flower-beds. There's standing room in the rear, though you're likely to be tapped on the shoulder and asked if you're in line for the coffee cart, the pedestrian mall's fuel cell, manned tonight by a skinny, brisk girl in a tartan skirt and black Converse high-tops, her sharp elbows jerking and slicing air as she wrenches filter handles into their sockets.

Alex came here hoping to feel embraced, integrated, a member of the human family, but he feels isolated and lonely. Kelly has gone to Davenport for the weekend to visit her older sister, who has just had a baby. Alex's friend Rob is on a bike trip, and Luther, with whom Alex occasionally prowls the bars, isn't answering his phone.

Alex allows Otto to wander out into the crowd, giving him all the play his leash will permit. A flotilla of college-age girls — summer sessioners — passes by, flaunting bare, tanned shoulders and midriffs, their faces velvety with makeup, leaving an invisible wake of perfume. A little girl in a stroller gropes for Otto until her parents, needlessly wary, scoot her away. An older man wants to pet Otto but can't bend his body to the necessary angle. A familiar voice off to the right splashes Alex's attention: "Hey, I know you, don't I, pal?"

Alex looks, sees. A few feet away, approaching Otto. Jasper. His headphones emit a metallic clicking. Slung over his shoulder is a purple gym bag that needs to be washed or ironed or maybe just thrown away — an enormous shriveled prune. He's wearing a baggy blue T-shirt, khaki cargo shorts, the complicated running shoes with air bubbles in the soles.

Alex feels like a fool, a reckless idiot. He knew he ran the risk of encountering Jasper on the pedestrian mall — any public place was risky — but hoped he'd be lucky enough not to. This is the price he pays for making it a policy not to let Jasper's existence — the fear of running into Jasper — dictate his movements.

Jasper gropes at an MP3 player clipped to his belt until the metallic clicking stops. He bends at the waist and holds out his hand to Otto. Otto sniffs, steps forward, licks. Jasper laughs. "He remembers me."

"He'll lick anything," Alex says.

Jasper reaches his arms high over his head and stretches his body, twists his torso, yawns, balls his fingers into fists, extends his fingers, rotates his wrists, bends his hands backward. He looks like someone who's just gotten out of bed after a long, deep sleep. Slowly, with a feigned reluctance meant to conceal the inevitability of what's about to happen, he steps close to the bench. "Mind if I cash in here for a sec?"

There's something about Jasper's nonchalance that seems exaggerated, possibly manufactured, and makes Alex suspect that this meeting isn't as accidental as Jasper would like it to appear. "Can't you find another place to sit?"

Jasper unclips his headphones from his ears, as though they might have caused him to mishear. "Is this your personal bench? I thought these benches were owned by the city."

"Come off it. You've got fifty other benches to choose from."

"Just let me talk to you for a sec." Jasper sits down next to Alex and slips his gym bag from his shoulder. He clutches his belly in both hands, slumps toward the horizontal, and stretches out his legs. He's trying to appear cool and unfazed, but his lower lip is trembling, and pin drops of perspiration have broken out on his forehead.

Alex shifts his body to the far left side of the bench, as far away from Jasper as he can get, and tries not to emit a single mote of interest. He clenches his teeth between deep breaths, struggling against anger, vindictiveness.

"I love the ped mall," Jasper says. "There's an easy, relaxed, welcoming feeling down here, you know? If things could just be like this everywhere, all the time. Mellow. Inclusive." Jasper watches Magritte, the husky Albanian who operates the gyro cart, bobbing loosely from side to side, arms in constant motion, carving strips of lamb from a glistening vertical spit. "Gotta envy that guy, huh? That's the life. Set up a stand, hang out all day making Greek tacos. I make baked beans from scratch. That's my specialty. You've got to find the right bean, the right mix of tomatoes, nail the tarragon quotient."

Alex looks into the face chosen by — accident? Fate? God? — to be the face of the man who killed Isabel, and attempts to make a link between what he sees there and Isabel's premature removal from the world — a pattern in the arrangement of Jasper's features that might account for this, explain it: the reasoning, the logic, the larger purpose, the intent.

Jasper plants his hands turned-inward on his thighs, tips his head back, squints at the sky. "What would you do if the girlfriend of a really good friend of yours kept hitting on you while he was sitting right there? I was

289

out with this guy the other night and his very hot, very significant other kept giving me this tractor-beam look. At first I thought she had some kind of problem with her eyes, you know, with that part of your brain, what is it, the optic cord? Her boyfriend is one of these all-American blue-eyed lats-pecs-delts boys, so it's not like I'd have a moral problem. It's not like I'd *hesitate.* God!" As if in agony, Jasper clutches his thigh with both hands, squeezes, lets go. "Temptresses! Temptresses everywhere!"

Sometimes Alex wishes Jasper conformed more suitably to his image of a killer: long greasy hair, reflector sunglasses, a lewd tattoo, a scar on his lip, scraggly growth on his jaw. A loose, mucous cough. It would be so much easier for Alex to dismiss Jasper if he were foul, filthy, repulsive. "Thanks for sharing that with me."

"Thanks for listening."

"I wasn't really listening."

"Thanks for sitting there with ears on your head." Jasper's expression is daunted but resolute. He watches a sparrow hop across the bricks, peck at a crumb. "So how are things with the girlfriend?" he asks with a teasing, tantalized inflection.

Alex gawks at him, shocked.

"She's cute," Jasper says. "I saw you guys

downtown together the other night. I was sitting in Calamity Jane's. Thin, short brown hair? Nose stud? Nice work. Hope it pans out."

Alex feels a powerful mixture of astonishment and outrage at Jasper's profound insensitivity, his tactlessness, and wonders, in fact, if Jasper has some kind of personality disorder that renders him oblivious to the basic rules and boundaries of human social interaction. "You are seriously fucked up," Alex says. "Are you missing a part of your brain? Have you ever had a serious head injury? Or do you just inflict them?"

Jasper winces as though Alex has blown cigarette smoke into his face. "I was just wishing you well."

"Keep your wishes to yourself."

Jasper glances down at his right hand. For the past few minutes, Alex has noticed, this hand has been engaged in a solitary, compulsive activity, the thumb pressing against the insides of the adjoining fingers, as though texting on an invisible phone.

Jasper says, "I walk around all day wanting to tell you how sorry I am, but there's no way to express it. I just want you to know I feel it."

"Whatever," Alex says.

"You don't make it easy, do you?"

291

Alex thought he *was* making it easy. "What do you want me to say? Apology accepted?"

"Why not?"

"Because I blame you. I blame you for fucking up big-time."

Jasper lowers his head into a supportive brace of fingertips. After a few seconds he removes his hands from his face, blinks rapidly, and stretches his mouth open so wide it could accommodate a baseball. His jaw clicks, a sound like a chicken bone snapping in half.

"At the hospital. There was an event," Jasper says. "With your wife. Curiosity at work here. Don't take it the wrong way." Jasper taps his chest with his hand. "Thumpathumpa. A change of heart."

The steady, ambient gurgle of the pedestrian mall grows suddenly louder, as if by some radical readjustment of the acoustics of the place.

Jasper says, "You *know*, right? I'm guessing you had to sign something."

Alex, enveloped in a soggy net of stupefaction, feeling exposed and violated, can't think how to respond. He winds the loose play in Otto's leash tightly around his left wrist.

"Look, I overheard you and your wife's mother talking about it in the waiting room," Jasper says. "I'm sorry, it's not like I was trying to overhear. I just did. I don't know where your wife's heart went, if you're worried about that."

This last statement comes out sounding like reassurance, an apology, but the longer it hangs in the air the more it feels like a question.

"You're not supposed to know *anything*," Alex says. "Even if you did overhear, it's none of your business. Is this why you showed up at my apartment? Is this why you're here now? To pave the way for an interrogation? To soften me up with bogus apologies and sympathy? Why do you care where my wife's organs went? Why are you interested?"

Jasper leans forward and peers down at the ground, drags the outer edge of his shoe toward himself along the bricks. "I just am. I'm interested in the heart. I'm involved. Unfortunately, but I am. So I think to myself, Hey, maybe some good came out of all this. Not good for *you*," Jasper clarifies. "But let's be honest. Somewhere out there somebody got a major break. If they survived."

Of course she survived, Alex wants to say, and for the first time has a sense of the disappointment he'd carry around if Janet

Corcoran hadn't survived, if Isabel's project had failed and he'd had some way of knowing. But he doesn't want to discuss any of this with Jasper. He won't offer up this thing that belongs to him, to Bernice, to Isabel. To Janet. It's sacred, isn't it? By virtue of its connection to Isabel. To Isabel's intentions, Isabel's body. It's private. Isabel didn't sign anything on her donor card that said, *Feel free to tell the person who kills me anything he or she wants to know about the ultimate destination of my body parts.*

"I don't know where the organs went," Alex tells Jasper. "They kept that confidential. Which is fine with me. I don't want to know where anything went. But if I did know, I sure as hell wouldn't tell you."

Jasper looks puzzled and disappointed. "Wouldn't it be kind of cool to know? Where her organs went? I'm sure Isabel would have wanted to know."

"Don't use her name. *You* don't say her name."

Alex has had enough. He rises from the bench and leads Otto away.

"What the fuck," Jasper says. He's following Alex, talking to his back. "Hold up. Quit *freaking* out for a sec."

Alex increases his speed, hoping to shake Jasper off, but an intersection and a stream of traffic stop him short. Jasper pulls up alongside, wedges himself between Alex and the crosswalk. "Will you chill out? We're just having a conversation. You can't deny I'm involved. I have a right to know."

Alex realizes that he and Jasper are standing in exactly the same spot where he, Alex, was standing a little over a year ago when he turned and looked back across the pedestrian mall and saw Isabel alive for the last time.

Alex crosses the street and continues down the sidewalk. Jasper keeps pace with him, sniping at his back: "Will you quit walking away from me? You're starting to piss me off."

Jasper hits Alex on the arm, a kind of desperate slap-grip at his biceps. "Just stop and hear me out."

Alex drops Otto's leash and lands a hard, right-handed punch squarely in Jasper's face, knuckles striking cheekbone, causing Jasper to stagger backward with one hand plastered to his eye and the other protectively outstretched. Alex teeters on the sidewalk, adrenalized, rigid, feeling a visceral delight in the success of his punch — he hasn't thrown one since junior high school. Jasper is still standing, albeit unsteadily, his feet constantly rearranging to stay beneath his weight. From the way he's clutching his face you'd think he was stopping up a severed artery. Hesitantly, he lowers his hand, squints into his palm as though it's a mirror in which he's inspecting the damage. There's no blood. Jasper's cheek and eye are flushed but structurally intact. Jasper glares at Alex, mortified and indignant.

Feel it, Alex thinks. *Even though it's an insignificant minuscule fraction of what you inflicted. Feel it just the same.*

TWENTY

Alex and Kelly are hanging out in his living room, settled at opposite ends of the couch, their bare feet mingling in the middle. On the coffee table are two empty plates, minutes ago heaped with Singapore mein fun. Otto sprawls contentedly on the floor, a fortune cookie in his stomach. Modest Mouse is playing on the stereo, a CD Kelly brought over and stealthily slipped into Alex's player. When Kelly asked him, after a few songs, what he thought of the music, he told her, "I'm OK with it," and Kelly gave him an admonishing look, as though there were something snobbish in his ambivalence. He hadn't meant to be snobbish; he'd only voiced a reaction he realized was not entirely his own. It belonged to Isabel. She spoke unbidden in his mind, offering her thoughts and impressions, her opinions. He contained her. A large part of her. Did Kelly realize, sitting there on the couch leafing through an REI catalog, that she was actually in a room with two people? That she was, in effect, dating a couple?

"We should go camping," Kelly says, enticed by page after page of top-of-the-line sleeping bags and tents. "I haven't been for so long. I have an awesome tent. Sort of like this." She points to a lightweight two-person tent called the Big Agnes Mad House 2. "I have a sleeping bag, too. Do you have a sleeping bag?"

"I have an old crummy one."

"Maybe we can get you a new one. Or borrow one. Do you like camping? Not like, 'Let's go out to the nearest state park and pitch a tent and get wasted.' I'm talking about finding a trail and disappearing into the woods for a few days. Backpacking."

"I'm game. A few years ago we went down to the Ozarks with Rob, my rock-climbing buddy Rob, and his girlfriend. That wasn't really backpacking, though. Just camping and a little hiking. Day trips."

"You ought to try the real thing. We should go out west." She gasps excitedly and grabs his arm. "I just read an article in the June issue of *Backpacker* about these underappreciated trails, and there was a photograph of this meadow, this amazing valley full of flowers and surrounded by peaks, you had to hike two days to reach it, and I thought, *I have to see this place before I die.* It was so beautiful. I think it was in Colorado. I couldn't believe this place was in my country. And just a few hours away by car. Well — ten or fifteen hours. But still, reachable."

Alex thinks of Isabel, in the Ozarks, in the middle of a stream, each hiking-booted foot planted on a rock, straddling a sun-flickery platter of water toward which she bent her upper body and craned her head so as to see more closely and clearly the polished stones, the fish so still they looked frozen, encased in ice.

"Let's do it," Kelly says definitively, slapping the REI catalog down. "Do you have anything going on at the end of July? Can you take time off?"

"Just so you know, I'm not some kind of superexperienced backpacker. I've never walked into the wilderness for five days with nothing but a pack on my back. I wouldn't even know half the stuff to bring."

"I know what to bring. My family used to go on backwoods trips like this every summer, for vacation. We went all over the west, mostly in Colorado and Wyoming."

"I'm not sure I can get time off. My

supervisor's saying no vacation time right now."

"What about in July?"

"I don't know. I'd have to check."

"Check." Kelly, grinning, jazzed, gives him a collegial punch in the shoulder.

Alex asks, "What about Otto?"

"We'll take him."

"I'm not sure he can handle the trail. Depends how hard it is."

"So we'll find someone to watch him. Marta can watch him. Marta loves dogs."

Alex hears Isabel say, *Her roommate? You're going to leave Otto for a week and a half with your new girlfriend's* roommate?

He says, "I'm not going to leave him with just anybody."

Kelly looks insulted and hurt. "Marta isn't anybody. She's my roommate, and one of my oldest best friends, and she's incredibly responsible and reliable."

"Yeah, but *I* don't know her."

"Yes, you do. You've had conversations with her."

"I've smoked a bong with her."

"So . . . you're worried she'll get stoned out of her mind and forget to feed your dog?"

"I don't know. Like I say, I don't know her."

300

"*I* know her. And you know me. It's a chain of knowing. A chain of trust. Do you trust me?"

"Sure. I'm just saying, I'm not leaving Otto alone for a week with someone I hardly know."

Alex's tone is unnecessarily combative, and has less to do with Otto's safety and well-being than it does with his uncertainty about going on a vacation with a woman who isn't Isabel.

Kelly bends down and gently strokes Otto's head. "Otto, can you tell your overprotective, hypervigilant owner to relax? Can you tell him no one's going to do anything to hurt you?"

Alex wants to keep fighting back, but he's grateful for Kelly's humor, her patience with his dullness and irritability, her enthusiasm, her ability to motivate him. Why on earth does she bother?

"Oh — I love this song." Kelly springs from the couch and turns up the stereo's volume, filling the room with music — a tinny, plaintive voice and jangly guitar. She sits cross-legged on the floor beside the stereo. She closes her eyes, bobs her head, taps her hands lightly on her knees in a way that strikes Alex as adolescent, affected, designed to impress. But why shouldn't her enthusiasm be genuine? He likes the song too. Or did, until that ringing started. He realizes it's his phone and flinches under the influence of that strange but familiar set of anxieties triggered by the sound, foremost in this instance the fear and shame that it's Bernice, who for the past few days has been calling and asking how he's doing, inviting him and Kelly over for dinner. He hasn't called her back.

Kelly turns the stereo's volume down and gives him an inquisitive look. *You going to get it?*

The machine picks up. The message is one Alex recorded a month or two after Isabel died, the message from which her name was dropped. His voice sounds frail and destroyed. He wonders if maybe it's time to attempt something more upbeat.

There's a pause after the beep, then a female voice, one Alex doesn't recognize.

"Hi. Alex. This is Janet Corcoran. You probably got a card from me a while back. Maybe another couple of cards and a letter before that. I'm calling" — she hesitates, breathes, uncertain — "I'm just calling."

Her voice is forceful, declarative. Alex is stunned. She has a lot of nerve, coming at him like this. He sits partway up on the couch and lowers a foot to the floor, his body still, wanting to hear and resisting a strong compulsion, one he never would have anticipated, to go pick up the phone.

"Tell you what," Janet says. "If you feel like talking, you can reach me at three one two, two two one, four three five nine. I'd love to hear from you. I think we might have a lot to talk about. OK. Sorry I missed you. Hope you're doing OK. Under the circumstances. Have a nice evening. Bye."

Her disappointment is unmistakable and interferes with Alex's righteousness, his determination to ignore her.

Kelly turns up the music slightly and allows her head to resume its bobbing, trying to give the impression, Alex senses, that she's not the least bit curious about the phone call.

Alex picks up his and Kelly's empty plates from the coffee table and piles the soiled napkins and curry-stained chopsticks on top. He carries the plates into the kitchen and sets everything, trash included, down in the sink. When he returns to the living room Kelly's eyes are waiting for him.

"Old friend of yours?" she asks.

"Hardly."

" 'I'd *love* to hear from you. We have a *lot* to talk about.' " Kelly gives him a sly, cheeky look.

303

Alex is inclined to lie, to make up a story, to tell Kelly that Janet Corcoran is Isabel's sister, with whom Isabel was fighting at the time of her death. This sister, who didn't come to the memorial service, has been trying to get in touch with Alex, determined to repair relations with him and with her dead sibling. To explain her side of the story.

But he doesn't see the point. Why shouldn't Kelly know what he's dealing with?

"That woman, Janet Corcoran, she got my wife's heart. Isabel's heart. After she died. Isabel was an organ donor."

Kelly takes the news solemnly. She turns the music down until it's barely audible. "Where does she live? Janet?"

"Chicago."

"And she's been trying to get in touch with you?"

"That's the first time she's called. She usually sends cards. She sent a letter first. She works through a back channel, too. Her mother and my ex-mother-in-law e-mail."

"Bernice?"

"Right."

Kelly drags her fingernail along a groove between floorboards. "It must be kind of weird for you. Weird and hard."

"It is."

304

After thinking for a moment, Kelly says, "I don't know if I want anyone taking my organs after I'm dead. I was born a specific, organic thing, and I want to die that same thing. Me. All of me. All my parts. They were formed together in the womb. I want them to decompose together back into the earth. There's something peaceful and natural about that."

Alex feels instinctively defensive, and surprised to hear Kelly express such New-Agey sentiments. "Yeah, OK, but the dream of dying you, the same physically pure you that you were born, good luck with that. You're going to lose zillions of skin cells and brain cells and who knows what other kinds of cells — teeth, hair, blood, bone — you're going to have fillings in your teeth and stents in your arteries, you're going to have chemicals and toxins in your body, you're going to be a completely different physical being when you die. You're going to be a soiled, cracked vessel. You're pretty much decomposing as you go."

"Yuck. That's a cheerful way of looking at it."

"I'd say realistic."

"So I'm going out with a guy who thinks he's decomposing."

"I *am* decomposing. So are you. Not

decomposing. Decaying, really. Gradually breaking down."

"Maybe if you stopped falling from rocks and punching people in the face you'd break down a little more slowly."

"Ha-ha."

Kelly studies the palms of both hands, her inward-turned arms, as though looking for flesh peeling from the bones. "I think I'm holding up pretty well."

"You're twenty-five. Wait till you're sixty-five."

"OK, so what's your point? We're all decaying or whatever, use it or lose it . . . Are you saying I *should* donate my organs? Are you going to donate yours?"

Alex has never considered this question at length. When he does, two factors present themselves for consideration: one, Isabel signed her donor card in what was clearly a noble, generous act; and two, shortly afterward she was hit by a truck. He knows it's ridiculous and illogical and superstitious, but he wonders sometimes if signing her donor card was what killed her. "I wish I knew what Isabel would want me to do. If she'd encourage me to sign my donor card or if she'd say, Hey, don't worry about it, you've already had one awful experience, that's enough for both of us."

"Was it an awful experience?"

"Her death?"

"No. Obviously. The organ stuff."

"It all happened on the same night. It was all one big mess."

Kelly nods toward the phone. "Do you feel a connection with her?"

"That wasn't Isabel. That was a complete stranger."

"Not a *complete* stranger."

"Don't go there."

Kelly lets the subject drop. She touches a finger to the stereo's volume knob but doesn't adjust it. She has the hesitant, uncertain look of a person who's just realized there are a lot of people at this party she doesn't know. Shyly, with an air of mischief, she rises from the floor and saunters over and straddles Alex. Leans her face in close to his. "You know, before you decompose too much further, I'm wondering if you wouldn't mind donating a certain organ to me. . . ."

She touches it through his jeans.

Alex pushes her off. He doesn't know how to account for his revulsion.

Kelly, wedged between couch and coffee table, half-sitting, half-kneeling on the floor, scowls up at him. "Hey. *Chill.* I was just trying to cheer you up."

"Well, you didn't," Alex says.

A few nights later, around ten o'clock, Alex is doing dishes, trying to remove a tough, hard-to-reach stain on the bottom of a tall glass by cramming a sponge down there and grinding it around with the handle of a wooden spoon. He's beginning to make progress when the phone rings.

He sets the glass down carefully in the sink. It's late to be getting a call. As he rinses his hands and shakes them dry he wonders if this is finally it, Isabel calling from the ends of the earth to tell him she's still alive, it was all a terrible mix-up, she's at an airport, all she needs is his credit card information so she can buy a ticket.

He picks up the phone. "Hello?"

"Alex?"

The voice, female, sounds vaguely familiar. "Yeah?"

"This is Janet. Janet Corcoran. Is this a bad time?"

Alex steels himself against a wave of irritation. If he wanted to talk to her, he would have called her back. "It's no better or worse than any other time."

"Do you mind me calling? In principle? I know you probably do, but I'm asking if you'll tolerate it." She laughs nervously, hopeful. When he doesn't answer she says, "I've been wanting to call you for a long time. Since last spring. But that would have been too early. They told me it would be better to wait if I tried to get in touch with you. People aren't encouraged. Recipients. Probably you can understand why. On the other hand I don't know how people manage not to know anything. There's so much guilt. Let's come right out with it, huh? It's more of a presence than I thought it would be. You can't just go about your business." She pauses, as though expecting some response. "So how are you? Obviously awful."

Her question requires an answer Alex isn't ready to give, an answer too lengthy and complex. "I wouldn't say awful."

"Listen, I don't want you to get the wrong idea," Janet says. "I'm not calling up so you'll tell me you're fine and I can relax and not worry anymore. I thought maybe . . . maybe you'd enjoy talking."

She sounds like she thinks she can help him. Presumptuous. "Why would I enjoy talking to you?"

"I don't know. I . . ." Sigh. "So how long have you lived in Iowa?"

Part of Alex wants to hang up on her right now, before she gets under his skin. But cutting through his vindictiveness is a trace of fascination. He thinks, *This woman has Isabel's heart.* She's no longer an abstraction, a distant writer of cards. She's talking into his ear. Alex can't help falling prey to an odd, surrogate thrill — the excitement Isabel would feel if she were here, if she had donated and somehow lived. If Isabel were here, she'd be trying to grab the phone away from him.

"I've lived in Iowa forever," he says. "I grew up here. Went to college here. Got married here. Everything here."

"Is it pretty? Athens?"

"I guess so. I saw a dead squirrel in the road today. It looked like a slab of mud. That's not pretty."

It's an odd offering, but Janet works with it. "In the school where I teach, down in Pilsen, there's a big rat that lives in a hole in the floor behind one of our kilns. My students and I named him Big Al. I have to stay away from Big Al, since he's probably carrying bubonic plague and I'm immunocompromised. I take drugs to make sure my body's antibodies don't attack my heart, your wife's heart, which the antibodies see as a foreign body."

Alex intended to absorb this little science lesson but the words *your wife's heart* catapulted his mind down the windpipe from which the words were emerging, and he thought, *It must be right here, close by, wrapped up in this voice.*

But she's stopped speaking.

He tells her, "My dog likes to eat dead things. Dead animals. I have to keep an eye on him."

"What kind of dog do you have?"

"Golden retriever."

"What's his name?"

"Otto."

"Otto. That's a handsome name."

A long silence makes Alex think of all the sky and cornfields between them.

"You and Bernice are pretty tight, aren't you?" Janet asks.

"What do you mean by that?"

"Nothing. I just get the impression you're close. Closer than a lot of guys and their mothers-in-law."

Alex is tempted to correct her, *ex-mother-in-law,* but he isn't sure that's right, and doesn't like the way it sounds — as if Bernice is dead too. "I'm closer to Bernice than I am to either of my parents."

"That's nice."

"Depends on how you look at it. Most people would like to be close to their parents."

"Where are your parents?"

"Council Bluffs." He thinks to mention that they're his adoptive parents but stops himself. She's unworthy of such confidences. "Where are your parents?"

"Milwaukee. Suburbs."

"And you're in Chicago?"

"Right. Wicker Park. It's northwest of downtown."

"And you're home now?"

"Yeah," Janet says, as though this were obvious. "You didn't think I was still lying around in the hospital, did you? I've been home since a year ago May. I go to the clinic regularly to get checked out, but that's no big deal. The worst is over. The worst has been over for a long time. For a while there I didn't think I'd get out of the hospital. I thought I was going to die in the hospital."

"Lucky you," Alex says.

"I'm sorry. That didn't come out well."

Alex tries to set aside his bitterness. "So when you say the worst is over, what does that translate into day-to-day-wise? Are you up and around and stuff? Can you do normal things?"

"Oh, yeah," says Janet. "I'm *fantastic.* If I can say that without lording it. I do everything imaginable. As opposed to lying around useless and sick all day like I used to. I'm up early, I go to work, I teach a full load of classes, I do more extracurricular stuff than I've ever done before, and unless it's been a knockout stressful day I'm not tired until late at night." Her tone of voice isn't exactly boastful, but she does sound as though she's trying to sell herself, to convince him that she's worthy. "It's summer now, so school's out, but I'll be teaching in the fall. I just had the first vacation I've had in three years, my husband and I. We went up to Wisconsin for a few days. It was a big deal for me. Just to have the energy to do it — to travel, to hold up through the days. We walked on the beach, we hiked, we rode bikes" — she stops herself, resumes in a more modest tone — "I'm making it sound like a second honeymoon. The point is, I'm physically capable of doing just about anything a normal person can do."

Alex feels queasy. "I believe you."

"I'm sorry. I get carried away. I just want you to know how great your wife's heart is. How powerful. I'd give it back to her if I could. I didn't want her to die."

"Could you give it back? That would be nice."

When he doesn't laugh or retract she says, "Sort of a seppuku kind of thing? Carve it out with a big knife? Ritual suicide?"

She's interrupted by a male voice in the background, and Alex hears a hushed, urgent exchange — Janet offstage, neutralizing the voice with a barrage of whispers. A door slams. She comes back sounding stressed. "Sorry. Please. What were we talking about?"

"Seppuku. Ritual suicide. You were going to kill yourself."

"Oh, right. Well, what good would that do either of us?"

"What if it would bring my wife back? Would you give it back?"

"The heart? And die myself?" She hesitates. "No."

Alex was ready to hang up if she said yes.

She says, "I decided not to die a long time ago."

"And look how magnificently you've succeeded."

Janet laughs uncomfortably. "I'm getting the impression you have it in for me. I guess I shouldn't be surprised."

"It's not easy, talking to you. The *idea* of you."

"What can I do about that?" It's an offer, not a retort.

Alex feels suddenly exhausted, as though he's been on the phone for hours. "I don't know. I have to work in the morning."

"Of course. I'm sorry to call so late. Can I say one thing before you go? I want you to know" — she pauses, considers — "I want you to know how truly sorry I am. And I want you to know I don't take any of this lightly."

Alex doesn't know how to respond. He wonders how she would react to the news that her donor's killer is looking for her.

"Good night," Janet says. "Sleep well."

"I sleep alone. You sleep well."

"Actually I don't. Sleep well."

Alex hesitates a moment, acknowledging her assertion, before hanging up. There's something harsh and abrupt about the severing of the connection. He feels a pang of remorse. If it's true that somewhere in Chicago, in the chest of the woman he was just talking to, Isabel's heart is agitated, uneasy, insomniac, then he blew a chance to comfort it.

To love and cherish, in sickness and in health, till death do us part.

What has death done to them, anyway?

TWENTY-ONE

She was hasty. She rushed it. She rushed *him.* Why on earth, Janet wonders, did she submit to her urge to call Alex when it clearly would have been smarter and more productive to wait until he was ripe for contact? Her mother had warned her — a warning that had originally come from Bernice. Not that Janet should have needed any warnings. Alex hadn't responded to her initial letter, or to any of her cards. He hadn't responded to her phone message. Couldn't she take a hint?

On the other hand, the conversation had its moments. Alex expressed interest in her well-being, whether she was up and around, whether she could do normal things. She sensed this interest struggling against resentment and bitterness, a feeling of injustice. Probably she went overboard in touting her physical capabilities. But she was only trying to express her amazement with her new life, and her gratitude, and to make Alex understand that it was his wife's generosity that had made the difference.

David doesn't say anything when she gets into bed. He's lying on his stomach with his head turned away from her, eyes closed, possibly asleep but more likely pretending. Clearly he was willing to talk a short while ago, while she was on the phone, but if David thought she was going to interrupt her phone conversation with Alex to argue about whether she ought to be having a phone conversation with Alex, David was mistaken.

Janet allows herself to make some noise settling into bed, even tugs repeatedly at a sheet trapped under David's leg. She'd like him to wake up. She'd like to talk to him. The Alex issue needs discussion, as does just about everything else. She feels naïve for having hoped a few days' vacation in Wisconsin would repair all the damage, restore peace. The lakeside restaurants, the steamed fish and cold beers (forbidden, in her case, so doubly delicious), the sun-soaked days sailing and biking and wandering streets and shops — this steady, trance-like procession of activity induced a contented amnesia about their troubles, an illusory harmony that failed to survive the car trip home. Perhaps this was partly her fault. She made the mistake of mentioning, in a moment of hopefulness somewhere just north of Milwaukee, that she was thinking about calling Alex in the near future. David turned to stone. Recalling his face now, his hard, Easter Island profile, and associating it with Alex's voice — *Could you give it back? That would be nice* — she wonders if there's something about herself she's un-aware of, some offensive quality or feature. Or is everyone just hypersensitive? She doesn't understand why David won't give his blessing to a relationship with Alex. She doesn't see how she can proceed without David. When she finally does arrange to meet Alex and Bernice in person — maybe here in Chicago, maybe in Iowa — it will be a catastrophe if David is impolite or disre-spectful. She'll need him on board. Com-pletely.

The next morning they're standing at the kitchen counter drinking coffee and watch-ing the kids eat breakfast when he says to her, with obvious disapproval, "So I gather you called him."

"You gather correctly." She's tempted to blow the discussion wide open by adding *I gather you've been talking with a Realtor* — a woman who called the apartment yesterday

318

and asked for David. Janet wanted to ask this Realtor, *Do you know the wife's not on board?* She'd like to ask David, *How dare you start into this process secretively, on your own?* But she's afraid of the answer she'll get.

David doesn't ask her how the conversation went, probably because he knows she wants him to.

"It's not going to be easy," she says. "It was rocky."

"I always told you he'd be thrilled to hear from you."

"Are you always going to be so weird about this?"

David glances at Sam and Carly, who are perched on stools nearby, slurping up Cheerios. They're lost in their own conversation about whether the pieces of cereal are perfectly circular. David says, "Maybe now's not the time."

He's trying to dodge the discussion. Sadly — or, in this instance, fortunately — Sam and Carly have grown accustomed to a certain tension in conversations between their parents. Conversations that used to halt child activity and elicit concerned gawking now barely register. Janet can only suppose that over the past few months (or has it been longer?) the baseline tone of parental discourse has become taut, urgent, even nasty. She wonders how much damage she and David are doing. Still, she wants this discussion. "They're not paying attention," she says. "Anyway, you brought it up."

"It concerns me."

"What concerns you?"

David grimaces as though she's suggesting they undertake an unpleasant and possibly treacherous task. He checks his watch. He looks at it far longer than necessary to ascertain the time. "I'm going to be late."

"Clearly it's not my well-being that concerns you, or you'd warm up to the idea of allowing me some contact with this man."

The slow, deliberate extension of David's arm as he sets the coffee mug down makes him look like he's resisting a competing urge, perhaps to hurl the coffee mug across the room. "Clearly it's not *my* well-being that concerns *you,* or you'd be sensitive to the idea that maybe I have good reasons to be apprehensive about this guy and his family."

"He hardly has any family. It's just him and his mother-in-law."

"Isn't that enough?"

"What do you mean, enough?"

Janet hasn't realized how stiff and tense David is until a breath escapes his mouth like a deep, long-trapped pocket of gas. "Here's this guy, he's probably a nice guy, I'm not saying he's not a nice guy. He's lost his wife in a terrible accident. He's miserable. We're talking about the exact kind of misery I came very close to. And now you want me to wade right back into it? To experience it? I thought the whole point was *not* to experience it. I'm scared. Honestly. I'm afraid to look the guy in the face. I can't even think about the mother. What am I going to say to the poor dead woman's mother?"

Janet, having forced him to lay out his motives, feels a little ashamed not to have expected this. She'd suspected a disinclination to reflect, a guardedness about his family, a kind of tribal insularity and loyalty, a reluctance to embrace unknowns, even a dash of male competitiveness and jealousy. Why hadn't she thought of fear?

"You're right, it's scary," she says. "I'm not denying that. I guess I feel like we owe them. You know, to buck up and take the pain. So we can approach them and thank them. Pay the price. No one ever said it was going to be a cakewalk."

"Exactly. It's going to be hard and messy. Why do you think the organ procurement people go to such lengths to ensure that it doesn't happen? Why do you think they have a veil of anonymity? Obviously someone envisioned and probably experienced this kind of scenario a long time ago and learned some lessons, and rules were devised as safeguards. Which you circumvented, on your own. That was *your* choice. Why do the rest of us have to go along?"

"Because you got something out of the deal. Presumably. Or don't you see it that way?"

"Hey, whatever I got out of the deal — I got *you* out of the deal," he clarifies in this obligatory aside. "Whatever I got, I pre-paid for, big-time, all those months you were sick."

"Do you honestly think you paid as much as they did?"

David glares at her. It's been difficult and scary to watch David coming to terms with his overly optimistic expectations for their post-transplant life — expectations she's forgiven him for, since that optimism propelled him through the long, difficult wait for a heart. The question now is, Can he adjust? Can he come down off those expectations and learn to be happy with what they have — which is, in her opinion, a lot?

"I'm not saying we don't owe them thanks," David says. "I'm saying we don't owe them therapy."

"That seems stingy. Their lives have been destroyed."

"And you're going to repair them? Janet Corcoran, miracle healer?"

"I just want to talk to them."

"Don't pretend you have modest hopes."

"What's wrong with high hopes?"

David brushes muffin crumbs from his tie. "Nothing, as long as you allow me my hopes, which I think are pretty modest. I hope not to be directly exposed to the bereft. I hope not to sit in a room with them discussing their dead wife and daughter. I hope not to have to suffer the experience of them looking me in the face and thinking, *Hey, you made out pretty well, didn't you?*"

"No one asked you to sit and talk with them," Janet says quietly, allowing herself to sound hurt. She's disappointed. This isn't going well.

"What does 'approach them' mean?" David says, deftly quoting her. "What does 'Pay the price' mean? No one asked me anything. That's the whole point. You ran off half-cocked and set all this in motion without making any effort to sound me out or take the measure of how I felt about it. Up until recently you've acted as though my opinion didn't even factor in."

"I'm sorry, but I did *not* set all this in motion. I got sick, and I got a heart transplant. That set everything in motion."

"You tracked down your donor. Against the advice of the organ procurement people. *That* set everything in motion."

Should she say, out loud, what she's thinking, which is that if she'd known the issue was going to become so divisive she might never have gone searching for her donor? Or would this be a lie? Her forehead feels hot, as though she's spiked a fever. Her heart is galloping. It's funny, she usually doesn't feel this crummy, even when she's upset. Even when she and David are in the thick of it. "OK, so I did. Get off my back. Would it really kill you to sit in a room for an hour or two with the husband and mother of the woman who saved my life?"

"No, it wouldn't kill me," David concedes with a readiness that could only be credible if he were secretly resolving to allow himself other options.

She's got to be brave. "Then I'm going to keep in touch with Alex, if it's OK with you."

"Don't pretend like you're asking me. You're issuing a policy statement."

Janet shrugs. She doesn't like feeling autocratic and unfair, but she wants to be honest. "Maybe I am."

"OK. As long as you understand that I might not be so involved with that."

"How are you going to be involved with me and not be involved with that?"

It's a good question, David's shrug admits, and one he doesn't care to grapple with at this hour of the morning, in his kitchen, with his children present. His body language says they're adjourned. He carries his coffee mug to the sink and sets it down with a clatter. The children's heads come up. David studies the refrigerator calendar for a moment before flipping the month forward from heavily scrawled June to July's clear block of cube-shaped days. He's three days premature. It's only the twenty-eighth.

"Down the juice and let's hit the road," he tells Sam, jiggling his shoulder. "Train's leaving the station."

"Trains don't drive on the road," Carly says.

"My train drives on the road," David answers.

Sam scrambles to finish his juice and cereal, pack his book bag. David loads papers into his briefcase.

"Are you coming home after work tonight?" Janet asks. Lately he's been working more than usual, sometimes late, till nine or ten.

David says, "I'm going to the gym."

Recently he joined a health club down-town, where he goes some evenings to lift weights and do cardio. A few nights ago Janet and the children dropped in on him — Janet wanted to make sure nothing human was getting his heart rate up — and there he was on the treadmill, running and watching ESPN. He doesn't get home on gym nights until after eight, sometimes nine, leaving Janet to deal with the kids. Every Monday night he goes to an international relations class at Loyola, which keeps him out till ten. In short, between work and the gym and his class, he seems intent on spending as much time away from home as possible.

"Hey, no problem, I'll handle everything here," Janet says sarcastically. "Build up your biceps. Change the face of Internet law. Study international relations. Have you ever thought of taking a course in domestic relations?"

David exhales with annoyance, closes and latches his briefcase. Sam finishes packing and organizing but doesn't present himself to Janet for a kiss, following some invisible emotional cue from his father. The two of them go out the door together.

"Daddy didn't kiss me good-bye," Carly complains after they've gone.

"Daddy didn't kiss me good-bye either. Daddy's distracted. Don't take it personally. He'll give you a big kiss tonight when he comes home."

The prospect seems to satisfy Carly. "What month is it?"

Janet goes over to the refrigerator and flips the calendar page back. "It's June. June has thirty days, not twenty-seven. There's only one month that has twenty-eight days. Do you know what month that is?"

Carly thinks for a moment. She doesn't.

"February," Janet tells her. "That's a good thing, because we want as many months as possible to have lots and lots of days. What kind of crazy person would want to take days out of the month?"

"What's a miracle healer?" Carly asks.

Janet, feeling dizzy, helium-headed, bends and leans her elbows on the counter and rests her cheeks in her hands. "There are no miracle healers. Not the way I see it. Healing is hard work."

Carly reaches out and presses her hand to Janet's forehead. "You're hot."

"Am I?" Janet touches too. "I can't tell. The whole room feels hot." She places her hand on her chest and feels her heart skittering, burst out of its rhythm. She sits down and draws deep, even breaths. This has been happening lately. The sudden fevers and out-of-the-blue arrhythmias. Not normal.

"Is Daddy a crazy person?" Carly asks.

"Nooo," Janet says, emphatic and silly. "Daddy's not crazy. Daddy's . . ." She nearly says *Daddy wants everything to be easy.* But she needs to be careful. It will get back to him. "Daddy wants everything to be normal."

"I want everything to be normal too. And I want to have fun."

"Of course you do." Janet struggles to keep her breathing even, suppressing an urge to panic as her heart sprints toward some unforeseeable finish. She takes Carly's hair between her fingers, guiding the strands downward behind the tiny, intricately lobed, radar-sensitive ear. She may not see this girl start high school. How do you squeeze a lifetime with your daughter into five or ten years? She feels an urgency, a fierce impatience with anything that might prevent her from achieving this, even as she notices, with incredible relief, that her heart is beginning to slow, to return to a normal rhythm. "We are going to have fun," she tells

Carly, feeling like she's been too neglectful and serious — feeling like she's focused too much attention on Alex and Bernice and not enough on Carly and Sam, her own children. Her palm, after wiping her forehead, comes away slick with sweat. She wipes it on a nearby towel. "We're going to have lots of fun. That's going to be priority one. From now on, life's a party. Deal?"

"Deal," Carly says enthusiastically.

Fortunately Carly doesn't ask Janet how she plans to hold up her end — how she plans to distribute her attention fairly and evenly, how she plans to manage so many responsibilities and allegiances. How she intends to stay healthy.

Fortunately Carly doesn't ask whether Daddy's coming to the party.

TWENTY-TWO

When Bernice offers Alex a birthday dinner at the restaurant of his choice, he opts for Los Rancheros, bustling and popular. The waiters and waitresses, the hostess and bartender, the cooks in the kitchen visible through an archway in a wall — all are members or beneficiaries of a large, boisterous Mexican family. They joke and tease and snipe in Spanish while attending to their customers, who are treated so cordially and served so quickly that they sit complacent as churchgoers amidst the Mariachi and the madness.

Bernice orders chicken enchiladas — she could dine on the tomato sauce alone — and Alex, beef fajitas. Their margaritas arrive in glasses the size of soup bowls. Bernice toasts Alex's birthday, his thirty-first. "To a peaceful thirty-second," she says. "No more crazy stalkers. No more punching out crazy stalkers. Even if they deserve it."

"To the inventors of tequila," Alex says, raising his glass.

"Any more run-ins with that nut?" Bernice asks, referring to Jasper.

Alex shakes his head no.

Bernice raises her glass. "Here's hoping he goes to jail sooner or later."

"Hear hear."

They drink deeply, and with what feels like more than the usual need. Bernice's heart is thudding. She's been upset to hear about Alex's encounters with Jasper — the first one at his apartment on the anniversary of Isabel's death, the second on the pedestrian mall. She was alarmed that Alex had punched him. She was glad Jasper hadn't punched Alex back, that Alex hadn't been hurt. On the other hand she understood why Alex had lost his temper. Jasper had badgered and provoked him. Bernice would have hit Jasper too. She nearly did hit him the night of the accident, at the hospital. He seemed stupefied to learn that Isabel was going to die, as though he'd expected her to just get up and walk away after being hit by a truck. Wobbling from side to side, unsteadied by alcohol or by shock — Bernice wasn't sure which — he attempted to apologize with a profuse, slathering incoherence that made Bernice livid. She couldn't believe his nerve, approaching her at that moment.

Alex looks handsome tonight, dressed in khaki shorts and one of those long, elegant, quadruple-pocketed guayabera shirts, lime green with vertical embroidery. Bernice wonders if he's going to see Kelly later on or if this is for her, the fancy shirt. *He looks good, doesn't he, honey?* Bernice observes to Isabel, whom she invited to this party. *He looks healthy. Don't you think? He's doing OK, honey. I know he still misses you, but he's doing OK. I miss you too. Yeah, I'm hanging in there. We both are. We're doing our best to pretend life doesn't totally suck without you.*

"So how do you feel?" Bernice asks. "Different? Older? Wiser? Feel those muscles starting to decay? Senility setting in?"

Though she bombards him with these questions in jest, because it's his birthday, she might as well be asking seriously, on account of the fact that she hasn't seen him face-to-face for a couple of weeks.

Alex sinks forward and caves in his shoulders and makes doddery motions with his head, affecting dementia.

"So tell me more about your conversation with Janet," Bernice asks. "What did you two talk about?"

Alex shrugs dismissively. "Stuff. She told me how she was doing, I told her how I was doing. Your basic exchange of information."

Bernice tries not to show her frustration with his reticence. She was alarmed by the news, received a few days ago in an e-mail from Lotta, that Janet had ignored Bernice's recommendation and called Alex. Had Janet blown everything by moving in prematurely? Bernice called Alex in a panic and clumsily felt out what had happened. He was curt and evasive, but she managed to glean that neither he nor Janet had completely turned the other off. Which was a positive result. Which was progress. Bernice ought to be satisfied, but she wants to know more. She's never spoken with Janet, and she's sitting across the table from someone who has.

"So what's she like?" Bernice asks, going for lightly inquisitive. "Is she nice? Friendly? Funny? Interesting?"

"We didn't go on a date," Alex says. "We talked on the phone for maybe ten minutes, tops. Yeah, she was nice. She was friendly. Nice and friendly to get what she wanted. She was smug, too. And presumptuous."

"Smug?"

"I'd say so. Telling me how great she's doing, how active she is physically and all that."

"I'm sure she didn't mean to be smug."

"How are you sure? Do you know her? Have you ever talked to her?"

Bernice feels a flutter of dread. What if, after all she's hoped for, after all the exchanged e-mails and confidences with Lotta, all the cards and letters from the Corcorans and the cards Bernice sent back in good faith, perhaps blind faith — what if after all this Alex turns out to be right, not spiteful or bitter but just right, that Janet is smug and presumptuous and who knows what else. A bitch. The scenario is too upsetting to contemplate. "I'm sure she didn't mean to come off that way. I'm sure she didn't mean to rub anything in. Why would she do that? Even if she is calculating and manipulative, it's a lousy strategy, it doesn't get her anywhere with you."

"I asked her if she'd give the heart back. If it would bring Isabel back to life."

"Oh, Alex, you didn't."

"She said she wouldn't."

"She *wouldn't?* Give the heart back?"

"Right. I have to say, I respected her for that."

Bernice takes a moment to consider what this implies about Janet. "She was straight

334

with you. She wants to live. Who doesn't?"

"Let her live all she wants. Just leave me alone. I want her to let *me* live."

Bernice is quiet for a moment, reckoning with his attitude, which isn't without justification. "It must have been hard for Janet to call you. To present herself. To expose herself. Think about it. You'd have to be pretty brave to call up the husband of your organ donor on the phone. A lot of recipients might not bother. They'd write the perfunctory anonymous thank-you through the organ procurement organization and leave it at that. Get on with their lives."

Alex plucks a tortilla chip from a red plastic basket and uses it to scoop refried beans and rice from his plate. "I think it would be harder for her *not* to call. The difficult, noble thing would be to leave us alone. But she feels guilty, she can't get on with her life, and she wants us to tell her it's all good, we're good, we're sad Isabel died but happy something positive came of it, you have our blessing. It's the same with Jasper Klass. He's after the same thing. It's selfish. Don't you see? We're supposed to perform the laying-on of hands. We're supposed to forgive and heal. I'm not ready to forgive and heal. I don't have the inclination or the power. And it's not my responsibility. I don't owe them. If anything, they owe me."

"So maybe that's why Janet's pursuing you. Us. To give us what she owes. To give us our due. I don't know what Jasper wants to give us. *He* can leave us alone. That I'm OK with."

"What Janet owes me is a gesture of appreciation, which she gave me, and peace. Which she hasn't."

"So . . . it's really no big deal to you that Isabel's heart, her *heart,* is still alive and beating inside this woman's body? Listening to you it's easy to get the impression that Janet got one of Isabel's toes. Or maybe a kneecap."

Alex slouches back in his seat and lets his head flop to one side, beleaguered, transmitting a silent distress signal across the restaurant. "Is this one of those places where the waitstaff comes out and sings happy birthday in Spanish? Maybe put a big straw sombrero on my head? I could go for that right now."

Bernice is ashamed at how badly, and how quickly, she's failed to maintain a celebratory mood for Alex's birthday. "Sorry. I guess I could try to be more fun."

"Yeah. Come on, fun lady," he says, pretending to chide her.

Is his implication that he doesn't expect her to be fun? She can't decide whether to be relieved or insulted. She's aware of conversations around her, the steady murmur of speech and laughter, the ubiquitous chatter that connects all people, that expresses and defines people, couples leaning toward each other across tables, families huddled into booths, children, and she has the feeling she's being slowly cut off from it, losing the frequency.

"So how's Kelly?" Bernice, nervous, so overloads the question with enthusiasm that it comes out tipsy. "Am I ever going to meet this mystery princess?"

Alex sours with annoyance. "She's fine. We've been having a lot of fun. Just hanging out. She's cool. It's relaxed. Nothing serious. We're planning a backpacking trip. Out west. To Colorado."

Bernice has trouble interpreting his description. Trouble with the language. What does "having a lot of fun" mean? Having a lot of sex? What about "hanging out"? *Stop,* she tells herself. He's telling her that things with Kelly are going well. "Colorado? That's a long way. When are you going? How long for?"

"A week or so. Kelly read about a trail out there that's supposed to be awesome.

There's this one meadow she's all jazzed up about. It's sort of a quest for the meadow. We'll drive out there and hike in for a few days and then hike out. It's funny, when she first suggested the idea, I was kind of cold about it; I think my enthusiasm in general is just so low. But I've really started looking forward to it. I'm really feeling like I could use the break."

"You do deserve a break. I'm happy for you." Bernice wouldn't mind driving out to Colorado. She envisions herself sitting with Alex beside a fire, flames flicking upward casting sparks into a dark sky fringed with staggering, snow-capped peaks.

"You don't have to be happy for me," Alex says, revealing a perceptiveness she's grateful for and surprised by. Is she that transparent? "I *want* you to be happy for me, but I understand it's complicated for you. It's complicated for me, too."

With a fingertip Bernice swipes salt off the rim of her glass, licks the finger. "Is it?"

Alex gives her a puzzled look. "What do you mean?"

"I don't know. You've got your girlfriend, and that's great, and you're going backpacking in Colorado, great. You have a life, you're on your way, you're making a break for it, all great. What's complicated?"

338

Alex appears unsure what she's saying, exactly, and moreover what's motivating her to say it. "You're the one who's always telling me to get out and do things. So don't beat me up now that I'm actually doing it."

Bernice supposes she is guilty of a certain hypocrisy. "So what do you think about the fair?" she asks, hoping a change of venue will brighten her spirits. "Wanna go check out some livestock? Chow down a funnel cake?"

The county fair has been running all week at the fairgrounds outside of town, and earlier she and Alex discussed the possibility of going. Alex glances at his watch. It's nine fifteen. He gives Bernice a hesitant look and says, apologetically, and also as a kind of advance warning, "I told Kelly I'd meet her at ten."

She doesn't like this, this delicacy, this walking on eggshells, the way he's hyperconscious of her fragility. "Fine," she says as agreeably as she can. "Some other time."

"Hey," Alex says, gently reprimanding, reaching across the table to take her hand. "This has been a really nice dinner. Thanks."

It has, Bernice thinks. "You're welcome. I've got a present for you at the house. Just a little something. There's cake, too. Stop by tomorrow if you want. Or whenever."

"I will," Alex says.

Kelly, on top of Alex, astride him, naked except for the silver necklace with the amber pendant he's never seen her take off, elbows locked, hands planted on his chest, fingertips digging in, his hands on her chest, cupping and stroking her breasts, lightly pinching her nipples, her neck and cheeks flushed, one side of her upper lip furled upward, snarl-like, eyes closed, veins trembling in the lids, a shank of hair sweat-glued to her forehead and the rest swinging forward, forward, forward with each onslaught of her hips, which Alex meets halfway with surges so furious he's sure he'd hit the ceiling if it weren't for her weight, feeling himself so deep and large inside her he's sure the head of his cock must be right up there beneath her bellybutton, which makes him imagine growing farther up into her and fusing with her spine and radiating ecstasy up through this trunk and out branches of nerves to every cell. He keeps his eyes on Kelly's face, because when he closes his eyes Kelly recedes from the prominence and exclusivity she deserves and who should appear but Bernice: Bernice's face and trim sculpted arms and naked breasts. Alex springs his eyes open, thrilled and ashamed, to reassert Kelly, and he comes in delicious pulses. He does his best to hang on for Kelly, who's close and panicking but finally arrives, letting out a hysterical laugh-shriek — that's her sound — as her lips peel back over her teeth.

They lie side by side on their backs, recovering. When Alex looks over at her she tweezer-fingers an invisible cigarette, brings it to her lips, and sucks it in a pantomime of wanton post-ravishment. "What was in those margaritas? You were nuclear."

Alex looks at her blankly, smiling. "Am I normally subnuclear?"

"Well, yeah. Sorry pal. Not like that. I'm not complaining. I'm going to start taking you to Los Rancheros all the time."

He stares up at the ceiling, where a galaxy of tiny stick-on stars glows faintly in the semi-dark. They were up there when he and Isabel moved in, put there by, or for, a child, or maybe a whimsical adult. Sometimes he and Isabel would turn off their bedside lamps after reading and the stars would shine with pearly light, and if they happened to be lying on their backs looking up Isabel would say, *Don't the stars look pretty tonight?* The funny thing was, they did.

"Are you thinking about her?" Kelly asks.

341

"About Isabel?"

Her tone suggests sympathy and concern, but the frequency with which she's asked this question lately tells him there's irritation, maybe even jealousy.

She tells him, "It's OK if you are."

"Is it?" Alex asks. "I wouldn't be OK if you were thinking about someone else right now. Some ex-boyfriend."

Kelly gives him a puzzled look. "Isabel was your wife. And she died. She's not just some ex-boyfriend. So to speak."

"That's true," Alex says. "Are you getting impatient?"

"With you? Thinking about her?" Kelly considers. "No."

Alex isn't sure he believes her. "I'm not sure how long it's going to take. To get over her."

"I don't know if you'll ever get over her."

"You know what I mean."

"Actually, I don't." Kelly rolls up onto her side to face him, propping herself up with an elbow. "How do you plan to get through this? Do you have a strategy? Do you have a plan? Have you ever thought about seeing a counselor? Someone you can talk about all of this with?"

Alex is taken aback by the barrage of questions. "I talk to Bernice."

"You hardly ever see Bernice."

"I talk to you."

"We hardly ever talk about it. And when we do, hey, let's be honest, I'm no professional."

"What's your point?"

"I want you to get the help you need."

"I need help?"

"You're going through a rough time."

"I've got you."

Kelly laughs with trepidation. "No pressure."

"There isn't any," Alex insists.

Kelly stares at him with a kind of affectionate exasperation. "There wouldn't be if I didn't care about you. But I do. So there is."

Alex, grateful for her concern, brushes his hand across her hair. "You're saying you're in over your head."

Kelly takes a moment to think. "With you? Maybe. With life in general? You're in way deeper than me."

TWENTY-THREE

After a rough day at U.S. Exam, Alex is inspired to give Otto a little more than the usual, dull walk, and drives him to a local park, where he lets him run around off leash in a huge field, chase squirrels into the woods, sniff deer urine, romp with other dogs. When they get home, Alex finds a copy of *Backpacker* magazine that Kelly has slipped under his door, the issue in which she originally saw the photographs of the secluded, Edenlike meadow in Colorado. Alex sits down on the couch and opens the magazine to the article and begins reading, though he's soon distracted by the photograph of the meadow, which is indeed striking — amazing: a flat, apparently endless vista of flowers rimmed by steep, high mountains whose gray corrugated peaks pierce the clouds.

When the phone rings he deviates from normal policy, which is to let the machine get it, and picks up, expecting a call from Kelly, who's at work, and will want to know if he found the magazine. *Does that meadow look awesome, or what?* It does, he wants to tell her. He can't wait to go.

"Alex." Bernice exhales dramatically, gratefully, as though she'd been unable to breathe before reaching him. "Hi."

Alex tries to conceal his disappointment. "Hi. What's up?"

"Not much. What's up with you?"

Alex can tell from her voice this isn't a social call. "What's wrong?"

"Oh, Alex, I don't know. I'm sorry. I know you don't want to hear it, but I just got some upsetting news about Janet."

Irritation and anxiety tighten Alex's chest. "I'm listening."

"She's in the hospital. She's rejecting Isabel's heart. I just got an e-mail from Lotta. Janet was admitted to the hospital Saturday night. She's been in the hospital for four days."

Rejecting Isabel's heart. Alex pictures Janet holding her hands out defensively as a disbelieving physician offers her the bloody organ. "Rejecting? What, she doesn't want it?"

"Of course she wants it. Her antibodies are rejecting it. Attacking it. The heart is under attack. That's how Lotta explained it." Bernice's tone is crisp and impatient.

"OK, hold on. We know Lotta has a reputation for exaggeration. Are you sure this is serious? I just talked to Janet on the phone, what, a week, two weeks ago? She was fine. She was great. She made herself out to be the healthiest, most physically fit woman on the planet. I about puked."

"Alex, I'd really like you to read Lotta's e-mail. I printed it out. Can I bring it over?"

"Bring it *over?*"

"Please."

"Honestly, Bernice, I don't want to read it."

"I'm not asking you to write back to her. I just need a second opinion."

Alex realizes it's going to be hard to enjoy the rest of the evening knowing he refused Bernice, and that she's not only upset, but upset with him. "Fine. OK."

She arrives at the door inside of ten minutes, agitated and huffing a little but clearly relieved to see him, carrying her keys in one hand and a folded-up piece of paper in the other. She's wearing lime green flip-flops with ladybugs on the straps and maroon athletic shorts and a black T-shirt with THE METROPOLITAN OPERA in white letters across the front. She unfolds the piece of paper and hands it to Alex. "Just tell me what you think," she says.

Hi Bernice,

How are you? Hope things are going well. I read something in the newspaper yesterday morning about "Global Warming Action Day" and thought of you pledging your $20. I'm glad there are other citizen environmentalists out there. Did you save some money for Alex's birthday present? I seem to recall that his birthday was the 6th. Hope it was a happy one (as happy as it can be . . .)

I don't want to alarm you, but I thought you should know that Janet was admitted to the hospital Saturday night after several days of low-grade fever and cardiac arrhythmias. The doctor says she's having a rejection episode — her antibodies are attacking/rejecting the heart — and that while this happens often in the first year post-transplant it's not so common after that. The upside is they're treating her with anti-rejection medications and assure us that she should be home soon. So there's no cause for panic. This isn't the first time Janet has landed back in the hospital for one reason or another. She's handling it all fine — going to the hospital is like going to the grocery store for her — but Bud and I drove down to help David cope, and to help manage with the kids.

I'm writing to you on my new laptop from the hospital lobby, which has wireless. Pretty soon we won't even need the computers — we'll just access the Internet and send e-mail directly from our brains!

Take care. I'll keep you posted.
Lotta

Alex nods judiciously. "Nice focus, content is relevant, ideas well-organized, good control over sentence structure and word choice, no mechanical or usage errors. I give her a five."

"Ha-ha. Seriously. What do you think?"

"She doesn't want to alarm you. Look, right here." He points out the phrase, then several others. " 'The doctor . . . blah blah blah . . . assure us that she should be home in a day or two.' 'There's no cause for panic.' 'Janet's handling it all fine.' She's been in the hospital before." He gives Bernice a put-upon look. "What are we worried about, again?"

Bernice sits beside him on the couch and leans in to read the e-mail, which he considers handing to her but leaves on his lap, amenable to having her close. She rereads the message with a puzzled expression on her face. Her lower lip drops and unfurls slightly, revealing its moist, plump inner surface. "What about this thing about rejection episodes not being common after the first year? And this, 'The upside is . . .' An upside implies a downside, doesn't it?"

Alex is pleased to see that what was only minutes ago Bernice's distress and alarm has tempered to curiosity, a childlike eagerness to collaborate with him in decoding this secret, urgent message relevant only to them.

"Well, sure, the usual downside: everything could completely fall apart," Alex says. "But it doesn't seem like it's going to. I think we're overanalyzing. Overanalyzing and overreacting." He flicks the paper with a thumb-sprung middle finger, as though to jettison a bug. "I don't think this is anything we need to be concerned with."

"So, OK, here's my next question." Bernice draws back and turns to face him squarely. "What *would* we need to be concerned with? More specifically, what would you need to be concerned with? Would you be concerned if Janet took a turn for the worse? Would you be concerned if Janet were close to death? What if Janet died? Would that send a ripple across your pond?"

"Why are you beating up on me?"

"I can't believe you're so detached."

"I can't believe you're so *a*-ttached."

Bernice takes a deep, equalizing breath. "I'm thinking of driving up there."

The declaration takes Alex off-guard: he experiences the psychic equivalent of stepping onto a rapidly moving conveyor whose presence he wasn't aware of. Bernice has him fixed with an intense, resolute look whose challenge to him is unmistakable.

"I'm not," Alex says, half-suppressing a laugh that calls the idea of accompanying her preposterous. "I'm *not*," he repeats. His reasons are too complex to explain, but the central reason is a presentiment, a very real fear, that going with Bernice to see Janet and Janet's family will drag him back into his own nightmare of acute grief and suffering. "You go if you want. I understand it's important to you. As long as you understand it doesn't have to be important to me. It's perfectly acceptable for us to have different ways of dealing with this."

Bernice looks crestfallen. "Is it? Part of me wants to say it is. Another part of me wants to say you're callous."

"You know, if this is your attempt at subtle

diplomatic persuasion, it's failing."

"Diplomatic persuasion isn't getting me anywhere." Bernice folds Lotta's e-mail in half, in half again, on into smaller and smaller squares. "I'm scared too, you know. I'm not thinking it's going to be a big easy fun fest, or that Isabel's going to shoot out of Janet in a ray of light. I'm expecting it to be hard and unpleasant and depressing."

"Me too. That's why I'm not going."

"*And* rewarding. I hope."

"I hope so too. If Isabel shoots out in a ray of light, call me."

Bernice glares at him. She seems, for the time being, to have resigned herself to defeat, and slips the piece of paper into her pocket, scoots to the edge of the couch, fiddles with her car keys, prepares to go. She stares fiercely across the room. "Why do you keep that?" she asks, nodding at the Turkish kilim hanging on the wall. "The rug. Why do you keep it prominently displayed in your living room so you can see it every day?"

Alex makes a weary, dubious face, determined to resist whatever point she's angling toward.

"Because it was Isabel's," Bernice says. "Right? It belonged to her. It was important to her. So you treasure it."

"Yes. True. And? . . ."

Bernice's tone is sharp. "It's made out of wool."

They were in Venice, of all places, coming out of a tiny street in San Polo, when they spotted the Turk and his wares. They had been in the city for three days, walking endlessly and visiting museums and palaces and stopping for espresso and taking long, indolent naps followed by sex, dinner, late-night strolls along the canals. It was March, but they'd been lucky with the weather, which was sunny and mild. It was the first time Alex and Isabel had taken a vacation alone together since their honeymoon — a week in St. John — so they'd decided to splurge. It was Alex's first time in Europe, Isabel's first time in Italy (she'd gone to Paris senior year of high school with her French class). They stood on the Rialto Bridge and watched the gondoliers in striped shirts pace back and forth in front of their gondolas, chatting on their cell phones. They saw a priest in black vestments kicking a soccer ball around with some kids in front of a seventeen-hundred-year-old church. They arrived too early for dinner at a restaurant they'd read about in the guidebook and had the privilege —

mostly Isabel's — of watching the entire staff, a dozen young Italian men with chiseled jaws and lustrous black hair, sit together at a long table slurping spaghetti like brothers in a large country family. Isabel dragged Alex into a supermarket, where they beheld aisles and aisles of dazzling, indecipherable labels, and they lost themselves in a game of guessing what was inside the stylish packages and svelte cartons. "Hey, Iz, I think this is *yogurt,*" Alex said at one point with a thrill, as though he had discovered a rare archaeological find.

They were interested in the history of the city and spent a lot of time reading the guidebook. It seemed incredible to Alex that the early Venetians had driven pinewood piles — long wooden poles — in close-packed clusters down into the clay at the bottom of the lagoon and then built on top of them with bricks and stone. And it was all still here, still standing, if barely. Many of the buildings were severely decayed. On the stone and marble and brick, just above the waterline, you could see horizontal bands of residue and grime. The colors of these bands were strangely beautiful, delicate and varied — pale blues and greens and reds. "Probably algae and salt crystals," Isabel said. "I don't know. Gypsum? Toxins?" She was mesmerized by the day-to-day life of the city: boats of all shapes and sizes and colors plied the canals doing the duties that cars and trucks did on the concrete streets of the rest of the world: collecting garbage, delivering mail, ferrying goods. There were buses and taxis, ambulances and police and fireboats. They saw one boat delivering an enormous red sofa wrapped in plastic. There were the Venetian equivalents of pickup trucks carrying two or three men, plumbers or electricians or contractors of some kind, with their tools and equipment, thermoses and cigarettes. It was obvious when Alex thought about it — how else could such a city manage? — but astounding to behold.

So they wandered and marveled, they stared up at buildings and counted stone lions, they ventured into more museums. They refueled with *macchiati* and tiramisu and set off again into the labyrinth, and late one afternoon found themselves coming out of the tiny street in San Polo onto the piazza where a thin, dark-skinned man dressed in a red-and-black A.C. Milan jersey stood beckoning to passersby. Before him on the bricks was spread an expanse of clear plastic the size of a two-car garage, and laid out on the plastic were what looked like Persian

rugs. Alex would have walked right past —
rugs weren't on his radar — but Isabel
drifted toward them. Soon Alex was following her down the narrow paths between the
rugs admiring their subtle, quiet colors,
blues and greens and reds, and geometric
patterns. The man greeted them in German,
then switched to English and explained that
the rugs were from Turkey. They were called
kilims and had been hand-woven in a remote province. "I myself am from Erzincan," the man said proudly, and then wrote
the word down for Isabel on a scrap of
paper, and though neither Alex nor Isabel
knew where Erzincan was, they nodded ap-
provingly. Alex worried that the man was
being dishonest with them, and that the
rugs had been machine-made somewhere
within fifty miles of the spot where they
were standing. Isabel thought the fabric's
intricate weave, the richness of the colors,
and the sharpness of the designs marked
the kilims as genuine. She was attracted to
one in particular, about two feet wide and
three feet long, its central design a pistachio
green diamond inlaid with flowers and
hourglass shapes. The man, with whom Isabel was becoming fast friends, explained
that kilims were used for rugs, prayer mats,
and even swaddling for babies. Isabel asked

Alex, "What do you think? We could hang it on the wall." Alex thought that instead of paying the equivalent of three hundred dollars for a hand-woven Turkish rug that was in all likelihood neither hand-woven nor Turkish, they should spend their money on something Venetian, like a carnival mask or an antique map or a piece of Murano glass. But he didn't say so. Whether the rug was real or not, Isabel was infatuated with it, and buying it would make her happy.

"Let's blow some euros," he said.

She smiled, then clouded with doubt. "Is it silly, going all the way to Italy and bringing back a Turkish rug?"

"It's not just a rug. It's a piece of art. Besides," Alex said, adopting a professorial tone, "Venice was the center of a maritime empire with ancient trade links to the East. We're doing something quintessentially Venetian, buying Turkish goods."

"You're spending too much time with that guidebook."

"It's all up here," Alex said, tapping his head with his forefinger.

"Should we use cash or put it on the credit card?"

"The ancient Venetians didn't have credit cards."

Isabel rolled her eyes and gave the man

four hundred-euro bills. The man rolled up the kilim carefully and secured it with tape and handed it to her. "Happy visit," he said.

"*Grazie,*" Isabel said. And then to Alex, "Hear that? I'm practically fluent."

They continued across the piazza, and looking at the soft evening light on the buildings, hearing the cries of children playing around a fountain, Alex felt wistful and immensely grateful for his good fortune, enraptured by this life. He stopped and folded Isabel into an embrace, then pulled back and held her head in both hands and pinched her earlobes lightly between his forefingers and thumbs and kissed her once, twice.

"I'm going to take you back to the hotel," Isabel said, "and strip off your clothes and wrap you up in our new kilim. Just like the ancient Venetians did."

"I bet it's scratchy."

"Oh, no," Isabel insisted. "The guy said they were soft enough for babies. And you're my baby."

The evening following Alex's conversation with Bernice, haunted by her disappointment, and by her accusation that he was callous and detached, he drives out to the highway, ramps on, and heads east. He gets off after two exits and cuts south to Rural Route 7, a narrow two-lane that gently rises and falls southwest toward the fringes of Athens. The corn is high, the car rolls like a pellet between barricades. There are farms set back at the ends of long driveways, pastures dotted with cows, ravines where oaks and willows sulk.

He starts up the hill, slowing as he approaches the crest. He sees Isabel riding alongside, struggling with the incline, crouched low on the bike, head down, fetal against the frame. He can't stand the prospect of seeing this image shattered — any second now, at the top of the hill — so he dissolves it, aware in a peripheral way that he was having trouble filling in her face.

He pulls over at the top of the hill and turns off the engine. Insect noises fill the open windows.

He throws open the door and climbs out. Shuts the door gently, wary of any harsh impact. Walks around to the front of the car, stands at the edge of the ditch. A moth, white as snow, spins and pitches above the soybeans. In the distance are fields of corn, ridges lined with trees, farmhouses, more fields, radiant green. He wonders what this land will be like in a hundred years, a thousand — what will be here, if anything.

A scorched desert. A nuclear wasteland. The past is more certain: ten or twenty thousand years ago he would have been standing in a forest of birch trees. The air would have been chilly. He would have been a hunter-gatherer cloaked in animal-hides. What would he have been doing in this spot where a woman would one day be mauled by a mechanized beast? Eating a meal? Killing an animal? More likely just trekking past.

Bernice had a point that night at dinner, on the year anniversary of Isabel's death. Standing on the side of the road midway between the Proterozoic and Earth's final, inevitable incineration, five hundred million years and countless millions of people on either side of him, it's comforting to Alex to realize how incredibly fortunate he was not to have missed Isabel entirely.

He descends into the ditch. Crickets flee his footsteps, flinging themselves into the air and scrambling to gain their footing on tall, tipsy grass blades. All the squeaking insects sound like they're in the sky, invisible in the air around him. At his feet are scattered bunches of red and yellow flowers, clover and moth mullein. Her body came to rest somewhere here, he'll never know exactly where. On his first visit to this place he did a quick excavation and uncovered a tiny pearl shard of wheel reflector, a black dime-sized gearshift lever cap. He still makes a habit of scanning the ground for clues, for something that may have escaped notice or appeared since: a sign, a message.

He aims his head at the sky and listens for her voice, quiets his mind to receive her emanations, more rigorous than usual in his effort to distinguish between the voice of his mind, animating her, and a real, external voice. He closes his eyes. Can she reach him? Can she touch him? A cool breeze brushes the left side of his body, fills his ear. The resolute silence of this place used to make him crazy. He'd close his eyes and see her face right there, fully formed, real-as-life, then open his eyes and see nothing — empty space. He felt like he was hemorrhaging. He wanted to curl up on the ground and wait for the sun to burn itself out.

He can't seem to work himself up to that pitch today. The pain doesn't feel as sharp as it used to. The voltage has dropped. Part of him doesn't want the pain to go, wants it to be perpetually fresh and scalding. If the pain is diminishing, isn't it a sign that his physical and emotional attachment is diminishing too? A sign that he's beginning to let go?

He wonders what Isabel would want him to do, what she would say if she could speak to him.

That's a silly question. I want you to be happy.

Then he should welcome this diminishing, shouldn't he? Not resist or counteract it, no matter how much love and memory and nostalgia — and Bernice, and Janet — urge him otherwise.

TWENTY-FOUR

Onstage, a chunky woman in a tight, red, midriff-exposing top is singing "Dust My Broom." Her voice is shrill and reckless, but she's determined, with enthusiasm and swagger, to sell the song. The backing band is first-rate, all talented musicians, and they're laying down a rollicking groove, but Jasper, listening from the crowd, can't lose himself in the music. The sound is raucous, a clatter of crunching, whining guitars, and there's a persistent thudding in the drums, whose texture and pitch mimic a sound from the accident, the sharp knock of a dislodged bike part against his windshield.

It's Monday night, Blues Jam night at Calamity Jane's, where smoke creeps along the low ceiling and the booths are cheap black vinyl and the carpet is something you don't want to get too close to. The place is jammed with musicians and hangers-on. Jasper sits in a booth with three other guitar players, dressed in his white pleated-front tuxedo shirt, black 501 jeans and snake-print cowboy boots, drinking a pint of Amstel Light, awaiting his turn to take the stage. When his friend Paolo called him at the last minute and invited him to go down to the Blues Jam and offered a ride, Jasper accepted. How could he not? He'd just had one of the worst days of his life. On the bright side, he wouldn't have to go to work tomorrow, or any other day. Not at Best Buy, anyway.

He hasn't been playing his guitar much lately, or well, but Paolo told him he had to get back on the horse. Paolo was one of the strange people who for some reason never tired of Jasper, who kept coming back for more. He was a fearsome guitar player himself. Still, slumped in the booth with Paolo and the others, listening to the ruckus from the stage, feeling demoralized and volatile and scattered, thinking nasty thoughts about Steve Schultz, Best Buy store manager, the ignorant, uptight fuck who fired him today . . . given this state, Jasper wonders if it might have been smarter to get back on the horse some other night. He doubts he'll play well. His confidence is at a record low. He's not even enjoying the tech talk, which is usually his favorite aspect of Blues Jam night. He's having difficulty following the conversation. He stares at his companions' moving lips without receiving the meaning of their words.

"It won't be long before some engineer at Fender or Marshall cracks the solid-state code. All they've got to do is get the digital sampling down to smaller pictures. Then the tube amp's history."

"People will always buy tube amps. It's vintage mania. People want that old, clean sound, and even if you can get it with solid state, why not pay a few extra bucks and get it the old way?"

Jasper closes his eyes and massages his jaw, which is tight and sore. It's hard to care whether transistor amps replace tube amps. The question he'd like answered is, *Why does this always happen to me?* Every time he gets a job, every time he starts going out with a woman, every time he attempts any serious project he seems, at first, appreciated and trusted by the people around him. Then, sooner or later, something erodes. People start treating him differently, with distrust and suspicion, as though unbeknownst to him he's been slandered by a third party. Strangely, the more that people around him distrust or slight him, the more he feels they're no longer worthy of him —

not worthy of his time and effort. By which time the situation is usually fucked. So he thinks to himself, *Why not go out with a bang? Why not pluck something from the wreckage?*

"It doesn't *have* a master volume. It's got a five-knob front panel with graphic EQ, pull pots, optional foot switching, and a progressive linkage control in the output stage that lets you toggle between two 6V6s or four EL84s."

Chunky Midriff and Co. finish "Dust My Broom" and slip into "Stormy Monday," doing it gently, sweetly, with lovely rainlike trickles from the guitar. Jasper leaves the booth and makes his way to a secluded corner of the room littered with guitar cases. He finds his guitar case, springs the latches, lifts the lid. He likes his Stratocaster's pristine white color, the arctic white pick guard. It's a Jimmie Vaughan Signature Tex-Mex, and the design reflects Jimmie's preference for simplicity and a traditional playing style. The Stratocaster is Jasper's most treasured possession. He's grateful to it for sticking with him, for staying in one piece, for enduring the mess of his life. He takes the guitar gently onto his knee, plugs into a digital tuner, and carefully tunes each string.

Chunky Midriff and Co. wrap up "Stormy Monday" and leave the stage. Jasper's on. He angles through the crowd with his guitar, mounts the stage. He plugs into one of the amps and doodles to check his sound. Evan, drums, and Nausherwann, the only Pakistani bass player Jasper's ever met, are warming up. Paolo, dressed as always in oily-looking jeans and a tattered T-shirt whose short cuffs display muscular biceps, is zipping out riffs on his red rosewood Telecaster.

Lou, voice and harp, wants to do "Messin' with the Kid," and they walk down in, fat and slinky. Jasper finds a little G9 thing up around the tenth fret that ornaments the main riff without obscuring it. Paolo takes the first solo. He climbs to a crystal-clear bent sustained peak, breaks it cleanly, and slides like ice off a roof into a line that meanders from side to side and concludes in a five-note wheel that gains speed and intensity and vectors into a dizzying spin. The crowd tosses hoots like bouquets.

Jasper's turn. He grabs a note and pinches it hard. He doesn't feel up to creativity, and clicks open riff files from memory, one after another, stringing them together, feeling scattered and inept. Phrases straggle through his head but most aren't promising, and the ones he tries to replicate on the fret board he mangles. It's shameful that his hands should produce disjointed, plaintive squawks from an instrument he's been playing since he was fourteen. He attempts a trilly, reel-like thing up on the high E string but his fingers, now trembling, jumble and clump. The band is willing to give him as many eight-bar cycles as he needs to get off the ground, but he wants out of the nightmare now. He manages to hang on until the end of the second eight, which takes forever to arrive, and bails.

His face is hot with embarrassment. The faces of fellow musicians watching from the crowd are smug and mirthful, tasting blood. A few girlfriends-in-tow give him enthusiastic, sympathetic smiles — the kind of smiles mothers award their toddlers for walking onto a stage dressed as vegetables. Jasper turns his face toward the stage lights and feels their heat on his eyeballs, sweat in the corner of his mouth. Closing his eyes, he thinks what a relief it would be to be incinerated by an all-consuming fire, to have his body, his anxieties, all his screw-ups and failures and shame, reduced to ashes, a heap of dust.

The moment the set's over he locks his guitar in his case like a misbehaving pet and heads for the bar. He finds an empty stool and orders a rum and Coke. He's struggling inside a vision of himself as continually unlucky, repeatedly screwed, the victim of one injustice after another. Did he really deserve what he got today? Did he really "cross the line" as Steve put it? Did he deserve to be described as "not giving a shit" and "clueless" and "irresponsible"? Though the infraction for which Jasper had been called into Steve Schultz's office and fired — stuffing five DVDs into his gym bag and walking out one of the service entrances with them — was what had done him in. Jasper felt, in the midst of his disbelief and creeping déjà vu, that Steve Schultz was only the latest mouthpiece for a much larger, more damning accusation of disgracefulness.

The rum tastes divine, and the Coke's just in the way. Jasper makes his next drink straight rum. Beneath the bar, without first being conscious of it, he's pressing the end of his right thumb against the fleshy pads on the insides of the adjoining fingers, dialing the ghost of the phone. He recalls with an electrical panic the way it suddenly slipped out of his grasp, jumped out like a frog. Is he the only person in the world who's dialed a cell phone while driving?

Hardly. He was calling Angela Koretsky, firming up plans for later that night — plans that never ended up happening. Of course if he had it to do over again he'd put off calling Angela, even put off his plans for the evening, stay home in bed under the covers where he couldn't possibly hurt anyone. He'd dialed three or four digits when the phone slipped and dropped to the floor. He checked the road ahead — clear — then glanced down and reached his right arm between his legs and groped. As he was coming up with the phone he saw the woman on the bike hurtling toward him.

Don't forget, Jasper reminds his accusers, *she was halfway out into the road.* She was reckless too. *Nice job, bitch. You know how many lives you fucked up besides your own?*

He imagines a woman, a stranger, sitting down next to him, right here at the bar. She gives him a knowing, sympathetic look. Her face is gentle and nurturing and aglow with intangible promise. He knows without asking who she is. *Don't blame yourself,* she says, laying her hand on his. *It could have happened to anyone. You were just unlucky.*

Then, *You saved my life.*

Jasper orders another rum and raises it into the air in front of his face and tells her, *Don't give up on me. I haven't given up on you.* The bruise below Jasper's eye, from Alex's punch, hurts — a reminder of Jasper's botched operation. Why didn't he hold his cards close to his chest and gain Alex's trust before asking about the heart? Instead he kept badgering Alex even when it was obvious that Alex didn't want to talk anymore. Then Alex lost his cool.

Idiot, Jasper chastises himself, pressing his finger to the bruise, purposefully exacerbating the pain. *Well done. Now what are you going to do?*

Apologize? Beg? Grovel?

Jasper has considered the dog. He could follow Alex on one of his walks, wait till Alex ties the dog up outside New Prairie Coop while he goes inside, which Jasper has seen him do. Then Jasper could swoop in and untie the dog and take him away. Call Alex and tell him, *I'm walking your dog. Thought maybe you'd forgot about him tied up there outside the Coop. I was going to take him down to Animal Control and tell them I thought he was a stray, unless . . . Tell me who got the heart. Tell me right now. If you want to see your dog again.*

Jasper could never do it. He likes dogs. He likes Alex's dog. And no dog has ever slighted or harmed him, whereas people, people have. So many.

Paolo stops by and tells him not to worry, he played OK, he'll do better next time. Jasper is grateful, and eager for further consolation, but Paolo, approached by an admirer, turns and floats away in her gravitational pull.

Jasper scoots off his stool and retrieves his guitar and slips out the back door into the alley. The air is warm. Lurching sidewalks make for tricky walking. He's got to be careful not to collide with other people. His guitar case, heavy and unwieldy, pivots and dips, taxing his wrist. The farther he gets from downtown the more the night reduces to darkness and foliage and shifting, breathing shadows. Jasper strays off the sidewalk onto a lawn, weaves back. He walks five blocks, crosses a busy street, walks five more. It's a radical idea, a departure, but brilliant in its way. Jasper picks up his pace. He turns onto Clark Street. Third or fourth house, if he remembers right. Here: tall, brown brick. He stares up through the trees, casing the place. A light in a curtained upper window. A dim light downstairs. He navigates the walk and mounts the porch and stands unsteadily, gripping the rail. He looks for a doorbell and finds it set in the circular curl at the end of a pewter gecko's tail. He presses and hears a buzz within.

He's breathing hard from anxiety and exertion.

The porch light comes on, and Bernice Howard opens the door a good two feet, creating a space large enough for Jasper to see her fully. She's wearing a white T-shirt that hangs low over jeans rolled up into cuffs. Her feet are bare. The intensity with which she remains gripping the doorknob makes it appear as though her shock, and the perfect stillness of her body, are a result of voltage flowing up her arm.

"Good God," she says.

"Can we talk?" Jasper's alarmed to hear his voice come out mushy.

Bernice looks as if he said, *Can I burn down your house?* "We don't have anything to talk about."

Her fingers are trembling. Is she scared of him? He's dumbfounded and offended. "I think we do," Jasper says. "Just hear me out."

He sways forward as though tipsiness has gotten the better of him and steps into the house, his guitar case swinging forward like a battering ram, though it hits nothing. Bernice, alarmed, lets out a little yelp and lets go of the door, backs up against a piano, raises her hands protectively in front of her.

"I just want to talk," Jasper reassures her.

With a swift motion Bernice reaches behind her and grabs a wrought-iron table lamp and slides it forward to the edge of the piano top, cord trailing.

"Hey, take it easy." Jasper sets his guitar case down as a gesture of peace and displays empty, harmless palms.

Bernice's fingers clench and unclench around the base of the lamp. "I want you to leave. Get out."

"I've tried with Alex. He has opinions. And a pretty good punch." Jasper winks at her with his injured eye. "Let me say . . . saying it cheapens it, or whatever. But I'm sorry. Lame, huh?"

"How sorry are you when you're sober?"

"It's harder to express."

"You express it by coming to my house drunk at eleven thirty on a Monday night?"

Jasper would deny that he's drunk if he felt he could do so without slurring his words. Besides, he's not entirely embarrassed. He takes a certain spiteful satisfaction in living up to this woman's mistaken impression of him.

"Never underestimate the motivational powers of alcohol," he says.

Bernice looks ill. "My neighbors are out on their front porch. One good scream will

bring them running. Then we'll get the police."

"How about you offer me some other options."

"Step back onto the porch."

Jasper steps toward her. "You've got me
all wrong. You think I'm a drunk. You think
I was shitfaced weaving all over the road. I
wasn't. *This* is shitfaced," he says, and points
to his face. "Just so you know the difference. This is five or six drinks. That night I
had one, and I'd eaten first. Maybe I was
going too fast — OK. Five miles over the
speed limit. Don't tell me you've never
driven five miles over the speed limit. No,
no, not you. You're the Holy Ghost. You
want to know why you've never killed
anyone? Luck. Dumb luck."

Bernice's face curdles. "So I'm supposed
to consider you the poor, sad unfortunate?
It sounds like you've absolved yourself of all
responsibility."

"You think I'd be here if I'd absolff . . ."
The word resists articulation. "Ab*solved*
myself?"

"So why do you feel responsible if it was
only bad luck?"

"Good question. Excellent question. *She*
was the one riding her bike in the middle of
the road. Didn't you ever tell her not to ride

374

her bike in the middle of the road? What's the first thing a parent tells a kid when she gets on a bike?"

Anguish spreads across Bernice's face. She releases her grip on the lamp and rests her hand on the edge of the piano to support her weight as she lists to one side.

"It was windy," he tells her in a consolatory tone. "Gusty. Blowing everything all over the place."

"Maybe she shouldn't have been riding at all," Bernice says.

Jasper shrugs. "It's not your fault. I was shooting my mouth off. What I really wanted to talk about is, I thought you might let me in on" — Jasper taps his hand on his chest — "who got it. Your daughter's heart."

Bernice looks mystified and appalled. She doesn't seem able to speak.

"I'm looking for some good news," Jasper says.

"You want some of the credit," says Bernice, her voice leaching disgust.

"Negative," Jasper says.

"And yet you claim it was an accident."

"It was."

Bernice laughs scornfully. "Then you can't take credit."

"I just want to meet her."

"Meet her? As if Janet" — she cuts herself

375

short, continues more cautiously. "What makes you think this person wants to meet you?"

Stunned, thrilled, Jasper stares at the space just to the side of Bernice's head.

She mistakes his unresponsiveness as incomprehension. "This person *wanted* to get in touch with us. Obviously she felt there would be beneficial aspects. Why would she want to get in touch with you? What good would it do her?"

As it happens, Jasper has considered this question at length, in more lucid moments. Obviously this woman, Janet, the recipient of the heart, can't be desperate to thank him. To openly show him gratitude for conveniently dispatching with an organ donor would be disrespectful. On the other hand that gratitude must exist. Secretly. It won't be easy to tap. No one wants to embrace a killer. It must be essential for this woman's peace of mind to protect the belief that she profited from the kind of random death that happens hundreds of times a day, and to keep that death distant and sterile. Jasper threatens to bring the death close, show her how ugly it was. He understands why Alex and Bernice want to shield her from him, really. On the other hand what they're all really doing is pretending. Pretending it was clean and tidy.

But he couldn't possibly explain all this now. "Look, I'm not the victim of all this, but I am *a* victim. You can lose your life without dying."

Bernice looks momentarily stunned, as though he's struck a nerve. "Welcome to the club."

"Thanks," Jasper says, and feels suddenly dizzy and unsteady. "I've been waiting to hear a thing like that. Now, a member of the club, members of the club —" He loses his balance and tips to one side, reaches out blindly and palms the shade of a Tiffany table lamp. His weight knocks the lamp over but he catches it. Righting it seems complicated, so he just lays it down. "It's OK," he assures Bernice. "So. Anyway. Don't members of the club have certain privileges? As far as access to certain luminaries?"

Bernice's torso cranes toward him. "Get out. Get out or I'll scream my bloody head off."

Jasper is fed up with being told to get out. He lunges toward Bernice. "Tell me who it is! I'm tired of fucking around!"

Bernice backs against a wall and holds her hands out protectively in front of her. After evaluating her situation for a second she says, "Janet. Janet Corcoran. She lives in

Chicago. There. Is that enough?"

Jasper catches his breath, tells himself not to get greedy. Even through his fog of drunkenness he has a feeling he's pressed too far. "It is. Thank you."

He picks up his guitar and stumbles out the door.

He hasn't been home for more than a few minutes — just enough time to set down his guitar, grab a beer from the fridge, and write the words "Janet Corcoran, Chicago" on a piece of paper — when there's a knock on the door. Through the window Jasper sees a tall, wiry man with short brown hair. He's wearing a dark blue uniform. Jasper glimpses the shield-shaped patch on his sleeve. A police officer. Jasper tries to sober himself and opens the door.

The officer steps forward into the doorway. "Jasper Klass?"

Jasper sees a second police officer standing behind the first one.

"Are you Jasper Klass?" the first officer asks.

"Are you coming in here? You need a warrant."

The first officer rolls his eyes as though Jasper is being needlessly dramatic. "Were you just over on Clark Street at Bernice

Howard's house?"

"We were just talking," Jasper says. "We were having a conversation. We know each other."

"OK, let's go." The officer detaches a pair of handcuffs from his belt, takes hold of Jasper's shoulder, turns his body around, and fastens the cuffs to Jasper's wrists. The metal bites into his bone. Jasper says, "Hey — what the . . . *hell?*" The second officer grabs Jasper's other shoulder and says, "You have the right to remain silent." He's so close, Jasper can smell his breath, which is fresh, minty, like Listerine. "Anything you say can and will be used against you in a court of law."

"What am I being arrested for?" Jasper asks. "What am I charged with?"

"Aren't you listening?" the second officer chides him. "Anything you *say* can and will be used against you."

The first officer, escorting Jasper out the door, says, "Criminal trespassing, simple assault, public intox, and anything else I can think of."

"I want a lawyer," Jasper says.

"Smart move," says the officer.

Alex is awakened from the beginnings of sleep by his ringing phone. He picks up.

"Hello?"

"Jasper just came to my house and threatened me." Bernice's voice is agitated and breathless.

"What?"

"Jasper. He came to my house and barged in and threatened me. I was so scared, Alex."

"Jesus. Are you OK? I'm coming over."

"I'm fine. The police officers just left. They're going to go find Jasper and arrest him."

"Good. I'm still coming over. Give me five minutes."

They continue the conversation in Bernice's living room. She's angry and distraught; she sits on the piano bench drinking ice water and staring. Alex spends a long time assuring himself that Bernice is OK, that Jasper didn't hurt her.

"Why did you keep this to yourself?" Bernice asks. "That Jasper knew about the heart?"

"I didn't want to upset you."

Bernice laughs. "Well, I have to tell you, it was more upsetting to have him show up at my door drunk at eleven thirty at night and shove his way in and demand that I tell him where my daughter's heart was."

"I couldn't think of a good reason why you needed to know — a reason that would outweigh the anxiety knowing would cause you. Also, I was hoping he'd just forget about it or get distracted by something else."

"Well, he hasn't forgotten about it."

Alex is furious at Jasper — furious enough to hit him again, this time harder, and with a warning attached: stay away from Bernice. He feels negligent, as though he's failed to protect her, endangered her by failing to foresee and prevent this.

"So when did you find out he knew?" Bernice asks. "How did *he* find out?"

"He overheard us in the waiting room. Talking. About Isabel donating her organs. That's what he says, anyway."

Bernice is quiet a moment. "I don't remember talking to anyone in the waiting room. Not about that. Who was I talking to? You?"

"It must have been. Who else was there?"

"Who else would I have been discussing a subject like that with?"

Alex bristles defensively. Is she implying that it's his fault for participating in a discussion that happened to be overheard? "Look, it doesn't matter how he heard about it. He heard about it. He knows. But he doesn't know who Janet is, or where she is."

"Actually, he does," Bernice says. "I told

him. I thought he might hurt me. It was like being mugged. I just handed over my wallet."

"It's OK," Alex says. "You did the right thing."

"It's *not* OK," Bernice says. "It's not right that he should know. You know what he plans to do? Find Janet."

"I wonder how she'd react to that."

"She'd tell him she didn't want any contact with him. Out of respect for us."

"You sound pretty sure of yourself."

"What? You think she'd fling her arms open to this guy?"

Alex tries to think how to make his point without coming across as cynical, which he is, or disrespectful to Isabel, which he's not. "It's not like Jasper did anything to hurt Janet. Exactly the opposite. Let's face it, if it weren't for Jasper, she'd be dead."

"If it weren't for Isabel. She'd be dead if it weren't for *Isabel.*"

"Right. But from Jasper's perspective, he set the whole thing in motion. And if Janet wants to be fair . . ."

"Isabel set the whole thing in motion. By signing her donor card."

Alex decides to stop arguing. He takes Bernice's empty water glass and goes into the kitchen and refills it.

"And by the way," Bernice says when he comes back, "since I'm guessing you're not going to ask me whether I've heard anything about how Janet's doing, I'll tell you. I have. She's still in the hospital. She's still fighting the rejection episode."

"I'm sorry to hear that. I hope she gets better."

Bernice's silence oozes disapproval. "You know, maybe I should call Jasper and tell *him* Janet's in the hospital. I'd probably get a more concerned reaction."

"You'd get a conversation with a maniac, is what you'd get. Look, even if he does know who Janet is, she's not at home. Maybe he won't be able to track her down in the hospital."

Bernice gazes at him as though his logic is skewed. "Why do you even care?"

"What?"

"Do you honestly care if Jasper finds Janet? Tracks her down? Talks to her? Maybe even has some kind of relationship with her?"

"Sure. Sure I do."

"I believe you. Now tell me why. Tell me why it matters to you."

Alex sees her trick, her clever rhetorical checkmate. "Good question."

TWENTY-FIVE

The plush, elegantly furnished offices of Blanck, Kowal & McVeigh have become an antidote to, and sanctuary from, the hardships and gloom of David's personal life. At some point over the past year, coming into the office surpassed going home as David's favorite time of day. He throws himself into his work. He actually thinks, as he shuffles papers and reads documents, *I am throwing myself into my work.* His current cases include defending a Chicago couple charged by an Alabama prosecutor with transmitting obscene sexual images through the phone lines, which were downloaded by a federal inspector in Birmingham — issues of jurisdiction are at stake — and defending an on-line bulletin-board operator in Winnetka accused of distributing copyrighted software.

David is proud to be an associate at one of the first firms in the country to focus on information technology law. He enjoys the chaotic, uncharted territory of e-commerce — software protection, content licensing, electronic data exchange, network and data security — a field where often the only law is an absence of law. He and his fellow attorneys are making the law as they go along. They're *creating* law, in collaboration with the courts. It's a tremendous opportunity — and a tremendous responsibility.

David's close to making partner. Another year or two, if he puts in the time and effort. If he doesn't get bogged down in his personal life.

Unfortunately his personal life *is* a bog — a sticky quagmire that started pooling around his ankles on the day Janet was diagnosed with dilated cardiomyopathy — one in which he feels increasingly submerged. He believed the new heart would be the solution, the miracle cure, the hand that would reach down and pull them out of the muck. It was certainly billed that way. David does vaguely recall several physicians cautioning that life with a transplanted heart would be just as difficult for Janet, if not difficult in the same way, as life with a diseased heart, but it was hard for David to believe them; it was as if they were trying to convince him that life with a million dollars in the bank would be just as difficult, if not difficult in the same way, as life with a thousand dollars. He became secretly convinced that the new heart would restore Janet to health, restore their marriage to health, restore their life.

Things haven't worked out that way. Janet is still sick. True, she's not as sick as she used to be, but for him, and for her, living with the new heart requires just as much effort and causes just as much anxiety as living with the old one. Life is an unrelenting succession of clinic appointments, late-night emergency room visits, hospitalizations, biopsies. Infections — respiratory, sinus, strep — strike continually. Even when Janet's not sick, she's sick — with nausea and headaches and tremors, side effects of her medications. David's married to a woman who rarely feels good for more than a few hours at a time. She is susceptible to sudden, debilitating exhaustion. Her menstrual periods are frequent and unpredictable, and can cause profuse bleeding. She has wild, roller-coaster mood swings; she feels elated one moment and despondent the next. She invests an enormous amount of effort into convincing her family and friends and coworkers that she is undaunted, courageous, normal — able to do everything that healthy people do — but then persecutes those same people when they fail to understand how difficult and miserable her life is. This terrified, envious, fulminating Janet confides freely in him, but he doesn't feel free to confide in her. He doesn't want to compound her fear with his own, so he conceals it. Also, he doesn't feel entitled to his fear. How can he, when he's comparatively healthy — a fact Janet is always happy to remind him of? In the future, in addition to the usual illnesses and infections, she faces the very real possibilities of cancer, kidney failure, diabetes, and vasculopathy — a coronary artery disease that inevitably develops in transplanted hearts. And, finally, death. True, she might not die for five or ten years. She could also die tomorrow. The way Janet looks at it, she's been given a reprieve. While David understands this, and feels happy for her, he's filled with dread at the prospect of having to live through the past three years, the worst years of his life, all over again when she declines.

Is she declining now? Is this the beginning of the end? Dr. Maslowcya told him last week on the phone that although Janet had been hit hard by the rejection episode, she would probably come through fine and that in the future such episodes would be less likely. David felt a spike of guilt and resentment at the words "hit hard." He's only been to visit Janet twice since she was admitted to the hospital a little over a week ago, and he last talked to her on the phone on Saturday. It's now Tuesday. He's hardly been home. Janet's parents are staying in the apartment, taking care of the kids. Last night, tired of their company, he slept in a nearby studio apartment he had rented recently on the sly — not for illicit purposes, unless you count the need for a refuge illicit. When he's lying there on the single mattress in his tiny, Spartan room, watching television or napping, his cell phone switched off, he feels his anxiety dissipate. He realizes that renting the studio was a step in a certain direction. But the step felt necessary for his health and well-being, and he tries not to analyze it too closely.

As evening approaches, as the hands on his antique desk clock turn past six and start toward seven, David's stomach flutters with dread. He hurries to close up shop. He stacks documents in piles, saves files on his computer, fires off essential e-mails. He's going straight from here to see Janet at the hospital. It's the last thing he wants to do, but his increasing detachment from the family requires some explanation.

He packs up his bag and turns off his lights and walks down the hallway to the elevators. He stops in to say good night to a young attorney who's helping him with the Winnetka case — a twenty-eight-year-old Yale grad who is brilliant and energetic and, it can't be avoided, attractive, though it's the pleasure of her company David enjoys, the easy conversations. The other day she asked if he wanted to play squash. He wanted to accept but didn't, feeling that he would be crossing a line, getting sporty with a female subordinate while his wife was in the hospital.

The revolving doors spill him onto the street into boisterous downtown, where crowds of people stride through the balmy air toward trains and buses and taxis and cars that will deliver them safely home. David gets his green Subaru Forester out of the garage and heads west in thick traffic. At Parkland-Wilburn he finds a parking spot on the first floor of the garage and crosses to the main entrance. Wasted on David are the efforts of the hospital's architects and interior designers, who borrowed from styles of buildings with more cheerful associations — hotels, museums, airport terminals — to disguise and distract from this structure's implicit menace. *You're not fooling me,* David thinks as he walks past the illuminated fountain into the bright lobby with its creamy walls and saccharine artwork, its berry-colored carpeting, the sparkling gift shop, the rows of purple armchairs flanked by tall, robust plants. Ever since he started coming here with Janet nearly three years ago this place has become an affliction all its own, whose symptoms David feels the moment he walks in: anxiety, inexplicable fatigue, stomach knots, a tightness high in the chest.

He takes the elevator to the fourth floor and walks past the atrium, the mirror-walled funhouse around which people gather to stare at reflections of themselves and of others. He turns into Medical Cardiology and immediately gets a chipper, "Well, hello there!" from a familiar nurse, who waves to him with a clear plastic package in which he glimpses a coiled, invasive-looking device. David, feeling incriminated, nods sheepishly. He walks past an old guy whose cough sounds like a flushing toilet. In one room a seventy-something woman sits on the edge of her bed, head hung limp, veiny milk-white legs dangling just short of the floor. She appears to be deep in thought, she's rocking one foot back and forth as though swishing her toes in a warm, shallow tub, until David realizes the poor woman can't get up, she can't get that foot to the floor. Just then an elderly man appears from behind a curtain and helps the woman to her feet. He's one of the caretakers, one of the dutiful, tireless, infinitely patient husbands who accompany their sick wives on endless clinic visits, spend hours leafing through magazines in waiting rooms, keep long vigils at the bedside — who dedicate themselves to serving their sick wives as thoroughly as monks dedicate themselves to serving God. *Hats off to you,* David thinks. He means it sincerely. These are no ordinary men. He should know: he's not one of them.

Janet is sitting up in bed sipping water from a paper cup through a straw, her hair massed against two stacked pillows. He's always thought she had extraordinary hair: red, ringleted, luxuriant — an Irish princess's mane. An equally red eyebrow lifts curiously as he enters. Her cheeks are gray: it's as though her skin is slowly turning to clay. Her body is stuffed waist-deep in sheets. She lowers the paper cup slowly to her lap, and though her eyes are exploring his face he can see that her attention is focused solely on guiding her arm through its uncertain descent.

"Well, well. What's your name again?" she asks.

He wants to kiss her, touch her, lift her out of that bed and untangle her from her IV lines and carry her away. At the same time he wishes he were on the other side of the universe, or in a different universe where he's never met or known her — never formed this terrible, painful attachment to a creature so precious and perishable.

"How are you?" he asks.

"OK. You?"

He exhales dramatically. "Busy."

"Thanks for taking time out from your busy schedule."

David positions his body near the window and stares out at a sheer concrete-and-glass face.

Janet asks, "Anything interesting out there?"

"It's a terrible view. Could they switch you? Give you a different room?"

"Is that why you're here? To make sure I have a nice *view?*"

"I just thought I'd ask."

Janet lifts the plastic cup from her lap, extends her arm, and brings her cup to a shaky landing on the bedside table. She retracts her arm, carefully trailing her IV, which David can't help thinking of as an actual vein hanging out of her skin. She burrows her hand down into the sheets and up under her gown, which rides her wrist and exposes her abdomen, the scar from her C section, and above that, ascending between her breasts, the larger scar from her transplant. *Life is carving her up,* David thinks.

"Can you do something for me?" she asks, her arm jammed up under her gown at a freakish angle. She's trying to scratch an itch she can't reach. She directs him to a tube of hydrocortisone, then to a blotchy rash just below her collarbone. He smears cream over it, trying to constrict his field of vision so it won't include the staple-sized incision on her neck, or the white silicone tube emerging from the incision just below her right bicep. The clear plastic Tegaderm covering this incision is finely wrinkled like the skin of an old woman. What an appetite he once had for this big white dinosaur bone of a body, this formerly magnificent expanse of flesh — he wanted to rain down on it with every nerve. The sex came first, gave birth to everything else, and was always the easiest, most reliable part of their relationship, a common tongue when all other languages broke down. Unfortunately they haven't spoken it for ages.

He finishes rubbing cream on her rash

and, finding her face beautiful for a moment, close to his hand, brushes her lightly on the cheek.

"Where have you been?" she asks with exasperation and concern. "Mom told me you didn't come home last night."

"I slept at the office."

Janet scrutinizes him. "On your couch? That must have been comfortable."

"Surprisingly peaceful."

"Are you planning to do that often?"

"When I need to."

Janet glares at him. "You got all over me for not consulting you about tracking down Alex and Bernice, for not getting your official go-ahead, but you never consulted me about joining the gym, let alone spending three evenings a week there, or taking your class — you just signed up and went. And now you're spending nights away from home without telling me. What's next? All-night raves? Trips to the Caribbean?"

"Boy, that sounds nice," David says.

"You also didn't tell me you were going to get in touch with a Realtor. I know about that. She called one day when you were out. I guess you thought you could just plan the family future on your own."

"That was about something different," David says. That Realtor had screwed up —

she wasn't supposed to call him at home. He switched to a second Realtor, who found him the studio downtown.

"What 'different'?" Janet asks. "David, what's going on? You've never spent a night away from home without calling me."

"It was eleven o'clock. I didn't want to wake you up."

"So you woke my mother up?"

"She *was* up. Reading Sam a story."

"Because he couldn't sleep, probably. Because he can't figure out where his parents are. *You* should have been there reading to him, David."

"Don't accuse me of neglect. You're hardly coming through for them."

"I'm *sick*."

"I'm unhappy."

Janet gathers a clump of sheets in one hand and massages it like the scruff of a puppy's neck. Her eyes are thoughtful and full of fear. "I know."

"I can't go on like this. Living with you and your illness. I admit it, I'm not up to the challenge. I don't measure up."

"Yes you do," Janet says unconvincingly.

David's known for some time that he falls short in her estimation as well as his own. "Thanks. But I don't."

"You could if you tried harder."

"I'm tired of trying."

Hurt, flustered, Janet collapses her head back against the pillows, rolls it to one side, and stares at the door as though waiting for someone — an earlier, more committed version of her husband, maybe — to come through it.

David says, "I want a different life."

"I get the picture," Janet snaps.

I have a choice. You don't. You're trapped. I'm not. But it's too ruthless for David to say. He tells her, "You're different. Different than you used to be."

"Of course I am. I went through a huge ordeal, a major transformation. How could I not come out different? I nearly died. I nearly die every couple of months. I need to be different to survive."

"I understand that. You're tougher, stronger, more focused and driven. You're also less sensitive to the feelings and needs of people around you. You're more stubborn, too. And inflexible."

"I could make exactly the same claim about you."

David shrugs. "Maybe so."

"I am who I am," Janet says.

"So am I." David draws a deep breath, slowly exhales. "I've rented an apartment downtown. Near my office. Just a studio.

396

I'm going to be spending some time there. I'll probably go by the apartment in the next few days to pick up some of my things."

"What are you saying? Are you saying you're leaving me?"

"No," he answers, though to be accurate he should say *I'm not sure,* or *I think I may be, yes.* "I'm saying what I just said. I rented a place. I'm going to spend some time there. That's all for now."

Janet's face turns pink, and her eyes well up. She lifts the hem of her sheet with both hands and presses it to her face, drying and concealing herself. Then she thrusts both hands palms-out in front of her as if to block an attacker. Her eyes are clenched shut, her mouth twitching at a corner. "I can't have this conversation right now. I'm in this fucking hospital suffering from a *rejection* episode, David. I need support. I need consolation."

She coughs a wet, sloppy cough. He doesn't know what she expects from him. He's lost his capacity for cheerfulness and optimism, she depresses him so thoroughly. For years she could recharge his confidence and assurance just by talking with him, by being in the same room with him, but now she makes him feel fragile and endangered.

"I'm sorry," David says. "I'll go."

Janet looks surprised, as if this wasn't the response she expected. "What are we going to tell Sam and Carly?"

"For the time being? That I have to spend some extra time at work. For a big project. I'll go by tomorrow and see them. I'll take them out to dinner."

Something about this prospect makes Janet wistful. "I miss you, David."

Her face is full of longing and need and he can feel it exerting a gravitational pull on his chest.

"I miss you," David says, thinking of the woman she used to be, the old, healthy Janet, the person who couldn't be saved.

TWENTY-SIX

The afternoon before Alex and Kelly plan to leave for Colorado, Alex is at work grading an essay about an epileptic mother who sleep-fugued into a busy street and got hit by a car, when Diane appears at his side looking weary and officious. "Can I see you in my office for a minute?" she asks.

He follows her down the aisle between the rows of tables. She ushers him into a small, airless, windowless room — a sensory-deprivation chamber masquerading as an office. The surfaces and walls are bare of decorative flourishes: no framed art, no family pictures, no knickknacks or doodads or toys. Clearly Diane doesn't expect to be here long. Alex sits without asking in a stiff armless chair facing Diane's desk. On the desk is a single, half-inch-high stack of essays. Diane sits down and gives Alex a perfunctory smile — a flinch, really — before beginning to leaf through the essays, preparing her speech.

Alex asks, "Are all those mine?"

"Every single one."

"Jeez, I've really been going at it."

Another smile, this time genuinely amused. Diane gives the stack of essays an exasperated shove out into the middle of the desk and tips back in her chair. She studies him, curious. "What *have* you been going at?"

"Excuse me?"

"When you first started here your scores were consistently low, and now they're consistently high. We're talking about *very* elevated scores, Alex. You gave every one of these essays a six, and the panel gave every one of them a four or below. Most of them are ones and twos. We can't tolerate this kind of disparity. Now, you tell me. Is this a case of overcorrection? Your profile's still unbalanced, it's just top-heavy instead of bottom-heavy."

Alex should have expected this. For several weeks now they've been working on a new shipment of essays from Arkansas in which the writers have been asked to describe a significant event in their lives. Alex doesn't mind the upbeat significant events — the vacations and school trips and athletic triumphs, the awards and prizes, births of younger siblings. The problem is that so many of the significant events involve accidents and illness and death. The writers describe strokes, heart attacks, cancer, surgeries, prolonged hospitalizations, bedside vigils, funerals. Alex found it impossible to grade these essays. How could you fault a little girl whose father had recently died of ALS for having no apparent control over sentence structure and word choice? For weeks after Isabel died, Alex could barely speak. He started giving the little Arkansans fives and sixes. He thought of these kids as his little brothers and sisters in the great big family of the wronged. It was his duty to protect them from the oblivious brutality of the blessed, no matter how poor their syntax was.

"I guess there's been some correction going on, sure," he tells Diane. "It's tricky, with this new shipment. Are other graders giving higher scores?"

"We saw a spike with Arkansas, yes. Our responses to these essays can be very intense and emotional and sympathetic. But most of our grader profiles adjusted after a few days. Yours didn't."

"Some of these kids, Diane, they've had such awful things happen to them."

"I know. But we're not evaluating their

personal lives. It's our duty to evaluate their writing, to evaluate it objectively, and give them the scores they deserve, even if it means giving them a low score."

"I can't do that."

"Can't . . . ?"

"I can't give these kids low scores. I can't score them low. Not the ones who've been badly hurt already."

Diane, sensing his sincerity, brings her chair up close to the desk and leans an elbow on it, props her cheek on her fist — guard down, thoughtful. "I think you could be a good grader, Alex. We need good people. Smart people. I think if you tried to read the harder essays and just put the writer's personal pain aside and focused on the writing, you'd adjust, you'd acquire a perfectly acceptable profile. We have a lot of work coming up. There's a shipment due from Nevada in October that's going to keep us busy through February."

Alex lets out a sigh, mostly to buy time. He's not strong enough to put any twelve-year-old writer's pain aside; he's not even sure it's right to do so. The whole *point* of the writing is to communicate the pain. These kids, weren't they writing under the premise that they were going to make themselves — their situations, their suffering — understood to someone? No one told them, *Don't bother putting all your personal shit in there, you're just being graded on how well you manipulate the language.*

"I'm going to take the rest of the afternoon off," Alex says. "Get an early start on my vacation."

Diane leans back in her chair, palms flat on the desk sliding back with her, the soft uncertainty in her face suggesting it's a reasonable request that unfortunately can't be granted. "We've got a lot of work out there. I know you're going to be away for the next two weeks, and we're going to accommodate that, but I can't encourage you to leave early today."

"You don't have to encourage me," Alex says cheerfully, rising from his chair, having reached that precipitous workplace moment where one thinks, *Anything but this.* "And I won't be coming back. Ever. Accommodate that."

He gets home earlier than usual and catches Otto napping on the couch, sprawled on his side across the cushions. The dog lifts his head in surprise, one ear turned inside-out, eyes coming sluggishly to. "Ready for Colorado, pal?" he asks Otto, petting him on the head. He and Kelly did some research, and the trail they plan on hiking to Kelly's meadow is low to moderate difficulty, and pets are allowed if leashed. So Otto's going. Alex has been making sure to take him on daily walks, and increasing the length of the walks, to get both himself and the dog in shape.

Alex surveys the camping gear he's been laying out haphazardly on the floor all week: clothes, rain gear, boots, tent, cookware, utility knife, weather radio, assorted tools and doodads. He needs to pick up a first-aid kit and insect repellant. There's a message on the answering machine from Kelly reminding him that they need to run errands tonight. "I was thinking we could go to Fin and Feather or Syler's and find you a sleeping bag if you're still up for the purchase. I'll stop by when I get off work. Hey, maybe we could get one of those two-person sleeping bags? That'll get us through the cold mountain nights. Hmmm . . . I don't know. Two-person bag. That's a big commitment. I'm not sure I'm ready."

Her voice is peppy and flirtatious. She's excited for this trip — "pumped" is the word she uses. She's researched the trail; she's made a list of necessary gear, assembled what they own, and borrowed the rest; she's written out a rough menu and divided the food they need to purchase into items they can buy here, in town, cheaply, and items they can wait and buy in Colorado; she's taken her car in for a tune-up and trip check. Alex has done little except marvel at and feel grateful for her enthusiasm and hard work. Especially her motivation. He would never have thought to take such a trip, or proceeded so far with the planning, unless Kelly had suggested it. Apparently he was sunk so deep in the rut of his circumstances that he had lost his sense of the possible, his awareness that up there, just over the lip of the trench, was the world — a world into which he could venture, and which would reward him enormously if only he could muster the energy and will to lift himself out. Kelly, standing above on two firm legs, reached down with her hand.

Alex goes into the kitchen and gets a beer and plops down on the couch next to Otto. On the coffee table is a short note he received from Janet Corcoran a few days ago. The plain white envelope, creased and smudged, looks like it was handled by at least ten different mail carriers. The unadorned paper and Janet's muscular black ink give the impression of indisputable seriousness.

Dear Alex,

I'm sorry if our phone conversation upset you or rubbed you the wrong way. Maybe I shouldn't have called. I just thought that if I could talk to you it would help you understand what I've gone through over the past few years and what I'm thinking and feeling now and most importantly that I'm not a selfish un-empathetic predator.

I think we got off to a bad start. Don't you?

Yours,
Janet
312 221 4359

Alex feels there's something arrogant about her use of the word "start" — something that presumes a future acquaintance. Does she imagine it possible, given the circumstances, that they could have gotten off to a *good* start?

He wonders when she wrote the card, and determines from the postmark that she must have written and mailed it after they spoke on the phone but before she went into the hospital. Why has it taken so long to reach him? He wonders if Janet's still in the hospital. He hasn't talked to Bernice since

Tuesday, the day after Jasper forced his way into her house.

He goes into the kitchen and gets another beer and returns to the couch. He thinks about going over to Kelly's to see if she wants to leave right now, right away, run their errands and get on the road. They could be across Nebraska by morning. But he's not packed, and Kelly doesn't get off work till seven. It's only four.

He sips his beer, lies down on the couch with Otto. He closes his eyes, pictures highway stretching out in front of him, the majestic ascent into the west: plateau after plateau, hills and rocks and finally mountains bursting out of the plain.

He's startled awake by an alarm clock going off in a momentarily unfamiliar room. It's his room. His life. The phone. He's too groggy to beat the machine.

"Hi Alex, it's me. Bernice. Call me when you get this message. Please. It's important. Bye."

Alex is getting sick of these urgent, breaking-news phone calls and wonders whether there's been some new development with Janet, or maybe with Jasper.

"What's up?" he asks when he reaches Bernice.

"It's Janet. I just spoke with Lotta. She's

not doing so well."

"Lotta or Janet?" Alex is purposefully obtuse.

"Janet." Bernice explains that, according to Lotta, who just called her, Janet's rejection episode has been more intractable than anyone expected. Her doctors are giving her an extra course of IV medications and thinking about moving her to intensive care. There's also something going on with her husband. Lotta was evasive and mysterious, but the gist was that he'd moved out. Lotta used the word "bailed." "I didn't even know they were having trouble," Bernice says. "I don't think Lotta did either. Of course when you're having trouble like that, you don't call up your parents right away and tell them. Usually. *I* didn't. You try to hide it as long as you can."

Alex absorbs this news with annoyance and impatience as well as stirrings of sympathy and satisfaction, that Janet may get a chance to see what it's like, losing a spouse. "Wow. That's awful."

"No kidding. Awful that she has to go through all this at the same time. She must be miserable. I know it's silly, but I worry about Isabel's heart. It must be under so much strain. Not only from the rejection episode but from the anxiety. If her family's coming apart."

Alex wonders if Bernice realizes how much strain she's putting him under. "Yeah, well, you and I both know about families coming apart and divorce and losing spouses and all that stuff, and you get through it. I'm sure Janet's doctors will get her fixed up and back home."

"What makes you sure? I'm not sure."

"You've been pessimistic about this from the beginning."

"I have not," Bernice says, insulted. "I've just been concerned. If you were at all invested you'd be concerned too. You *are* invested, of course. You just don't realize."

"It must be nice for you to have this trumped-up crisis to use as leverage."

"Is that what you call this? A 'trumped-up crisis'? You think I'm crying wolf? You think *Lotta's* crying wolf?"

"OK, I don't want to have this conversation right now."

"Right now is when we're having it." There's a tense, preparatory silence. "I'm driving up to Chicago in the morning," Bernice says. "I've decided. That heart began life the size of a poppy seed in my uterus. It pumped for thirty-eight weeks inside my own body. I can't just sit here."

"So don't."

In the silence Alex senses Bernice waiting for some apologetic elaboration or qualification. She releases a breath that seems to contain months of accumulated frustration with his intractability. "I'd like you to come. It would mean a lot to me. And to Janet."

It has the ring of a final appeal, her ominous tone flashing a threat of dishonor.

"I'm driving to Colorado in the morning," Alex says. "You know that."

"I do. Don't you think this is more important?"

"Going to Colorado is important. For me."

"How so? To run away?"

"I'm not running away. I'm taking a vacation with my girlfriend. I'm trying to have a life. I'm trying not to get bogged down in the past. Why do you have a problem with that? If you want to see Janet, go see Janet. If you think Isabel opened a door for you, walk through it. Get religion. Believe what you want to believe."

"I think this transcends personal choice, Alex. It's a matter of duty."

"I have a duty to myself."

"What about Isabel? I think Isabel would have wanted us to go."

"Don't use Isabel against me. Isabel would have wanted me to be happy. To get

410

on with things. It's been over a year. I can assure you she didn't donate her organs so I could be permanently obsessed with worry over the health of all the people who received them. What's next? Are we going to go find the people who got Isabel's kidneys and liver? Her lungs and skin and corneas and pancreas? Make sure they're all OK? Make sure they're not in intensive care? Those organs all grew inside your body too. Hey, I have an idea. Why don't we go skipping all over the planet and put her back together again?"

If Alex's intent was to decimate Bernice, he appears to have succeeded. The silence on her end of the line feels fathomless and absolute, as though he's listening to the sound of deep space. Finally she asks, "Shall I give Janet your regards?"

"Of course. Please."

A pause, as though to give him the opportunity to reconsider, to change his mind. "See you in a few days. A week — whatever. Happy camping."

"Drive safely."

He waits for the "You too," but it doesn't come. Instead that messy stutter-clack of the receiver dropped carelessly, perhaps spitefully, into its cradle. Then a dial tone.

■ ■ ■ ■

Deep in the multifloor, mazelike interior of Syler's Sports, Alex and Kelly stand in front of two dozen sleeping bags hanging side by side, head ends down, like human-sized cocoons. North Face, Kelty, Marmot, Sierra Designs. Kelly, excited by the imminence of a major purchase, moves from bag to bag, reading labels assiduously, pinching pillow-lets of down between her fingers, stroking linings, tugging zippers, carrying on a continuous murmuring dialogue in which she compares qualities and attributes of the different bags. "OK, this one's three-season, down filled, rated to fifteen degrees, water-proof, lightweight, *check,* but I don't see anything about ripstop nylon. Do you care about ripstop nylon? Alex?"

"Hmm?" He's floated over to a glass case full of orienteering compasses. "Ahh . . . yeah. That might be good."

"Well, this one doesn't say anything about ripstop nylon," Kelly says, dropping the tag and moving on.

Alex gazes at the compasses superimposed over topographical maps and wishes one of them could tell him which way to go, wishes a needle would swing over a map of Iowa and point defiantly west. His phone call with Bernice left him wracked with self-doubt. He has to admit, she got to him, made him feel that by going to Colorado he would be neglecting her, neglecting Isabel. On the way out to Syler's, bouncing west along the interstate in Kelly's car, Alex stared out the window at the sun burning low and red in the sky, lights coming on in the colonies of duplexes crowding the highway. The world — or maybe it was just him — felt sad and desolate. He could recall driving this very patch of interstate with Isabel, going out to the mall to shop or see a movie or to their favorite pancake house, and he was sure he had been happier then than he ever would be again. So what was the point?

By the time he walked into Syler's, he was missing Isabel acutely — more than he had in a long time. Assaulted by the glare of the bright lights, he felt himself regressing, slipping back over an invisible border into that region of intense grief and helpless attachment he hoped he'd escaped, and the fear of which had made him determined to avoid Janet. Bernice was right: he *was* detached. But wasn't the goal to detach? Didn't one have to detach to survive? Bernice ought to let him, if he's ready. Maybe she should work on being more detached herself. Maybe she'd be happier.

He and Kelly decide on a sleeping bag, a three-season Marmot she's thrilled he'll get for twenty percent off, and after picking up a few other supplies — a first-aid kit, a fire starter, insect repellant, sunscreen — they head home. It's just after nine, and Alex is relieved, looking out over the land from the highway, to see that the mellow colors and hazy textures of twilight have been replaced by unsentimental dark. Returning through town, the streets thick with Friday-night traffic, the sidewalks busy with people, lighted signs, and interiors of crowded restaurants and bars and coffee shops — the entire scene, oblivious to Isabel's absence, makes him want to reanimate her, seat her in the window of the coffee shop with her botany books and her laptop, her café au lait and her almond biscotti.

"Are you going to be this quiet all the way to Colorado?" Kelly asks. "I don't think I can take it. I'll fall asleep at the wheel."

"I'm just tired."

"Rough day with the kids? Too many significant life events?"

He hasn't told her yet that he quit his job. "Way too many."

"Relax. By this time tomorrow, we'll be in

tucking them into an open suitcase. He imagines her driving to Chicago alone, the radio on for company (talk, not classical), adding up the numbers on license plates to pass the time, and to distract herself from what she's driving toward.

Alex glances over at the couch and sees Isabel lying there ashen-skinned with her head resting on a pillow and a blanket covering her body as she used to whenever she had a bad cold or the flu. She says to him, *My heart's under attack.*

Alex lowers his head and massages his temples with his fingertips. It's profoundly disturbing to think that part of Isabel, part of a dead person, still exists to be injured and hurt.

In sickness and in health. Till death do us part.

When Kelly comes over the next time she finds him like this, sitting cross-legged on the floor, head in his hands.

She kneels beside him but not too close, and she doesn't touch. "Alex. What's wrong?"

He doesn't want Kelly to see his face. His face is a wet clay thing with everybody's fingers in it. His face will tell Kelly he's still in love with someone else.

"Janet's in the hospital," he says.

It takes a moment for Kelly to catch up. "Janet. The woman who got your wife's heart."

"She's sick. She's not doing well. Bernice is driving up there in the morning."

"And you . . . ?"

"I don't think I can go."

Kelly exhales with relief and sympathy. Finally, an explanation for the sullen mood she's been enduring all evening. She rubs his back. "You don't have to go. If you don't want to, you don't have to. Simple as that. Anyway, you have an appointment with the Rockies."

But she misunderstands.

PART IV

July 2006
Twenty-Seven

It's not until the words stumble disorganized out of her mouth — "Yes, hello, good morning. I guess it's afternoon. We're friends of a patient. Not really friends. Acquaintances. She knows we're coming. We'd like to visit her. Janet Corcoran. That's the name. C-O-R-C-O-R-A-N" — and the clerk behind the information desk squints with annoyance . . . it's not until this moment that Bernice understands how nervous she is. She takes a deep breath through her nose, fully inflating her chest, and empties her lungs. Her fingers rest on the edge of the high counter, thumbs tapping in sync. She was fine driving up here in the car — edgy and scattered, but fine — riding the wave of delight that had washed across her when Alex appeared at her door at seven this morning looking sleepless and distraught and told her, "I can't let you go through this alone." His hug nearly crushed her, and she cried with happiness, and with guilt: true, she'd encouraged him to do what she felt was the right thing, but she'd ruined his vacation, she knew, and possibly his relationship with Kelly.

Now as the clerk behind the information desk types on his keyboard and stares into his monitor, Bernice remembers the anguish she felt when she arrived at the hospital on the night of Isabel's death, the immediate and terrifying solicitude with which the clerk at a similar information desk in a similar lobby — a fortyish man with graying hair and sky-blue-tinted glasses — treated her the moment he learned her daughter had been hit by a truck. As if he'd been alerted by a red flashing message on his computer screen: PATIENT IS DOOMED. HANDLE FAMILY WITH CARE.

The clerk at Parkland-Wilburn in Chicago scrawls some arrows on a hospital map and hands the map to Bernice. "Medical Cardiology, Fourth Floor East. Elevator F."

Alex is standing a short distance away beside a tall fronded plant. He's standing so close to the plant that one of the huge curling leaves is practically draped across his shoulder. He appears to be hiding.

"OK. That way," Bernice says, pointing

across the lobby toward a branching corridor.

"Is she here?" Alex sounds surprised.

"Were you hoping she wouldn't be?"

"I don't know what I'm hoping."

There are four lanes in the corridor, but the rules are opposite those of the highway: slow lumberers occupy the middle lanes while those in a rush zip along the outside, skirting the walls. Elevator F turns out to be popular. A dozen people await the opening of the doors. Bernice and Alex wait for the second car and ride up to the fourth floor, which is less crowded. The signage directs Bernice and Alex left. They pass an atrium whose mirrored panels contain their reflections and those of walkers on floors above and below. Opposite the atrium is a large window through which they can see part of the elevated highway that brought them here, and which causes Bernice to think back on what a long distance they've come. Four and a half hours in the car. The monotony of I-80 shooting east through Iowa past corn and soybean fields and across the Mississippi into flat, featureless Illinois. Conversation with Alex was sporadic and strained. Alex, who had finished his coffee somewhere in Eastern Iowa, continually flicked his thumb against the bottom of the cup. "Could you please stop?" Bernice asked. Alex expertly employed the same phrase against her later when he grew tired of her tinkering with the air vents. She hadn't realized she was doing it. It had to be at least ninety degrees out; the sun was beating down on Bernice's chest and lap, and she was sweltering, her armpits moist. The air-conditioning couldn't be working properly; she was dissatisfied with the force and direction of the flow. They decided to crack the windows. They hit traffic. They'd turned north onto I-55, joining the arterial surge toward the city, cars sweeping left and right, inches off one another's trunks and hoods.

Bernice thinks how nice it is to be out of that car. She pauses in front of a large mirrored sign that reads MEDICAL CARDIOLOGY, studies her reflection. She's wearing a white silk shirt, Isabel's jade cabochon around her neck. A matching pair of jade earrings. Makeup. Dark chocolate poplin pants, leather slingback sandals. She worries she may have overdressed for the occasion, but she wanted to look respectful and prosperous, not in any way damaged or pitiable. She'd like to find a restroom and clean up a little.

"You look great," Alex tells her. "Seriously.

Anyway, I'm here to make you look good." He gestures downward at his own clothes: gray T-shirt, army green cargo shorts, Birkenstocks that look like they were worn during the Peloponnesian War.

Bernice adjusts her hair, which has picked today of all days to misbehave, and makes sure there's nothing stuck between her teeth. "You're going to freeze. You know that, don't you?"

They turn left off the main corridor into Medical Cardiology. Televisions chatter from hidden corners. Bernice glimpses, through half-open doorways, bodies mummified in sheets, chalk-white heads half-sunk in pillows like heads toppled from Greek statues. Bernice feels as though with every step she takes, gravity gets stronger. She wants to slump against a wall. She slings her arm high around Alex's shoulder and uses him for support. His arm finds its way around her waist. He's eager, and grateful, to use her the same way.

The nurses station is a chest-high, semicircular barricade manned by nurses and doctors and assorted personnel. Bernice and Alex detach and approach. After a moment Bernice realizes she's approaching alone. Looking back, she sees that Alex has stalled.

She goes back to him. "You OK?"

"You sure we want to do this?" His face is pale. Sweat glosses the skin just above his eyes. Bernice can't help feeling relieved that this isn't easy for him, either. She settles her hand high on his back. "Take some deep breaths. We'll be fine."

They make a second run at the nurses station, but en route, Bernice's attention catches on a five- or six-year-old girl wearing a baseball cap, red polo shirt, and blue jeans with animal patches sewn onto the denim. She stands with her back military-inspection straight, arms rigid at her sides, chin slightly upturned, and revolves clockwise tiny step by tiny step. The girl's baseball cap is fitted on top with a bubble-like compass similar to one Bernice's father used to have mounted on the dashboard of his Buick, and as she revolves, the vertical white needle moves from SE to SSE.

Bernice thinks she recognizes the girl from a photograph Janet sent. "Carly? Are you Carly Corcoran?"

The girl looks out curiously from under her cap brim.

Bernice explains who they are. "We're here to visit your mother."

The girl's gaze intensifies. She turns and walks purposefully away, though whether her purpose is to guide her inquisitors or

426

ditch them Bernice isn't sure. Bernice and Alex follow. A corridor leads to an octagonal space that services three patient rooms. The compass-capped girl disappears into one of these rooms, and a few moments later a sturdy, thickset woman emerges, her silver hair cropped short. The woman wears baggy khakis cinched at the waist by a braided leather belt, a blue denim shirt that looks several sizes too big for her. She has a pudgy, kind face. Arctic blue eyes behind tiny, egg-shaped lenses. "Bernice?"

"Lotta?"

"Welcome!" Lotta spreads her arms wide and splays all ten fingers. Bernice moves in for a hug. Alex stands aside as the two women first clasp hands and let out nervous, self-deprecating giggles. They hug firmly but quickly: someone who didn't know better might guess they were two old friends who haven't seen each other for years. Bernice introduces Alex. Lotta extends her hand. Alex shakes it. Lotta tells him, "We're so glad you're here. We were so thrilled to hear you were coming. Did you . . . you found your way OK?"

"Oh, easily," Bernice assures her.

Lotta watches them expectantly, smiling, eyes wide: one of them will surely have more to say. Bernice isn't sure how to fill the silence. Alex is staring into space. They've expended every last drop of energy getting themselves here, presenting themselves, and now they're too drained to think. Bernice is relieved — glad for some stage direction — when Lotta says, "Well, would you like to come in and meet the gang?"

The name *Janet Corcoran* is written in red ink on a dry-erase placard on the door. The room is polygonal, illuminated by ceiling fluorescence, the walls an airy blue. The bed, its thick, cakelike mattress frosted with linens, is backed up to a control panel in the wall outfitted with air-pressure gauges and graduated canisters, buttons and switches and dials. Janet lies in the bed with a white sheet loosely draped over her waist and legs, one knee raised like an Andean peak. Bernice's first thought, which leaves her crestfallen, is that the woman isn't Isabel, isn't her daughter. She never would have admitted that she expected to find Isabel here — alive and in the flesh, lying in a hospital bed — but her disappointment suggests that somehow, on some level, she did.

"The Iowa delegation has arrived!" Lotta announces to her family, ushering Bernice and Alex into the room.

Janet scrambles to sit up, using her foot's purchase against the mattress and her hands planted on either side of her hips to scooch up against the headboard. A large, obelisk-like man who looks too old to be Janet's husband — her father? — slides a pillow out from behind her back and transfers it to her lap. This man asks Alex and Bernice to please wash their hands at the sink by the door, explaining that Janet is extremely vulnerable to infection. Bernice and Alex grapple with a dysfunctional soap dispenser and splash water all over themselves. They turn around to find Janet hugging the pillow to her stomach and soaking them up with big brown eyes, cheeks flushed. "Wow. *Wow.* I'm so glad you came." Her voice is nervous but clear and surprisingly strong. "I can't believe you're actually here. It's amazing."

Alex isn't sure what to do with Janet's effusiveness, as he can hardly match it, and feels instead a contrary urge to dampen her enthusiasm — to let everyone know, right from the start, with a noncommittal shrug and a grimace, that he's wounded and confused, and that what she'd call amazing, he'd call strange.

Bernice appears to feel no such restraint. Already she's approached the bedside, and presses Janet's hand between her palms like some object she's been searching the Earth for. "I can't believe I'm finally meeting you," she says. "Are you OK? Did we come at a bad time?"

"Not at all. We're holding together."

"In the grand family tradition," Lotta adds.

Janet rolls her eyes at her mother's patriotism. "My rejection's under control. That's the main thing. I'm going home tomorrow."

Lotta says, "The cardiological high priests have ascertained its mysterious roots."

"That's wonderful," Bernice says.

Lotta grips the railing of her daughter's bed with both hands and leans in, allowing her elbows to bend slightly. "A man called the day before yesterday from the organ procurement organization in Iowa checking up on her status. It was awful having to tell him Janet was in the hospital. He seemed shocked, which surprised me. Surely they hear about people rejecting once in a while. Or maybe he had a personal interest in the case. I was thinking I should call him back and let him know she's OK."

Alex can't help feeling he and Bernice were misled as to the severity of Janet's condition. He expected to find her weak and sick, barely able to move or speak, fighting off death. On the verge of a move to intensive care. Were he and Bernice lured here by false urgency?

"You must be Alex."

Janet's speaking to him. He doesn't know what to do with her face. The fiery red hair, the abundant freckles, prominent cheekbones, powerful jaw. Her face doesn't make any sense to him, doesn't register or resonate. It's the face of a stranger. It's a face that could have been drawn out of a hat.

"I must be," he says.

Janet aims her voice directly into his unresponsiveness. "You have no idea how much this means to me. You coming here. The two of you. This is huge."

"It was an easy drive," Bernice says, as if it was the distance that had prevented them from coming all along. "We couldn't have asked for better weather. It's a beautiful day. Crazy hot."

All eyes turn to the window, where the only weather is a shaft of sunlight bisecting a concrete wall. Next to the window is a table full of get-well cards, neatly arranged like a flock of birds.

"I'm Bud," says the large man who was arranging Janet's pillows, extending to Alex a thick, hairy, gold-watched arm. "Janet's father. Welcome to Chi-town."

Bud's firm, slightly prolonged grip seems to assure Alex that he's welcome but that his movements, vis-à-vis Janet, will be carefully monitored. Alex wants to tell him, *My wife saved your daughter's ass.*

"Sit, relax, do whatever you want to," Janet blurts, seeming at a loss as to how to proceed. "Make yourselves at home. Dad, can you get some seats? We're terrible hosts."

Bernice accepts a stool from Bud, cheerfully lets him show her how to work the up and down, and draws it up to the bedside near Janet's head. Bernice sets her purse on the floor. Alex declines the offer of a stool, which will position him closer to Janet than he's ready to be.

"What a huge hospital," Bernice muses. "I bet a lot of people get lost."

"I did at first," Janet says. "Not so much anymore."

"She's got the whole labyrinth memorized," Lotta says.

"I was going to say, you must be an expert by now."

"Too expert. I'm here a lot. Coming for clinic visits is OK, but staying overnight gives me the creeps. I worry I'll get stuck, that I'll have to spend four months here again. I don't think I could do it. I'd go nuts."

"Were you here that long? I guess I'd

forgotten."

"December to April."

"Probably not the worst place to spend a Chicago winter."

"True. Plenty of homeless people would have killed for my room. You miss the outside, though. One day a nurse brought me a snowball because I'd mentioned something the day before about wishing I could make one."

"Who'd you throw it at?"

"There are a few doctors I could have thrown it at, I can tell you."

Bernice laughs harder than the quip warrants. Alex can't decide whether he's relieved or disturbed to see how easily she's bantering with Janet. Bernice's natural facility for small talk and the need for human contact have met obliging, reciprocal forces in Lotta and Janet.

"You could have thrown it at Sherman," Lotta says to Janet. "He deserved a good whack in the head. What a crank."

Janet rolls her eyes. "He was a character, that's for sure. He got his heart, though. Finally."

Bernice asks, "Friend of yours?"

"More like competition. But yeah, a kind of friend. Brother-in-arms. We were up here waiting together."

He got his heart. There's something Alex doesn't like about that. As though hearts were common, readily available, not harvested from human bodies. *He got his degree. He got his baccalaureate.*

"Sam, can you say hello to Alex and Bernice?" Janet is speaking to an eight- or nine-year-old boy sitting in a red rocking chair holding an electronic game up to his face and frantically jamming his thumbs into the buttons. "Sam? Do you remember what we talked about?"

Sam doesn't feel inclined to indicate whether he remembers or not, but greets the visitors obediently.

A look between Janet and Lotta debates whether the boy should be pressured to ramp up his congeniality. The decision is to let it go. Alex gets the impression the boy might have some legitimate reason to be uncommunicative. Something to do with his absent father?

"You've already met Carly," Lotta says. "Our advance scout."

"Compass Head," Bernice says. "I ought to get a cap like that. Maybe then I wouldn't get lost so much."

"How can you get lost in Iowa?" Bud asks. "It's just one road, isn't it, going through the cornfield?" He winks.

434

"Not far from the truth," Bernice says.

A silence ensues. Alex knows the conversation might get going if he got involved, but he feels quiet. Janet is staring down the length of her bed at her feet. The expression on her face is tense and resolute but not entirely confident, like that of a gymnast about to launch a difficult routine. It dawns on Alex that she's probably as anxious about meeting them as they are about meeting her.

"I hope you're not worried about me," Janet says, noticing his attentiveness. "I'm fine. Really. I could be so much worse off. I *have* been so much worse off."

"I'm not worried about you," Alex says, and envisions Isabel's body — stripped naked, head shaved, face bruised, lips swollen, eyes syrupy, breathing tube jammed between her teeth — superimposed on Janet's, stretched out in the hospital bed. "You look great. I like your stylish little packets." He nods toward two slim IV bags hanging from Janet's hook. "At least you don't have tons of shit stuck into every conceivable orifice."

"Young ears," Lotta says.

"Janet's not dying," Bernice reminds Alex, picking up on the implicit comparison. "Janet's going home tomorrow."

"I can see she's not dying," Alex says.

435

"She came closer than we'd like," Lotta says.

Is it Alex's imagination, or is Lotta smug? It bothered him, that remark about young ears. He'd like to tell Lotta that if you compare whatever's unpleasant or profane about the word "shit" to whatever's unpleasant or profane about certain gruesome events — let's say, his wife getting hit by a truck — you have to admit the young ears are getting off lucky, not having to hear about the mess that saved their mother.

On the drive here, just before crossing the Mississippi into Illinois, they drove over the remains of a deer that had been killed in traffic. The fan blast of vomit-pink blood rushed them out of nowhere, rode the concrete like a conveyor right up under the car. In the splatter Alex glimpsed a few resilient chunks that had escaped the leveling of tires.

Maybe Lotta would like to hear about that?

Bernice is trying to restart a pleasant, diverting conversation with Janet. Is that IV in her arm the only one she has? What's going into it? Does she like her doctors and nurses? Are they the same doctors and nurses who took care of her while she was waiting for a heart? Alex, bored and bristly, trying to avoid Lotta's eyes, stares up at the monitor over Janet's head, where her vitals are displayed in gold and red and blue digits. The arrangement of these numbers is familiar to Alex from Isabel's bedside, and he's oddly assured to realize he can read them. Janet's blood pressure is 122 over 85. Her oxygen saturation is 98 percent. Her heart rate is playing around in the low nineties. But it's Janet's electrocardiogram that draws and holds his eye — a robust, leaping green waveform that looks like it could bound off the screen and across the city of Chicago if it wanted to.

Alex feels light-headed, a little dizzy. He has yet to confront it. That's *Isabel's* electrocardiogram. That's Isabel's heart rate. Isabel's heart is in this room. How is he supposed to accept such a preposterous notion? How is he supposed to believe that the leads hidden beneath Janet's gown, attached to her chest, are receiving electrical signals from Isabel's heart? The heart of a woman who lived and died hundreds of miles away? The heart he used to live with, sleep with, felt thudding after sex when he lay with his hand between Isabel's breasts?

Bernice has noticed Alex's interest in Janet's monitor, and is also admiring the waveform. Bernice must have more faith or imagination or both, because she asks Janet, "So how does it work?"

"Great. Just great." Janet struggles up onto an elbow and looks fondly at the waveform. "I couldn't have asked for better. My old heart was such a lemon. You have no idea. It got me through thirty-two years OK, but then it quit. I wasn't getting any oxygen to my body. It felt like someone was slipping me an elephant tranquilizer every morning in my cereal. This heart pumps like crazy. It's like having a Maserati in my chest."

The process of propping herself up and turning sideways has allowed the neck of Janet's gown to flop downward, revealing what looks like the head of a long, pink worm crawling up her chest. Alex's eyes are due back at Janet's face but they won't go. It's hard to believe a cut in a human being could be so large, that a person could withstand such a slashing. The scar's centrality, smack in the middle of Janet's chest, so dangerously near the heart and lungs, makes it seem so threatening as to be disallowable, like an active fault line running through the most populous area of a city.

Janet has noticed Alex staring. With a swiftness that takes him off guard she undoes two buttons of her gown and peels it open just wide enough to reveal the full length of the scar. It's pink, waxy in texture. It's about a foot long, and runs straight down her sternum to just below her breasts.

Alex's face feels like the paper shade of a hot lamp.

Bernice's cheeks have gone albino, and a barely perceptible quivering in her eyes makes Alex think of the tiny green lights on the fronts of computers that flutter when the hard drives are stressed.

He sways forward and grips the bed's railing.

"I'm sorry," Janet says, and buttons up her gown. "I just thought you'd like to see."

Her apology, though sincere, has a chastening crispness, as if she doesn't mind having shown him evidence of her own suffering. Alex is impressed. "So that's where it went, huh?" He nods at Janet's done-up buttons. "They just crammed it in there?"

Janet smiles, appreciative of his interest. "It was a little more complicated than that. The surgery took six hours. They had to put me on bypass, then cut out my old heart, then put in the new one, then start it. Which took a while. Apparently it was reluctant to start pumping."

"Reluctant?" Bernice has the look of a mother who's just been informed by a teacher or fellow parent that her child has misbehaved.

"They have to start it again," Janet explains. "After it's been in the cooler. In transit. With an electrical shock. Sometimes it takes a little patience. But then it got going, and I was on my way."

Alex watches Janet's electrocardiogram jump-plunge, jump-plunge. Why can't he feel anything? A connection? A presence? The leaping green line reveals nothing. The leaping green line refuses to claim or signify or give evidence, and in his chest Alex feels the tension of the disparity between its ordinariness and its mystery.

"She kept trying to yank out her ET tube," Lotta says. "When she woke up. ET stands for endotracheal. It's a tube that goes down your throat to help you breathe. She was like a wild animal. They had to tie her wrists to the bedrails with Velcro straps."

Janet performs a dramatization: she grips, with orangutan-like mischievousness, an imaginary tube protruding from her mouth, rolls back her eyes, and violently yanks the tube free. Bernice laughs. Lotta and Janet join in. It's effusive, sloshy laughter, and makes the three women seem like allies. Alex feels conflicted and righteous. He doesn't like the sight of Bernice sitting forward on the edge of her stool with her hands draped over Janet's bedrail like a mesmerized novitiate; he doesn't like the delighted, approving smiles Janet and Lotta are awarding her in return. He worries he and Bernice are being tricked, coerced.

"We know what an ET tube is," he announces for Lotta's benefit. "Isabel had one. She was on a ventilator. I don't know if you've ever seen a brain-dead person, but they can't breathe on their own."

"I have seen a brain-dead person," Lotta says. "I worked my way through college as a nurse's assistant."

"Don't go there, Mom," Janet says.

Alex wants to go there. "It's different when you see a member of your own family brain-dead. Your wife, say, or your daughter."

Lotta gives him a confrontational look. "I watched my daughter come very, very close."

"And presto, here she is." Alex makes an unveiling motion with his arm. "Fixed."

"Alex, please," says Bernice.

Bud settles a loving, restraining hand on his wife's shoulder and gives Alex a cautionary look that's also respectful, as if he understands the link between Alex's loss and the body of the woman he, Bud, is touching. Bud nods at the window. "Think it's up to ninety yet? Weatherman said we'd hit it today."

Everyone seems to prefer looking at the sun-flooded window to continuing the conversation. Alex wouldn't mind being transformed into one of those particles of light and floating off to the far reaches of the universe. He feels, regarding his exchange with Lotta, a mixture of satisfaction and shame.

"So your mother, Janet . . . Lotta explained to me . . ." Bernice, in salvage mode, can't seem to formulate the question. "Lotta, you've been telling me that the heart is rejecting . . . that your *body,* Janet, is rejecting the heart?"

"That's right," Janet says tersely. "First of all, *I'm* not rejecting the heart. It's not a conscious decision. I want the heart. I love the heart. It's my antibodies that are the problem. They recognize the foreign antigens and attack, figuring the foreign entity is something dangerous, like a virus or a bacteria or a fungus. The immune system isn't smart enough to know that the foreign entity has been put in my body to keep me alive."

Alex wonders how she can love the heart. What does she know about the heart? Yet running alongside his incredulity is gratefulness for that love, however she comes by it. It would be worse if she didn't give a shit.

"Like guard dogs in a yard," says Bud. "They'll rush the fence and bark their fool heads off even if it's the UPS man bringing your Christmas presents to the door."

"Right. Thank you, Dad," Janet says.

She lets her head sink back into her pillow, smiles apologetically at Bernice and Alex, closes her eyes. Apparently they're going to stay closed. Lotta gives Alex and Bernice a look that asks for indulgence, then tells them in a hushed voice, "She's had a hell of a week." All eyes migrate to the children. Carly is staring up at a baseball game playing on a muted TV hanging in a corner. She mimics the pitcher's windup, hurls an invisible ball at the wall, nearly loses her balance during the follow-through. Sam is walking a green plastic dinosaur along a wall. Alex wonders where their father is. Gone for good? Still involved? Will he show up later?

Alex is inclined to believe Lotta's suggestion that Janet is entitled to her exhaustion, given how quickly and seamlessly Janet has sunk into sleep, or something like it. A vein trickles across a closed eyelid. A little slack appears in her lower lip. Her heart rate gradually descends from the low nineties into the high eighties, progressing through a series of advances and hesitations and retreats, 91 to 90, 90 to 91, 91 to 89, 89 to 90. Janet's children play contentedly, Bud fiddles with the broken soap dispenser, Lotta goes over and stands behind Bernice, who turns 180 degrees to face her so they can talk without disturbing Janet. Alex, left to himself, watches Janet's electrocardiogram flinch, flinch. Between the large, obvious spikes he notices smaller, reappearing nubs and jags. There's a preparatory, lightning-fast bump and dip before each spike, a crevasse into which each spike directly descends, a double-swell into the next cycle. He thinks of the projectile points he used to study and occasionally dig up during his years of fieldwork. By carefully noting each point's size and shape, stem and notches, flaking and fluting, he could tell one type from another; he could distinguish between, say, an Agate Basin and a Sedalia. He wonders if people's electrocardiograms are equally distinctive, or whether waveforms are more or less the same from healthy heart to healthy heart. If only Dr. Pagano were here, the physician from Iowa, from Isabel's bedside — thin, decorous Helen Pagano, who listened patiently to his questions and tried to explain whatever he didn't understand. She arrives and stands close at Alex's side, a spirit only he can see. With the confidentiality of an old friend he asks her, *Is that Isabel's EKG? Can you tell? Can you remember?*

"Narf wants a hamburger." Sam has appeared in front of Alex, and holds the green plastic dinosaur up toward him, making the jaws open and shut by pressing a button on its belly.

"Narf?" Alex asks.

Sam nods proudly.

"Narf's a brontosaurus," Alex tells him. "He's a plant eater. An herbivore. He wants to eat some lettuce, maybe some tomatoes. He'll pass on the ground beef."

Sam says, "Hamburgers come with lettuce and tomatoes. If you ask for them."

Carly lunges toward Alex. "Sam named him Narf but I named him Sam because he looks like Sam's face!"

"He wants to eat your *brain,*" Sam says, thrusting the dinosaur toward Carly's ear.

"Sam. Easy." The commotion has woken Janet, whose face is doughy and crimped. "Dad, maybe these two need a workout on the playground."

For an instant Alex imagines, ridiculously, that he and Bernice are being invited to go off to a playground with Bud — which doesn't sound all that bad. Bud, who has been struggling to repair the defective soap dispenser, seems eager to abandon the project in favor of solo time with his grandchildren. He asks Carly and Sam, "Anybody want to go ride the slippery slide?" They erupt with enthusiasm. Sam spins on a foot. Carly does a wriggling dance. After making a few preparations, and taking a few instructions from Janet, Bud herds the kids out the door. Their jubilant wake sloshes against the walls. Janet shouts after her kids, "Behave yourselves!"

Bernice is overcome with envy and nostalgia, watching them leave. Was Alex right all those times he insisted, to her irritation and dismay, that he and Bernice were the losers, and that Janet and her family the winners? Though Janet surely has her problems, and possibly Lotta, there's no question they gained or regained from the whole ordeal exactly the kind of life Bernice and Alex were deprived of. A life full of children, family, laughter, good times.

"All we've talked about is me, me, me," Janet says. "Tell me how you two are doing."

Bernice goes to the net. "I'm OK. Puttering along. Nothing big to report. Work's OK. We're gearing up for *L'Orfeo,* the summer opera. And we've got *La Bohème* coming up in the fall."

"Mom told me you worked in a costume shop, but I didn't realize you did costumes for operas. They have operas in Iowa?" Janet smiles, lightly mocking.

"We sure do," Bernice says. "We put on three a year. We're not the Met, but we do our best."

"Are you an opera fan, Alex?" Lotta asks.

"Not really. People moaning in languages I can't understand? No thanks."

Janet asks, "What kind of music do you like?"

"I don't know. Whatever suits my mood. I don't listen to a lot of music these days. In the car sometimes, driving to work."

"What kind of work do you do?"

He wishes Janet would back off, refocus her attention on Bernice. "I grade writing tests." He hasn't yet told Bernice that he quit.

Bernice says, "Alex's background is in archaeology."

"Really? What period?" asks Lotta.

Alex tells her Late Mississippian America.

Janet says, "When — and maybe I should ask where — was that?"

It's going too far, it's moving too fast, it's easing too quickly into a familiarity that could seduce him into forgetting the injustice and lead them to conclude that he's on board. "Look, I don't feel like going into a whole summation of my stalled career, OK?"

Janet, scorched, bows her head and presses the balls of her thumbs together. Lotta turns brusquely away, her body language pronouncing Alex a sourpuss. Bernice gives him a look of baffled reproach, as if to ask, *Didn't you agree to come here? Didn't you agree to be my ally?* Yes, he'd like to answer. But he may have been naïve and foolish. He failed to anticipate that meeting Janet would generate so many complex discordances. Or maybe he did anticipate it but came anyway. Unfortunately he's nowhere near ready to concede Janet's existence, let her off the hook, celebrate her. Anyway, don't they seem a little too pleased with themselves, these Corcorans?

Janet is holding her head, one hand over each ear, like a fragile glass bowl. "I'm not even going to pretend to know what it must be like for you," she says. "It must be a nightmare. I'm so sorry. And here I am rambling on asking you inane questions. I haven't *thanked* you. How long have you been in the room? Half an hour? You must think I'm an ungrateful bitch."

"No, no," Bernice says, shaking her head.

Alex doesn't think Janet's ungrateful. He thinks she's playing for sympathy, which might be even worse.

"Thank you," Janet says solemnly, forcefully, intending to generate a sense of occasion. "I want to thank both of you officially, right now, in person, though definitely not for the last time, and definitely not that it'll fix anything or that I'll ever be able to thank you enough. But I've got to do it. Thank you. For everything you've done."

Bernice mumbles acknowledgment, then makes a brave, courteous speech about how glad she is that something good came out of all this, it's what Isabel wanted, what she planned for.

Janet turns her gaze to Alex. In her eyes he sees Isabel's huge, inky, blown-out pupils. He hears the dog-whistle whine of an electric saw, sees blood trickling over her nipples and running down onto her stomach and pooling in her belly button as the harvesters close in.

"Don't thank *me,*" he says, mortified. "I didn't do anything. What am I supposed to say? You're welcome? You're not welcome."

Janet glares at him, wounded and indignant.

"Alex, please," Bernice says. "She's not

asking you to say 'you're welcome.' "

"What's she asking me, then?" he says to Bernice, and to Janet, "What do you want me to say? You can't expect me to pretend I'm happy about the way all this worked out. If it had been up to me you'd be dead and Isabel would still be alive. I'm sorry to say it, it's nothing personal, but it's true. Or maybe it *is* personal. Maybe there's no way around you."

Alex is surprised to see Janet's eyes turn glossy, to see her chin and lower lip tremble. Lotta's glare accuses Alex of being needlessly brutal. Bernice glances up at Janet's monitor, her face tense with concern. She turns to Alex. "That's not the way the calculus works. You can't go back and trade Janet for Isabel. Isabel would have died no matter who else did or didn't."

"Could you rub it in a little?" Alex's face is hot. He feels bitter and aggrieved and spiteful. He feels *entitled* to feel bitter and aggrieved and spiteful. This bitterness, this spite — is *this* the evidence? Of Isabel's presence? Is this the proof?

He misses Isabel intensely, precipitously — a slosh of longing. Bernice extends a comforting hand but he swats it away. He doesn't want her hand.

"If you think you're doing any great

service to Isabel, or to her memory, you're wrong," Bernice says. "You're not being faithful to her. Far from it."

With a jerk of her head she suggests he take a look at Janet's monitor. The waveform is zipping along at a brisk clip, the heart rate straining toward 110. Wasn't Janet's heart rate only 92 or 93 when Alex first noticed it? Bernice raises her eyebrows meaningfully, and he gets her implication.

The sense that there's no connection to Isabel through Janet, no access, no way for Alex to get to her, swings jarringly into a fear that there is, and that he's been reckless, even abusive, with his power.

"Do we need to call a nurse?" Bernice asks ominously, studying the waveform.

"Don't worry about it." Janet, breathing rapidly, hand on her chest, glances up at her echocardiogram with familiarity and something like trust. "The heart's denervated. It gets all its news by hormones and chemical messengers. Whatever it's doing now is a reaction to whatever happened a few minutes ago."

Bernice looks confused. " 'Denervated'?"

"It's not connected to her nervous system," Lotta explains. "Not as intricately as a normal heart. The heart a person is born with."

When Bernice fails to nod or show any sign of comprehension Janet says, "The hookup's too complex. It takes nine months in the womb to weave it all together. The surgeons couldn't equal that in four hours. They couldn't stitch her nerves to mine."

"Oh. Of course." Bernice stares at Janet's chest, devastated.

Alex is dumbstruck. Is Janet telling them that Isabel's heart, once so tightly knit to Isabel's emotions and senses, was denuded and stuffed into its new recipient like a meatball inside a ravioli? Is Janet telling them that Isabel's heart is now an insensate drone, severed from the brain's continuous sensory updates — from everything it once read the world by? From everything and everyone?

From him?

Sadness sluices through Alex's body — an irradiation of sorrow so intense, he's sure it will crush him.

He turns and gropes for the door latch and bursts out into the hallway.

TWENTY-EIGHT

Even if the past hour had gone smoothly, Janet would have been exhausted by now, given the unexpectedness and stress of the event piled onto the upheavals of the preceding days. Alex's incriminations have left her teetering between anger and shame, righteous indignation and self-doubt. As if she'd had some agency in Isabel's death. As if she could have made it otherwise. By doing what? If she could travel back in time, what would he have her do differently? Take herself off the waiting list? Decline a heart and die? Would that have prevented a car accident from happening three hundred miles away?

After Alex left, Bernice apologized for his behavior, then went off to look for him. Janet's mother pulled the blinds in Janet's room, shut out the lights, and left, intending for Janet to sleep. Janet was whipped. Unfortunately she's too agitated to drift off.

Is she mistaken, or did she receive a gift? A gift given freely and deliberately by a woman acting under her own will. A woman whose husband endorsed her decision. So the husband can hardly turn around and blame Janet for accepting the gift. The gift was *intended* for her. Would he rather she'd refused it? Would he rather she'd died? He essentially said so.

Of course she felt for him. Once or twice, when she met his eyes, they took on a nearly imperceptible gloss, and his lower lip flinched as though tugged by a thread. Would she always evoke such sadness in the man? She hoped not. She felt sorry for him. How could he have known what he was getting into, coming up here to meet her? How could he have predicted with any accuracy how difficult or painful such an unorthodox encounter would be? Maybe David was right all along. Maybe meetings like this between recipients and donors' survivors weren't meant to happen.

Sleep. *Sleep.* The conditions are perfect: dark room, drawn blinds, closed door. Delicious quiet. No children. Who knows when she'll have another chance?

She wonders if she made a terrible mistake, damaging her relationship with David by insisting on contact with Bernice and

Alex. On the other hand she doubts things would have improved with David even if she'd given up on her donor family. Alex and Bernice aren't the issue. She and David are the issue. And now he's moved out. Her mother gave her the details when she came to the hospital late yesterday evening: David had called the apartment the previous morning and arranged to have Lotta and Bud take Sam and Carly out for the afternoon, and when they returned David had taken some clothes and toiletries and other personal items. He had also taken a few small pieces of furniture. Janet clutched her mother and wept. She didn't know whether to be grateful or enraged that she hadn't been home for the event. Janet had a talk with Sam and Carly and explained to them, as David had, that he was moving out for a while to be closer to his office. She felt horrible lying to them and wanted to reveal more but didn't feel up to the repercussions. The truth would have to wait until she got home. Until she felt better. Until she was fully prepared to give comfort.

She wishes the cosmic serendipity responsible for the timing of these things had managed to delay David's departure and her hospitalization until after Alex and Bernice's visit. As far back as she could remember she'd envisioned greeting her donor's family at the door of her pretty loft apartment, stylishly dressed, radiating health and vitality. She would proudly introduce her husband and children — her solid, supportive, intact family. Instead she was forced to undergo the humiliation of greeting Alex and Bernice in the same hospital where she'd once been a dying inpatient, and where she was once again inert, bedridden, pillow-haired, dressed in drab hospital garb, confined in a room smelling of antivirals. Of course if she hadn't landed in the hospital Alex and Bernice might not have had such a powerful impetus to come. Still, she hated to greet them with the news that her immune system was throwing a hysterical, self-destructive fit — that she was rejecting the rare, precious heart their dead girl had given her. *Oh, and by the way, my husband just dumped me.* She wishes her mother hadn't told Alex and Bernice about her troubles with David. She doesn't want their pity. She's glad the subject didn't come up while they were here, though it might have been easier if it did: she found it difficult, while talking to them, not to make any reference to the gaping crater in her personal life, and was at times so preoccupied with worry that she couldn't give Alex and

456

Bernice her undivided attention.

Sleep. Force yourself. Clear your mind.

She might have drifted off if this person coming in had taken more time with the door and opened it carefully, quietly, instead of stumbling through like a clumsy prowler. At first Janet thinks her musings have summoned David, that he's come here to check on her, maybe even ask if he can move back in. But this person is shorter, more bulky. Janet strains to make out the face in the shard of light from the doorway, extinguished when he closes the door behind him. Probably a new housekeeper who hasn't yet learned the art of slipping stealthily into patients' rooms to empty the trash. But there's enough light to see he's not wearing the gunmetal gray housekeeper's shirt. He's wearing a long, loose, red T-shirt. Jeans. Cross-trainers. He's breathing hard, as though he just charged up a flight of stairs. He stands motionless by the door, his head aimed toward the bed, waiting for his eyes to adjust.

"Who are you looking for?" Janet challenges. "I'm trying to sleep."

The man steps backward, startled. The heel of his foot clunks against the base of the door.

"Turn on the light," Janet says. "The

switch is right there by your hand."

Her visitor seems happy to turn on the light, and in the blaze from overhead they inspect each other. Janet's never seen this man before. He's hefty, twenty-five or thirty pounds overweight for his height. His forehead glistens with sweat. His cheeks are flushed. His little round mouth sucks breaths: his lungs and heart are doing hard, forced labor. He plunges a fleshy hand into his hair and gapes at Janet with amazement and disbelief; he has the look of a person who's come a long way to deliver a message but can't remember what it is.

"Do I know you?" Janet asks.

"Do you *know* me," the man answers with something between offense and bemusement. "No, you don't. Not exactly. You *ought* to know me. There's a connection. You are Janet Corcoran, aren't you?" He seems momentarily uncertain of being in the right place.

Janet's first impression, which may be rash and uncharitable, is that this man is a fugitive from Adult Psych — that somewhere over on Five South there are panicked nurses wandering the halls looking for him. "I am. Are you a patient here too?"

"A patient? I'm from out of state. I drove up here from Iowa."

Janet hoists herself upright in bed and frees her arms from the sheets. "Iowa? How do you know me?"

"I don't know you." He studies her appraisingly. "That's why I'm here."

"So let's meet," Janet says, nervous. "I'm Janet. And you are . . . ?"

He takes himself on a brief tour of the room, ends up over by the window. "Can you see the lake from here?"

"It's in the other direction."

"Really? I thought I was . . ." He turns, extends an arm, turns again, attempting to find his bearings.

Janet asks, "How long are you going to keep me in a state of total mystification as to who you are?"

The man's head makes a recoiling motion. "*I'm* hardly the one who kept you in a state of mystification. You should know who I am, let's put it that way. In a just world. But certain powers won't reveal all the identities involved. Sure, they'll forward your letters to the family of your donor, and if you're lucky, like you were, you'll find out who your donor family is. But they don't want you to know about me."

Though Janet's still not sure what he's talking about, she feels a creeping anxiety, as if her life has just morphed into a drama involving undercover agents and clandestine organizations. "So what do I need to know about you?"

Her visitor approaches the bed and extends his hand. "I'm Jasper. Jasper Klass."

Janet feels like she's encountered that name before, but she couldn't say where or when. She declines the handshake. "Would you mind washing your hands? I'm immunocompromised."

"I knew that."

Jasper turns the water on too hard — droplets splatter the mirror — and studies the soap dispenser for a minute before locating the foot pump.

Janet says, "So you're not from an organ procurement organization?"

"Let's just say I was involved in the procurement process."

"In what way?"

"Not in any official way."

Janet's beginning to find his elusiveness disturbing. She reaches above and behind her to the Call button on the wall. "So in what unofficial way were you involved?"

Jasper finishes rinsing and drying his hands, wads the used paper towel into a ball, searches for a garbage can, and shoots. "That's three," he declares. Then he sees her hand on the call button. He freezes.

460

"Don't do that."

"Tell me who you are."

Jasper stands perfectly still for a moment, trying to decide how to proceed. "I'm the guy who drove a truck into your donor," he says. "A year and three months ago. April twenty-first, 2005. Ever wonder who did it? Well, I did. I'm your man."

Janet feels herself breaking out in disbelief and fear, a nerve alert spreading across her skin. She's shocked to hear him get the date right. *Jasper Klass.* She remembers the name faintly, she thinks, from a newspaper article about Isabel's accident, which must have mentioned him. *The driver of the vehicle.* She would have tried to forget that name. She takes her hand off the Call button. It's hard to believe this is him, her donor's killer. She's stupefied. It's astonishing and disturbing to think she might be dead if it weren't for this man's recklessness, or whatever it was. "Do Alex and Bernice know you're here?" she asks.

"No. Are they here?" Jasper seems alarmed.

"No," Janet lies, figuring maybe they'd rather he didn't know.

Relieved, Jasper steps toward her bed and rests both hands on the footboard. It's an intimate act, touching her bed, and Janet

461

isn't comfortable with it.

"It was an accident," she says. "So you didn't mean to do it. To kill anyone."

Jasper taps his fingers on the footboard. "She was in the middle of the road. In the middle of *my* lane. I didn't have time to stop. I didn't even have time to slow down. She was hidden by a hill. I just came up and over and —" He claps his hands together sharply.

Janet can't help wondering whether Jasper is telling the entire truth. Is he omitting details less to his credit, such as his speed and his failure to see the bicycle, for which Alex or Bernice might hold him accountable? She'd have to be braver to explore these questions herself. She's scared, talking about the accident — terrified of what this man, the only eyewitness as far as she knows, might tell her. Reveal to her. Details she never wanted to see, details she'll go on seeing for the rest of her life. Blood, cracked limbs, gore.

"It must have been awful for you," she says. "You must have been terrified."

"I was scared shitless. I could hardly make myself turn around and go back. It's not like I didn't know what I was going to find."

A perverse curiosity takes Janet by the hand. "What did you find?"

"You really want to know?"

"Not really. But I get the feeling you want to tell me."

Jasper shrugs as though he'd be happy to talk about anything. "She was flung out on her back in the grass. One arm beneath her all crooked. Crickets on her chest. An ear filled with blood." He stares at Janet in a kind of trance. "I've got to tell you, to see you alive as a result of that, it's pretty amazing."

Janet's body feels suddenly weightless, insubstantial. "I don't like the word *'result.'*"

Jasper comes around to the side of the bed. "She was hit by a truck. You're aware of that, right? You got her heart as a result." He measures the length of her body with his eyes. "She was about your size. Her heart must have been a nice fit."

Janet tugs her sheet up over her chest. "I don't talk about the heart like it was a shoe. It's great that it was the right size for my body, but there was more to it than that. We were the same blood type. We had a four-antigen match. That's rare."

"You like that, huh? The blood type? The antigens? It makes the whole thing feel warm and fuzzy?"

Janet steels herself for an argument. "Are

you trying to suggest I'm not aware of the fact that I wouldn't be alive right now if you hadn't killed an organ donor? I get the picture. You can quit selling me."

"I'm not trying to sell anything." Jasper presses both hands flat outward against the air, emphasizing his eagerness to avoid a blow-up. "I'm just trying to make sure we don't have any illusions."

Something about the way he uses the word "illusions" makes her hear David's voice, in a recent conversation, accusing her of being stubborn and inflexible.

Jasper wanders over to a supply nook in the wall, picks up a tiny plastic pill cup from a counter, and jiggles it on the end of his forefinger. "You know what's funny? Here we are, getting all worked up, feeling guilty and anxious and upset, but none of us, not *one* of us, did anything wrong."

He launches into elaboration, but Janet has trouble focusing on what he's saying. She's busy asking herself whether she really is stubborn and inflexible.

"— driving a hundred miles an hour with my eyes closed high on crack swerving all over the road," Jasper says, squeezing the pill cup between his thumb and forefinger. "I *wasn't* driving my vehicle in a reckless manner with willful or wanton disregard for the safety of persons or property. That's section 321.277 of the Iowa Code, which I was never charged with violating, by the way. The point being anyone coming over that hill would have hit her. And you, you just happened to need exactly what she'd offered in the event of exactly such a situation. So why are we all bent out of shape? Why are we all miserable?"

"You tell me."

Jasper stares at the floor, looking vulnerable and ashamed. "It's hard to enjoy your life when you've obliterated someone else's."

Janet rubs her thumbs lightly together, then less lightly, curious as to how little contact is required to produce feeling. She's thinking about how, when she was in this hospital a year and a half ago, waiting for a heart, she and the other Status 1's used to joke about wishing drivers would be more reckless.

"I bet it was festive up here that night," Jasper says.

"It was." Janet decides to be honest. "It was celebratory." She's appalled to recall how she felt. "People stopped by to congratulate me. There was kissing and hugging."

"No one stopped by to congratulate me. No kisses and hugs for Jasper. Not that I was expecting any." Jasper wanders over to Janet's IV pole and studies the med fusion pump that is feeding Janet her antirejection drugs. He reaches out as though he's going to press a button, finger extended. "On the other hand, if you accidentally kill someone whose organs go off and save lives, you think you'd at least get something. A phone call. A letter."

"Don't touch that," Janet says.

Jasper withdraws his finger. "Don't you think?"

Janet steadies herself with a deep breath. "Look, Jasper, I don't want to discount what you . . . gave me." She inwardly winces to think how Alex and Bernice would react to her saying this. "But you don't want to start down the slippery slope of rewarding people who kill other people, accidentally or not. There's a huge enough fuss whenever someone suggests that *donors* ought to be compensated."

Jasper pulls a stool up to the bed, sits, swivels experimentally while allowing his eyes to travel up and down her body, surveying her form beneath the sheets. "Donors. Donors are amazing, generous folks. But let's face it, donors are just people with cards in their pockets. You need more than a donor. You need an agent of destruction.

466

The organ-procurement system, the health-care system, whatever system you're talking about, no one in those systems likes to talk about the system that really makes it all work, which is the American Automobile Death System."

Janet sits up straighter and draws her legs up, removes as much of her body as possible from view. "A certain number of automobile deaths are statistically bound to happen."

"Oh, that's nice. Are you saying it was statistically bound to happen to me?"

"I didn't mean that. I just meant . . ." She's not sure. She's too tired to be having this conversation. When will someone — anyone — come into her room and rescue her?

Jasper gets up from the stool and pushes it aside and takes a few steps toward the door. "Don't you think it's too bright in here?" he asks, and flicks off the lights. "Don't get me wrong, it's amazing you're alive. You're my silver lining. You're my flower that grew out of the ashes."

"I'm not your flower. Turn the lights back on."

Jasper looks hurt. He takes a few steps toward her. "OK, Isabel's flower. But I planted you."

"No, you didn't," Janet says. "You can't claim to have had the same foresight and generosity that she did. If you're going to claim the accident was an accident — if you're going to claim it wasn't premeditated — then *none* of it was premeditated. Anyway, how could I thank you? It's unseemly. It's obscene."

"I don't want you to thank me," Jasper says, his voice leaching anger. "I just want you to . . ." He doesn't seem to know. He looks confused and disoriented; his eyes explore the room as though he's seeing it for the first time. His attention returns to her. He comes over to the bed, stands close to her with his big hands hanging at his sides. His fingers are stubby and blunt. There's a thin, pink, crescent-shaped scar — a cat scratch? — on his left wrist. His eyes hone in on her chest, and to Janet they seem to well up with complicated, disorganized need.

"Can I feel it?" Jasper asks.

Janet prepares to scream and thrash. "I think maybe you should go."

"Hey, come on," Jasper says calmly, and with a flicker of anticipation. "I just got here."

TWENTY-NINE

Bernice has searched Medical Cardiology's honeycomb of hallways and pods, checked the waiting room near the main entrance to the unit, walked down the corridor past the atrium to the elevators she and Alex rode up in, walked back in the other direction, past Medical Cardiology, past the neurology clinic, Surgical Intensive Care, ducking into more waiting rooms, scanning more sitting areas, looking for Alex. No luck. She's more irritated than worried. How on earth does he expect her to find him? He has a new cell phone, but she doesn't — she'd have to stop and use a hospital phone to call him. Which she's going to do. Soon. She's already walked what feels like a mile.

Then she spots him, sitting alone in a row of chairs near a large window. He's sitting back in the chair — pressed back, it looks like — as though a stiff wind were holding him there.

"Where have you *been?*" Bernice asks. "I've been looking all over for you. Where did you go?"

Alex is bewildered by the onslaught. "Sorry. I had to get out of there."

Bernice sits down beside him. "Are you all right?"

"Yeah. It's just all so bizarre."

"That's one word for it."

Alex regards her curiously. "What's your word?"

Bernice considers. "Jarring."

"No kidding." Alex stares blankly out the window into the harsh glare of the day. "I think we're being too nice to them."

"They're being nice to us."

"You were practically worshipping Janet."

"Worshipping?" Bernice feels insulted. "Alex, that's ridiculous. I'm simply trying to treat her decently. Isabel's heart is in her body."

"It's not supposed to be. It belongs in *Isabel's* body. Don't you see how fucked-up that is?"

"Look, just because I don't say nasty things and storm out of the room doesn't mean it's easy for me."

"I didn't mean to be nasty. I'm sorry."

"Don't tell me. Tell Janet."

"I just want to go home."

"And leave things like this? We can't."

"Why not? What — we owe them more?"

Bernice sighs, exasperated. "It'll depress me for the rest of my life. And it'll hurt Janet."

"Janet, Janet, Janet. It's all about Janet."

"No, it *isn't.* It's all about Isabel. You know what's happening right now? Those chemical messengers Janet was talking about, the hormones, when you left the room they started toward Isabel's heart, and by now they've reached it, and she's upset and anxious and beating like crazy."

The expression on Alex's face is grave and concerned. His eyes search hers as if to ask, *Will it get easier?*

"Come on," she says, slapping him on the knee. "We don't have to stay long."

Alex, returning with Bernice to Medical Cardiology, feels sheepish and docile, like a thirteen-year-old boy who's thrown a tantrum in front of strangers, been chastised for his behavior by a parent, and forced to make amends. On the other hand, it's easier in some way to let go of his bitterness and annoyance and focus on pleasing Bernice, to whom he at least feels allegiance.

Alex is surprised she remembers exactly where Janet's room is, exactly how to get to it. The pod outside is empty. Janet's door is closed, her room dark. "I wonder if she's sleeping," Bernice says. She and Alex approach the door. They hear voices from within. Janet's, and also a male voice. Bernice gives Alex an inquisitive look. She goes to the door, peers through the window. "Oh, God," she says, stepping back. She cups her hand over her mouth as though she's going to be sick. "I don't believe it."

Alex steps forward and looks through the window and sees Janet sitting up in bed in the dark talking to — is it? Jasper. Perched sidesaddle on the bed with one leg lifted, knee resting on the edge of the mattress. His left hand is gripping his left thigh for support, but his right arm and hand are out of sight, hidden by his torso. From the contour of his right shoulder, from the way he's leaning in toward Janet, that hand appears to be somewhere on her body. Then Alex sees Jasper's hand on Janet's chest.

She sees Alex in the doorway. She waves and calls out his name as though he's her best friend in the world, finally arrived after a long absence. Alex opens the door and steps into the room. Jasper cranks his head around and smirks with a strange mixture of annoyance and triumph. He keeps his hand on Janet's chest.

"What the *fuck,*" Alex says. "What are you doing here?"

"Just talking," Jasper says cheerfully.

Behind Jasper's back Janet mouths silently to Alex, *Help.*

Bernice draws up alongside Alex, and though he extends an arm to restrain and protect her, she doesn't back off. She stands glaring at Jasper with her head dipped to one side, her face pained and incredulous. "You monster. Janet, do you have any idea —" The enormity of the explanation deters her. She says to Jasper, "How did you find her?"

"We're talking about a certain amount of detective work, sure," Jasper says, redistributing his weight on Janet's bed in what seems a partially conscious effort to sustain his claim to it. "It's not like I was getting a lot of help from you people."

"How long has he been here?" Bernice asks Janet, exploring the extent of the betrayal.

Janet glances up at the clock on the wall. "I don't know. I was asleep. He came in and woke me up."

"It's not like I forced myself on her," Jasper explains to Bernice. "We've been having a nice mutual conversation."

"I'm afraid I can't trust you when you say

473

you didn't force yourself on her, given that you recently forced yourself on me," Bernice says. She asks Janet, "Are you aware that this man has been stalking us? Trying to figure out who you are?" She unloads on Janet a brief but exhaustive inventory of Jasper's recent behavior: his intrusion into her house, his threats, his arrest, the charges she's pressing. Jasper interrupts to defend himself but Bernice bulldozes over him. "Criminal trespassing, assault, criminal mischief, public intoxication. Why aren't you in jail?" she shouts at Jasper. "You're not allowed to be here. There's a protective order against you."

"They're not giving you the whole story," Jasper tells Janet. "And the protective order doesn't apply in Illinois."

Janet has scrunched herself into a ball, drawn her knees up tightly to her chest, encircled her shins with her arms, clasped her hands together. She looks shocked, repulsed. She tells Jasper, "You need to leave."

"Right," Jasper says dismissively. "One minute we're laughing and joking and the next minute you're kicking me out."

"We weren't laughing and joking," Janet says. "I was scared."

"Get away from her," Alex tells Jasper,

who is still sitting on Janet's bed.

Jasper extends a hand toward Alex and gently pats the air. "Easy, Superman. Chill out." He rises slowly from the bed, as though doing so only because he wants to. "I just want some understanding. I just want to be part of all this." He gestures expansively at the room around him. "Is there anything wrong with that? Can't we all just get along?"

"No," Alex says.

Bernice laughs in his face. "No way in hell."

Janet tells Jasper, "You need to leave, or I'm going to call security."

Jasper glares at her as though she's needlessly escalating. "Seriously?"

Janet reaches up and behind her to the red Call button on the wall.

"Hang on," Jasper says. He holds his hands up in a gesture of surrender. He turns uncertainly, starts toward the door, pauses at a supply cubby in the wall. He studies the items on the counter: a graduated container, plastic medicine cups, a plastic bowl stuffed with bandages and alcohol pads. On the shelves above are stacks of towels and washcloths. Jasper pulls open a drawer and peers down into it. Alex wonders if he's searching for a weapon. Will he find scalpels or razor blades? Jasper slams the drawer shut and turns around. He stands motionless, numb, his face ugly with anguish. "What a fucking bust," he says. "Why does this always happen to me?" He stares at Janet and Alex and Bernice, expecting a response. Not one of them speaks. Janet presses her Call button. Jasper's eyes enlarge. His face floods red. He reaches out and grabs Janet's IV pole and throws it to the floor.

Janet shrieks. Her medicine pump, big as a car battery, attached to the top of the pole, falls farthest and hardest, dragging her IV lines with them — Janet thrusts out her arms and lunges forward to prevent any of the lines from being yanked out. The pump crashes to the floor, and a shard of plastic — a broken-off corner — whizzes across the room. The fallen pump beeps calmly and flashes a red light. Jasper stands paralyzed, shocked and pleased by what he's done. Alex tackles him at waist-level, driving hard with his legs and using all his weight to bring Jasper to the floor. Alex lands on top and clenches Jasper tightly in the vise of his arms. Jasper struggles and squirms and says, "Get off me, you fucker, get off me." He jabs Alex hard in the ribs with an elbow. Alex groans and snakes an arm up under Jasper's and manages to get him into a half nelson. Jasper is strong, and Alex doubts he can hold him down for long. He hears shouts, new voices in the room, more shouts. He yells for someone to call security. He can't see anything going on above him. His chin is wedged into Jasper's upper back. When Jasper struggles and rears up, Alex's mouth gets mashed to Jasper's neck, forcing him to taste slick, salty skin. They spend what seems like five or ten minutes entangled like this, Alex pinning Jasper to the floor, Jasper cursing and struggling and then tiring, relaxing, briefly closing his eyes and breathing with a steadiness that makes him seem peaceful, even content, lying there in Alex's embrace. Finally Alex is yanked to his feet by powerful arms. Janet says, "No, the one *underneath.*" Two beefy security guards with guns and nightsticks on their belts release Alex and haul Jasper to his feet, one guard to an arm. Janet confirms that Jasper knocked over her IV pole, and Bernice adds that he has charges against him in Iowa, and a protective order. Jasper doesn't defend himself or resist. He looks humiliated and spent. "I need a drink of water," he tells the guards as they escort him out of the room. "I need to go to the ER. I think I broke my rib."

Irrepressible shudders run up and down Alex's arms. He's coursing with anger and adrenaline. Bernice, who somehow managed to stand up Janet's IV pole and organize her lines while Alex was battling Jasper, now helps Janet's nurse, a wiry Latina named Mara, assess the damage to Janet's pump. Janet has her left hand up under her gown, on her heart. She's breathing deliberately and staring into space with a resolute expression. Alex glances at her monitor. The waveform leaps, leaps. Her heart rate is 105.

"Are you OK?" he asks.

"The adrenaline's coming," she says, a little breathless. "Just need to talk myself down."

"Can you talk me down too?"

Janet smiles. "Thanks for doing that. I don't know what I would have done if you guys hadn't come back."

"I have to admit, I kind of enjoyed it," Alex says.

"Did he hurt you?" Bernice asks.

"I've got some pain in my side."

"You should stop down to the ER."

"I will if it keeps hurting."

Janet's nurse leaves the room to get a replacement medicine pump.

"I'm so sorry this happened," Janet tells Alex and Bernice. "It must have been awful for you, walking in and seeing him."

Bernice approaches the bed, rests her hands on the side rail, and slumps forward. "It was. It must have been awful for you, too."

"I didn't welcome him with open arms," Janet says. "I didn't even know who he was, at first. Then he got creepy and threatening and asked to feel the heart, and I figured I could calm him down and buy time by letting him."

"We're just glad you're OK," Bernice says.

Janet's adrenaline comes on, and she breathes through it, hand on her chest, focused inward. Bernice and Alex stand vigilantly on either side of her. Alex watches Janet's jouncing waveform and feels relieved when it begins to settle. Bernice notices too, and gives him a smile.

THIRTY

Sitting in the tub, in piping hot water, islets of foam floating between her upraised knees, Bernice washes herself with a soapy sponge. She scrubs her face, her shoulders and arms, her chest, her legs, and as she does wishes she could scrub her insides too, wishes it were possible to clean off all the accumulated grit and grime inside her — grief, sadness, envy, anger, unpleasant memories — as easily as she dispenses with the day's perspiration and odor.

She rinses thoroughly and rises from the tub. The water releases her with a startled slosh. She towels off and swaddles herself in a white bathrobe that has the hotel's insignia on the breast. The hot, steamy bathroom makes her feel claustrophobic. She opens the door quietly, suspecting Alex may be asleep, and enjoys the first step into cool air, which hits her skin and lungs like a reprieve, like liberation from suffocating entombment.

Alex is sprawled facedown on the bed nearer the door, legs hooked at the ankles. One arm is pinned beneath his body, the other flung above his head, fingers splayed against the headboard's pillowed leather. Bernice thinks of her son, Clancy. She can remember discovering him as a boy asleep in his room in similarly awkward, torturous-looking positions, and how she would approach the bed and disentangle him, carefully lifting and freeing limbs as though defusing a bomb. She has to resist the inclination to approach Alex and do the same.

She walks across the ochre carpet and sits in an armchair by the window. The window overlooks Wacker Drive and the Chicago River from nineteen floors up. Bernice booked this hotel on Priceline, and while the view is spectacular, as promised, she can't get excited about it. The river's bile-green viscosity bothers her stomach. The Michigan Avenue Bridge, with its quartet of dark stone towers, seems to await a funeral procession. The Wrigley Building looks like something accomplished with a massive surplus of salt.

Alex stirs in his bed and lets out a desultory murmur. His mouth has that slack, gravity-induced lopsidedness that signifies deepening sleep. Bernice would like to wake him — she wouldn't mind a little conversation — but she appreciates his need for rest. As he descends deeper into sleep, he brings up his knee and turns partway onto his side, freeing the trapped arm and extending it in front of him, palm up, fingers curled, in a way that makes him look supplicating and almost unbearably vulnerable.

Bernice gathers a change of clothes from her suitcase and returns to the bathroom. She closes the door and dresses. She puts on minimal makeup, brushes her teeth, flosses. When she emerges from the bathroom Alex is still asleep. Bernice sits on the edge of her bed and puts on her shoes. She sits watching Alex sleep and trying to think of something else she can do, some other preparation she can make. Finally she leans forward and squeezes Alex's hand until his eyes open.

"Where are we?" he asks, stupid with fatigue.

"Chicago," she says. "We've had a rough day. Want to go get some dinner?"

On Michigan Avenue, constellations of lights ionize the warm night air. The sky, propped up by skyscrapers, is a peach ether.

Cars and buses and taxis lunge. It's nearly nine. The sidewalks are crowded with people, sharp dressers and brisk walkers enjoying a Saturday night out.

Bernice notices a funny, glazed attentiveness in Alex's face, and wonders if, like her, he's a little stunned by the traffic, the crowds, the noise. The dense, frictional energy, the aggregate voltage of all these human beings crammed into so little space.

"So what do you want to eat?" Alex asks. They're walking north on Michigan after a brief sojourn south into the Loop. "I could go for a cheeseburger."

"A *cheeseburger?* What's the point of coming all the way to Chicago for a cheeseburger? We can have any cuisine in the world. Polish. Lithuanian. Ethiopian."

They leave Michigan Avenue at Huron, walk west past hotels and parking garages, searching for ethnic cuisine among the chophouses and bars. They turn north, then west again, discussing restaurants they come upon, peering into windows, reading menus. Bernice finds herself thinking about the fire, the Great Chicago Fire of 1871, in which nearly the entire city burned to the ground. She saw a documentary about this once on PBS, or maybe it was the History Channel. Engineers and architects — Sullivan, Adler,

Burnham, Root — flocked to the charred ruins and built one magnificent skyscraper after another, reinventing the city from scratch. And now look at it, over a hundred years later: a sprawling palace of iron and steel and concrete. Stronger than it ever was. Talk about a recovery.

"Here we go." Alex draws to a halt in front of a small, bustling pizzeria. "Compromise. I get my cheese, you get your ethnic. Italian is ethnic. Not the most exotic ethnic, but technically ethnic."

"What the hell," Bernice says, tired of walking, ready for a glass of wine.

Red-and-white checked tablecloths, stucco walls, arches over the passageways. There's a thirty-minute wait, but the pizza looks saucy and spicy, so Bernice and Alex find two stools at the bar. Glass in hand, the taste of Merlot in her mouth, surrounded by conversation and laughter, horns from the street, the evening unfurling in the surrounding neighborhoods — the cumulative effect makes Bernice giddy and self-conscious. How long has it been since she sat having a drink at a bar on a Saturday night? With a man? She can't even remember. Eons.

Conversation takes the path of least resistance. There's so much they could talk about, so much they could discuss — so much they've been through in the last eight hours — but to do so would necessitate reexperiencing and reconfronting, and neither of them has the energy. So they talk about the wine. It's good. They talk about Chicago, which makes Athens seem sleepy. "Remind me why we live in Iowa?" Bernice says. They talk about cocktail napkins — how some of them cling to the bottom of glasses and some don't. Alex thinks it ought to be possible to design a cocktail napkin that could get wet and not cling.

"Maybe there's no market," Bernice says. "Maybe people don't care."

"I care," Alex says, holding up his wineglass, which his cocktail napkin has persistently ridden on every trip to his mouth.

He's so young, Bernice thinks. That's the thought brought to her by his thick hair, his nearly blemishless skin, his slim body. He's hardly set out on the voyage. In twenty or thirty years this entire experience will take the form of a grim anecdote rarely told. *That was just after my first wife died.* By then Alex will have another wife, probably, and a different mother-in-law. He'll have children and grandchildren whom he'll know more thoroughly and intimately than he knows her, who will mean more to him than she does, maybe even more than Isabel did. This life will take place in a house far away on a quiet street where the evenings carry voices from yard to yard. So many days and nights, so many experiences, and Bernice will miss them all.

Maybe not. She hopes they'll be able to stay friends. Or will it be too painful for Alex? Will seeing her, hearing her voice, always bring back unpleasant memories?

A waitress approaches, carrying two menus pressed to her chest, barking Alex's surname. Presently Bernice and Alex are installed in a secluded booth with a basket of breadsticks and fresh glasses of wine. Bernice opens her menu and studies the pizza sizes and crust types and toppings. So many options, so many combinations. She's surprised to glance up and see Alex staring directly into her eyes with an astonished, haunted expression on his face.

"You OK?" she asks.

"I was sitting with Isabel in a pizzeria like this when she signed her donor card. Zambrotta's. Same tablecloths. I was having a flashback."

"Do you want to go somewhere else?"

"I'm OK. Just don't tell me you want to become an organ donor."

"Not at the moment." Bernice studies her

menu, unable to extract meaning from the lines of tiny, flowery script. She closes the menu and slaps it down. "I can't figure this out. I don't care. You choose. I'll eat anything."

Alex gives her a pitying look. "I feel terrible. A while ago you were all set on some exotic ethnic food, and now you're telling me you don't care, you'll eat anything."

"Alcohol." Bernice holds up her glass. "And I think I'm just realizing how hungry I am."

"We'd better get a large, then. Pepperoni? Sausage? Extra cheese?"

"Wow. No one's going to be transplanting your heart." Bernice suggests they go half and half, her half with extra tomato sauce, green peppers, and mushrooms. "And let's have a few paramedics standing by in case your arteries clog up."

A wave of sadness sloshes through Bernice as she remembers something Lotta told her earlier in the day. "You know what? In five or ten years, Janet's coronary arteries are going to occlude, and there's nothing the doctors can do about it. Vascu-something or other. Vasculopathy? Lotta told me."

From the way Alex is staring blankly at her, slate-faced, you'd think she'd just informed him of his own impending death.

" 'Occlude.' You mean clog up."

"I'm sorry. It's depressing."

"*Isabel's* coronary arteries."

"Yes. The only workaround is to have a second transplant, to get a second donated heart, but Janet's said she won't take one."

Alex raises his eyebrows and bumps the air lightly with the side of his head, as if to suggest that Janet is less selfish than he thought.

Their waitress arrives and takes their order. After she leaves, Bernice asks Alex, "Did you think she was pretty?"

Alex gives her a puzzled look, then turns to look across the room at the waitress. "I guess so."

"Not her. Janet."

"Oh." Alex gives the question thought. "Yeah. Striking. The long red hair."

Bernice didn't anticipate such a positive endorsement. "I'd kill for that hair."

"What's wrong with your hair?"

"Everything." She rubs a few brittle strands between her finger and thumb.

Alex is looking at her tenderly, smiling. "You're way too hard on yourself."

"Think so?"

"Yes."

Bernice takes a breadstick from the basket and lays it across the rim of a small bowl filled with sugar packets. Alex lays a second breadstick across the bowl, parallel with the first, leaving an inch or two of space between them. Bernice balances a third breadstick perpendicularly across the first two, and Alex adds a fourth, completing a frame. They continue adding breadsticks, one at a time, with increasing delicacy and precision. The emerging structure is precarious, but the salt flakes on the breadsticks provide traction and prevent them from sliding off one another. It's Bernice's unsteady hand that brings the pagoda crashing down. *"Shit,"* she says, enjoying the frank, unbridled sound of the expletive. Alex gathers the fallen pieces and starts again, positioning the first breadstick across the bowl. As they proceed, he and Bernice urge each other to be careful, chide and tease if the other is careless. The teasing turns into playful intimidation designed to sabotage the other's concentration. When the breadsticks tumble, they shriek and cover their faces with their hands. They're vaguely aware that they're annoying adjacent diners, but don't care. Maybe it's the tension of adding breadstick after breadstick to the rickety structure, or the emerging futility of building beyond five stories, or the fact that they're starting into their third glasses of wine on empty stomachs, but each collapse is more amusing than the last. Bernice and Alex giggle and flip breadsticks in the air. Bernice is amazed she's able to feel this silly, to act this silly after a day like today, and feels giddy with relief to know that there's a force in reserve inside herself, and presumably inside Alex, that deploys to the surface when it decides the body has taken enough.

The pizza arrives just in time to halt the unimpeded consumption of alcohol. For a while Alex and Bernice, ravenous, focus solely on feeding themselves, scooping slices onto their plates and wolfing them down. It's not long before they're slumped back in their seats, bloated and stupid, their conversation reduced to an exchange of confessions of how tired they are.

When the check arrives Bernice whips out her credit card. Alex tries to pay but Bernice insists. "It's on me. You can buy breakfast."

The sky outside is dark. The city's myriad lights and noises and movement — people everywhere, in vehicles and on foot, jamming the streets and sidewalks — make Bernice think of a giant pinball machine into which thousands of balls have been sprung. A massive amusement device. Gusts of music and voices from the doorways of bars packed with twentysomethings —

chesty, well-scrubbed men bobbing like buoys around glammed-up women displaying tanned arms and cleavage. Bernice gets a sick feeling seeing all these healthy young women advancing into their lives, enjoying themselves so thoroughly, eligible for opportunities and adventures and happiness.

"You won't believe this," Alex says as they maneuver through a throng of revelers spilling from an Irish pub, "but you know what I'm worried about right now? Jasper. Running into him. This is exactly the kind of place he'd pop up."

"I don't even want to contemplate that," Bernice says.

A block of boarded-up storefronts, trash and broken glass on the sidewalks, disheveled homeless men slumped in doorways, passes like a diorama that has been set up to remind the prosperous how the other half lives. All the black faces make Bernice feel provincial, detached, sheltered from the nation's racial *Sturm und Drang.* She thinks about Janet teaching her underserved Mexican kids, dedicated to the struggle for social justice, social equality — not reading about injustice in *The New York Times,* not contemplating injustice as she strolls with a full belly toward her room at the Hyatt, but devoting her life to its eradication.

Is it reasonable to think that she, Bernice, has contributed in some way, through Isabel, to Janet's efforts? By giving birth to Isabel, by raising her to be empathetic and generous?

"I quit my job," Alex says. "Yesterday. I didn't tell you."

He's tipsy, Bernice notices. A little floaty on his feet. His lips struggle to keep up with his words. "Your job at U.S. Exam?"

"That's the only job I have."

"Really? You really quit?" She's not sure whether to be pleased or concerned. "I didn't even know you were thinking about quitting."

"I wasn't. Until yesterday." He explains that a new shipment of essays arrived from Arkansas a few weeks back, bringing news of a thousand tragic events: car accidents, heart attacks, strokes, cancer, rare diseases. "It's carnage down there, I'm telling you. Carnage in every essay. I couldn't grade the kids objectively. Diane caught on. The way I see it, you ask kids to communicate their suffering and pain and then penalize them because they didn't do it with syntactical flair — what's *that* all about? I'd rather make lattés."

"You can do better than making lattés."

"Lattés must be made."

492

"Well, anyway, it sounds like you quit for a justifiable reason. I never thought that job was good for you. It doesn't have anything to do with your field, with your interests. And it kept you inside all day. You ought to be outside more. That's important to you, isn't it?"

"Maybe I can pick up highway litter."

"Don't be ridiculous. You've got a great education and lots of experience. You'll find a good job."

"Hardly likely, in Athens. Two major employers, the university and the hospital, a handful of small corporations, one of which I just ditched. Unless you have a PhD or an MD, anywhere you look you're pretty much support staff."

"Well . . . sure. I can't deny that's true. It took me years to find my job. On the other hand, it can be done."

They walk on in silence. Alex, hands thrust in his pockets, alternately scowls and grins at some private truth revealed to him by inebriation. He stops short at the inter-section of Ontario and Michigan and gazes north at the buildings reaching skyward, shadowy pillars draped with fleeces of light.

"Just think," he says, riding a mysterious lightness, "if you live here, anytime you want to see this, you just come down here and look at it."

Bernice feels queasy with dread. She yawns and turns away from the view. "We've got a big day tomorrow."

"Maybe we can walk down to the lake in the morning after breakfast."

"If you want."

"I like the lake. It's unlikely, isn't it? Un-*lakely*. Right there at the edge of the city. Like a tide came in from nowhere and never went out."

"It's OK," Bernice says. "It's not the ocean."

"Many bodies of water are not."

"That's profound."

"Thank you."

As they cross the Michigan Avenue Bridge, Bernice takes Alex's arm. He asks if she's OK, and she tells him she feels light-headed. She doesn't tell him that her stomach is a clenched fist of muscle, and that her mind is cycling panicked through thoughts of Isabel and Todd and Clancy and all the others who have left her.

In the hotel, riding up in the elevator, Alex puts his arm around her and gives her an affectionate, inquiring squeeze, as though worried he's responsible for her sullenness.

At the door to their room, Bernice can't get the key card to work. Three times she inserts the key, removes it, and tries to turn the handle without success. Finally, defeated, she scrapes the card against the door in a parody of her ineptness.

Alex opens the door on the first try.

"How did you do that?" Bernice asks, dumbstruck and irritated. His success, contrasted with her failure, feels critical to comprehend, despite the trivial stakes. "I did *exactly* what you did."

"It's all in the wrist."

"No, seriously, how did you do that?"

"Relax."

They collapse on their respective beds with dramatic groans and exclamations of exhaustion.

"What an interminable, whacked-out day," Bernice says.

"It was your idea," Alex says good-naturedly. "Coming up here."

"What was I thinking?"

Bernice stares up at the ceiling, wondering what fills the space, what's there that she can't see or apprehend. Atoms? Molecules? Radiation? What else? In the days when she attended church, the minister used to say, quoting Christ, *Whenever two or three are gathered in my name, I shall be among you.* Does this hold true for the beloved dead? "Do you think she's here?"

she asks Alex. "You think she's with us?"

Alex speaks groggily, as though she's disturbed the onset of sleep. "I don't know. I really can't say."

Bernice glances over to see him lying in exactly the same position she is: flat on his back, limbs sprawled like a starfish, staring up at the ceiling.

She draws up her knees, clasps and massages her ankles. "I'm not asking scientifically. You don't have to unravel the mysteries of the universe or anything. Just tell me what you feel."

"I don't know what I feel. I wasn't thinking about her, but now that I am, it doesn't mean she's floating around in the air above my head. It's a scientific question, you can't avoid it. Does she exist only in our minds, in our memories and thoughts, in our neural circuitry, or does she have some tangible, physical existence out there in space? Outside of our minds?"

"In this case she definitely has some tangible physical existence out there in space."

"The heart is a muscle. It's debatable whether you can call that existence. The way a whole person exists."

"Didn't you feel her presence in Janet's room?"

"I was having trouble feeling it, to be honest."

Bernice allows a respectful pause. "Maybe you need to give it more time. Circumstances were hardly ideal."

"When will circumstances be ideal? Tomorrow?"

"I'm just saying maybe if you spent a little more time with her, one-on-one, something might click. We're in the presence of an incredible thing. It's an incredible thing to have saved another person's life. It's an amazing accomplishment."

"Isabel was her own amazing accomplishment. Not Janet."

"I know. It's just that what's happened with Janet . . . it really is something. And you have to admit it took a lot of vision and empathy and foresight."

Alex lets out an impatient sigh. "You talk sometimes like the donation was the supreme crowning achievement of Isabel's life. Her life's work. It wasn't. The donation was her death's work. Her life's work was her. Don't give her short shrift."

Is Alex suggesting that she doesn't appreciate her own daughter? "I understand that," she says. "Obviously her main goal in life wasn't to sacrifice it for a stranger. The thing is, all her other projects are gone. This is her only surviving work." *Also this, Alex and me, this friendship.* "So it has significance for me."

Alex doesn't respond.

"Don't you think Isabel would have liked her?" Bernice asks.

"Janet? I don't know. Sure. Maybe." He yawns deeply. "Is this still the same day that started this morning?"

Bernice is sloppy in the bathroom, a brisk, perfunctory tooth brushing, a splash of water on her face. She changes into sleepwear, a T-shirt and boxer shorts. She emerges from the bathroom to find Alex out cold on his stomach under a sheet, the blankets heaped at the foot of his bed and his jeans, T-shirt, and sandals tossed on the floor. His bare arms thrown overhead encircling the swirl of his hair on the pillow. Again she thinks of her son, Clancy. She wonders where he sleeps now, and with whom. A doom-tinged sadness pools behind her sternum, making her separation from her son feel like a thing she couldn't possibly live with, even though she does.

The Wrigley Building glows like the moon against a firmament of lights. The Tribune Tower's solid trunk decays, at its faintly illuminated summit, into a skeletal fabric of colonnettes and pinnacles and tracery, an exposed gothic core: the structure sheds mass and surface as it approaches the sky, tapering toward a spire that never appears.

Bernice closes the curtain and slips into bed. Props herself up on a pillow, draws the sheet up over her stomach. The darkened television stares back at her. She wishes she could turn it on and see Isabel's electrocardiogram on the screen. Fall asleep in the glow of those little green wavelets.

She finds the remote and turns on the TV. Assured of its glow, she extinguishes the lamp on the night table. She surfs channels, the sound lowered to a murmur. She hoped the people and chatter would soothe her anxiety, but there's something about the garish colors and vapid, thrusting faces that cheapen, rather than distract from, the events of the day.

Alex's breathing is stuttery and irregular, nearly snoring. His face is sunk so deep in the pillow it's a wonder he can breathe at all.

Bernice turns the TV off, lies down flat, closes her eyes. It's not easy being left with her thoughts, which range back over the day, and which settle, finally, on the conversation she just had with Alex. *Don't give her short shrift.* The accusation needles. *Has* she been heaping attention on Janet, directing too much attention and praise to the success of Isabel's donation while slighting other, earlier successes, foremost among them Isabel's success at simply being herself? It's just that Janet's recovery and prosperity were so attractive, so irresistible — the perfect refutation of Isabel's destruction. The perfect refuge from it. From Janet's first card, from Lotta's first e-mail, a channel opened to a bright parallel universe whose inhabitants believed that a miracle had occurred, that the awful tragedy had been averted. And who was the messiah of this bright parallel universe? To whom did the Corcorans owe their salvation?

Isabel.

Bernice basked in the glory. A little. In the attention. The fuss.

The proud mother got out of hand.

Isabel's face appears, Isabel's voice, pleading for attention and love.

I'm sorry, Bernice tells her. *Forgive me.*

The silence feels immense. Bernice would like to dissolve into it, and resolves to get as close as the living can. Sleep. She shifts and turns in bed, curls up fetal, stretches out like a plank, casts off sheets, tugs them up, determined with each new strategy to switch off her mind. But a channel has opened to a cascade of images and memories of Isabel, which aren't here to be fussed over but to make a case for themselves, to say, *This is who I was.*

Bernice thinks of Alex lying a few feet away in the dark, his sleeping body under the sheets, his breathing. All she'd have to do is touch that body, make contact with any part of it, and she'd have enough on her mind to force out everything else. The inhibition is strong, and she vaguely apprehends consequences, but it's dark, and she's in an unfamiliar city high in a hotel room indifferent to the activities of its occupants — a secluded, permissive space into which broadcasts of propriety barely penetrate.

It's like bench-pressing a heavy weight, raising her body and crossing the space between the beds, but she does it, heart pounding, an electrical thrill flickering in her muscles. She sits on the edge of Alex's bed and settles her hand on what turns out to be his back. Waits.

He turns over. Takes her arm down near the wrist, as though to confirm it's her. "You OK?"

"Can I sleep over here?"

He hesitates a moment, and in the darkness Bernice can feel astonishment coming off him like heat. He shifts over without saying a word, creating space. He lifts the sheet to let her in. Bernice inserts her legs and hips into the bed's snug sheath and directly finds one of his feet with one of her own. From there they come together like a zipper: she presses against his body and slips her arms around his torso and presses her face to what ends up being the base of his neck, to soft skin warmed by sleep, which she kisses naturally, reflexively — what mouth wouldn't, when presented with a neck? His chin stubble scratches her forehead. His fingers on the back of her head, working down into her hair. "It's OK," he says. "It's going to be OK." It may not be an invitation to converse, but Bernice lifts her head and looks into his face, which fills the darkness like a monument. His eyes close and his lips move uncertainly, betraying a hint of intention. She takes the kiss humbly, at first, but his lips are tender and agile and it's not long before she's feeding delicately on the circle of his mouth. Hands on the move touching cheeks and backs and during a brief interlude apart, her chest, a tentative brush of his hand against her breast, which frightens and excites her into another interlocking of mouths. His leg arrives on top of hers, hooking over, extending, his heel against her calf. She feels delicious and combustible. She could consume this man, sweep across him like a brushfire. But there's a line she can't cross.

You fucked my husband, Mom.

He's kissing her neck, light suctioning touches, each kiss like the activation of a hidden, enervating switch.

Mom, what are you doing? Stop.

"Alex," Bernice says. "Let's just sleep."

His hand travels up under her shirt and cups a breast. His fore and middle fingers lightly pinch her nipple. She strokes his bare chest, his stomach, her pinkie brushing rough, curly hairs. She kisses him more deliberately and lets her hands roam his skin hunting warmth and contour when, in an unanticipated unwanted upsurge of emotion, she begins to cry. Alex takes it with surprise and concern and presses his hands to her cheeks as though to make sure the fragile vessel of her head won't spill or shatter. He holds her securely, kissing her forehead and telling her *OK, OK, easy,* until she deflates against him, washes up on his body.

"I don't think she'd understand this," Bernice says.

Alex breathes unevenly, composing himself. "She's not us."

"Lucky for her. In some ways."

Alex maneuvers an arm around her, holds her close. She settles her head in the shallow well of his shoulder, lays her arm across his chest. She closes her eyes, breathes deeply through her nose. She likes the smell of Alex's skin. She wishes she had someone to lie with like this all the time.

"Do you think I'm sad and lost?" she asks.

"Why would I think that?"

"Because I'm here. With you."

"I'm here with *you*," Alex says, mildly indignant.

"Are we sad and lost together?"

Alex takes a moment to consider.

"Just sad," he says.

THIRTY-ONE

Janet swings her legs over the edge of her bed and pulls on a pair of fuzzy blue slippers. She probes the floor with her feet, tests it, as though the floor, not her, is likely to be flimsy and unstable. Finally she grips her nurse's arm and rises, teeters a little before establishing her balance.

This is the first time Alex has seen Janet out of bed, standing up. He looks at her in the bright sunlight from the window. He's taken aback by her height and size. She's nearly a head taller than he is, big-boned, substantial through the shoulders and hips. The friction of sliding out of bed has hiked her blue-flecked hospital gown up her backside. Janet's nurse, an equally large, blond woman named Zoë, tugs the fabric down and helps Janet into a lightweight blue bathrobe. Janet takes a few tentative steps. Assured of her stability, she says to Alex, "Let's boogie."

Janet is required to take two therapeutic walks daily, and even though she's going home this afternoon — her doctors surprised her early this morning with the news — she's determined to stick to the regimen. Alex has agreed to walk with her. Janet invited both him and Bernice to come along, but Bernice passed, suggesting to Alex with a meaningful glance that this was an opportunity for him.

He follows Janet out of her room, and together they start down the corridor. Her steps are solid. Her balance is good. There's no need for anyone to accompany her as far as Alex can see. Except for the bathrobe and flimsy hospital pants, she might be an ordinary civilian. He walks awkwardly beside her, his hands, for lack of anything better to do, stuffed in his pockets. Janet stops by the nurses station, where she's greeted with "Going home today, are you, superstar?" and "Who's your friend?" Janet introduces Alex to several nurses, a surgical resident, and a unit clerk — all who have known her for a long time. The reactions are admiring. Alex gets the impression that donor families aren't a common sight around here.

The farther they travel, the more Alex sees why he was invited along. Though Janet walks well, she does so slowly, deliberately, with barely detectable unsteadiness, as if she's getting used to a pair of cross-country skis.

They pass an elderly-looking man returning to harbor, laboring behind his IV pole, his infrequent steps separated by long pauses in which he stares down at the carpet, planning his next footfall. His nurse leans close to his hairless head, straining to comprehend his muffled utterances. As Janet passes, he happens to glance up with a look of incomprehension.

"Hi, Octave," Janet says, careful not to expend too much breath.

Octave isn't going to expend any. He tips his head forward and opens his mouth as though to let something drop out. There's a hinge-like wheezing in his throat that Alex would rather not think about.

When Octave is out of earshot, Alex asks Janet, "What was that guy's problem?"

"He needs a new heart," Janet says.

They leave Medical Cardiology and turn into the main corridor, which is crowded with hospital staff. Alex and Janet hug the right-hand wall, Janet on the inside, Alex on her flank. Octave's wheezing has left Alex spooked. He imagines Janet's heart thudding away under the folds of her gown, under layers of skin and muscle, its chambers obediently contracting, struggling to meet the necessity of moving her legs. His mind registers the increasing distance of Medical Cardiology and its staff. What if something were to happen to Janet out here in the middle of nowhere, on the high seas, on his watch? What if her heart works too hard and bursts like an overhandled water balloon? Alex dips his head inconspicuously toward Janet's body and monitors her breathing for signs of strain, her face for flushing or wincing, while keeping an eye out in the corridor ahead for obstacles: bumps in the carpet, doors that might swing open into Janet's face, hospital personnel approaching on collision courses with carts or machines. He allocates a slice of peripheral vision to Janet's feet, making sure they stay separate and parallel. Having her in his custody — coordinating his movements with hers, matching her steps, worrying that she might fall — forces him to partially inhabit her damaged body, whose fragility must feel strange and foreign to her, too. He doesn't feel like he's taking Janet for a walk. He feels like he and Janet are walking a third person.

"Is this pace OK?" Alex asks. "I don't want you to overdo it."

"I should have started more slowly," Janet admits, the words riding out on a breath. "The heart needs a few minutes to figure out what I'm up to."

"To figure out . . . ?"

"It's denervated. Remember?"

"Oh. Right." A cargo of hope, which Alex hardly realized he was carrying, drops in his stomach. Why is it so hard to be reminded that Isabel's heart isn't attached to Janet as closely as it could be? Because then he has less chance of reaching it. Affecting it.

They pass the atrium with its high, mirror-paneled walls, a well of reflections and refractions and indirect sight lines. Janet suggests they go up to the roof deck. Apparently there's a view. They have the elevator to themselves. Riding up, face-to-face with Janet, Alex worries that somehow she'll figure it out, that she'll be able to tell just by looking at him what happened with Bernice last night. It's paranoia, of course. Even crazier, Alex worries that somehow Isabel's heart will know.

The doors on the twelfth floor open onto a gallery furnished with couches and armchairs and lamps. Alex holds the door open to the roof deck while Janet steps through. Sunlight bakes the concrete. The furnishings are spare, and suggest minimal use:

scattered pieces of lawn furniture, a frail-legged patio table sheltered by a tipsy umbrella. A woman in green scrubs dozes in a chaise parked in a slab of shade.

Janet goes to the railing, grips it with both hands, locks her arms, and levers her body forward like a gymnast. Her feet leave the ground. A flutter passes through Alex's chest; what if she tips over the railing and plummets to the ground? He peers steeply down. Directly below, twelve stories below, is a concrete patio furnished with benches and plantings. He wants to take hold of Janet's arm but restrains himself. He's relieved when her feet touch down.

"It's great to get out of that room," she says. "I'm so sick of lying down."

"You must be looking forward to going home."

"Totally. A transplant's great, but the trade-off is you spend way too much time in a place like this. It's hardly a normal life. It's a weird life. But I'll take it."

Janet unties her bathrobe and holds it open wide like a pair of wings, gently swings the fabric to and fro, airing it in the breeze. Alex looks out over the city, the rooftops and chimneys and antennae, the jagged foothills rising unevenly to downtown's clustered peaks. "Isabel hated hospitals," he

gers, bikers and Rollerbladers, babies in strollers, dogs. Alex and Bernice followed the shore south. Their conversation consisted of trivial observations and musings. They carefully avoided their mutual preoccupation. Above, skyscrapers stood sentinel-like, guarding their Sunday utopia: copper-backed volleyball players leaping on the beach, swimmers carving lanes parallel to the shore, sailboats perched like moths out toward the flat, featureless horizon.

Alex tries to discern, from his position on the hospital roof, where in relation to the buildings near the lake he and Bernice were walking. He can't. He doesn't know the city well enough. His eyes are drawn to a narrow, octagonal tower that rises from a wider building like a rocket ensconced in launch scaffolding. The building's surface is complex, intricately sculpted, and makes him think of a cathedral. He says so to Janet.

"That's Seventy-five East Wacker," Janet tells him. "You're right, there's some nice Gothic stuff happening up top. I like the tiers, and the buttresses at the base of the tower."

"Wow. You've got some vocabulary."

Janet shrugs dismissively. "Architecture's not my thing. I like it, but I don't know much about it. Living in Chicago you can't help picking up a little. Seventy-five East Wacker's one of my favorite buildings. I used to be down there fairly often. David's office is right around the corner."

The expression on Janet's face is grim, stoic. Alex finds himself increasingly curious as to how strongly she feels about this man, whose words and actions have the power, however circuitously, to affect Isabel's heart.

"So David's a lawyer?" he asks.

Janet nods. She's busy reaching behind her head, gathering her hair in her fists. She clamps it with a barrette. "Information technology law. E-commerce. Nine times out of ten, he's defending someone who's been accused of transmitting or distributing something they shouldn't have been. Copyright stuff. He's good at it. It's demanding work. He loves it."

Alex's spirits and self-esteem briefly sag. How long has it been since he had a job he loved, or even liked? How long has it been since he felt the exhilaration of a challenge — of absorption in a task matched to his talents and interests?

He asks Janet, "How long have you been married?"

Janet squints at the sky. "Twelve years. How long were you and Isabel together?"

"Six," Alex says. "Married for three."

Janet winces compassionately. "It must have been much worse for you. David and I, we're cracking under the stress of a long, difficult period. But you two . . . Isabel was . . ."

"Stricken down at the height of our marital bliss?"

"I'm so sorry."

Alex understands that she means to acknowledge that he got a worse deal than she did, and to be sensitive to the particular nature of his suffering. Still, it feels like she's rubbing something in. He says, "It must be hard when your marriage crashes and burns."

Janet gives him a defensive glance. "It is. At least you have the comfort of knowing that Isabel's death was no reflection on you. It's not like she woke up one morning and said to herself, 'I've had enough of Alex. I can't stand him anymore. I can't stand being married to him anymore.' Which is presumably what David woke up and thought. I'll always have to live with that. With the mystery of why."

"Is why a mystery?"

Janet's laugh cuts. "What do you mean? Do *you* have the answer?"

"You said yourself that you destroyed his

life. That it's not easy living with a person who has a chronic illness."

"I also said I expected him to rise to the occasion."

"So that's the mystery? Why he didn't? Whether he would have for someone else?"

"Thank you for putting it so succinctly. Do you have anyone in mind?"

"I'm sorry, I don't know why I said that."

"I see where you're going with this. Isabel would have been worth the effort. You said you'd give anything to have her alive with a chronic illness. Is that the implication? That David would have hung in there for me, had I been her? Had I been her equal?"

Alex meant to imply no such thing, and can't imagine how Janet construed that he did. "How can I answer that? I've never met David."

"You would have hung in there for Isabel. If she'd had a chronic illness."

"Of course."

"Don't be so sure," Janet says sharply, as though rebuking the hubris of a child. "You have no way of knowing. Don't be so quick to declare yourself the better man. You have no idea what David went through. It was a lot more than just walking me up to the roof deck."

■ ■ ■ ■

It's embarrassing to Janet, how slowly she moves, how tired she is after her short, undemanding walk to the roof. Alex, who's entitled to be more irritated with her, is patient and solicitous, and when she nearly stumbles over a raised strip of metal in a doorway he grips her arm at the triceps and steadies her. From there on he walks close, his near arm partially raised, hand open, wary, attentive, ready to come to her aid again.

"I could get used to this," Janet says. "Have you ever wanted to be a personal assistant?"

"Does it pay?" Alex asks.

"Actually, my mother would feel slighted if I hired you. That's her job. And she takes pride in it. She enjoys the glamour. The glamour and the drama."

"I know I'm feeling pretty glamorous right now."

Janet laughs, and then, in a kind of hiccup, reverses, swallows it, her eyes having ventured down the corridor ahead. She wonders for a moment if she's seeing an apparition, if she's experiencing some kind of stress-induced hallucination. But that *is* David, pacing near the entrance to Medical Cardiology with his arms hanging close to his body, hands flapping like little flippers, drumming on his thighs. He's whistling under his breath, his nervous whistle. Carly and Sam orbit, dazzled, riddling their mysteriously absent father with requests and observations. The sight of David, the fact of his presence here, gives Janet a subcutaneous thrill, a glimmer of hope, as if he might have come to apologize and atone — as if he might have been miraculously transformed into an earlier, sweeter, more committed version of himself. He's wearing his Teva sandals and an ancient, faded pair of khaki shorts she's probably folded fifty times. The yellow Angel Eco Tours T-shirt from the trip they took to Venezuela before they were married. She remembers the wet, green, luminous hills, jagged black peaks, waterfalls that seemed to flow from the sky.

"Well I'll be damned," Janet says to Alex. "You're going to meet my husband."

Janet's surprise, or an unrelated loss of balance, causes her to waver to one side, and though she instantly self-corrects, Alex's hand jumps to take hold of her arm. "That's David?"

"That's David."

David spots them approaching, straight-

518

ens, and stares. He gives Janet an affable smile. "Hey. How's it going?"

The intensity and exclusivity of his gaze tells Janet he's trying not to look at Alex, trying not to dignify him with interest. How does David even know who Alex is?

Janet asks, "Have you been back to the room? Did you talk to my mom? Did you meet Bernice?"

David nods wearily. "They told me you were on a walk. I was out here waiting for you and I ran into your dad coming back from the playground with the kids. He went back to the room."

Janet's sad for herself, but also sad to see him standing out here alone, estranged from his family. What resources does he have? Who will he lean on?

Carly hurls herself affectionately, hard as a linebacker, into Janet's thigh.

Janet says to David, "Well, lucky you. You finally found me. If you'd come any later, I would have been home."

His eyes give her a down-up. "You look good. Up and around."

"David, Alex," Janet says, introducing. "Isabel's husband. Remember?"

"Of course. Nice to meet you." David's tone is polite but restrained. He shakes Alex's hand. "I'm sorry about your loss."

Alex acknowledges the condolence with a barely perceptible nod. Janet gives David a moment to say more, and when he doesn't — when he fails to allow a single drop of gratitude or appreciation to fall from his lips into the excruciating silence — shame and embarrassment soak her bones.

"What are you up to today?" Alex asks David with a civility that makes Janet both grateful and nervous.

"Not much," David says. "I thought I'd drop by and see how she was doing. See the kids. It's been a crazy week at work."

Janet tells Alex, "The tyrants he works with, they won't let you visit your wife in the hospital."

"Not true," David says.

"Well, there you go."

David flops his head to one side as though his neck has snapped. He stretches his eyes wide and makes a goofy, frazzled face for Alex — an invitation to join in a solidarity based on a shared recognition of, and exasperation with, his wife's flaws.

"We went up to the roof deck," Janet says. "It's gorgeous out. First time I've been outside since Tuesday."

"I hear you had a biopsy this morning. It came back OK?"

"I should know in an hour or two. They're

expecting everything to look good."

"You had a *biopsy* this morning?" Alex asks. "Isn't that a big deal?"

"Not really. I've had dozens. They snake a wire down through a vein in my neck and . . ." Probably Alex doesn't want to know. Probably he doesn't want to hear how they clip off a piece of cardiac tissue and mount it on a slide and study it under a microscope. Janet substitutes a dismissive, trifling wave of her hand. "Check stuff out. Piece of cake."

"Everything's a piece of cake for her," David tells Alex.

"Isn't that to her credit?"

"Depends on your point of view."

"And your point of view is . . . ?"

"Everything's *not* a piece of cake. The truth is those biopsies hurt, and in the past she's had arrhythmias and nearly died."

Alex looks to Janet for verification. Janet rolls her eyes dismissively but with a certain bravado.

After an awkward silence, Alex announces that he's going to head back to the room — a move that seems born equally of discomfort and an inclination to leave them alone. "Can you get back OK?" he asks Janet.

A fabric of possibility, intricately interwoven with her nerves and deepest needs, is

521

coming apart in front of her, despite her efforts. So this is it. Alex and David have met, and now they will part. She gives David a look that asks, *Is that all? Is that all you have to say to this man?* Evidently it is. "I'll be fine," she tells Alex. "Thanks for the walk. I enjoyed it. Really."

"Nice to meet you," Alex tells David.

"Likewise."

After Alex has gone, David gives Janet an arch, bemused look.

"What?" Janet challenges.

David shrugs and keeps to himself whatever disparaging comment he'd been on the verge of making. "It's funny, seeing you two together," he says with genuine sincerity. "It makes me nostalgic. Is that crazy? You two getting to know each other, talking, taking walks. It reminds me of old times. Does it remind you?"

Janet's face is hot. She's determined not to cry in front of him. "How much does it remind you?"

David smiles sweetly, but it's an apology. *Didn't mean to get your hopes up.* "I love you. I miss you. I think about you all the time."

From his tone of voice, whose gradations of pitch and timbre she knows better than any other, she realizes he's truly, genuinely in pain — that he believes in and suffers

522

from a version of what's happened between them, and why it's happened, whose truth is as real and convincing to him as her version is to her.

"Spare me," she says, barely able to speak.

Carly and Sam have been entertaining themselves admirably but now find themselves out of ideas. Carly attaches to Janet's robe and squeals, "Can we have an elevator race?" It's something the four of them used to do in happier times, in whatever large building they were in: one adult and child ride up in one elevator, the other adult and child in a second elevator, first team to reach the objective floor wins. "Carly, sweetie," Janet says, "why don't you and Sam go back to the room. Dad and I are talking. Sam, can you walk back with Carly? Go catch up with Alex."

They're reluctant at first, but after more prodding, they morosely depart. Sam, out of an urge that's partly protective and partly domineering, tries to make Carly take his hand. Janet's pleased to see Carly resist and ultimately refuse — pleased to see her daughter insist so firmly on her autonomy.

"They seem to be holding up," David says.

"What have you spent, like, ten minutes with them?"

David checks his watch. "I'd say twenty."

"The past few days have been really tough on them. They could have used you."

"I know. It's been busy. I talked to them last night on the phone."

What does he mean by "busy"? *Busy in my brain. Busy avoiding you. Busy with my agenda.* "They need more from you than a few minutes on the phone. They need reassurance that you're not about to disappear forever. They're worried. They're restless. They aren't buying the smokescreen. Especially your boy. I think we should tell them the truth."

"I'll talk to them."

"What are you going to say?"

"That you and I aren't getting along, we're both under a lot of stress, we're going to spend some time apart. That's not a lie, is it?"

Janet wonders if the same frailty and weakness that rendered him unfit to face the hard realities of her illness will also render him unfit to face the hard realities of their separation. "I don't think we should tell them any kind of lie. And we should talk to them together."

"When are we going to do that?"

"You tell me."

David stands with his weight on one leg, arms folded across his chest, staring into space with grudging forbearance.

"Look, David. When I get out of here today, we're all going back to the loft to have a party. No big deal. Very casual. Why don't you come? Just hang out for a while. Mom's going to cook sukiyaki. We won't talk to the kids tonight, but at least you could spend some time with them. You could spend some time with Alex and Bernice. They're nice. And my parents would love to see you back in the game."

"They're thrilled with me, I can tell."

"They'd be relieved if you came. It would give them hope, even if it's only hope that you're going to be around for Carly and Sam."

"I'll pass."

Did he say *"pass"*? A small, intimate celebration of her survival, a long-hoped-for union with her donor family, her amiable parents, her adorable children, who were also saved from loss and grief; a home, a room full of people who love him, or are willing to try — did he say *"pass"*?

Janet drops her face into her hands and allows herself a moment of release. She wants to sob, she wants to collapse to the floor and cry out, *I can't believe this is happening,* but she'd only add to David's conviction that she's a physical and emotional liability, a drag on his well-being, when she's determined to prove it's the other way around. She yanks her hands down and straightens up and looks at him full-on, trembling with disbelief. "OK. That's it. I'm going back to the room."

"Oh — OK." He's surprised. He seems to have expected this conversation to continue. "Keep in touch, huh?"

It strikes her, with a wallop, that he's come here to be assured that it wasn't necessary for him to come. That he needn't feel too guilty. He wanted to witness her strength and self-sufficiency, and to go on record with himself as having said certain things at certain junctures — *I love you, I miss you, I think about you all the time* — that will, in retrospect, make his behavior seem more noble.

"Stop worrying about me," Janet says.

THIRTY-TWO

Hardwood floors, tall windows with views of rooftops, a high ceiling, exposed vents. Paintings done in bold, vibrant reds and yellows and blues. A dark, oxidized tin mirror with sea-green, inlaid tiles. A shelf loaded with books. A fish tank. A Berber rug.

"What a *lovely* apartment," Bernice says, magnetized, floating into the space.

Alex can't help thinking it: Isabel would have loved this room.

"Welcome to my humble abode," Janet says with a dramatic sweep of her arm, ushering them in, wondering if she'll be able to afford to keep living here. She showered at the hospital, washed and blow-dried and brushed her hair. She put on a white linen wraparound blouse, an Aztec-patterned skirt, strappy leather sandals. She intended to dispel from Alex's and Bernice's memories any visions of her hobbling around in sad hospital fashions.

"Would anyone like a glass of wine?" Lotta is standing at a black granite counter that separates the kitchen from the living area. She's holding a knife. On a cutting board in front of her are chopped celery and onions, beef sliced into thin strips. There's an open bottle of wine, too, and several empty glasses. "I've already had a glass. Help yourself."

"What are you making?" Bernice asks, lifting the bottle of Shiraz and inspecting the label. Alex pulls up alongside, ready for a drink.

"Sukiyaki. I've always wanted to visit Japan. All those beautiful Shinto temples."

Janet, on a brief tour of the apartment, reacquaints herself with the space, eyes peeled for changes and aberrations. Often, when left in charge of domestic operations, her mother relocates decorative objects she feels would look better elsewhere, and then, when confronted, explains her reasoning in a prepared speech fortified with references to practicality or tradition or aesthetics. Evidently this week she's been too busy. Everything is exactly where it should be.

Except David.

"Excuse me. Opening windows. Hot as an oven in here." Bud slips in front of Janet and heaves open a sash. The sash squeals and cracks on the way up.

"Go easy on those, Dad. They're old. We go easy on you, don't we?"

"I have the worst trouble with my windows," Bernice tells Lotta, sipping wine. "Some of them won't even open. God knows what I'd do if there were a fire."

"Climb out one that opens," Alex says.

Sam and Carly shriek and giggle and chase each other around the apartment like a pair of cooped-up dogs released into a yard.

Janet pours herself a glass of wine. "There's not a cardiologist in the room, is there?"

Bernice and Alex exchange a glance of concern, as if this might evidence a reckless side of Janet that she hasn't yet allowed them to see.

"It's OK," Janet assures them. "It's red wine, after all. And I'm just having a splash."

"Party on," Alex says, weary of her flushed, beaming face, her transparent delight. All the way home from the hospital, captive in the back of Bud's minivan, he was forced to listen to her rhapsodize about her freedom. *It's so great to get out of that place. It's so great to smell real smells. God, I could eat a piece of fried chicken!* Carly gazed up at him moonily, flirting, from the car seat into which she was strapped and buck-led every which way — she would have been the safest girl in the world hanging from her ankles inside this hulk of steel — while Sam, greedy for attention, whined incessantly about being cold even though it had been sweltering until Bud turned on the air.

"I didn't realize when we moved in what a great neighborhood this was," Janet tells Bernice. "The loft came first, and we knew it was a pretty happening area, but it wasn't until after we'd moved in and taken a look around that we realized, Hey, Wicker Park's really cool."

"Look, I got it!" Sam displays for his mother a small puzzle whose objective — to jostle a thin, loose chain to form the nose and mouth and chin of a woman whose cartoon profile has been left incomplete from forehead to neck — he's just ac-complished.

"That's the kind of toy I used to have when I was a kid." Bernice leans close over the boy's shoulder. "No batteries. No silicon chip."

Yes, good, Janet thinks. *It's important for Sam and Carly to have a tangible experience of these people.* To reinforce the idea that their mother wasn't saved by an abstract medical procedure.

Carly announces that she's discovered a funny-looking bug on the windowsill. Lotta joins her to examine it, bending at the waist and bowing low over the specimen. Carly's head hovers close to hers. Lotta answers her questions in whispers. Alex hears the words "prothorax" and "nonjointed antennae" and "wings."

Bernice finds herself wishing, watching Lotta and Carly, that you could turn off your memory, if you chose to, at particular times when you didn't want to deal with what it might dredge up. In this case, the old Randall's Grocery, circa 1971, huddling head-to-head beside the cart, voices low, Isabel struggling to pronounce the ingredients of a juice or a cake mix.

"Tell me it's not a cockroach, Mother," Janet says.

"It does share similarities with *Blattaria*, but there's no dorsal plate, and no multi-jointed antennae. It's missing the joined cerci at the end of the abdomen. I'm guessing *Hemiptera*."

Bud leans slowly and deeply over the coffee table, groans as he plucks a chip from a bowl, and stands wincing with pain. "I think I hurt my back."

"That's what happens when you go around beating the hell out of my windows,"

Janet says. "Are you OK?"

"Your windows beat the hell out of me."

"I've never understood why so many people have bad backs," Bernice says. "You'd think evolution would have managed to build us strong, decent backs. We obviously need them."

"Evolution decided walking upright was more important," Alex says. "Bad backs are the price we pay to have our hands free."

"Is that really true?" Lotta asks. "That's fascinating."

"I'd rather go around on all fours," Bud says.

Lotta laughs, and Bud smiles and massages her shoulder as if that were the only result he cared about. They exchange a weathered, grateful smile. It's the first time Alex has seen Lotta's face timid and sad, the corners of her eyes and mouth downturned in unison. Is she going to cry? Their daughter's safe. It's all they care about. Obviously. And they're still sweet on each other.

Janet hears Sam's Game Boy bleeping and thinks for a moment it's an alarm on a pump she or her nurse ought to pay attention to, then realizes it's only a toy. A toy!

Alex stares into the fish tank. Slowly, gently, the costumed beauties lift and sink, shimmying against gravity, dainty tails twitching. Eyes roll toward Alex's face. "That's Ziggy. She's a clown triggerfish. That's Mom's favorite fish." Sam is standing beside Alex, his Game Boy on pause. He's talking about a preposterous-looking, yellow-lipped creature whose sagging belly is covered with gray-blue, jellybean-shaped spots.

"What's this guy?" Alex taps the glass near a fish shaped like an arrowhead with black zebra stripes.

"Don't tap the glass. It scares them. That's Lancelot. He's a Wimplefish. This one's Guinevere." Disc-shaped, yellow, with plumelike fins. "She's a Yellow Anthia."

"Lancelot and Guinevere. I get it. Do they . . . Are they . . . ?"

Sam stares at Alex, bewildered. Alex reaches out and cups his hand to the side of the boy's head, just above the ear. Sam's hair is soft and fine, his skull hard and warm. What would his and Isabel's child have looked like?

We are fools, Bernice thinks. Fools to fall captive to hopes and dreams and above all to expectations. Expectations depend on the future, and the future is a loan shark: callous, usurious, unreliable. What makes us believe we can construct and fathom the future? Why do we ogle its promises and enticements, when the present, in so many cases, is everything we could have asked for? Later in life, after the present has become the past, we'll long for it, and for its people.

She's watching Alex and Sam over by the fish tank. She's in the kitchen helping Lotta, stirring a skillet simmering with beef and onions, mushrooms and potato noodles.

Alex catches her eye and wanders over. Bernice's stomach clenches. She thinks how much worse it would be if she and Alex hadn't managed a brief conversation, a partial release of pressure, before leaving the hospital. Janet was taking a shower. Bernice and Alex went downstairs in search of decent coffee. They were returning with not-so-decent coffee along a deserted corridor when Bernice couldn't stand the evasiveness — his or hers — any longer.

"About last night," she said. "I don't know what that was."

Alex looked at her as though her face might know more. "Let's not analyze it. I don't have any regrets."

"I feel embarrassed."

"Why?"

"Not exactly behavior becoming of a mother-in-law."

"After all we've been through? Who says?"

534

Bernice said gratefully, "I like it that you stand up for me."

"You stand up for me."

Bernice's greatest fear is that their physical intimacy last night, which she's decided, contrary to certain dissenting desires, ought to be a singular event, will cause each of them to feel so uncomfortable and awkward with the other that their friendship, which Bernice values above all else, will regress and deteriorate.

Alex, standing next to her at the counter, can't believe that her body, so ordinary now in daytime, covered in clothes, humble, plain, effectless, your typical four-limbed human model, is the same body that last night, in the dark, in vivid, tactile memory, was galvanic and exquisite. He worries that in a strict sense he betrayed Kelly, and maybe even Isabel. Though Isabel, unlike Kelly, might understand.

He wonders what will happen with Kelly. He called her yesterday after storming out of Janet's room and left a message in which he said, essentially, with some equivocating, that he was sorry, he wished he'd gone camping, everything up here was a mess. But she hasn't called him back.

He points to a dark, thick leaf on the counter. "What's that?"

"Kelp." Bernice tears off a bite-sized shred and lifts it to his mouth. "Want a taste? It's sweet."

He tries to take the kelp from her hand.

"Relax," Bernice says, pulling it away.

Alex opens his mouth. Bernice drops the kelp onto his tongue and gives him a reproving smirk. *That wasn't so hard, was it?*

"*Konbu dashi,*" Lotta says, like a blessing.

Alex and Bernice both look at her, bewildered.

"Japanese for kelp," Lotta says.

Dinner is served buffet-style. Janet and Lotta and Bernice sit one-two-three on the couch in front of the coffee table, Bud reclines in a sling chair with his plate perched high on his stomach, Sam and Carly sit on the floor at either end of the coffee table like the miniature master and mistress of a country estate. Alex is given a comfortable armchair near Janet. Conversation sputters to a start and lights out for uncharted territories. Plates and wineglasses are refilled. Lights are turned on against the darkness. The breeze slipping in through the windows cools. Janet gets up and puts on some early Miles Davis, which injects energy and velocity and serves as a bulwark, in Alex's mind, against the sadness likely to germinate in quiet.

536

He works on his second plate of sukiyaki, concentrates on savoring the taste. Voices grow loud and boisterous, straining against the walls, especially Lotta's and Janet's, fueled by Bernice's loose, helpless laughter and Bud's cheeky one-liners. Maybe it's the alcohol, or the food, or the accumulation of time spent together, but a barrier has been crossed, and they're speaking to one another with familiarity and a kind of trusting carelessness, less afraid than before of causing offense.

Alex's reflex is to chafe against this levity, feeling everyone ought to be more quiet and respectful in deference to Isabel. But that's not what Isabel would have wanted, is it? A room full of silent, morose, excessively reverent people? Isn't that exactly what she was determined to prevent? His mind travels to a different scenario, the negative image of all this happiness and prosperity. A pocked, smoking ruin. Janet has died. Her family mourns. Lotta, having lost her daughter, is Bernice. Carly and Sam are motherless. Janet's husband, like Alex, aimlessly circles the wreckage. It's astonishing to think that it was Isabel who prevented this darker scenario by signing her name in blue ballpoint pen on a piece of paper only several square inches in size, and by being prepared to accept the consequences. It's incredible to think that such power and possibility are contained in a single decision, a single organ of the body. And that Isabel knew it.

Brownies arrive, hot, capped with berets of melting vanilla ice cream. The coffee is hot and strong. For a long time the group is silent except for purrs of delight. One by one the sated lay their forks on empty plates and slump back. A post-meal torpor ensues in which the children, sugar-buzzed, provide a floor show. Sam expounds on the abilities of different Power Rangers. Carly takes off her shoes and socks and demonstrates Tae Kwon Do patterns. After a while, Janet falls asleep. Voices respectfully soften. Watching her chest rise and fall, Alex hears, through the open windows, car engines, scattershot voices, the *phump* of a shutting door, the clatter of an El train in the distance. And now Isabel's heart one more sound in the mix of this city.

Sam and Carly are playing marbles on the carpet.

Bud asks Lotta what time they ought to think about driving home.

Bernice looks at her watch.

It's a shock to Alex, seeing Bernice do this. Despite his unease, despite the difficulty of the circumstances, he hasn't given a thought to leaving. Before long he and Bernice will have to rouse themselves and say good-bye and drive the long, bleak stretch of I-80 back to Athens.

Janet's head is tipped back against the cushion, her chin lifted, hands clasped across her stomach. Her skin is fair, with an unlikely translucence — the translucence one sees in the skin of infants. Smudges of pink in the cheeks. Even with its more pressing responsibilities, the heart attends to this small cosmetic matter, so important in evolutionary terms. Freckles scattered across her nose. A few dry patches, lightly dusted with white, on her neck under the overhang of her jaw. A mole the size of a pencil point. A tendon rises, an artery shifts beneath the skin.

Her chest rises, falls. Rises. The top of the scar is visible in the deep open neck of her blouse.

She wakes to the clack of marbles, a hard shot of Sam's. She's surprised to discover Alex sitting forward in his chair, elbows on knees, his face slack and lifeless, scooped-out eyes staring at her chest as though it were a television screen on which some terrible catastrophe were unfolding.

Blinking her eyes, coming to her senses,

she can't believe she hasn't thought to offer, can't believe the idea hasn't occurred to her.

She places her hand on her chest to assure herself she's correct about his object of interest. "Do you want to listen?"

It takes a moment for the invitation to sink in. Stunned, thrilled, afraid, he rises slowly from his chair and sinks to his knees in front of her. She slides forward to the edge of the couch and parts her legs to create space for his body. She's still holding her hand over her sternum, and Alex is close enough to see faint blue veins crossing tendons and threading among knuckles. Janet laughs, shaking off self-awareness — a laugh like the silky ripple of a horse's flank. Her eyes inquire how he'd like to proceed. He kneels up, arms stiff at his sides, and edges forward close to her, positions his body against hers like a cello. "Is this OK?"

"Put your hands here, if you want," Janet says, indicating the couch on either side of her thighs. He does, reaching over her thighs, embracing her.

The room has gone absolutely still. Bernice and Lotta have seen what's going on and spread the word, and everyone has gathered at a respectful distance. Only Carly blurts with suppressed mystification,

"What's he *doing?*" and Lotta quietly explains. Bernice, whose shock won't wear off — a mixture of shock and unease that may or may not be jealousy — notices that Carly is uneasy too, seeing Alex so close to an area on her mother's chest to which she used to have near-exclusive access. The girl is chewing hard on the tip of her pinkie and digging the toe of one foot into the heel of the other. Bernice takes her hand, and Carly gives it an accepting squeeze, as though it were only natural that they ought to witness this together.

Alex glances up at Janet, a last-minute request for clearance.

"Go for it," Janet says.

He turns his head sideways and presses it to Janet's chest just inside the open neck of her blouse. Her skin radiates heat. He's touched down on firm ground, right on the sternum, though there's a cushioning rise on his cheek where her right breast ascends. He can feel the seam of her scar, a rough ridge against his ear. The only sound is a faint, muffled rumbling, like a distant avalanche heard through a snowstorm. Alex closes his eyes to help himself concentrate. He plugs his exposed ear with a finger, effectively appending his head to Janet's body: the outside world is now the inside of her.

He waits for a rhythm to rise from the distant roar. "Don't hold your breath," he tells her.

Her stomach rises. She was. He adjusts the angle of his head and increases the pressure of his ear against her chest until the seal is tight — too tight, it turns out: he's plugged his ear. He backs off slowly, and there it is, right there: firm, rhythmic, duo-syllabic. *Frum*-pum, *frum*-pum, *frum*-pum.

His head tingles as though ice-cold liquid were being poured slowly down over his hair. "Hey there," he says.

Janet asks, "Do you hear it?"

"I do."

The room is so still it sounds like everyone has gotten up and left. *Frum*-pum, *frum*-pum. Alex is discouraged not to hear something distinctive about the beats that might definitively identify the heart as Isabel's. Then again, he's not sure what that distinctive quality might be. In any case, he's not inclined to doubt. He wants to believe. But this belief requires a payment, a concurrent relinquishment. The beats are deep, deep down. Lungs and arteries and veins, muscle and tissue crowd around, muffling, claiming. *Ours.* The heart belongs to Janet. To Janet's body. Isabel's body is incontrovertibly gone. It must be, if this isn't it.

Frum-pum, *frum*-pum, *frum*-pum.

If only there were some way to insert himself in that sequestered space where the heart lives, to be dissolved and subsumed in its rhythm. To merge with it, to *be* it. To be part of a human being instead of a whole one, which feels, at this moment, far too difficult.

He circles his arms around Janet's waist and buries his face in her blouse and hugs her tightly. He breathes down hard, sucks air into lungs that feel like they're filling from the bottom with helium. Janet has settled her hand on his head. He's grateful for the presence of that hand, the warmth and fragrance of her skin. "It's OK," she tells him. "You're going to be OK." His skull is hot as a meteor coming through the atmosphere. She cradles it securely to her chest, consumed with the ridiculous fear that it will burn up. All at once something switches and she feels she could forfeit her will to exist. She'd give anything not to be an obstacle, a barrier between this man and the sole surviving remnant of the woman he loves. She aches to open the vault, to give it up. To disappear, sacrifice every molecule, disintegrate entirely around her precious core.

Alex feels a third hand on his shoulder.

543

Too many hands for one person. He's not ready to come up, not ready to go. Desolate, broken, he ascends from the impenetrable depths and detaches his ear from Janet's chest.

Bernice is standing bravely above.

"My turn," she says.

Two Years Later
Epilogue

Earlier in the day there was sun, but after lunch, walking back to work from town, where she'd met a friend from her book club, Bernice saw that the sky in the west was black, and two hours later the air outside turned sea-green and every lightning flash in the costume shop's basement window briefly illuminated lashing rain and wind-whipped trees.

A tornado warning followed, forcing Bernice and her staff — Cari and Ralph and a graduate student named Eileen — to take shelter in the shoe room, a tunnel-like subbasement where they were soon joined by administrative and technical people from the auditorium's upper floors. The crowd sat on the floor with their knees drawn up to their chests and their backs resting against the stacks of cardboard boxes that faced each other across the narrow space and overflowed with Roman thongs and medieval poulaines and women's damask heels and a hundred different styles of boots. If they died, Cari joked, they would die in an avalanche of leather. The tornado warning expired, and the shoe room refugees emerged unscathed. Theatrical endeavors would proceed. Costumes would be altered and fitted. The summer opera — *Le Nozze di Figaro* — would go on.

Now it's after five, and everyone has left. Bernice moves among the dress forms and sewing machines and ironing boards, turning off lamps and fans, picking bits of netting and thread off the floor. She tidies draper's tables, straightens pattern pieces. These are things she could do Monday, or not do at all — their custodian is a dream — but Bernice is stalling. She feels melancholy, listless, in no hurry to leave. She often feels this way late on Friday afternoons, reluctant to part with the workweek's compulsory activity and socializing. She doesn't feel up to the impending Saturday–Sunday gap, a desolate stretch of terrain in which her deprivations — lack of family, the absence of an intimate companion — will swell and hurt.

Outside, the sky has cleared, and the sun is reclaiming ground. The grass is wet and lush. Trees drip. The river rushes and churns, invigorated by rain, its color like milky tea.

Bernice crosses a bridge over the river and climbs the hill into town. University Books, Franklin Optical, Murphy's Bar, Ulla's Scandinavian Imports. Weathered benches on the sidewalks, trees arcing up from grates. Bernice is grateful for the essential immutability of this place. Over the years she's become accustomed to the luxury of her familiarity with it, and in return for her fealty she's received a feeling of entitlement and ownership and safety that would take years to accumulate elsewhere. Some days she tries to imagine leaving Athens, as Alex did, but the prospect of uprooting and moving to a new place, a town or city where she knows no one, knows nothing, fills her with dread. Hasn't she already lost enough?

She looks up and sees a man waddling unhurriedly toward her on the sidewalk, a heavyset thirtysomething with buzz-cut hair, and for an instant, before he recedes into unfamiliarity, she thinks it's Jasper. Her body goes light. She discharges her held breath. Run-ins with Jasper Klass, though infrequent, are, like the long gray winters, the brief, fleeting springs, and the menace of tornados, an inescapable drawback of life here. The last time Bernice saw Jasper was

547

earlier this summer, downtown at the Arts Festival. He was playing his guitar in a blues band. He was wearing a white Stetson hat and playing a white guitar — playing it well, Bernice had to admit. A small crowd was gathered, a few people in front shimmying to the music. Bernice wanted to lunge onto the stage and grab the microphone and announce to everyone that the guitar player was a sociopath. She found it hard to accept that Jasper wasn't still in jail. She had discovered, to her dismay, that you could damage property and attack people if you were willing to spend a few hundred dollars for the privilege, and at the very worst a few months behind bars. Jasper had spent a meager three months in an Illinois prison for his outburst in Janet's hospital room, and the misdemeanors committed at Bernice's house, to which he'd pled guilty, had cost him only a thousand dollars.

As Bernice watched Jasper playing at Arts Fest, grinning and tapping his foot, basking in the applause, she could only hope that somewhere, under that facade, he was suffering.

At the Public Library, Bernice checks out Barbara Tuchman's *A Distant Mirror: The Calamitous 14th Century* — lately she's been interested in medieval history — and a video: *Prime Suspect,* starring Helen Mirren as a hard-bitten London detective. She stops into New Prairie Coop, and her spirits lift at the sight of the colorful produce section, the cheery handwritten signs. The checkout is as busy as a toll plaza at rush hour, harried cashiers whipping items across bleeping scanners, customers carrying on conversations in line, between lines, in the aisles where they load their carts and baskets with vegetables and fruits, meats and fish, bread and cheese and wine. It's Friday night, and on Friday night Bernice buys herself a bottle of wine. She chooses a Pinot Noir, and to accompany it, a baguette, a jar of mango-jalapeño chutney, Camembert. There's a veggie pizza in her freezer she can have for dinner.

Her new neighborhood is one of the oldest in Athens, tucked in a remote corner of the street grid, perched high on a hill overlooking the river. Redbrick streets, wrought-iron fences, fussed-over flower gardens. Stately Victorians. Of course it would be wonderful to live in one of these gorgeous old houses, but Bernice *did* live in a gorgeous old house, and it had become too big for her, too burdensome, too expensive, too quiet. Especially after Alex left. The rooms sulked. The walls greeted her stiffly when she came in the door, as though she had interrupted them grousing. The house had had enough of her. The house wanted arrivals, children, pets, commotion, noise — a young, growing family. It deserved better than a sixty-two-year-old single woman with no close relatives and a torpid social life.

You haven't given me what I hoped for either, she told it.

She likes her new condominium, which is cute and solidly built and has all the amenities. The modest-sized rooms — kitchen, living room, bedroom, bath — seem happy to accommodate and provide for her, enthusiastic about her newly streamlined existence. Bernice unloads her library materials and groceries onto the kitchen counter. She opens the bottle of Pinot and pours herself a glass.

A loud thud shakes the ceiling. The three-year-old boy upstairs has a habit of driving his tricycle into walls. Bernice doesn't mind. Her neighbors' thumps and bumps are a pleasant change from mausolean silence.

She wanders into the living room with her wine. The furnishings, most of them new, financed with the profits of a massive garage sale, are simple and spare. On a round table with a braided-wire base stands the bust of

Mozart wearing his green and white Pioneer Hi-Bred Seed cap. Bernice adjusts the cap on his head — she likes to keep it at a jaunty angle — and asks, "How was your day, Wolfgang?"

The view from the living room window is one of the main reasons she bought the place. Just below is a small, grassy front yard and a flower garden a committee of residents tends to. Across the street is an 1883 Queen Anne with decorative millwork around the bay windows, gable-roofed dormers, and a central turret whose fish-scale-shingled bell roof glimmers with sun in the morning. On either side of this house is ample space for Bernice to see down the slope across the tops of the trees to the river, the green expanse of city park, a corner of the city pool gleaming like an emerald. High on an opposite ridge are several large sorority houses, and farther to the left, nestled among the trees, is the new nursing building — a crystalline structure surfaced in stainless steel — and the law building with its observatory-shaped dome. Also visible, behind the law building, poking like molars out of a distant hill, are two of University Hospital's five pavilions.

Anyone who knew Bernice and her history might imagine that she wouldn't want to look out her living room window every day and see the hospital where her daughter died nearly three and a half years ago. But the opposite is true. Standing here looking out across the river and the trees at the hospital is not unlike standing vigil at a grave, the way Bernice sees it. She hasn't told a soul, not even Alex, who she doesn't think even noticed, the times he's been back to visit, that you can see the hospital from this window. She worries he might think her sentimental or obsessive or morbid. What she'd say, if she had to explain, is that her intention to live out the rest of her days in this place where Isabel lived her days, to depart this life in the hospital where Isabel departed it, to stay with Isabel, attend to her, never abandon or forsake her — this commitment makes Bernice feel attentive and purposeful, dutiful and true. Maybe Isabel doesn't need her. Maybe Isabel would bless and approve of any desire Bernice might have to leave Athens, to seek out a place where she might be happier. But Bernice can't imagine such a place. Isabel's spirit is here. Sometimes she alights quietly, butterfly-delicate, inspiring fondness and yearning; sometimes she plunges into Bernice's gut like a saber. Isabel can be tender; Isabel can be cruel. Either way, Bernice continues to experience her. Which is all you can ask from the dead.

Alex lives on Chicago's north side, just off Clark Street. His apartment is small, and his bedroom window overlooks a school-yard, noisy on weekends with thudding basketballs. But there are hardwood floors, and the rent is reasonable, and downtown is fifteen minutes away on the El.

He works downtown, in an office on Madison and LaSalle, for a small company that schedules rentals of surveying equipment, some of it used for archaeological purposes. It's not fascinating or glamorous — he described his work to his friends in Athens as "sporadically interesting" — but he feels lucky to have the job, considering his erratic employment history. The money is decent — better than waiting tables, which he did when he first moved up here a year ago last April. He keeps his eye out for other openings — he'd like something more interesting, more directly related to his field, something that gets him outside more — but for the time being he's content. He likes his boss, and with one or two exceptions, the people he works with. The atmosphere in the office is laid-back and convivial. By a stroke of good fortune, Alex has a corner cubicle whose window overlooks LaSalle. He likes to sit at his desk in the morning with his coffee and check his e-mail. Skim through the *Tribune* online. Tidy up his databases. He likes the absolute certainty that at no point during the day will he be asked to read an expository essay written by a seventh grader.

When asked whether he's glad he moved to Chicago — mostly it's Bernice who asks — he says he is. He likes being in a place that's completely, thoroughly new to him, fresh, overgrown with distractions and diversions, densely inhabited, brimming with energy and activity and noise and movement, with shiny textures and surfaces, wattage. Infinite possibility. Or the feeling of it. "If you get that — that feeling," Bernice said sagely, "that's enough. Stay there." He's working on friends. A guy he knew in college who's married with three cats in Wrigleyville. A wry, quipping office-mate with whom Alex occasionally male-bonds over cheeseburgers. A friend or two at the coffee shop near his apartment. Dog owners Alex sees repeatedly at the fetch beach. He's established routines, developed interests, inaugurated pastimes. He likes riding the El to work in the morning, watch-ing the city accumulate in the windows as

courage and holding a private ritual, a devotional, a kind of binge-purge in which he remembers everything about life with Isabel that he possibly can, all at once; endures the entire randomly spliced montage until it either exhausts itself or exhausts him, usually the latter, breaking him down, squeezing him out. It's not pleasant. It's never a happy film. The images and scenes appear in gray and charcoal tones, as though his entire life with Isabel occurred on a bleak, rainy day. He knows this isn't true, but his mind, for the time being, wants to deny the era color and light. One day, Alex hopes, when there is more color and light in his present, the deserving patches of his life with Isabel will reacquire their rightful brightness, and he'll be able to linger over them fondly, without fear.

Maybe that explains why he's made such a concerted effort to brighten up his new apartment and to fill it with color. He's repainted the walls off-white; their original pale aqua-green made him think of the bottom of an abandoned swimming pool. In a junk shop he found several antique mirrors of various sizes and shapes; he polished them up and hung them on the living room wall opposite the windows, creating, with their reflections, the illusion of a second external wall. In the afternoon, when the living room floods with sun and the mirrors cast beams, it's a Jacuzzi of light. He bought some plants: an African violet, a heart-leaf philodendron, miscellaneous ferns. He hung prints and posters on the walls, among them a large, framed, color photograph of Machu Picchu and a map of pre-Columbian North America. He hung Isabel's Turkish kilim in the front hall. He could hear her say with bemused amazement, *Well, look at you, Mr. Decorator Man. Look at you, Mr. Green Thumb.* When he found out Bernice was planning to visit, he splurged on a rattan armchair, so one of them would have a place to sit in the living room other than the couch. He picked up a rust-colored jute rug to cover the ancient water stain on the floor. The last time Bernice came up, in May, he was still living in the dank, mildew-colonized basement apartment he'd been renting since the previous spring, when he first arrived in the city. Now that he has a new place, he wants to send Bernice home with a more pleasant, reassuring memory of his surroundings.

Bernice arrives on a Friday afternoon. Settled in the new armchair, sipping a beer, petting Otto, recovering from her five-hour drive, she surveys the apartment with admiration. "I like what you've done," she says. "It's so cheery. What a change from that dungeon you used to squat in. I love the mirrors. This is all new paint? I didn't know you had it in you."

Alex shrugs. "I've had time, is what I've had. I don't have the busiest social life in Chicago. I spent a lot of Saturday nights painting."

"Well, when your social life does get busy, you'll have a nice place to invite friends over to." Bernice presses her beer bottle against one cheek, then the other, to cool her skin, or at least demonstrate that she's hot. She studies a plant spilling from the top of his bookcase. "Is that an Algerian ivy? I had an Algerian ivy once. I think it died. As do most of my plants."

"How's your philodendron? That always looked healthy."

"It's fine. Philodendrons are indestructible."

She's thinner than she used to be, even more lean and wiry, if that's possible. Alex guesses it's the new exercise regimen. He's glad she's taking care of herself, though he worries, with a dutiful, custodial gravitas he doesn't feel about his own parents, whether she's eating well, whether she's depressed, whether her health insurance, which she's assured him is top-notch, will cover her in the event of illness or injury, God forbid. She's wearing a plain white T-shirt whose neckline is just low enough to allow him a view of her collarbones, which look fragile, in high relief against the wells behind them. The bump of vein in her neck. How did such an important conduit of blood end up so close to the surface, so exposed and vulnerable? It doesn't make sense. You'd think evolution would have wanted to bury it deep down. Seclude and protect it with muscle and bone.

Bernice is gazing at Machu Picchu with curiosity and awe. Neither of them has spoken for what must be a minute. It says something to Alex that after all they've been through, after all their disagreements and disputes, after that night in the hotel room two years ago, it's remarkable that they can sit in a room together alone, in silence, without awkwardness.

Midafternoon they go out for a walk. The day is hot and humid, the sky clear, the sun bright. Alex has learned to appreciate the sight of Otto trotting merrily in front of him, and tries to emulate the canine's unflappable high hopes, the handy obliviousness to the future. Bernice seems tired from her drive, and less cheerful than she might otherwise be. Walking with her, Alex feels the weight of her sorrows alongside his, compounding and accentuating his, drawing them to the surface. Alex has no doubt she feels something similar. It's the price they pay to be together. Alex isn't sure it would be good for either of them to be together all the time. But these visits, and their occasional phone calls and e-mails, lift each other's spirits more than they dampen them, so both of them come out ahead.

They buy dried cherries and pistachio nuts at the Persian grocery and walk down Clark Street nibbling out of paper bags. Couples stroll sipping iced drinks, chatters and readers hang out on the benches and stoops — scruffy alterna-hipsters wearing layers of tight shirts and expensive ripped jeans. Not exactly Alex's crowd, Bernice thinks. A little young, a little pretentious. But she agrees that the neighborhood has an eclectic, arty, laid-back feel. They take Otto into a tiny, cramped hole-in-the-wall, a dog bakery where a variety of exotic treats, prepared on the premises, are displayed on shelves and in bins. Bernice picks out a carob cookie, which Otto detects and wolfs down before she has a chance to pay for it. There's a Swedish bakery up the street into which Bernice ventures while Alex and Otto wait outside; she wanders the immaculately clean aisles ogling liqueurs and glögg, chocolates and candies, cookies and biscuits, marmalades and jams. She buys a bar of Marabou Mjölkchoklad and some Önos lingonberry jam and stumbles out into the day, her eyes swimming with umlauts.

That night she and Alex eat dinner in a Persian restaurant called Resa's, just a few blocks down Clark Street from Alex's apartment. The atmosphere is convivial, alive with conversations and laughter, and the food — radishes and feta cheese and pita bread smothered with hummus, shish-kabobs afloat on huge beds of dill rice — is delicious. A few glasses of Syrah, a Palestinian wine Bernice has never heard of, get her talking about the costume shop, this year's finicky prima donnas, the setbacks they've had getting ready for *Le Nozze di Figaro*. One of these days, she says, she'd like to come up to Chicago and see an opera with Alex at the Lyric. "It's one of the great opera houses in the country. Maybe even the world. It's where Maria Callas made her American debut."

Alex looks disoriented. "I think I work right around the corner from the opera house. It's on Wacker, right? Big chunk of limestone? More columns than the Parthenon?"

"It might be on Wacker. I'm not sure. I haven't been to the Lyric since . . . what a shame. Ages. Do you know . . . I drove up here with Ellen Frankel and Susan Delahunt in Susan's white Opel in what must have been, good lord, 1961 or '62. We saw *Lucia di Lammermoor* with Joan Sutherland and Carlo Bergonzi. Wow. That was the golden age."

"I'm game for an opera," Alex says. "As long as we don't have to see one where people are dying right and left."

"I'll see what I can do." Bernice raises her glass as if to seal the deal. "I'll buy the tickets. We have to sit up close so we can see the costumes."

At seven the next morning Alex picks up Bernice at the bed-and-breakfast where she's staying, and after stopping for coffee they drive down to the lake. Otto circles frantically in the Jeep's towel-carpeted back. The sky is gray and overcast, the air refreshingly cool. The lake is cold and choppy and full of dogs. At the fetch beach Otto and a dozen other water-lovers plunge and swim robustly out to hurled rope toys and tennis balls and other rubbery floatables while their owners, Bernice and Alex included, huddle like a coaching staff, slurping at their coffees, talking, comparing fetching styles and swimming ability with a geniality not entirely free of competitiveness and pride.

Later, toward noon, they leave Otto pleasantly exhausted on the living room floor and drive down to Pilsen to meet Janet for lunch. Sam and Carly will be there too. During the school year Sam and Carly live with their father in Elmhurst and spend every other weekend in the city with Janet. Now, during the summer, they're with her more often. In Elmhurst the kids have school and friends and music lessons and sports; downtown they have museums and exhibits and concerts and festivals. Parks. The lakeshore. Janet hopes it will be good for them, growing up in two different places, exposed to so many different things. She hopes they'll end up better people. Bernice, who hears all of this from Alex, worries they'll end up damaged and bitter, like so many children of divorce. Alex, who sees Carly and Sam from time to time, and even babysat them once, is more optimistic; he thinks they're resilient. He worries about Janet. As he and Bernice leave 94 South and take a right on Halstead, a left onto Eighteenth Street — Bernice is impressed with Alex's knowledge of the route — he explains that Janet had a lesion, a squamous cell carcinoma, removed from her left ear three weeks ago. For all intents and purposes, she's having an outbreak of skin cancer, to which she's especially vulnerable, being immunosuppressed. Alex warns Bernice that Janet suffers from nosebleeds, and often carries a ziplock bag full of bloody tissues. "OK, maybe I'm dumb," Bernice says, "but how does cancer on your ear give you a bloody nose?" Alex explains that Janet's doctors started her on a psoriasis drug to control the cancer, and that the drug dries out her nasal passages, as well as her eyes and mouth. "Jesus," Bernice says, feeling obscenely healthy.

They find a parking space on Eighteenth Street and walk west. Bernice gazes up at the Czech-inspired buildings with their oddly shaped gables, hears mariachi music and boisterous Spanish from the open door of a *taquería,* thinks of the Persian grocery and Swedish bakery she and Alex visited yesterday. She has the sense of a jumbled, mongrel world, a mosaic of disparate parts in which no pure, unalloyed thing exists.

Alex has his hands shoved deep in his pockets, elbows locked, shoulders hunched. His eyes scan actively ahead. He exhales through his mouth, cheeks puffed.

"You OK?" Bernice asks. She would give his arm a comforting squeeze, but she doesn't touch him as readily, as freely, as she once did.

Alex smiles, caught. He's come to appreciate having a person in the world who knows him as well as Bernice does. "I still get nervous."

"Of course. Me too."

"You don't look it."

"I'm a good actor."

"Hey, there they are."

Out on the sidewalk in front of the Cuernavaca, the restaurant where they've arranged to meet, Janet is wearing a burgundy-colored dress with a Polynesian floral print. Her hair is pulled back and loosely bound. She looks elegant and strong. Whenever Alex sees Janet, he doesn't think first of what's inside her, but what's inside him — a sad, tender sensation of displacement, of serendipitous deliverance and ingress. He arrived so randomly in this city, and now lives a life — a fairly good life — that he could not possibly have foreseen only a few years ago.

Janet sees Alex and Bernice and waves.

Carly is hopping and skipping along the sidewalk nearby, head down, obeying some logic of lines and cracks. Sam, who has been mashing his face against the window of the Cuernavaca, trying to see inside, turns and registers Alex and Bernice's presence and goes back to his spying.

Janet hugs Bernice, the traveler of longest distance, first. "It's so good to see you."

"It's so good to see *you*," says Bernice. "What a beautiful dress."

Standing back, struggling to contain her emotions, she watches Alex and Janet embrace. They do so affectionately but formally, with deliberate seriousness. Reverence. Bernice watches for the move, and it comes as Alex and Janet part. Without ceremony, as if in passing, Alex places his right hand high on Janet's chest, the heel of his hand on her sternum, his fingertips touching the bare skin below her neck. Janet's right hand settles briefly on his. Then, in the space of a second, it's over.

The first time Bernice saw Alex touch Janet like this, on one of her early visits, she tensed and nearly panicked. Had Alex and Janet become lovers? Had Isabel, through an unforeseeable sequence of events, an extraordinary convergence of munificence and disaster, replaced herself?

Bernice has since come to learn: it's just the way they say hello.

ACKNOWLEDGMENTS

My deepest thanks to Pamela Dorman and Ellen Archer at Voice for bringing this novel into the world. They made every day of labor worthwhile. A second thanks to Pamela Dorman for urging me to look deeper into the novel than I had previously, and for her excellent suggestions. Sarah Landis has been an extraordinary editor and a helpful guide at every step of the way. I'm grateful to all the other talented people at Voice and Hyperion who have given so much to the publication of this book, especially Laura Klynstra for the beautiful jacket art. I'd also like to thank Rachelle Mandik for her meticulous copyediting.

Lisa Bankoff lowered a rope out of the light and hauled me up. I'll never forget.

Thanks to James Michener and the Copernicus Society of America for support during the writing of this book.

Margot Livesey has given me encouragement, support, and wisdom for nearly twenty years. She bravely engaged this novel when it was bloated and unwieldy, and as usual her suggestions were indispensible.

Nam Le gave one of the closest, most intelligent readings I've ever received. Kevin Kelley's filmmaker's perspective helped me enliven a dull section of the book.

Thanks to Deborah Eisenberg for setting the prose standard, Ethan Canin for once suggesting that good fiction ought to be interesting (something I'd failed to think about seriously before), and Frank Conroy for opening a very large door. Kim McMullen got me on my feet. I'm deeply indebted to them all.

Thanks to these writers and friends who encouraged and believed at various points along the way: Merrie Snell, Amy Margolis, Erik Huber, Scott Anderson, Curt Mark, Bekki Lee, Lan Samantha Chang, Connie Brothers, Deb West, Caryl Pagel, Jeanne Stoakes, Kim Wall, Rod Mickle, and Dan Lind.

For help getting the facts straight: Brian Manahan, Brett Engelke, Susan Zickmund, Linda Cadaret, Wayne Richenbacher, Guillermo Delgado, and Bonnie Jenkins.

Thanks to the incredibly talented writers at the Iowa Young Writers' Studio — students, teachers, and counselors — who continually reassure me that writing and reading will never die.

Miranda gives me a life outside of my head, and makes all of it beautiful.

Thanks to my brothers, Timothy and Brian, and their wives, Victoria and Cathy, for their faith, and for always taking me seriously.

Last and most deeply, I wish to thank my parents, Edward and Barbara, who gave me so much. They are truly irreplaceable.

ABOUT THE AUTHOR

Stephen Lovely graduated from Kenyon College and the Iowa Writers' Workshop. For seven years he worked as a night clerk in the pediatric intensive care unit at the University of Iowa Hospitals and Clinics, where the idea for this novel was born. He lives in Iowa City, and he is the Director of the Iowa Young Writers' Studio. This is his first novel.